MW00614430

TAIL OF THE LIZARD

CRAIG DAVIS

TAIL OF THE LIZARD

*STRANDED WITH JFK'S ASSASSIN
IN A STRUGGLE FOR SURVIVAL*

A Novel

CRAIG DAVIS

This book is a work of fiction. Names, characters, places and incidents are either products of the author's imagination or used fictitiously. Any resemblance to actual events, locales, business establishments, or actual persons (living or dead) is entirely coincidental.

Copyright © 2020 by Craig Davis
Published by Craigslegz

All rights reserved. No part of this publication can be reproduced or transmitted in any form or by any means without permission in writing from Craig Davis.

First Edition

ISBN 978-0-578-67401-8

Also available on Kindle

Cover art and design: Fran Davis, Fortune Studio Design
Author's website: Craigslegztravels.com

For Fran, my love and partner on a life of adventure.

CHAPTER 1

Off the Southeast coast of Florida, January 1993

When the grits hit the porthole, Andrew Dallas Huston was standing at the stern of the 40-foot sailboat, one hand on the cool, aluminum safety rail, watching the remnants of the morning's coffee splashing into the wake swirling off the hull.

It brought to mind the drunk in the men's room of a seaside joint in Pensacola the night before he left pouring a beer into the urinal next to him. When Dallas did a double-take, the drunk squinted at him and bellowed, "I just hate being the middleman."

Something about the timbre of the drunk's laughter struck Dallas like a bucket of ice water. Wasn't that the story of his life? Always the middleman, never the one cashing the big chips. Always just passing through, or being passed over. He'd stood staring at graffiti on the wall, the drunk's laughter stinging his ears until someone shouted, "Yo, chief, ya gonna camp out there or what?"

Dallas shrugged it off and did what he always did when things got heavy. He got on a boat and left.

He smiled now as he spied a plump cloud that resembled the physique of the Pensacola drunk. Seemed like a good sign: more laughs ahead. Less than an hour and he'd be in Fort Lauderdale. He'd deliver the sailboat, pick up his check and find the nearest barstool with a view of the beach. Was it that bad being a middleman, as long as the reward was cold and refreshing on the way in?

Then why did this unease keep returning? Self-analysis was for neurotics of the 9-to-5 trap. Here he was getting paid to sail a boat from one place to another. How could you question that?

It had been an easy, uneventful run around the tip of Florida, about the best he could hope for on a mid-winter delivery. A bit chilly leaving Pensacola, but mostly chill since. Still standing at the stern rail, he glanced at the cloud again. It had transformed from squat and dumpy to something sleek and graceful like a jumping dolphin. No, more like a finger, pointed in his direction. The drunk's laughter echoed in his ears. He felt a chill run along his spine.

What? Why now? He had the boat and life on auto-pilot cruising on a hang-loose agenda. No worries, nothing pressing. He'd spend a couple of days in Lauderdale, then pick up a rental car and head to the Keys. Visit an old fishing buddy. Maybe hook into a tarpon. No matter, there was certain to be plenty of sunshine and beer.

And, wasn't that the problem he could no longer deny? On the cusp of 40 and no place he had to be, nothing important to do. The laughter of a drunk mocked him. A recent conversation with his sister, Linda, lingered like a dumpling in the gut: "Are you ever going to do anything meaningful with your life? Are you going to leave behind more than footprints in the sand?"

Linda had mentioned the vow he'd made to become a writer after he stopped being a pitcher. That was a dozen years ago. He knew she was right, but it was hard to give up the easy course he knew so well.

There was an offer to write some boating and fishing articles for a friend's new outdoors magazine. That was a mere extension of what he was doing now. Bold move would be to write the tale he'd only told a few close friends, usually late at night after many beers and a shot or three.

How many times had he said it: One day I'm going to write my own book about the assassination of John F. Kennedy? Most of them were written by people who weren't even there. They hadn't seen what he'd seen, the images that haunted him all these years. They offered theories. He'd witnessed it, the face behind the fence on the Grassy Knoll. The man, he was certain, who fired the shot that altered the course of history.

Time never healed, nor did it answer the nagging question: Who was that figure in the shadows, and what became of him? Imagine: He writes his account, and during a book signing a man approaches, their eyes meet and, it's him.

Would he become another chalk mark on the slate of mysterious deaths of witnesses and others who knew too much? But it was so long ago now. This November would be the thirtieth anniversary. If he ever was going to put his thoughts on paper it had to be, well, soon.

Dallas glanced at the pattern of waves trailing the sailboat and realized he'd zoned out like on the night in Pensacola. What a picture that would make from a passing cruise ship. It reminded him of something else Linda had said: "You're pissing it all away, Dallas."

Who would even be interested now or believe his historic tale? He shrugged and glanced at the cloud. It had curled up into a smile. He smiled back.

The next moment unfolded in slow motion, an explosion erupting in the belly of the boat, the deck rising and catapulting him off the stern.

In the two or three seconds Dallas was in the air, a stampede of disjointed thoughts rushed through his mind: a bill he needed to pay, the name of a teacher who once admonished him, football scores from the past. Then the realization: *Damn, the Cowboys are going back to the Super Bowl and I may not be around to watch it.*

Impact with the water took his breath away. He came up gasping, still clutching the safety rail. A lot of help that would be now. He let go and began flailing his arms like a windmill in a bathtub. Something heavy, probably a section of the mast, splashed down nearby. The ocean was cold and seemed to be sucking him in. Amid desperation, his mind seized on an old comedy record his mom used to play, the voice of God asking a reluctant Noah how long he could tread water.

How about it, Dallas? How long? *Don't panic, don't panic.* He kept repeating it like a mantra, trying to calm his breathing. It helped.

He turned back to survey the remains of the sailboat as the stern disappeared amid a frothy effervescence. Must have been a gas leak — the stove or the auxiliary engine. He recalled the name painted on the transom: *Peace & Quiet.* Now a more appropriate one would be *Bits & Pieces*, which reminded him of a classic Dave Clark Five song. Mentally humming the tune, he wondered about the fate of his four-foot-long pet iguana, Rambo, last seen lounging near the mast. Iguanas can swim, provided he's still in one piece, but how long can they tread water?

Dallas spotted one of the yellow U-shaped flotation devices that had been affixed to the stern rail and was swimming toward it when something else caught his eye.

"The hell is that?"

It was moving fast and silent on a northerly course a quarter-mile seaward of the wreck. Occasionally it skimmed a wave top and kicked up a shower of spray like a bionic flying fish or some sort of surface-to-surface missile.

Did one of those hit the sailboat? Whatever it was, it halted abruptly. Some type of boat, though unlike any he'd ever seen. With a streamlined profile hugging the waves it looked like a comic book spaceship. There was gold lettering on the side of the black hull, and Dallas saw a helmeted head pop up and turn his way.

Now something else was approaching from the south, moving fast, spurred by the whine of a pair of racing engines. This, at least, was familiar. By the side-to-side wobble as it bore in, Dallas recognized it as a high-performance catamaran, the type that had dominated the offshore racing circuit since the mid-'80s. The DEA had a small fleet of them, as did the drug runners they often chased in these waters.

Dallas waved frantically until a hand pointed his way. He continued waving as the sleek cat altered course toward him. It slowed, and a voice from one of two orange-helmeted occupants called out, "You OK?"

Dallas gave a thumbs-up, at the same time thinking this wasn't exactly his idea of OK.

"Anybody else aboard?"

"No, I was alone," Dallas shouted, then thought, poor Rambo.

The catamaran idled closer and its passenger tossed a line to Dallas. For the first time he noticed the name on the side: *Bad Attitude*. There was also a number, M-45, which marked it as a racing boat. The passenger, the one doing the talking, reached down and plucked Dallas — all six feet two inches of him, still in T-shirt, shorts and boat shoes, out of the water with surprising ease.

Less than ten minutes had passed since he left the galley where he was cooking breakfast to take a leak — a most fortuitous call of nature — and now he was standing on the deck of a very different sort of craft, feeling the vibration of 1,000 horsepower. All that was needed to complete a perfect hallucination was for one of his rescuers to pull off their helmet to reveal Kim Basinger while a voice from a bullhorn on a nearby barge yelled, "Cut! Print it!" But this was no movie scene and there was a beard framing the face of the driver. His companion, the one who yanked Dallas out of the water, was big enough to play nose tackle for the Cowboys. He was the one saying, "Saw the explosion. You're damn lucky to be alive."

So, Dallas thought, this is my lucky day. At the moment, what he felt was cold, hungry and thirsty. He touched the back of his head and realized the blast had singed his hair. Yeah, lucky. Lucky he'd gone off on that mental tangent and not immediately returned to the galley.

"Guess I'm lucky you came along when you did."

"I'm Rick, that's Carlos. Sorry we can't offer a towel, but here's a jacket you can put on."

Dallas peeled off his soggy shirt and slipped on the orange vinyl parka. Shivering, he pulled the hood up. Must have looked like a traffic cone. The driver looked his way and grinned. He had a lot of gold among his teeth. It didn't sparkle, so Dallas knew it was real. He wondered if Carlos spoke English.

"How 'bout a beer? It's all we got on board," Rick said. For a crew with an avowed bad attitude they seemed like hospitable swashbucklers.

Dallas would have preferred something hot, but the beer cut through the salty taste from the seawater he'd swallowed. He pulled the parka tighter, took another swig and stared at the strange craft bobbing in the gentle swell of the waves 100 feet away.

"Just wondering. What the hell is that, ah, boat over there?"

Rick studied Dallas for a moment, then glanced at the strange craft.

"Aw, that. It's experimental," he said, his voice gruff, gravely. "They're testing it."

Dallas eyed the two men. The driver was talking on the radio, the conversation unintelligible, but it sounded like English — more or less. Looking back across the water, he noticed something moving on the surface. Something squiggly, like a worm.

"Rambo!"

Rick followed Dallas's gaze but didn't comprehend.

"Looks like a snake."

Dallas immediately recognized it as the bottom third of an iguana, the part the lizard leaves behind in flight from a predator — or, from an explosion. Dallas couldn't reach it but could see it was moving on its own, eerily, eel-like. He scanned the water outward, but quickly lost hope. There was debris floating but nothing swimming that he could see.

Just then another black hull came into view, this one larger, converging from the southeast. He heard a voice amid the static on the radio say, "We'll pick it up. You take him in and wait for the Coasties at the sea buoy. Got it?"

Carlos said something into the radio. Rick said, "Where were you headed?"

"I was delivering the sailboat to Lauderdale."

"Well, you almost made it. The Coast Guard's on the way out from Port Everglades to get you. We'll take you part way in. Beats swimming."

The catamaran had stalled. One engine started right up again, but when Carlos cranked the other one he got a series of clicks.

"Fucker must be loose again," Rick said. "Hold on, let me check."

The big man flipped open the huge lid of the engine compartment as if it were a match cover, revealing the gleaming chrome of two massive power plants, one rumbling, the other still. While he worked, Dallas watched the arrival of the third member of the peculiar flotilla. It looked like a shrimp boat with the nets removed.

"Try it now."

Another rat-ta-tat of clicks.

"Shit. Hold on."

The shrimp boat — it said *Mary Lou II* on the bow — headed directly toward the experimental craft and idled alongside. A pair of crane-like booms swung out from the port side and lowered a harness that the pilot slid under both ends of the strange vessel. Dallas could make out the lettering on the side now — actually, letters and a number. It read: P-BJ-003. Was that B.J., as in Bond, James? Or, he had to laugh, blow job? Dallas always wondered why anyone would use those initials to name anything, such as a Texas bar he used to frequent because it had great chili, called B.J.'s Tavern. Dallas once made a crack about it to the owner, Bill Johnston, and got a dirty look.

"OK, now!"

The catamaran's second engine roared to life just as the *Experimental Prototype James Bond Blow Job Exocet H2O Starship Enterprise* was hoisted from the water by the *Starkist Spy Shrimper Ricky Nelson Say Goodbye to Mary Lou II Too*, both of which were now pointing bow-first toward the racing catamaran. The experimental boat had a catamaran-like hull, too, although unlike any Dallas had come across before. The twin hulls had tube-like openings with a flat-topped tunnel in between. Which brought Dallas back to the original question:

"The hell is that thing?"

"Huh?"

Rick closed the engine hatch as Dallas pointed toward the strange craft as it was being lowered onto a cradle on deck of the *Mary Lou II.*

"Never seen anything like it," Dallas shouted as Carlos revved the engines.

"Like I said, it's experimental." Rick shrugged and turned away.

Dallas noticed two men standing by the door to the wheelhouse of the shrimp boat. One had a light-colored beard and wore a cowboy hat, one of those Garth Brooks numbers with the front of the brim bent low almost covering his eyes. The other man, thickset with close-cropped hair, wore a dark-blue jacket and mirrored sunglasses, Secret Service standard issue. Cowboy hat was speaking animatedly, punctuating his monologue with head bobs and hand gestures. Mirrored Glasses stared toward Dallas. When the catamaran began moving away, Mirrored Glasses looked down at the water and something caught his eye. Dallas saw him move out of sight and return with a long-handled fish net. The catamaran was picking up speed, rising onto plane, but Dallas kept looking back, watching as Mirrored Glasses leaned over the side of the shrimp boat and scooped up something. Something, green?

"Hey," Dallas said to the nose tackle, "Can you talk to that boat?"

Rick glanced back and nodded.

"I had a pet iguana on board with me. It looks like they may have found him."

The catamaran slowed as Rick pulled a hand-held walkie-talkie from under the forward deck and made contact with the shrimp boat.

"This guy here had some kind of lizard with him. Did y'all pick it up?"

Dallas strained to hear the reply over the engine noise.

". . . what's left of it."

"What can I tell ya?" Rick said with a shrug. He nudged the driver and pointed toward shore. As the catamaran roared away, Dallas glanced back again and saw the glint of sunlight off the man's sunglasses. His stomach churned like before the blast. He continued to stare at the shrimp boat through the mist stirred by the powerful twin outdrives until the catamaran lurched over a steep wave and knocked him off balance.

"That's them," Rick said, pointing toward a boat with a flashing blue light framed between the twin condominiums marking the entrance to Port Everglades. As it got closer, Dallas could make out the distinctive angled orange stripe on the hull.

The catamaran slowed to idle and waited for the cutter's arrival. Just before it got close enough to throw a line, Carlos turned and spoke to Dallas for the first time since he'd been aboard.

"My friend, I think ya'd better zip your fly."

CHAPTER 2

Two days later, Dallas was seated at a Tiki bar in Islamorada in the heart of the Florida Keys sipping a watered-down draft beer with a scruffy crowd watching William Jefferson Clinton being sworn in as the nation's 42nd president. The government was putting pen to a fresh chapter. Dallas, too. Yeah, he'd drink to that.

It had been a memorable few days for him and the new prez. Slick Willie from Arkansas donned a tux and went to Washington. Soggy Dallas from Texas dried himself off at the Coast Guard station in Fort Lauderdale, detoured through Broward General Hospital for minor repairs and to Kmart for a new wardrobe. Good ol' American Express came through with a replacement card in short order. Praise plastic.

Getting his money for the incomplete yacht delivery was another matter, but he wasn't going to sweat it. He'd gotten a ride to the Keys from a guy he met at Southport Raw Bar who was taking a truckload of bonefish skiffs to Tavernier. So he'd seen a boat delivery through after all.

Dallas knew a captain, Zack Tomlin, who was running a charter boat out of Islamorada. They'd worked together on fishing boats in the Gulf of Mexico a few years back. Maybe he could find something to do down here while pondering his next move. Tomlin was out on a morning charter, so Dallas was hanging out, soaking up sun and suds. It was a lot more pleasant than frigid D.C.

"... and I will faithfully execute. ..."

Most eyes were on the fuzzy image on the 19-inch TV at the corner of the bar as the new president took the oath. Dallas was having trouble keeping his gaze off the backside of the barmaid. Hell of a fine caboose. He wondered about the penalty for entertaining such thoughts in this repressive age. Any day now, it seemed, the thought police would come up with a device to detect any brain transmission that registered to the left of accepted standards of political correctness, the latest catch phrase for societal constipation. Undoubtedly, some subversive entrepreneur would respond with a jamming device to market as a sort of cranial Fuzzbuster to preserve the sanctity of free thought.

In the meantime, Dallas vowed to take advantage of every opportunity to savor the last bastion of male chauvinism. So, disregarding caution, he took a brazen gulp of tepid Bud Light and thought loudly, now that is a damn fine backside.

"… so help me God …"

A patron across the bar caught him staring and raised a glass in his direction. "Can't beat the scenery around here."

Dallas blushed. When you've been alone at sea for a week and had the boat you were piloting blown out from under you — what the hell, no need to rationalize. Small nations have been invaded over less. At that moment, the crowd in Washington was applauding a new president. Dallas had his own standing ovation going on under the counter and flashed a jack-o'-lantern grin.

"You look happy today," the barmaid said, glancing up as she replaced the soggy cocktail napkin under his beer with a dry one. "Glad to see someone around here's having a good week."

"He's probably a Democrat," a patron with gray whiskers and a well-worn Greek fisherman's cap said. "Go ahead, do your celebrating now. Just remember, beware what you wish for, it may come true. There's always a morning after. The bill always comes due. If you get my drift."

Dallas felt himself shrink.

"To tell you the truth, this hasn't exactly been my week. The boat I was on blew up. And with it the delivery fee I was going to collect. I don't have a job. I don't know where I'll be sleeping tonight. But I was just thinking that, all things considered, I could be a lot worse off. I'm sitting by the ocean in January having a beer. There's a guy younger than the Beatles in the White House. I don't know how he's going to do — or me either, for that matter. I do know one thing right now: I'll have another beer."

As he spoke, he locked on the barmaid's eyes, a shade of blue he'd only seen in water of a certain depth in the Caribbean. She held his gaze as she filled a plastic cup from the tap, and he felt the urge to go snorkeling. Was that a blink or a wink? She turned to serve another customer, and Dallas noticed a small lizard tattooed on the back of her left shoulder. It reminded him of Rambo, his lost shipmate. His smile faded.

Clinton was into his inaugural speech now. Dallas turned his attention to the newly anointed most powerful man in the world, listening to the cadence of Clinton's delivery more than to his words. Good rhythm. Authoritative, if a bit raspy. Dallas fixed his gaze on the movement of the chin. Thinking, good firm presidential chin — it had better be.

Dallas, trying to find inspiration in the moment, instead saw Clinton's face morph into that of Senor Wences. He was envisioning a close-up of a lipstick face on a hand speaking when he heard Clinton say: "It is time to break the bad habit of expecting something for nothing, from our government or from each other. Let us all take more responsibility, not only for ourselves and our families, but for our communities and our country."

"Listen to that, he's trying to sound like Kennedy," said a beefy man near the television: 'Ask not what your country can do for you.' Damn poor imitation, though."

"Well, he's got one thing in common with Kennedy," the man's ruddy-faced companion said. "He likes to screw around on his old lady."

"Yeah, funny about that," the man in the Greek fisherman's cap said loud enough for everyone to hear. "Kennedy and Clinton, both Democrats, right? Real skirt chasers. What's funny, they say the hookers always do much better business at the Republican conventions than at the Democratic conventions. But all the Republican presidents, you can't picture any of those old buzzards ever getting laid. Hey, Claire, how 'bout it? I'm dying of dee-hydration over here."

Kennedy. Mention of the name jarred Dallas, as if from a trance. Senor Wences snapped his fingers, and Clinton's face dissolved to that of the previous youngest president. Such a compelling face. A face that to Dallas's young eyes always appeared vibrant, unfailingly confident, until the horrific moment on that street in Dealey Plaza. Ten-year-old Dallas stood by the curb with his mother and sister and watched the head of the president erupt in a shower of blood.

It happened so quickly, incomprehensibly, immediately after hearing his mother say, "There he is, he's looking this way." Then a sharp crack, staccato, like the snap of a finger. The mind didn't immediately register what the eyes were transmitting, until there was another. How many? Still not certain. But the last one — much louder, and closer — left a chilling mental echo resounding across three decades.

In his mind, Dallas was back there again, on the ground, peering up the little hill, a glint of something shiny catching his eye. Initially, movement, or a shift in the shadows above the fence. Then just for a moment it came into focus. A face. There was no doubt he saw it, the vision as clear now as it was then. Whenever it came to him, usually like this, unexpectedly, it was always the same: a distant yet distinct replay that never failed to jar him.

"Would you like some chips?"

It took an instant to register, to put the unsettling memory back in its folder and slam the drawer.

"Whoa, there. You still with us?"

The sights and sounds of the tiki bar came back, the wind rustling the palms, surrounding chatter, commentary on the television. The barmaid held a basket of potato chips in each hand.

"Yes, ma'am."

"Thought we lost you there for a moment. Would you like some chips?"

"Yes, ma'am. And another beer, please. Make it a Heineken this time. In a bottle."

She smiled up at him as she reached into the cooler. "Everybody as polite where you're from? Not from around here, that's for sure. What's your name?"

"Dallas. From Dallas. Actually, it's my middle name."

He'd started using it when he pitched for the University of Texas. Good baseball name. Before that, he'd gone by Drew, which he preferred to Andy. Only his mom called him Andrew.

"Nice to meet you, Dallas from Dallas. I'm Claire from California. Sorry to hear about your boat."

He got the idea she'd like to chat, but duty called again, the crowd working up a powerful inaugural thirst. Twelve hundred miles away, the presidential party was headed for the White House. Bet they couldn't wait to get inside and pour a drink. Wait, what's this? They're getting out of the car. And walking. On Pennsylvania Avenue?

"Check out the Mad Hatter," someone was saying. There was a close-up of Hillary Clinton, the new First Lady. "She looks like Soupy Sales."

"No, more like that goofy guy on that old show, 'F Troop,' " a fellow a couple stools away from Dallas said. "Corporal Acorn, or something like that."

"Agarn," Dallas said. "That was his name, I think. Corporal Agarn."

The mention of headgear on a president's wife made him flash back to Jackie Kennedy's famous pink pillbox hat. The one she wore that day. Seeing the Clintons, smiling and waving and walking out in the open caused Dallas to shudder again. For Chrissake, get back in the car, hurry on through the gate and go have that drink. A stiff one.

Dallas didn't have any particular feelings for Clinton. He hadn't bothered to vote. He did know it wasn't smart for any president to be walking the streets. And he couldn't help but feel sorry for the man, in all his blind ambition. The wag was right: Be careful what you wish for. Dallas couldn't fathom why anyone would wish for that job, to be the nation's whipping boy, a virtual prisoner.

Or a sitting duck, like JFK. The TV showed another view of Hillary, but Dallas was thinking about Jackie, a vision in pink, the sun on her face, waving, until the smile faded to bewilderment, then horror. When the limo sped away with Jackie and a Secret Service agent on the trunk, Dallas was on his hands and knees staring up the little hill toward the picket fence where he was sure the last shot, at least, came from.

He'd heard the bullet whiz past, no mistake about that. And for an instant he had a clear look into the face of the man who fired it.

Dallas cringed and took a sip of beer. The TV showed the inaugural parade, but few at the bar were still paying attention to it. A couple of guys got up and left.

"Hey, did you hear about Audrey Hepburn? She died." It was the guy in the Greek fisherman's hat again.

"Is that the one with the shaky voice?" said the beefy man.

"No, that's Katherine," Claire said.

"It was Audrey that died," Greek fisherman's cap said. "She was 63, they said. Cancer."

"Too bad. Much too young."

Dallas wondered if that was better or worse than getting your brains blown out. Cancer was certainly tougher on the person succumbing to it. Getting one's brains blown out was probably tougher on those who might witness it.

He was frowning at the Heineken bottle, envisioning it pierced by a bullet, crumbling onto its base. He imagined it blown to tiny green bits by an explosion. Both times he heard the muffled sounds deep in his head: The staccato crack of gunfire; the boom of an explosive. In each case, a beautiful sunny day, like this one. The death of a president. The death of a sailboat.

Who killed JFK, lone nut or evil conspiracy? How does a sailboat explode without warning? Maybe a faulty gas stove. Maybe fuel from the auxiliary motor leaked into the bilge. Still, the violence of the blast seemed unfathomable. As unfathomable as the Warren Commission's magic bullet theory.

Dallas recalled his internal angst just before the explosion. What did it mean? Was it an omen?

His mind was drifting again. Away from the tragic Kennedys. Away from the full-of-hope Clintons. Away from the ringing in his ears. He became aware he was staring at the lizard tattooed on the milk-white shoulder of the barmaid. He recalled the words of advice his mother gave him the day he signed his first baseball contract with the Baltimore Orioles and left home to pitch for their Rookie League team.

"Don't get a tattoo."

CHAPTER 3

Slosh, slosh, slosh … kick. Slosh, slosh, slosh … kick.

Dallas was on a mission for junk food, kicking the larger chunks of gravel on a late afternoon march along A1A to the Lil General. His head was still back at Mariner's End Marina mulling the strange tale Capt. Zack Tomlin had told about the day's fishing trip.

He'd gone there to tell Tomlin he was sticking around the Keys for a while. Waited on the dock with the tourist crowd when Tomlin brought the *Happy Flamingo* in from a charter with two good ol' boys from Missouri and a couple of giggly gals on the shady side of 40. They'd caught their limit of sun, a bonito, a barracuda and two small dolphin fish, which the restaurants list as mahi-mahi so nobody mistakes Flipper for the catch of the day.

Dallas waited until the tourists settled the bill and left, then came aboard while Tomlin hosed fish blood and bits of bait off the deck. They'd met at a fishing tournament in Cozumel a few years back, laid a few pitchers of margaritas to waste and struck up a friendship. Dallas worked as deck mate for Tomlin in a few marlin tournaments. Tomlin's passion for fishing was matched only by his love for talking about it. Dallas sipped a beer left over from the charter while his friend related the events of his day, routine except for one oddity.

"Damnedest thing out there today. We're working a little weed-line where we got the dolphin. I see some frigate birds diving a little farther out, and I'm thinking they might be on a bigger patch of weeds or some debris, and maybe there's more dolphin out there. Just as I'm about to head out, there's this big-ass explosion to the north. First, I see a flash, then there's a big 'blam,' and a mess of shit is flying up in the air. First thing comes to mind is what you were telling me about what happened to that boat you were on.

18

"Dick on the *Reel Thing* saw it, too. He was a little north of me. Didn't have his lines out, so he goes running up there right away. From what he could make out of the debris, it was some kind of old wooden boat that blew up, like the kind you see loaded with Haitians. But Dick didn't see any people or bodies around. He called the Coast Guard anyway. Pretty weird, huh?"

"Any other boats nearby?"

"Well, here's the thing, the other strange part. I decide not to go up there, and I'm looking for those birds again. All of a sudden I see something a little farther out going like crazy. I've seen those Blue Thunder boats the feds have, but this was a lot faster, and there was hardly any spray. I grab the binocs and zoom in, and the damn thing looks like it's flying. Never seen anything like it. Had to be some kind of crazy-ass hovercraft."

"How close a look you get?"

"Close enough to see there's some writing on the side, but I couldn't make it out. Fuckin' weird. Never know what you'll see out there. Guess that's why you keep going out. At least, that's what keeps it interesting." He shrugged. That's when Dallas noticed his boat shoes were getting hosed along with the deck.

Slosh, slosh, slosh … kick. Slosh, slosh, slosh … kick.

The sound mirrored the jumble of thoughts in his head. Here he was in the quirky tail of the most disconnected state, a haven for people who have spun out on life's highway or simply pulled over for a siesta. Dallas could count his share of spinouts, but since landing here he was feeling oddly inspired.

Earlier in the day, he'd put down first and last month's rent on a duplex apartment. After so long calling a post office box home and having to look over the transom to remember the name of the boat that happened to be carrying him to the next paycheck, it felt strange to have a home base that didn't float. Even stranger to not be feeling the pull of the nomadic life. Initially he thought it was the compulsion to confront the demon that had dogged him for three decades, to finally put down on paper what he'd seen when JFK was killed. Even if nobody cared to read about it, just for himself, to finally flush it out.

It was more than that, something else drawing him here. He thought about what Tomlin had seen, and the events of a couple days ago kept flashing through his mind. Explosions. Strange flying boats. Suddenly he wasn't feeling like a mere accident victim.

Slosh, slosh, slosh … kick. Slosh, slosh, slosh … kick.

Dallas didn't realize he'd walked past the L'il General until a voice broke the spell. He looked up, disoriented, and there were four faces staring at him from a car he hadn't noticed pull up. The accent was world's away from his own. Clipped rather than drawled. French but not Parisian. Of course — *Quebecois.*

"Par-*don*, can you tell us how to get to the Theater of the Sea?"

Dallas had been here for only two days and already was giving directions like a native. Nothing to it. Everyone comes and goes on U.S. 1, the one and only road to anywhere between the Florida mainland and Key West. Don't even need to know left from right, just oceanside from bayside. He thought for a moment until he placed the tourist attraction.

"You've got to turn around. Then go back about a mile and a half. It's just past Holiday Isle. Oceanside. Can't miss it."

A rear window rolled down and a woman peered out behind big, orange sunglasses.

"We wanted to try the Marker 88 Restaurant. Do you know where that is?"

"Well, let's see," he said, looking to see if one of the little green markers was within sight. "You're in the low 80s here, I believe. So what you've got to do is go back the way you came for a few miles. You should see it up there on the bayside around, oh, mile marker 88."

Chrissake, how did people this clueless find their way this far from Canada? Dallas watched them drive away, noticed the slogan in French on the license plate: *Je me souviens*. Probably the motto of French-Canadian tourists, he mused: "I brake for cheap souvenirs." The dusty tan Oldsmobile kicked up gravel as it wheeled around and darted into the flow of traffic, prompting a rebuke from a truck horn.

Inexplicably, a familiar ad slogan popped into his head: Not your father's Oldsmobile. Another blast from the disturbing past. He couldn't remember much about his own father, who'd split when Dallas was five. All that remained was a vague recollection of Alexander Huston in a similar brindle-colored car driving like a bat out of hell, not caring who he ran off the road. Gone in a cloud of dust, consequences be damned.

It occurred to Dallas, his old man could be in any of these cars and he wouldn't know him if he stopped to ask directions. He knew the face from old photos, but after 35 years there's no telling what he'd look like. If he somehow did recognize the old bastard, he'd tell him, "Take a left at the next turnoff. Keep going till your hat floats."

Dallas kicked another stone. He was trying to project the aging face of his vagabond dad, assuming he's still alive, and almost walked into a car backing out of a space in front of the Lil General. Someone was pounding on the pay phone in front of the store, trying to dislodge a coin from a call that didn't go through. Two boys ran past in pursuit of a black dog. Dallas kept walking, head down and tripped over the step by the entrance. He looked up as the door swung open and a woman walked out carrying two bags of groceries.

The surprise of literally running into someone he recognized in a place where he was a virtual stranger sent Dallas into a Chevy Chase stumbling routine. It was the barmaid who'd served him at the Leaky Tiki. Equally nonplussed, she lost grip on one of the bags, and a half-dozen items spilled onto the ground. Dallas scrambled to gather them up, and when he looked up at her face the first thing he could of think to say was, "You bought Ring Dings?"

"Oh, it's you. Texas, right?"

"Dallas."

"Right. From Dallas."

"Claire …"

"… from California."

He smiled sheepishly.

"So, you decided to stick around?"

"Yes, m'am. I rented a place just down the road. Ah, oceanside. You know, I love Ring Dings. In fact, I was thinking of picking some up."

Just babbling. Truth be told, he preferred HoHos. Didn't matter. She was smiling.

"They're for my son. He's in the car."

She pointed to a sandy-haired boy working on a monster Bazooka gum bubble in the passenger seat of a Toyota parked between two pickup trucks. Damn, she's married. Dallas felt his smile sag as his eyes searched the left hand for a ring. Just a small emerald on the pinky. Hmmm.

Finally, he had the presence to say what he should have said in the first place. "Sorry. Geez, sometimes I can be such jerk."

She laughed. "It's OK, I didn't see you coming either." She looked at her son, then back at Dallas. "We were just driving out to this place down the road to watch the sunset. It's where the locals go, away from the tourists. They call it Preacher Point."

"Oh, right, I heard of it. On the bayside, I believe," Dallas said, thinking, of course, you dope, where else would you go to see the sunset?

"If you'd like, you could ride out there with us. I mean, if you're free."

The words were barely out of her mouth when she blushed. The invitation caught Dallas by surprise. He felt a wave of heat on his face, too. Boy, was he ever free.

"I don't really have any particular plans. Let me just pick up a snack or something. How about I get some wine? And extra Ring Dings?"

It was turning out to be quite a day. He had a place to live and now a date to watch a world-class sunset. They had a bottle of wine (screw cap) and a bag of Ring Dings. Oh, yes, and her eight-year-old son in tow.

"Lyle and I come out here all the time. It reminds us of home, even though this doesn't look anything like the Pacific. We used to love the sunsets at Newport Beach. This is our link to that."

It was a short drive to Preacher Point at the edge of Florida Bay, less than a half-mile down a narrow side road off U.S. 1. Dallas sat in the backseat of the Toyota, behind Lyle, fixated on the glow of Claire's dark-brown hair in the late afternoon sun. He smiled to himself when she referred to her divorce less than a year ago.

"I call it my great escape. Packed up the car and headed east. Wanted to get as far from Southern California — and him — as I could without leaving the country."

"Can't go much farther than this."

"It's another hundred miles to Key West. But that's farther west, so we'd actually be getting closer to California if we went there."

"Yeah, and Key West isn't really part of the United States, from what I hear. What do they call it?"

"The Conch Republic."

Claire kept glancing at Dallas as she talked. Her eyes weren't on the road when something brown and furry bounded out of a palmetto thicket and onto the pavement in front of them. She saw Dallas wince in anticipation of impact an instant before the creature thudded against the right-front fender. Claire shrieked, Lyle yelped and the car rocked side to side as it skidded to a stop.

"Oh my God, what did I hit?"

Dallas ran the 50 yards back to the body and was stooped over it when Lyle arrived with Claire close behind.

"Mom, it's a monkey."

"Oh, my god. Is it dead?"

Dallas looked at her grimly. "Not your fault. There was nothing you could do. It darted right out in front of you."

She looked devastated, and Dallas felt almost as bad for her as for the animal.

"Do you have anything in your trunk I could use to dig a hole?"

Dallas picked up a large stick and was starting to push the dead monkey to the side of the road when he heard a rustling in the bushes and turned as another dark creature leaped toward him. Dallas reared back and retreated to where Claire and Lyle stood dumfounded as one monkey after another bounded onto the road. There were five of them clustered around their fallen comrade, each no more than 2 1/2 feet tall. They were jumping, squawking and baring their teeth at Dallas. In their anguish, the apes had fingered him as the culprit. The scene was so absurd it would have been comical if it weren't so damn sad.

Claire was clearly shaken. Dallas thought about pointing out the lack of a Monkey Crossing sign to break the tension but thought better of it.

CHAPTER 4

"I never killed anything before. I mean, except for, you know, bugs, ants."

Dallas looked down at her from his perch on the rock, so-called Preacher Point, which arced up from the sand like a pulpit at the water's edge. Claire was sitting on a fallen tree. He thought the distress on her face made her even more attractive. He watched her eyes staring toward the bay where the sun had dipped behind a bank of clouds, bathing them in an orange glow.

"You might expect a dog or cat to run out in the road. But a monkey, it's almost like a, you know …"

"A person."

"What are monkeys doing in the Keys? I remember hearing about some that escaped from a research lab in Miami during Hurricane Andrew last summer. But that's a long way from here. I don't know, I just feel so bad."

"Don't blame yourself. If it's anyone's fault, it's mine. It never would have happened if I hadn't been with you."

She looked up at him, puzzled. "What do you mean?"

He gazed at the water and smiled slightly. The colors in the clouds were changing quickly. He saw reddish hues to the south deepening to burgundy. It reminded him they hadn't opened the wine.

"I know it sounds crazy. I just have a knack. Like, an odd habit, or whatever. For some reason, weird things happen around me. And to me."

She studied his face.

"Tough to explain. Story of my life, you might say. So many things have happened. Strange things. Some terrible things. Well, not all of it bad. But it is uncanny. And scary, when I think back on it. Sometimes I can't help but wonder, what next? That's why I hate to fly. I avoid it if I can. So what happens? The boat

I'm delivering blows up. That's how I ended up here. And I meet you, and a monkey runs out in front of your car. I mean, a monkey? You have to admit, it's unusual."

She wiped a tear from the corner of an eye, smearing her eyeliner. Dallas wondered if he should point it out.

"What other sort of things have happened?"

"Wait." He fetched the wine from a paper bag on the sand. He filled two plastic cups, handed one to her and climbed back onto the rock.

"Cheers."

She smiled.

"Not bad for screw cap stuff, huh. OK, you want the big stuff first?"

"All right, tell me the big stuff."

"OK, biggest of all. When I was 10, I saw President Kennedy get shot. I was in Dealey Plaza in Dallas with my mom and sister. It happened almost in front of us. Some of the pictures in magazines and books, you can see us. I had on a dark blue sweater. My mom wore a red dress."

"My God, you were there. You saw it? That must have been horrible."

"Beyond belief. I saw … I heard the …"

He stopped and stared across the water again. The sunset was becoming more dramatic, the colors enveloping the clouds. A blue sweater? She was trying to recall pictures and film footage she'd seen. It was mostly black-and-white.

"Another time — I was 16 — I was visiting my cousin in upstate New York. We take off on our own, hitchhiking. We didn't know anything was going on. We're just looking for an adventure. We get picked up by some kids who say they're going to a music festival. We had no idea what they're talking about. Next thing you know, we're in the middle of Woodstock."

The sadness in her eyes had given way to wonderment. He loved their hue: travel-brochure blue.

"There were, what, half a million people at Woodstock? Nobody knows exactly. But I've often thought, I'm probably the only one who was present when JFK was shot and Country Joe McDonald led the Fish Cheer."

"What's the Fish Cheer?"

It was Lyle, back from exploring crab hideouts in the sand. He was holding an empty crab shell at the end of a stick. Dallas noticed he had big hands. Claire looked at him and laughed.

"Give me an F. Give me an I. Give me an S. Give me an H!"

"Yeah," Dallas chuckled, "Something like that. One, two, three, what are we fishing for? Don't ask me I don't give a darn."

"Sounds pretty dumb," Lyle said. Claire hugged him and he scurried away.

"What was Woodstock like?"

"Better to be able to say you were there than the reality of being there. I mean, it was an amazing scene. Great fun at first. The music, all those famous bands. Seeing so many people converging on one place, and the crowd kept getting bigger and bigger. It's true what you hear, people really did get along pretty good, for a crowd that size. Of course, most people were so stoned that after awhile they were just laid out like squid in a fish market, or wandering around with smiles and blank looks on their faces. After a day or so it got to be too much. You could hear the music but you couldn't see what was happening on the stage. And it turned into a big hassle if you wanted something to eat or had to, ah, use the bathroom."

"I bet that part was a lot worse for the women."

"Yeah, well, there were lines like you wouldn't believe. I felt dirty, and everyone started to smell bad and look ugly. I don't much like crowds as it is. They make me paranoid, like I sense something bad is going to happen. Probably has to do with what happened in Dallas. I feel much more at ease in the middle of the ocean. But Woodstock, it was an ocean of people, and eventually I just wanted to get away from there. You couldn't just hop a bus and split. Finally, I told my cousin I was walking out of there and he could either come along or stay, but I was leaving. We walked for hours. We were exhausted, but I felt more exhilarated the farther we got from that mob. We ended up sleeping in another field that night. It was chilly. I was just glad to not be hemmed in."

He remembered it well, the feeling that he'd never been so free in his life. So liberating, it even felt good to shiver in the damp night air, at peace under a canopy of stars, away from the madness and a sense of being trapped. It was a feeling he'd sought refuge in often since, whenever life closed in.

As he talked, Dallas could feel her eyes on him. They brought the same comfort as those stars.

"After that, my mom decided I should be a journalist. She said, 'You have a nose for news.' I don't know what she thought of Woodstock, but she was impressed that it was a big deal on the national news. She wanted me to be another Edward R. Murrow, reporting on big events all over the world. Either that or an astronaut. My mom loved the astronauts. I remember she took me to a parade in Houston after one of the first Gemini flights. I got Gus Grissom's autograph. But I knew I could never be an astronaut. Too accident prone. Look."

Dallas held up the index finger of his right hand. It made a detour between the first and second joints. If he pointed straight ahead and said, "Go that way," the actual course indicated would be off to the left.

"I sliced it off with a hedge trimmer when I was 14. They couldn't get it back on straight. Another time I rode my mini bike off a bridge and broke my collarbone. So, I don't think NASA would be too comfortable with me flying their space shuttle."

She shook her head, unable to suppress a grin. "Sorry. It's kind of funny thinking of you flying the space shuttle and the guys in mission control all nervous that you're going to put a dent in it."

"Or worse. Like I said, weird things happen to me."

"What about journalism? Did you go to college?"

"Yes, but I majored in baseball. Actually, that was a compromise with my mom. I could have signed with the pros out of high school, but the University of Texas offered a baseball scholarship, so I went there to make her happy. She always thought I was going to be famous. She used to say, 'Someday you're going to do something special, something that will make people take notice.' "

Dallas laughed. "I guess most mothers probably think the same thing about their kids. The reality is, fame can be more trouble than it's worth. I've come to believe that you're probably better off going through life as anonymous as possible."

"Were you a good baseball player?"

"I was a pitcher. This crazy finger actually helped. It gave my pitches a different spin than hitters were used to seeing. You always wonder how good you might have been. I blew out my shoulder, so ..."

He was skipping over a few details. Like the fact that he was good enough to make it to the major leagues with the Baltimore Orioles in the middle of the 1979 season. After several years in the minors he finally developed sufficient control of his unique breaking ball and it gave hitters fits.

The Orioles used him out of the bullpen at first. He was effective enough, earning one victory, that he was named to start a game in New York against the Yankees. Two nights before he was to debut in Yankee Stadium he accompanied two teammates to a party in Boston. He hit it off with a woman in a red leather dress with a zipper down the front. Couldn't take his eyes off the zipper. When his teammates were ready to leave, Dallas said he'd catch a cab later. He was still contemplating the possibilities of the zipper when the cops arrived in response to a complaint by a neighbor. Someone was handing Dallas a joint as they came through the door.

Yes, fame can be a curse. A misdemeanor earned him a 90-day suspension from the commissioner of baseball. It cost him the stage in Yankee Stadium and a chance to pitch in the World Series that year. After his reinstatement, he tried to throw too hard in an attempt to win his way back into the Orioles' good graces and injured his shoulder. Within a year he was out of baseball. He never did set foot in Yankee Stadium. But what saddened him most was seeing his mother's vision of fame dissolve into infamy.

It was almost dark and something was nibbling at his ankles. Lyle was back asking when they were going to leave. Dallas looked at Claire and saw her smiling at him.

"Geez, I have been rambling on."

He wasn't usually so talkative. Something about her melted his inhibitions. He sensed something different about this woman. More than easy on the eyes, she was easy to be with. He wanted to know more about her. Instead he'd been jabbering away like a disc jockey on truth serum. Maybe it was because she was an attentive listener. That was a rare quality in a self-absorbed world. It was rare to find someone who bothered to listen.

#

Claire let Dallas drive them back to Islamorada. Watching her peripherally, he said casually, "So, you're on your own now?"

"Yes, thank God!"

It wasn't just the answer that pleased him, but the force of it.

The inflection brought to mind Martin Luther King's free-at-last speech. After 10 years of oppression, that is exactly the way Claire felt. When the divorce was finalized, just before Halloween, they had a big costume party at the Leaky Tiki highlighted by a ceremonial burning of an oar bearing her married name, Claire Dvorak. She didn't even mind the headache the next morning.

"Sometimes you have to experience pain in order to appreciate how good you feel when it goes away. At least that's what I tell myself."

She, too, was glossing over key details. Such as how the previous spring, with the last batch of bruises still in bright bloom, she'd packed up Lyle in her '85 Corolla and headed for Florida. Actually, the departure wasn't quite so sudden, she'd been planning it for months. The decisive moment wasn't the latest beating but rather the arrival of a letter with the news that her ship, so to speak, had come in.

"We were living in Orange County. Like I said, when I dumped Dvorak, I wanted to get as far away as I could without leaving the country. I was looking through a travel magazine and saw an ad in the back that said, 'Treasure Hunt in the Florida Keys.' So, I sent for the free brochure."

The ad was placed by a firm called Paradise Expeditions, which offered opportunities to assist on archaeological work at various places throughout the world under grant money. The project that caught Claire's attention involved working with archaeologists employed by the State of Florida who were monitoring the salvage of a Spanish galleon off Matecumbe Key. The grant didn't pay enough to support one person, let alone herself and Lyle, so the job at the bar was essential. She had been working overtime there with the salvage project at a virtual standstill through the winter. The big benefit of the salvage work was cathartic. Sifting through artifacts during the previous summer had helped Claire bury her own past.

"They haven't found the mother lode yet. But I found my freedom. And I also got to learn scuba diving."

"And get a tattoo."

They had stopped in front of the duplex where Dallas was staying. In the yellowish glow from a streetlight he could see crimson flash on her cheeks.

"It looks good on you. It's, ah, distinctive."

She smiled shyly. "That was part of my declaration of independence. I just figured, if there are going to be any marks on my body, it's going to be my decision to put them there."

Dallas hesitated. "Did your husband hit you?"

"Near the end. Before that, for a long time, he didn't touch me at all. He just ignored me. I'm not sure which was worse. But that's all in the past."

She dipped her shoulder and glanced back at the inky figure that appeared to be crawling out of her sleeveless tank top.

"I know, it was impulsive. So unlike the way I used to be. My friend, she has an iguana. A man she knows from the Bahamas gave it to her. Sometimes it sits on my shoulder. I figured, what the heck. Weird, huh?"

Dallas was going to mention the lizard he lost in the wreck of the sailboat, but Lyle was becoming impatient in the backseat. Instead, he opened the door and said, "Thanks for the sunset."

He followed the walkway toward the side of the house leading to his entrance around the back. He heard her footsteps on the gravel as she went around to the driver's side. The car door thudded shut. Dallas stopped and looked back. Through the window he saw her face turned toward him. A beam from a streetlight caught a glint in her eyes. She smiled and waved. Dallas's gaze locked on the Toyota's tail lights. As she drove away, he thought about the strange events of the past few days. Was the sailboat exploding an accident? Or was it destiny?

CHAPTER 5

The sign hand-lettered on brown cardboard and taped to the inside of the old Caddy's windshield said, "RUMS GOOD." Dallas figured that meant it was ideal transportation for bar-hopping. He got a vision of Claire riding next to him, top down — the Caddy's — and her hair blowing in the breeze. Sold!

For $350 (according to the sign: "A STEEL!") he became the proud owner of a '75 Cadillac El Cheapo convertible. OK, it was an old gas-guzzling barge. Faded white, red interior accented with multiple cigarette burns. Dallas immediately dubbed it the Great White, basic transportation with a certain funky Conch Republic panache. It would also serve as the Keys mobile bureau of *Florida Nautique* magazine.

One week after his awkward arrival in South Florida, Dallas had a car, a place to live and a job. He'd picked up an ancient Smith-Corona typewriter at Salvager Ned's Second-Hand Shop in Tavernier and banged out a few ideas for his Kennedy memoir. Meanwhile, he couldn't live on a fortune he'd never made. So he called Kirby D'Arbonnell, a rogue editor/publisher in Pensacola for whom he'd filed occasional dispatches for D'Arbonnell's outdoors magazines from various deep-sea fishing tournaments he'd participated in over the years.

D'Arbonnell had more failed publications in his wake than Liz Taylor had ex-husbands. He knew it wouldn't be easy to keep the latest one afloat, so he had an angle to make it stand out from the other fishing and boating rags on the newsstand. He explained the concept when Dallas ran into him in a bar just before he left on the sailboat delivery.

"I was thinking about having a centerfold. Some hot tamale fighting a tarpon," D'Arbonnell said. "You know, give them a few tips on fishing hot spots, reviews of the newest boats on the market and a little T & A."

"Yeah, like they do in those motorcycle magazines, babes on bikes," Dallas said. "You could call yours, 'Fishing Tips and Tits.' "

D'Arbonnell laughed. "Nothing raunchy like that. More wholesome, but stimulating. You know, the girl's not topless. Maybe she's wearing a sleeveless blouse, loose-fitting, and you get a glimpse of boob from the side."

"Real wholesome stuff, huh. I thought fishing and boating were supposed to be family activities."

"Don't start with me about family values. All the politicians and TV preachers are so full of crap on that topic. That's a big reason Bush lost. Especially the way things are these days with all the diseases to worry about. Maybe people are afraid to screw around as much, but they still think about it. Especially boating people. Has to do with being out in the sun and fresh air. And in Florida, they're not wearing many clothes. They get out on the water, have a good time, a few drinks, they get horny. Nothing wrong with that. We'll put some beefcake shots in for the women, too. Guys in Speedos with good tans casting fly rods. I say, give people what they really want and they'll buy it."

"Isn't that what Henry Ford said?"

"See, great minds think alike. Hey, if you decide to stay down there for a while, I could use a correspondent in South Florida."

D'Arbonnell wasn't paying much, but he was eager for anything Dallas could produce in South Florida with a sexy outdoorsy angle. It wasn't quite what mom had envisioned, but an ember of her journalistic dream for him still glowed.

#

His first assignment for *Florida Nautique* was to cover the Middle Keys Mid-Winter Offshore Powerboat Race. It was a perfect D'Arbonnell demographic event. The powerboat crowd was young, hip, flashy and, no doubt by the end of the day, drunk and horny.

Dallas parked the Caddy in a dirt parking lot next to A1A (bayside), scurried through a break in traffic and trudged the quarter-mile to Whale Harbor where he was to board *Calypso*, a 65-foot party boat that would serve as a viewing platform. It was just past 10, almost two hours before the scheduled start, and already Islamorada had been jolted out of Saturday morning slumber by the rip-roar of high-performance engines and the beat of reggae music.

On the docks, where the racing engines reeked of excessive chrome and RPMs, everyone had a Bloody Mary in hand and multiple gold chains around their neck. It was a toss-up as to which was more ostentatious, the racing boats or their fans, many of them young Latinos from Miami. All fashionably tanned, impeccably coifed. And then there were the women.

The photographer D'Arbonnell hired would have a field day. Hopefully, he'd save some film for the race, Dallas thought as he made note of a driver moving down the dock with a woman on each arm, both of them amply accoutered with diamonds, hairspray and cleavage. The driver, handsome with raven-black hair slicked back, received a cheer when he stepped aboard a boat with a bright red hull and name lettered in gold: *Muy Caliente.*

"*Mita*, Ortega!" said a stocky man with a black beard and a hoop earring. "*Marinero fiero.*"

Ramon Ortega was the defending national champion on the offshore racing circuit in the superboat class. Like a heavyweight fighter or rock star, he came with the inevitable entourage of burly men and languid women, all of whom looked like leftovers from the old set of "Miami Vice." It was not necessarily an illusion. In the '80s, when "Vice" was the trendy king of prime time, TV cop Don Johnson could often be seen fitting about Biscayne Bay in his speedboat by day, while at night some of the notable professional racers were ferrying pot and cocaine through the ocean inlets of South Florida. Some of the real-life drama was more dramatic than fiction. One boat racer was chased through Miami on Interstate 95 during lunch hour and machine-gunned to death in his pickup truck by a Colombian drug gang. Once, in a clever ruse, racers used two identical boats to slip a load of coke past the feds during a race.

In his research for this assignment, Dallas came across an old newspaper clipping in which an exasperated Coast Guard official summed up the problem:

"During the day we're asked to patrol their race course during events for emergency reasons. But at night, we're chasing many of the same guys for smuggling. That used to be a joke. Now it's reality."

Some of the top drivers of that era were now serving time on drug-related convictions, and the sport was struggling to regain the million-dollar sponsorships it lost because of the scandal. But drivers such as Ortega were proof that offshore racing hadn't lost its flamboyance. The 29-year-old son of an exiled Cuban factory owner had a Ferrari dealership in South Miami and an older brother in the South Dade Stockade awaiting trial on racketeering charges. But Ramon's record was clean, except for one tax evasion charge that didn't stick.

While two sweating mechanics fine-tuned the twin 535-horsepower turbo-charged engines, Ortega stood with arms folded on the deck of his new 40-foot racing catamaran, preening for the shutterbugs. His jumpsuit matched the boat's vivid paint job. His name was embroidered in cursive on his chest. No grease under his fingernails; they were impeccably manicured. Dallas peered past Ortega into the cockpit and noticed a gold crucifix dangling from one of the throttles. The crowd on the dock played to his vanity.

"How's the new boat, Ramon?"

"Fast, very fast."

"Do you expect a tough race out there today?"

A glint of sunlight off a gold tooth accompanied his reply.

"There is no doubt who will win, my friend. The only question is, how far will we be ahead at the finish?"

In fact, the outcome was of little consequence. The regular racing season would not begin until May. This event had been conceived to help boost business at the resorts and restaurants in the Middle Keys during the lull between the year-end holidays and the spring tourist surge. The race course would be set in relatively protected waters inside the Keys' barrier reefs. Nonetheless, it can get sloppy in Hawk's Channel in January, so the race held appeal as an old-fashioned test of machismo that many drivers favored over the inshore flat-water dashes on the summer circuit. Those were a measure of horsepower; this would tell which crew had the biggest *cojones*. Dallas noted that Ortega's cockiness was unwavering even though his catamaran hull was better suited to calmer conditions.

"Rough or calm, doesn't matter. This is an appetizer. We want our opponents to get a taste of what they are going to be in for this season," Ortega said before donning his helmet and sliding into the cockpit beneath the protective canopy modified from an F-16 fighter plane.

The random blasts of engines revving grew into a relentless cacophony as crews began casting off and motoring out of the harbor. The noise and vibrations of the engines roused the spectators. They began a mass surge toward private and commercial vessels that quickly joined the racing boats in a disorganized procession toward open water, bucking and weaving on the waves and wakes. All around there were smiles, shouts, waves and fists pumping.

The level of excitement and anticipation was akin to that of Pamplona, Spain, for the running of the bulls. Here it was, Florida style: the running of the high-octane, mega-horsepower, Kevlar-skinned bulls. Dallas wasn't sure which held the greater promise of danger or rush of adrenaline, dashing bulls or racing boats. Both, wildly unpredictable.

The allure was hard to grasp. Dallas thought of Hemingway's Pomplona in "The Sun Also Rises," the incredulity of a waiter to the news that a man running ahead of the bulls had been gored to death in the interest of fun.

It happened in boat racing, too, usually with a head injury sustained from impact. Not often, but the possibility was the part of the excitement that incited the crowd on the docks.

Dallas shuffled with the flow of people boarding *Calypso*. He flashed his press pass and stepped aboard. A young blonde woman looking chilly in a white one-piece swimsuit handed him a can of light beer. He took it and, in the spirit of the moment, responded with the appropriate succinctness of a Hemingway character: "*Salud!*"

#

Calypso anchored inshore of the starting area. Dallas's credential afforded access to the media viewing area on the upper deck, though he and a reporter from the *Keynoter* and a Spanish-speaking woman from a society magazine in Miami seemed to be the only media representatives on board. The remainder of the spectators consisted of wives and girlfriends of racers and assorted hangers on. Most stood with a firm grip on the rail as the boat rocked in the three-to-five-foot swells. Some wore seasick prevention patches behind ears. A few already looked green around the gills, while others matched every sway of the deck with a swig of beer or Bloody Mary, reveling in the floating happy hour.

Fortunately, the wind was more easterly than northerly, or it would likely have been too rough for the race. Just the same, the thought of a 90-mph ride over white-capped speed-bumps made Dallas's back ache. He had once been asked to navigate in a race off Pensacola, but after a short test ride left him breathless and weak-kneed he declined. Might as well ride a barrel over Niagara Falls. These guys were loco. He'd asked the driver why he risked his neck and sacroiliac on a sport that cost far more than prize money and most sponsorships could hope to compensate.

The response: "Chicks dig the boats. The boats are sexy. The vibrations from the engines get them excited."

So why not just tie up at the waterfront bars and let the engines idle? It seemed to Dallas that the racing was a primal male power play, more expensive than arm wrestling but slightly less dangerous than a gun fight. To the victor went, a backrub? Whatever. There was no shortage of women aboard the *Calypso* eager to witness the spectacle. They were, of course, an integral part of it, though some seemed amused by it. Two women standing next to Dallas returned the wave of the driver of the pace boat as it passed close by on its way to the starting area. The silver-hulled speedboat was more than 40 feet long, sleek as an arrow. The woman closest to Dallas nudged her companion.

"He's such a jerk. He acts like that boat's a big prick."

Her friend smirked. "He just wishes he had one, but instead he is one."

The racers were milling, waiting for the pace boat to begin the run to the starting line. But Dallas's attention was drawn to the sky, where more than a dozen helicopters meandered like giant dragonflies. A few of them carried photographers, some bore race officials, others had paramedics aboard. Some of the racers, including all in the open and superboat classes, had a helicopter that was either owned or leased by the racing team, which would follow its boat around the course. Consequently, when that group of the largest boats in the race came roaring toward the starting line side-by-side, churning a swatch of spray and foam a quarter-mile wide, it was difficult to tell who was racing, the boats or the choppers.

This peculiar symbiotic relationship of raging horsepower in the air and on water created a stunning commotion. Dallas was more amazed by the helicopters, streaking low in consort with the boats, than by the boats themselves. It appeared the pilots, flying close together at high speeds, were at greater risk than the racing crews. Dallas was reminded of the helicopters in "Apocalypse Now". In fact, he thought *Apocalypse* would make a great name for one of these race boats. If war was hell, powerboat racing was hell-bent.

The din rolled across the water like thunder, and for a moment enveloped the spectator fleet. As the pack pulled even with *Calypso*, a boat that had been trailing on the approach suddenly shot ahead of the others, a red streak on the blue palette of sea and sky. Ortega was already where he wanted to be. Out front. Showing off. As the tidal wave of machinery passed, Dallas noticed the two women next to him exchange a smile. Ah, yes, those good vibrations. *Muy caliente.*

Turning to follow the rooster tails, he noticed something else, another familiar hull lurking nearly a half-mile to the south — this one black. He bummed a peek through the *Keynoter* reporter's binoculars to confirm his suspicion: Hello, *Mary Lou II*. Nice to see you, again.

CHAPTER 6

Offshore powerboat racing is like baseball in one respect, it doesn't demand undivided attention. It is like trying to catch a cab in New York City. You never know when the boats will appear, or from which direction they will come. And when they show up, they're going like mad. You wave, but they zip right past. You shrug and pop open another beer.

The only way to really watch a race, to observe the exhilaration, the bone-jarring, mind-numbing monotony that racers experience — short of being aboard one of the boats themselves — is from the air. For those in the spectator fleet it isn't a spectator sport at all, it's an opportunity to work on one's tan with a cocktail in hand. The race is somewhere over the horizon.

A man pouring French brut for a couple of Cuban girls in Spandex tights and white ruffled blouses looked up and shouted, "Anyone know who's winning?" Dallas smiled: It was Ortega's stocky admirer with the beard and earring. Whoops, didn't anticipate that wave. Now he's going to smell like a winery. The *chiquitas* rolled their eyes and shuffled away. Tough break. It's like that for the racers, too. One ornery wave can ruin your whole day, although the consequences are more severe than stained laundry.

This contest of machine and machismo was somewhere off to the southwest where the symphony of racing engines was barely audible. Dallas heard it as a faint hum that gradually became more distinct as the lead boats returned from the first 30-mile loop. Now Dallas invoked his fisherman's skills, scanning the skyline as if to spot a frigate bird that would reveal a school of dolphin. See the birdie? There, three dark specks aloft. 'Copters coming. Conversations were suspended, vantage points reclaimed along the rail.

"Who is it? Who's in first?"

The *Keynoter* reporter was trying to steady his binoculars.

"Looks like two of them pretty close together."

Dallas could make out the twin plumes of white spray on a parallel course maybe 100 yards apart. Two boats escorted by three helicopters, the choppers bracketing the boats, attitude angled slightly forward, tails higher than noses. One so low and close behind one of the boats it looked to be getting a shower from the bigger bursts of spray.

"The one on the left ... *Caliente!*"

Ortega's No. 1 fan had a keen eye or a pretty strong pair of binoculars. He was right. The other boat was yellow. What were they doing, 85, 90 mph? Hard to judge speeds on the water. They were skipping over a pretty good chop, periodic flashes of daylight beneath the hulls betraying dolphin-like leaps, the massive hulls rising completely out of the water and crashing down with a jolt that stressed the integrity of every component. It was mesmerizing watching them approach, mad mechanical sea serpents lunging and snarling out of the foam.

Something else was in the picture now, an element that didn't fit. It appeared from behind and seaward of *Muy Caliente*, looming there like a shadow or an apparition. Too low for a helicopter, but it wasn't behaving like a boat. Nonetheless, its appearance didn't surprise Dallas as much as it did the others watching. This time he didn't need binoculars to confirm another unannounced appearance of the *P-BJ-003*.

Fingers were being pointed, queries raised, shoulders shrugged. Who? What? Huh? Anybody got a clue?

"It's, ah, experimental," Dallas said, eliciting an incredulous look from the Keynoter reporter.

The boats were getting close now, an aquatic ballet of bounce and spray accompanied by the operatic crooning of engines and flutter of helicopter props. And the *P-BJ-Whatever-the-Hell-003* hanging right with them, only occasionally nipping a wavetop and kicking up a shower of droplets that gleamed like diamonds. Then, just before the stampede reached the area where most of the spectator boats were congregated, this phantom of the regatta slingshotted ahead so suddenly, accelerating so rapidly, that a gasp swept across the deck of *Calypso*. As they dashed past, bound for the northern checkpoint of the course, *Muy Caliente* surged away from the yellow boat and lit out after the intruder. Ortega had to know this strange craft wasn't part of the race, but his ego wasn't about to let him be shown up.

What happened next was reconstructed later from interviews with observers in helicopters and the crew aboard the yellow boat, *Bow-Wow*, driven by Dr. Herb Leventhal, the racing veterinarian from Great Neck, New York. The drama was played out beyond the horizon, out of sight of the spectator fleet, and resolved with stunning suddenness.

Ortega continued his pursuit for several minutes, bouncing desperately over the waves, steadily closing the gap. Then, just as *Muy Caliente* caught up to the experimental craft, it shot ahead again, pulling away effortlessly. Ortega called for more power, and his throttleman pegged the levers, spurring the engines to their limits. *Muy Caliente* was literally flying now, dancing over the wave tops on the edge of control. As waves are not created equal, each presented a different peril, a distinct problem for micro-second adjustment. It only took one peak a little higher than those around it to catch the tip of the right sponson and send Ortega's boat into a cartwheel.

It was a spectacular sight for the few who witnessed it, this huge hunk of space-age composite materials, 40 feet long with 1,800 horsepower raging at one end, flipping ass-over-applecart. Imagine the hand of Neptune grabbing a humpbacked whale by the tale and hurling it out of the ocean, and the splash it would make.

That was the grand finale of *Muy Caliente*'s Ballbuster Ballet. The judges scored it 9.0 on bold artistic presentation, but marked it down on technical merit. Alas, as this was not a regular-season race and wasn't being taped for television, nobody captured it on video.

"The most incredible belly-flop you've ever seen," is the way the pilot of the closest helicopter described it.

"How fast do you think they were going when they crashed?" Dallas later asked Leventhal, who stopped at the scene for several minutes. With paramedics descending from a rescue helicopter and taking charge of the situation, he continued on and won the race, which was black-flagged a lap short because of worsening sea conditions.

"They had to be up to 130, 135, which way was too fast on that water. We got just up over 100, and I just about broke my kishkas," Leventhal said with a grin.

Kirby D'Arbonnell laughed when he read that quote. He was ecstatic about the story Dallas turned in. He especially liked the contrast of the description of the scene outside the emergency room at Mariners Hospital with the two women — the same exotic-looking duo that accompanied Ortega on the dock before the race — teary-eyed and disheveled, with that of the post-race revelry at the Leaky Tiki. And the part when Ortega's navigator, seated at the bar amid an attentive gallery, still wearing his racing suit with traces of blood visible on a sleeve, one hand gripping a cocktail, the other in a sling, and with eyes opaquely glassed, succinctly summed up the day with: "That's boat racing."

Once again, it was Pamplona in all its outrageous excess. If nothing else, the spirit of celebration made perfect sense. Once again the bulls had run in all their mindless splendor. Everyone had a glimpse into the raging nostrils of death, felt its breath, watched it rush by. They saw someone get gored, or at least heard about it. The victims would recover. No actual deaths to put a damper on the mood of the festival. So they could all har-har and hoist another round, grab the nearest pert ass and bellow raucously long into the night.

D'Arbonnell couldn't have scripted it better. Dallas's story captured all the drama and debauchery. The photographer got a good shot of the crumpled remains of *Muy Caliente* when it was towed in bound and buoyed by floats to keep it from sinking. The crew was more fortunate than the boat, thanks to their enclosed cockpits. The racing association's chief medic cheerfully remarked that there'd have been three funerals to attend if not for the protective bubbles, which had become standard equipment since several racers were killed or seriously injured from impact injuries in the late '80s. It was the same reason presidents and popes no longer rode in open cars. If JFK had his bulletproof top on that day, his trip to Dallas would have merely been a 15-second clip on the evening news. Without it, he was a sitting duck.

Ortega sustained a concussion and dislocated elbow. Still groggy, and with his female companions nodding solemnly at each side of the hospital bed, he declared that not only would he be back in time for the first regular-season race in late April but guaranteed a victory. His throttleman had broken ribs to go with a concussion, which left him babbling incoherently about the nightclub bouncer he thought had cold-cocked him for no apparent reason.

"I'd of knocked the motherfucker's teeth out, if I'd seen him coming," he kept repeating, vowing revenge as soon as he got out of the hospital.

The navigator received a bloody nose and bruises but never lost consciousness. He was holding Ortega's head out of the water, trying to revive him when the rescue team landed. It could have been tragic. As it turned out, for an off-season race that didn't mean much and didn't offer much to see aside from the sideshows of the characters involved, it had been remarkably entertaining. And it left an intriguing riddle, which Ortega's navigator phrased in much the same way Dallas had after another boat ride that ended with a splash:

"What the fuck was that thing we were chasing?"

It was a very good question, one that stirred considerable debate and conjecture that evening as a chaser for beer, rum and assorted exotic concoctions. The P-BJ-003 had vanished as mysteriously as it appeared. Dallas had noticed the *Mary Lou II* chugging to the north after the crash. But neither it nor the experimental craft was spotted off Islamorada again the day.

CHAPTER 7

The answer to the navigator's question was close at hand, as Dallas suspected, amid the chaos in the carnival twilight that rocked the Leaky Tiki, a predictably contrived Keys outpost inspired by a line in a Jimmy Buffett song that referred to Gardner McKay's boat in the early-'60s television serial "Adventures in Paradise." There clearly had been a purpose to the dramatic appearance of the *P-BJ-003* in the middle of the race. If it was for show, there had to be someone around with something to tell, if you could sift through the din of alcohol-addled chatter.

Dallas stood at a corner of the main bar, trying to get a beer and his bearings when a muscular fellow with big hair wedged his way in and leaned across the bar. He held a rock-solid forearm out to a barmaid with Asian eyes and eye-opening curves who was packing a tray with gimlets, screwdrivers and sours.

"Hey, sweetheart, check out this new cologne. It's called, Come To Me. Get it? Come to me."

Without looking up from the drinks, the barmaid said, "It doesn't smell like come to me. Get it?" She picked up the tray and walked away."

The guy looked at Dallas and cracked up.

"That was good, I'll have to remember that," burly dude said and waded back into the mob. The next time Dallas noticed him he was holding an arm to the nose of an unsteady brunette, jabbering into her ear. She grimaced and smacked his arm. Mr. Muscles laughed so hard his shoulders shook.

The problem for Dallas in this scavenger hunt was he didn't know the crowd. In a sea of faces, none stood out as familiar, except for Claire, who looked harried behind the bar trying to keep up with the torrent of orders. These go-fast boaters drank with the voracity that their boats guzzled fuel. Dallas briefly caught Claire's eye and she forced a smile, then made an exasperated face.

He kept scanning and noticed Dr. Herb Leventhal at a table with a group gesturing at a man wearing a Stetson who was standing with one foot up on a chair. The man was drinking something brownish in a clear plastic cup. Dallas guessed Scotch. He drifted over, bumping through a maze of buttocks, elbows and one ample pair of breasts. He stood close enough to eavesdrop, facing away but watching peripherally. Something about the Stetson was familiar. Dallas fixed on the motion of the hat, the man's head bobbing as he talked and the exaggerated movement of his hands, as if they were connected to his jaw by a string inside his jacket. He reminded Dallas of one of those cymbal-playing mechanical monkeys. Then it dawned on him: It was the man with the cowboy hat aboard the *Mary Lou II* the day of the sailboat explosion.

"What can I tell you, it's a free ocean out there. We were testing. We had a right to be there. We weren't in anybody's way. It's not our fault if someone pushes their boat too fast for the conditions. Everyone has to take responsibility for his own safety. He was a damn fool."

Dallas had trouble hearing everything being said amid the music and party bedlam except for scattered words and phrases. "Experimental." ... "Unprecedented." ... "Revolutionary new system." And one boast that was repeated three or four times in the five minutes Dallas stood there: "This thing is going to be the new Detroit. I tell ya, the next Detroit."

A waitress deftly threaded her way through the crowd balancing a tray above head level. The man grabbed her other arm and ordered a round for Leventhal's party, punctuating his instructions with "darling" this and "sweetheart" that. Dallas had a sudden urge to get away and took a walk along A1A across the bridge to Whale Harbor. He had a fresh grouper sandwich on a sesame bun and washed it down with a Corona, pondering the origin of putting lime in beer. But, damn, it slid down easily. He had another while reviewing the events of the day.

Several rolls of mental pictures awaited processing, from the arrogance of Ortega to the boats and their attendant helicopters, to the ominous *Mary Lou II* and the man in the hat. It reminded him how witnesses to the same event can extract vastly different viewpoints. He drained the last few ounces of beer and plunked the bottle down firmly, in the process setting his resolve. If he was going to write, he needed to concentrate on details. He needed clarity.

When he returned to the boat crowd's bash there were nearly a dozen racers stripped to their briefs in the water at the poolside bar having a chugging contest. In friggin' January. Dallas shivered. It was well after dark and there was a substantial chill in the wind, which had shifted to the northeast and intensified since the race. Nobody seemed to mind. A crowd circled the pool cheering on the chuggers until one contestant vomited in the water. Everyone cleared out in a hurry, leaving the rube with his shame.

Back at the Leaky Tiki a reggae band had taken over the stage under the thatched roof, and the dance floor was shimmering with Latino girls. Their racer boyfriends, a few still wearing jumpsuits with their names on their chests, others in tight jeans and T-shirts, danced with drinks in hand, bumping every fanny within range. Dallas wended his way back to the bar, hoping for a word with Claire. He had called to ask if she'd have a drink with him later. She wasn't sure. It was going to be a busy night. She'd let him know. Now she was leaning over the bar in vigorous discourse with a tall, thin fellow with streaks of gray in a ragged, brown beard. Dallas could tell he wasn't part of the powerboat crowd. Less the peacock, though self-assured in a different way. He had the ruddy appearance of an outdoorsman and the demeanor of one who fancies himself an intellectual. A cerebral crabber?

Dallas felt his heart sink, but at the same time his curiosity was piqued. He turned away and plowed head-on into the man with the Stetson, dislodging the hat and knocking the drink out of his hand. Surprise turned to apology, and Dallas quickly picked up the hat and offered to replace the drink.

"Scotch?"

"Bourbon."

The man eased the hat back into place and laughed heartily. "Dang, I haven't gotten blindsided like that since I was covering punts for ol' Bear Bryant at 'Bama." By the look of him that was many bourbons ago.

"Edison Hawke. The Third," he said, holding out a hand and laughing again. The hand was tepid and a bit shaky, but the grip was firm. Two barstools suddenly opened up. Hawke seized one and motioned Dallas toward the other. "Do I hear a drawl? Where you from, son?"

"Dallas."

"I knew it. I can smell a Texan a mile away. I used to be in the oil business out in Houston. Made my fortune and got out before it all crapped out. Lots of poor bastards stayed in and lost their shirts. Now I'm into international investment and development, if you know what I mean. Look at these boat people, they all think they're hot shit. But I could buy 'em all and have 'em lighting my cigarettes and bringing me drinks if I wanted to. Now, I can tell you're not a boat racer, so I know you know where I'm coming from."

Dallas knew he'd hate to be stuck in a window seat next to this guy on a nonstop to LA. But for the price of a drink or two or three he hoped to learn a few things, although it might require hip-boots to wade through the malarkey. Hawke had his drink down to the ice and was waving it at the Asian barmaid.

"Like I was saying — hey, baby doll, get my good buddy here another beer, and make sure it's good and cold." Then turning back to Dallas, "Now ain't she the sexiest thing you've ever seen? Nothing sweeter than Asian honey, day or night."

The barmaid looked at Dallas and rolled her eyes as she served the bourbon and the beer in plastic cups.

"See? They can't do enough for you."

Dallas chose this moment to blindside him again.

"So what was the *P-BJ-Double-oh-3* doing out there today? Or does it have another name?"

This would be the first time, and hopefully the last, that Dallas would see a man spray bourbon through his nose. It made him think of the lunchroom in junior high and his buddies making him laugh as he was taking a drink of milk. The server saw it, too, and she froze with an expression of horror and amazement.

"Now what would you know about that?" Hawke said, wiping his face on his sleeve and adjusting his hat.

"I know it's experimental. P for prototype, right? But what's the BJ stand for?"

Hawke took a big gulp of bourbon and studied Dallas, his eyes suddenly in sharper focus than they'd been?

"Bobby Joe? Billy Jack? Big Jake? Baines Johnson? Billy Jean, she's not my lover? Blow job?"

"Now listen to this wise-ass Texas boy."

"Sorry, I'm just messing with you. I was on a sailboat that blew up off Lauderdale about a week ago. I think you were on one of the boats that stopped when I was picked up."

An odd look of recognition passed over Hawke's face and he began alternately sipping and nodding, the hat moving again in the cocksure bob.

"Aw, right, right! That was an unfortunate happenstance. Lucky thing you weren't hurt bad."

"So what's it stand for, the BJ?"

"If you must know: Behrent Juergens. That's the designer. He's a genuine German genius. He's come up with a whole new approach to speed across water. It's revo-*lutionary*. Know what I mean?"

"Is it a boat or a hovercraft or what?"

"Hell, it's no boat. Not in the conventional sense. Behrent's got some high-brow name for it. Surface-actuated something or other, based on some highfalutin hydro-dynamics sorcery or some damn thing. He's a crazy, brainy old bastard, but he knows his physics and shit. I call it a skimmer. I don't quite understand how it does it, but that baby flies. He calls it the Juergens Principle."

At this point, Hawke took a quick look to see if anyone else was listening, then leaned close and began speaking in a confidential, conspiratorial tone. The bourbon on his breath was overpowering.

"We're sitting on a gold mine and a powder keg at the same time. This thing is going to cause the world to rethink transportation. What we're talking about is the new Detroit. Know what I mean? The second Detroit."

He leaned closer still. The brim of his hat was almost brushing Dallas's brow.

"Of course, the old Detroit is going to fight it all the way. There's billions of dollars at stake, and lives and livelihoods, too. And the military is involved. We've got a proposal pending with them. But the damn Pentagon is dragging their feet. The chain of command is such a tangle of bullshit. It's going to cost them, too. We're talking to other governments. Someone else will jump on it if they don't act soon. I always say, waste time, you waste money. That's why I never sit still for long."

Dallas was trying to read the dividing line between fact and fiction here, and the influence of bourbon in the tug of war between ego and discretion. Right then Hawke was looking for more fuel, waving his empty cup and becoming agitated by the lack of response.

"Time and money's a wasting. It's like with this place. I've told John, the manager, as much. None of my friends will come here anymore because of this kind of crap. I don't know why I bother, but I see the potential here and I hate to see potential go to waste. I want to see them get back on course. I keep taking him aside and telling it as I see it. 'Cause that's the kind of guy I am. Hey, hey, doll!"

"How fast does it go?"

"You gotta take care of your loyal customers first, the locals, right. Huh?"

"The, ah, skimmer. How fast?"

Hawke was off on a rant, a barstool politician in search of a constituency. Dallas was doing his best to reel him back, like a marlin you bring almost within gaffing range only to have it take off again for open water. He paused and looked at Dallas, eyes lightly glazed.

"Oh, let me tell you, the imagination's the limit with that deal there. Now, if I could just ..."

"You know, I might be interested in doing a story on it for *Florida Nautique* magazine."

The hat stopped moving and Hawke studied Dallas for a moment, trying to focus through the alcohol haze.

"You're some kind of reporter? Son of a bitch! Should've guessed. You'd have the scoop of all time with this deal, if I gave it to you. But my investors wouldn't go for it. Not now. Too much still up in the air. But I'll tell you what I'll do, son. You give me your card and you'll be the first I'll call when the time comes. And you can take that to the bank, 'cause I'm a man of my word. And — well, thank God, I'm about to die of thirst."

The barmaid was back with his refill and Hawke was nodding again and complimenting.

"See, she's the best. Just put that on my tab, honey, and put another on there for my friend, Tex, whatever he wants. Did you know, he's a writer? Lotsa great writers from Texas. I always loved reading that Loo-ie L'Amour."

And with that he spun off the stool and lurched away, though he paused for a parting shot. "Remember what I said, you gotta take care of your loyal customers, 'cause that's where your bread's buttered. Otherwise, you're wasting time and you're wasting goddamned money. And that's a crime."

Dallas turned back to the bar grinning. The server was standing there with the same look of horrified amazement as before.

"Fuckin' Eddie and his tab."

"Quite a character."

"What he is, is bad news and a lot of B.S. 'Put it on my tab. Put it on my tab.' Then he tips his hat. That's the only tip you ever get. You a friend of his? I've never seen you here."

"I've just been in the Keys a few days, and he's no friend. I was just trying to get some information for a magazine story I'm doing. Name's Dallas."

"My friends call me Sami. I write, too. Poetry. It relaxes me. Takes my mind off this place and the B.S."

He liked the way she said B.S. He liked her eyes, as deep and dark as the Milky Way. He was trying to decide. Japanese? Definitely not Chinese. Maybe Korean. But something else there, too.

"Nice to meet you, Mr. Loo-ie L'Amour."

Dallas laughed. "Funny thing is, Louis L'Amour isn't even from Texas. I read a lot of his books when I was a kid. It says right on the book jackets, he's from North Dakota."

"But you're from Texas. It says so right in your name."

"It would be funny if I were really from someplace else, like North Dakota. It's confusing sometimes. Used to be worse when I still lived there. I'd have to give my name and address and I'd say, 'Dallas,' and they'd say, 'No, your name.' So, I'd say, 'Dallas Huston' — Huston's my last name spelled H-u-s-t-o-n. And they'd say, 'Well, which is it, do you live in Dallas or Houston?' It's like Abbott and Costello doing the 'Who's on First' routine."

"Who? Where?"

She didn't wait for the answer. Duty called. Dallas watched her walk away and lean over to reach into the cooler. Damn. What's her story? But then who'd guess his, or anyone else's here? Maybe they all had something in common, running away from some twisted past to the end of the world. Or close to it. Dallas used to know a fisherman who liked to boast, "I've been to the four corners of the world and seen monkeys fuck." But the fisherman was deluded. If nothing else, experience had taught Dallas that the mind misses as much as the eye sees. He also knew he had once again arrived at a strange corner of the world, and there was more afoot than sappy tourism and free-spirited escapism.

There were monkeys in the underbrush just up the road. Or was it down the road? Oceanside? Bayside? Whatever. Alcohol and fatigue were trying to steer him into weird philosophical tangents, where the ramblings of Edison Hawke III might even seem profound.

Dallas set his beer down. The diluted draft was beginning to taste like bilge water. He pushed it away and looked around. The crowd had thinned. The reggae band had finished its set and was moving its gear into the adjacent Parrothead Lounge. The Leaky Tiki was closing, the action shifting inside. Claire, Sami and the two bartenders were busy cleaning up. Dallas decided to try again with Claire. She saw him approach, and before he had a chance to speak she introduced him to a lanky black man, one of the band members, who was waiting for a rum-and-coke.

"This is the one I was telling you about."

"Aw, right, the boat captain."

The musician held out a hand with fingers as long and thick as cigars. His name was Keith, which didn't seem to fit with the dreadlocks and Caribbean soul. Someone named Keith should be a car salesman from Cleveland, not a Rastaman, Dallas was thinking as they shook hands and the man's fingers wrapped squid-like around his hand. He had noticed those amazing fingers earlier as they massaged some remarkable riffs out of a beet-red guitar.

"Keith works on the salvage project I'm involved with," Claire said.

This woman had some interesting acquaintances. Cerebral crabber. Guitarist treasure-hunter.

"Yeah, so there's a dude maybe you should meet. Old Captain Devereaux; he's the head of the salvage operation," Keith said. "He's looking for someone can handle a boat. Claire says you're new here, and that's good because the man don't want to hire any of the locals. But he wants to find somebody pretty quick. I could arrange for you to meet him right away. I mean, if you're interested."

At that moment Dallas was more interested in whether Claire was available for the remainder of the evening. But he was curious and agreed to a meeting the next day at some boatyard he'd need directions to find. He shoved the card Keith handed him into his pocket and continued pursuit of Claire, who had moved away again. He waited another five minutes before she returned. Was she avoiding him? The answer, when it came, wasn't reassuring.

"I can't. I'm sorry. Tonight's not a good night."

Dallas could tell she didn't want to explain. Her eyes were everywhere else, avoiding his. He took the hint and strolled to the entrance to the Parrothead Lounge where a reggae beat was spilling out the door. He thought he could pick out Keith's voice from the others, doing a passable Marley on "Stir It Up." Humming along and wondering why they always sang "steer" instead of "stir." Guess because Marley did. Glancing toward the Tiki bar, most of the lights out there were off now. Nobody left except Claire and one bartender, who was closing out the register.

Then the guy with the brown beard stepped out of the shadows. He and Claire had another brief but animated conversation before she grabbed her purse and they left together. She didn't look particularly happy but she had made the choice to be with him. Whoever the hell he was. Dallas cursed under his breath. Suddenly the night turned ugly, the music seemed to mock him, and his ears resounded with the discordant echo of piano keys randomly struck.

CHAPTER 8

Still aware of the beat but not hearing the music, Dallas shuffled along a path, the crunch of gravel adding to the percussion. Following the walkway to the resort's private beach and out onto the sand, thinking this is what it must feel like walking on the moon, except with more gravity. Up there, you'd never imagine all the shit going on down here.

He regarded the moon like he did the ocean, as a haven, at once inviting and forbidding. For Dallas, the sea was a point of reference, the only place he'd truly felt at home in a long time. He shivered in the wind rattling the palms and thought maybe that explained a sudden feeling of discord. Or was it something else?

He scanned the sand, bright in the moonlight. Something caught his eye. No, somebody. Shit, the racer who threw up in the chugging contest. Unconscious, though by the grace of Bacchus or some benevolent deity, still breathing. Dumb fuck's going to end up with hypothermia. Dallas looked around. All he could come up with was a tarp covering some beach chairs. He dragged it over and placed it over the man, who gave a snort but didn't move.

"You're welcome."

Anxiety abating, he walked back along the shore toward the yacht basin and sat on a wooden-slab bench, staring offshore at the wave tops dancing in the moonlight. He reflected again on the images of the day: Ortega's crash; Edison Hawke III and the mysterious skimmer; reggae Keith. And what of his own reaction to Claire giving him the brush? Out of character. Wasn't there always another intriguing barmaid in the next bar?

A shadow suddenly appeared on the concrete in front of the bench. Or maybe it had been there and he hadn't noticed. When he glanced back, it took a moment to make out the face because of the glare from the dock light. It was Claire's co-worker, Sami.

"I saw you sitting here, Mr. L'Amour. Thinking up the plot for your next book?"

He smiled. "Yes, just working out who all the bad guys are going to be. What I need now is a pretty girl. Accepting applications."

"Hmmm, perhaps," She said, joining him on the bench. "Or maybe I'd rather be a bad guy. Any law saying you can't have a bad guy who's a pretty girl?"

"Not at all, but I don't think you'd be a convincing bad guy."

"Maybe you just don't know me."

There was playfulness in her eyes that belied the end of a busy night of work.

"Maybe I'd like to get to know you better."

"What if you didn't like what you found out?"

"Maybe it's a risk I might be willing to take. All for the benefit of literature, of course."

He felt the smile all the way to his ears. She crinkled her nose at him.

"I do have my good points. Like, for instance, I give the best backrubs in Islamorada. Make that, in the whole Keys."

The remark surprised him. She noticed.

"It's my other, how you say, profession. I'm a masseuse. Part time."

So she wasn't just being friendly.

"You mean, like you write poetry."

"No, silly man. That's for fun. Massage, that's for profit. But that doesn't mean it's not fun, too."

#

By the look of her place, Sami wasn't doing badly in the profit department. She lived in a stilt house next to a canal on the bayside. Not palatial, but not too shabby, considering the premium on real estate in this part of the Keys. Dallas stood with a glass of wine inside the screened perimeter watching two cats scrapping on the dock while Sami showered. The water shut off, and a few minutes later the door behind him creaked open and she was standing there in a pink kimono holding a candle.

She took him into a room with more candles and told him to lie face down on a spongy mat. Naked. She left the room while he complied and returned with a folded towel but showed no interest in using it to cover him. Instead she straddled him, sending a jolt of excitement up his spine. His senses were aflutter with conflicting sensations: Her hands, soft but strong, so soothing on his back and shoulders, were turning him to putty, while the thought of her tender parts pressing against his skin stirred images and impulses he could barely contain. There was no doubt she knew the effect it was having on him. He sought a diversion.

"Is your full name Samantha?"

"I tell everyone that Sami is short for Samurai. So, better not mess with me."
She giggled.

"But you're not Japanese, are you?"

"Vietnamese. And American. My father was a G.I. I never knew him. My mother said he was killed before I was born. His name was Sam."

She paused, then added, "I do have a picture. And his eyes." She laughed again. "At least, I can tell."

Neither of them spoke again for several minutes. A cassette was playing on low, soft horns and sax. Her hands were magic. He was her pawn.

She gave him a playful smack on the butt.

"OK, that side's done, time to turn over."

When he did, she was still astride, on her knees. The kimono was gone. Her black hair hung down to the middle of her back. The pale light from the candles danced on her flawless skin. She was smiling at him.

"My, you are a healthy boy, just as I suspected. Does that mean you like me?"

"What do you think?"

His hands found her thighs and their smoothness made his appreciation grow.

"Because you are such a nice man, I am happy to offer you the deluxe massage at a special introductory rate."

"Deluxe?"

"Yes, the works. Payment in advance, if you please."

Good thing he'd stopped at the ATM in the morning on the way to the race. He watched her move about the room, quickly, gracefully taking care of the business side of their relationship without letting him feel like it really was business. She flipped the cassette over and returned to her previous position.

"Now, for pleasure."

The music was suddenly more vibrant, penetrating deeper into his consciousness, as if he were the sax and she the player. Her sprightliness excited him as much as her skilled fingers. His eyes danced from her face to every intriguing contour of her body as she took him from one breathtaking plateau to the next.

He tried to cling to the moment by holding his breath, but too soon it was going, going, gone. He could feel his heart pounding and saw her smiling down at him through heavy-lidded eyes.

"Happy?"

"Mmmm."

She left the room and returned with a warm, damp cloth that felt soothing on his skin. As she bathed him, his gaze roamed the room, seeing it fully for the first time in the flickering light. The cassette player was on a broad cabinet flanked by several candles. There was a love seat, a rocker and a wicker bookshelf. In one corner an elaborate piece of driftwood, and on it a shape familiar to Dallas.

"Is it real? The iguana?"

"It was a gift. Someone I know in the islands."

"That is a coincidence. I used to have one, too."

"I love lizards. All kinds. See?"

She raised a knee. On the inside of one thigh was a tattoo similar to the one on Claire's shoulder. How had he missed that?

"There were always lizards around when I was a little girl in Vietnam. I used to feed them and try to catch them. Most are harmless. Something about their presence is comforting. That's why I keep him in here. They don't make a sound, but they see everything. I think they are very wise."

It was difficult to see clearly in the dim light. Gradually his brain filled in the gaps in the shadows, and he saw that the iguana's head was turned in his direction, its eyes on him. Then, just as he was about to concede the stare-down, it bobbed its head and winked.

CHAPTER 9

Ramon Ortega wanted to get the hell out of Mariners Hospital and he was losing patience. It wasn't easy getting dressed with an arm in a sling, even with the help of Regina Martinez. He liked having the raven-haired beauty attending to him, though he liked it better when she was undressing him. Her scent was far more pleasant than the room's dominant aroma of rubbing alcohol and antiseptic, but he had other things on his mind; decisions to make, calls to place. He'd be much more comfortable on his 10th floor balcony in Miami overlooking Biscayne Bay. The helicopter should be arriving any minute to take him and Regina there.

She carefully tucked his injured arm inside the silk shirt and began working on the buttons, but her two-inch nails made progress slow. She flashed a quick smile when she noticed him scowling.

"*Pobrecito*," she said.

His frown softened. Something about the way the words rolled off her lips. The night had passed comfortably enough for Ortega, thanks to the medication and midnight TLC administered by Regina. Oh, yes, those luscious lips. His instinct had been correct to send the other one, the faux blonde, off to look after Raffy, his throttleman. Regina wasn't just a princess, she understood it wasn't enough to merely look good to maintain the interest of a man like Ortega. She had sat on the edge of the bed for hours massaging his scalp with those magic fingers until he had fallen asleep, then she curled up in chair until a nurse came in at daybreak.

Dr. Bubba, the Conch physician, hadn't shown up until 10:30, and Ortega was fuming. His head felt as if it were stuffed with cotton. The pain killer he took an hour ago was keeping the throb in his arm at bay but made him jittery. He needed fresh air. He needed a drink, but he wasn't supposed to have booze because of the medication. That made the need all the more urgent for a cigarette. *Come on, let's go. Let's go!*

Regina was zipping his trousers when the door opened behind him. Ortega figured it was the nurse bringing his prescriptions. The change in Regina's expression and the sound of two sets of footsteps on the linoleum indicated otherwise.

"If it isn't the one-armed man. I knew we'd find you sooner or later."

Ortega turned and his eyes narrowed when he saw the man in the cowboy hat.

"You shouldn't have come here."

"What? I'm just paying a visit to a friend in the hospital. I must say, you look like hell, Senor Ortega, but you've got the prettiest nurse in the joint."

"I told you I would contact you when I was ready."

"Time is a luxury few can afford. Even you, my friend. My partner is on his way out of the country. He needs some answers now."

Ortega focused for the first time on the other man, standing near the door, and a discomforting, unaccustomed feeling of anxiety swept through him. The man was solidly built, if not physically imposing. Not more than six feet tall, though his presence was somehow larger. Or, as Regina would say later, he had a heavy aura. Broad shoulders. Thick neck. Wide forehead. Gray beginning to overrun the black in his thinning hair. A bit of a paunch rested on his belt. This was not a young man; his physical prime was past. But Ortega correctly surmised it would not be wise to underestimate him.

What stood out were his eyes, cold and a chilling green, deep and dark. They didn't blink, didn't dance around. They bore right in, fixed and lethal like twin torpedo tubes under a heavy brow. The effect was powerful. Ortega felt a muscle in one of his eyes twitch. He wasn't easily intimidated, but he had to look away. He motioned Regina out of the room. When she approached the door she stepped quickly, keeping her distance from the man. The door clicked shut.

Ortega felt the weight of the eyes on him and suppressed a shudder.

"I know who you are. My uncle, Manuel Avillas, has spoken of you. He is the reason I'm asking for your help. Your services."

"I can assure you, he is the only reason I'm here."

The words were uttered brusquely, almost spat out. The tone sent a shiver through Ortega. The eyes were locked on him, relentless. It took an effort to maintain the usual Ortega 'tude.

"I, I'm interested in you — in your services because I was told you're the best. My uncle says you are the only one for the job. I trust what he tells me."

The eyes continued to probe. The wheels of a cart rattled in the hallway. The only sound inside the room was the ringing in Ortega's ears.

"I need to know if you are committed to this. This is not a game, like the one you were playing yesterday. I don't do business with clowns."

Ortega felt the sting of the last word.

"The money should tell you how committed I am. Fifty, large. That's serious cash. And if you succeed, then we will be ready to make our move. What is the feasibility?"

"It is bold, but it can be done. I had a look. The security is half-assed, same as with any government institution: Under-budgeted, under-motivated, unprepared for the unexpected."

The voice wasn't loud, more like an amplified whisper, yet each statement carried the impact of a sledgehammer and was accompanied by an expression that suggested a smirk. Ortega wanted nothing to do with this man, but he had little choice. Congeniality wasn't a prerequisite for this job. He wasn't interviewing a *maitre d'*. He fought through the force of the eyes to study the face. The man had to be near 60, maybe past. He seemed old for this sort of operation. There was no sag in the muscles, though; forearms solid as a drill sergeant's.

Ortega had little choice but to trust his uncle's assurances. Still, he felt queasy. His stomach rumbled. He couldn't wait to get out of this place. This meeting shouldn't be happening here. He struggled to suppress a rush of anger, to appear inscrutable.

"When can you go?"

"When I see the green. Twenty-five up front, the rest on delivery."

"I want to know the details of your plan."

"I am not teaching a clinic. You take your car to a mechanic, you tell him the problem. He fixes it, he tells you when to pick it up. I work the same way — if I decide to take the job."

"How do I contact you, mister, ah, what do I call you?"

"You don't call me anything. And you don't call me. You call him."

Ortega glanced at the man in the cowboy hat, who stood with his weight on one leg, arms folded, nodding.

"Don't worry, Ramon. Smile. It's all going to work out. Believe me, your uncle was right. It's going to be a piece of cake."

Ortega's frown settled deeper into his face. He hated dealing with this man Hawke. So full of shit. Worst part, once he started talking he wouldn't shut the fuck up. Unlike this other man, who said only what was necessary.

"There is the other matter to discuss," Hawke said. "I take it you were impressed by our demonstration yesterday. I told you you'd never seen anything like it. You shouldn't have tried to keep up. You have to recognize your limitations, Ramon. Like my friend said, that was foolish."

Anxiety gave way to anger. A muscle in Ortega's neck began to twitch. He was past being intimidated.

"Let's just see if you can pull this thing off, then we'll see how impressed I am."

"I must warn you, we have other potential clients. It would be a shame for this thing to go to ..."

The door swung open. A nurse walked in and looked at the two men with surprise. Hawke tipped his hat.

"Just leaving, ma'am. Ramon, it's sure good to see you're feeling better. When you're ready, just give a call and we'll arrange that fishing trip we talked about."

#

Ortega sat brooding and smoking, staring out the window as the helicopter swung over the ocean on a gentle arc toward the north. The day was bright and clear with less wind than during the race. His eyes scanned the surface, gauging the wave patterns. It all looked so benign from up here.

He imagined himself back in the cockpit seeing white-crested waves rushing at him, feeling the rumble of all that glorious horsepower and the surge of inner strength — call it ego — he always got from knowing he was in control, the Man going toe-to-toe with the sea. It really was very much like sex with a wild, vibrant woman, the unrestrained joy and exhilaration. In some ways it was better, because of the added elements of danger and competition. That made the conquest all the more satisfying; the sense of triumph over other men, their machines and the sea. Which made what happened yesterday all the more infuriating, a double humiliation. Who were they to show him up like that?

Fuck it. He opened the oak console conveniently situated for easy access from the plush passenger seats and fetched a bottle of Bacardi and a glass. He found ice in an adjacent compartment and orange juice in the compact refrigerator below. Regina looked up from filing her nails and grabbed his arm.

"Ramon, you're not supposed to have that while you're taking the medicine."

"This is medicine, too."

Forget that spicy bitch Bloody Mary. Nothing got his motor running better in the morning than a sweet kiss of rum-and-orange. He settled back in his seat and looked out again at the water, a jeweled palette of shimmering hues — aquamarine, turquoise, topaz and sapphire. He never tired of looking at the water. It settled his nerves. Sometimes he stood on his Key Biscayne condo balcony and stared at it all afternoon.

From the air he could trace the jagged reef formations visible in the clear shallows like submerged Rorschach blots. Even with all the abuse and pollution, there was still so much life in the fragile ecosystem of North America's only living coral reefs, a complex interaction of beauty and treachery, the fulcrum of any society at any level. To Ortega, the reefs had never been as much objects of admiration as obstacles to be avoided. He scanned the surface for things familiar — a fishing boat here, a sea turtle lounging on the surface there. And the most chilling sight from this vantage point, the occasional hammerhead shark slowly patrolling the outer reef line.

Sharks fascinated and frightened him. As a boat racer, his greatest fear wasn't crashing but the possibility of getting thrown into the water and being attacked by sharks. It was on his mind yesterday as he waited for the rescue team to pluck him from the water. Nonetheless, he identified with sharks; he envied their unquestioned claim to the upper hand in their environment. It was a status to which he aspired. Dominance. Admiration. Respect. Fear.

"Who was that man at the hospital?" Regina asked, continuing her quest for the perfectly sculpted fingernail.

"Huh?"

"The one with the scary eyes."

"He's a mercenary. He fought with my uncle in Cuba. Bay of Pigs."

"He gave me the creeps."

"He's a dangerous man, but he can be trusted. Uncle Manny told me about him. When they were training for the invasion, he had nothing to do with the other men. The only kindness he ever showed was to the wild lizards — iguanas, salamanders. He fed them, tamed them, carried them around on his shoulder. The men called him El Lagarto."

"What does he want with you?"

"Don't worry about it. It's business."

The helicopter was approaching the mainland of the Florida peninsula, the striped stacks of the Turkey Point nuclear plant ahead. Beyond it the emerald bowl of Biscayne Bay. Ortega could see the Miami skyline in the distance looming through the haze. He took a big swig of rum-and-orange and felt its tangy coolness spread down his throat. He was feeling better, more like himself the closer he got to home.

For the first time all day he smiled. Very soon he would be back to normal, once again the Man.

CHAPTER 10

With a little coaxing and the right blend of stimulants, his eyes were gradually coming into focus. A sip of coffee — Mmm, the aroma. A slurp of V8 Picante — as effective as smelling salts, and a hell of a lot more palatable. A bigger slurp, the tangy liquid slicing through the cobwebs. Perspiration forming a glaze on his forehead; he wiped it with the back of a hand.

Could have been worse. Dallas thought about the drunken boat racer on the beach. Imagine being inside his head this morning. He blew his nose on a napkin and squinted at the name on the card on the table between the coffee mug and the juice glass.

"Keith Richards Salmon — Musician, Salvage Expert, Catering, Snow Removal."

Snow removal? More picante. More squinting. Salmon? Is this a name or an entree? More coffee. He reached for the phone and dialed.

"If you want me to come over, you're going to have to send the snowplow to dig me out."

"Ah, it's alive."

"More or less."

"Wasn't so sure last night. Looked like you were on the ropes."

"Hell no, was just getting warmed up."

"No shit. The main event?"

"Forget about it. Just tell me one thing, what kind of a name is Keith Richards Salmon?"

"Yeah, yeah, yeah, sounds like today's special at the Hard Rock Cafe. Don't strain your brain, man, I've heard them all. And don't say Sah-man. The right way: Say, Sa-moan."

"Sa-moan? Sa-moan. Right, I remember when I was a kid there was a ballplayer with that name."

"Chico Salmon. My uncle."

"Your uncle? That's amazing. I was always getting his baseball card. Played for the Indians. I must have had 10 Chico Salmons. Probably had a bunch of them pinned to my bicycle spokes. You know, to make it sound like a motor."

"Real nice, dissin' my uncle like that."

Dallas jotted directions on a paper towel and took a shower before leaving for his meeting with Keith and this Captain Devereaux. The water pressure, as usual, was a piddle, but the water was hot and soothing on his shoulders and back. He closed his eyes and thought of Sami's incomparable hands, imagining her standing behind him, working him over.

By the time he was dressed and out the door he was fully awake and snapping his fingers with the reggae riffs of Keith's band playing in his head. "Stir it up." The lyrics running through his head as he tooled down U.S. 1 in the Great White turned his thoughts to Claire. He wondered about her night, feeling a wave of jealousy that gave way to a surge of guilt, both of which surprised him.

Keith's directions weren't as smooth as his guitar playing. OK, so the second turn to the left was after the bend to the right; at least he was in the right neighborhood. Difficult to get too far lost in the Keys. Only had to stop twice to ask for guidance. The first fellow, barefoot on a bicycle, looked as if he wasn't sure where he was, either. But then, Snapper Cove Boatworks wasn't exactly a major port of call for the yachting set. Dallas found it at the end of a narrow canal sandwiched between mangroves and a trailer park. There was the usual array of boats resting on blocks and cradles in various states of disrepair and reclamation inside a rusty chain-link fence. A dusty bulldog snoozed in the shade of a drydocked sailboat, sans mast, hull partially sanded below the waterline.

Dallas parked outside the gate near the water's edge. He shoved the door closed and took a step toward the gate when a loud thud near the front of the Caddy stopped him in his tracks. Then another, louder.

Thwop!!

This one, closer, made him jump. Damn, his feet actually left the ground. The sound of laughter spun him around.

"Not bad, not bad — for a white dude."

Dallas looked up, following the path of the gray crooked trunk of a palm tree. Just below the juncture of the fronds, nearly 20 feet above the ground, peeking around from behind the trunk, was the face of Keith Richards Salmon, a broad smile framed by dreadlocks. Kind of looked like it was connected to the tree. Only then did Dallas notice the ladder propped against the other side of the palm.

"Don't you know never to park under a coconut tree, man, unless you want one of these as a hood ornament?"

Keith held a coconut the size of a bowling ball at arm's length, palm down, as if he were Michael Jordan swooping from the rafters to jam it home through an imaginary hoop. Once again Dallas couldn't help but marvel at the man's fingers. They made the coconut look like a Granny Smith apple.

"Here, catch."

Fingers parted. The coconut hung in midair for an instant before beginning its descent. It was bright green and shiny, nothing like the shriveled brown coconuts typically displayed in the shell shops and roadside fruit stands. Dallas watched it fall, seemingly in slow motion. He took a half-step forward as if he actually intended to catch it and was glad he didn't try after it landed with a resounding thud.

He picked it up and was surprised by the heft. Dallas's hands were bigger than average, but when he tried to palm the coconut like Keith did it slipped and just missed crunching his toes. Keith's laughter rained down again.

"Watch yourself. You don't want to be trying to catch the coconut, man. It can bust your coconut wide open. That's why you want to make sure to get the coconuts out of the trees in hurricane season. Don't want these things flying around in a 150-mile-an-hour wind. Even a hundred. Get the picture? It could be ugly. Ugly! Be like Nolan Ryan throwing bowling balls like they're baseballs. Whooee. Knock your block off. Never know what hit you. Hell of a way to go."

Dallas felt the smoothness of the shell, waxy as if polished. Liquid sloshed when he shook it.

"This thing isn't ripe, is it?"

"Oh, it's ripe, you bet. It's just right. That's what you want, the green coconut, not the brown. Brown ones no good. Only white people eat the brown ones. Go anywhere in the Caribbean, all the native people will tell you the same thing: The green coconut, *mon*, that's the good coconut. You listen to me, *mon*, I don't lie to you."

Keith laughed again. He was affecting the sing-song island accent that he slipped into easily when he sang reggae. He dropped four more coconut bombs before bouncing down the ladder, two steps at a time.

"I thought the island people shinnied up the tree to get coconuts."

"Only the ones can't afford a ladder. I'm not risking my neck for coconuts. Here, I show you what I mean about the green coconuts."

Dallas was gathering them into a group, a dozen on the ground. He stepped back in surprise when he turned and saw Keith brandishing a wicked looking machete, the blade at least 18 inches long. It looked as if it had been through a few banana republic coups, but the honed edge gleamed like freshly forged steel.

"You could shave with this thing. I've seen people in the islands so good with one, they hold the coconut in one hand and chop the top off with one whack. Not me. I like my long fingers better than I trust my aim."

Keith wedged the coconut at an angle in a gap between two railroad ties next to a footpath. Using just enough force, he hacked a shallow V in the coconut with two short, quick strokes and flipped the divot aside with the tip of the blade to reveal the interior brimming with a clear liquid.

"See how pure this is?"

"I thought coconut milk was supposed to be more of a milky white."

"This isn't milk, this is coconut water. Milk is different: You got to grate the meat and soak it and boil it. It'll make you fat, and it's bad for the heart. This is the good stuff. Here, try."

Dallas held the nut with both hands and took a tentative sip. Some of the juice spilled down his chin and dripped onto his shirt. Sweetness flowed easily down his throat.

"See? Good stuff."

Dallas drank some more. Keith broke into his reggae voice and strummed an invisible guitar.

"Coconut water, drink it down, you feel fine. Make you strong, like a lion."

"Yeah, pretty good."

"Nectar from the gods. Drink a green coconut every day, it's good for the belly." Keith patted himself there, then down lower. "Good for your love life, too." He winked.

"I bet it would taste even better with some gin."

Keith cut another coconut open and chugged half the water. "Gin good. Vodka, too. Rum's best. C'mon, you talk to Captain Devereaux now, then we go to my boat and have some rum with coconut water. You'll see. It's the second-best afternoon delight."

CHAPTER 11

"This Devereaux, he's a funny cat. You'll get to like him. Eventually. If he don't know you well, he hardly says a word," Keith was saying. "You think, what's with this dude? Then you go hunt treasure with him and, you'll see, he turns into a little kid. Sometimes you come up from a dive, out of breath, tired, and he'll be jabbering like a fool. You want to say, 'Hey, shut up, ol' geezer.' Ya just gotta laugh. I think he gets drunk on the bubbles. He's funny, man."

Capt. LaRue Devereaux wasn't doing a standup routine when they found him in the battleship-gray, hangar-like main building of Snapper Cove Boatworks. They entered by a side door and Keith led the way through what looked like a morgue for outboard motors, past shelves cluttered with used propellers, anchors and assorted marine engine parts, all overdosing on rust and corrosion. They weaved through a maze of racks containing small fishing boats and runabouts stacked three high.

Devereaux was inside the big sliding door that opened to the gas dock and boat basin. He was stooped over, working amid a debris field of parts from what looked to be some sort of giant pump. Dallas's first impression was of Jacques Cousteau from hell, all leathery-tan, grease and curses muttered with a sort of crass French lilt. Dallas recognized it right away. Bayou French. Pure Cajun.

Devereaux was poking at a motor housing with a screwdriver, digging out some disgusting gunk. He gave a quick glance over his shoulder and continued to work without a greeting or any show of recognition. Dallas sensed that in one quick visual sweep, the man had sized him up and formed an opinion.

"This is the guy, Skeeter," Keith said. "Licensed captain. Name's Dallas. What is it?"

"Huston. Dallas Huston."

Devereaux stopped for an instant and began to turn his head, then went back to his work. A full minute, maybe two passed before he spoke.

"Hand me that manifold over there."

Dallas stood out of the way while Keith fetched the part and helped Devereaux position it. It took several minutes and half a dozen expletives to get it bolted into place.

"We're going to have to rebuild that motor. I'm goin' up to Miami this afternoon to get the parts. Gonna pick up a new hose, too."

Dallas shifted uneasily as Devereaux gave Keith a grim mechanical prognosis of the whatchamacallit, which was in too many pieces to be identifiable. With any luck, they'd be back in business in a week, the captain said, bitterly. There was an urgency about Devereaux that Dallas hadn't seen before in anyone in the Keys. The regional demeanor seemed to be: Ain't going nowhere special, no hurry to get there. It was summed up in a word that fit perfectly with carefree subtropical perspective: mañana. Often it was uttered with a shrug, as if to say, don't worry, tomorrow's another day.

Dallas studied the older man. Had to be in his 60s. His hair was fully silver, but except for a receding hairline it showed no sign of thinning. His skin was the dull bronze of a man who had spent his life working outdoors.

The tension in the air made Dallas uneasy. Devereaux was grumbling, the stub of a cigarette wagging between his teeth adding emphasis to the image of a man literally fuming. Keith squatted beside him, nodding, trying to be helpful. Dallas realized he was nervously tapping his own foot to music playing from what he at first thought was a radio but turned out to be a tape player. He knew the music well. Then he recognized the tune.

"Ah, Clifton Chenier. He's great. I saw him do this one at Muddy Waters's place. Rumblin' on the Bayou."

Keith and Devereaux turned and stared at him.

"You know, Muddy's. In N'awlins." Dallas said.

Keith rolled his eyes. Devereaux got up slowly and walked past him to a sink in the corner. He took his time, washing his hands with Lava soap while Keith briefed Dallas on the situation.

"Guy was supposed to fix that motor two weeks ago. But it's still fucked up."

"What is it?"

"That's the airlift. It's like a vacuum cleaner for sucking up treasure. Can't go treasure hunting without it."

Devereaux returned, wiping his hands on the cleanest corner of a greasy towel. He looked Dallas straight in the eyes.

"Where'd you say you're from, Houston?"

"No, that's my name: Dallas Huston. From Dallas."

Another uncomfortable pause. What? Dallas studied the face, deeply lined. Lots of mileage there.

"You planning to stick around here?"

"As long as there's a reason to."

"I need someone can run a boat, follow instructions, be dependable and be available whenever the weather's good enough to go out."

"I've run a lot of boats in a lot of places. Inboard, outboard, sail."

Dallas could sense the other man assessing him. It was uncomfortable but he didn't let himself appear intimidated. Finally, Devereaux motioned him to follow and began walking at a brisk pace toward the back of the building, past the outboard motor burial ground and the racks of boats. He didn't stop until he came to the most remote corner and pointed to an odd craft resting on a wooden framework.

"Ever run one of these?"

Dallas hadn't expected anything like this. For a moment he just stared.

"Where'd you get this?"

"I know a man built it."

There was no mistaking what he was looking at. Dallas had seen mini-submarines before, on National Geographic documentaries and once aboard a research vessel docked in San Juan. This one had a homemade, futuristic look about it that could have sprung from the imagination of Jules Verne — or a hallucinogenic vision of the Beatles. But Devereaux's submarine wasn't yellow, it was navy blue.

"You want me to run that?"

Dallas heard Keith trying to suppress a laugh.

"I want you to be able to. Not as hard as you'd think. Easy, really."

Dallas ran his hand across the hull. Fiberglass. The sub wasn't more than 12 or 14 feet long. Two robotic arms were folded and secured on either side of the bow. Devereaux climbed on top, using two steps inset in the hull, and popped open an entry hatch. He reached inside and flipped on a light. Dallas stood on one of the rungs and peered into the cockpit. Interior space was cramped, but he could see that it was set up for a crew of two.

"Mostly you'd be running our support boat," Devereaux said. "But I need someone can help with this, too. It really takes two to do what we need to do: one to position the sub and one to operate the arms and drill."

"Can't a diver do more than you can do with this thing?"

Dallas stopped looking inside the sub and focused on Devereaux's eyes, which were pale blue and darting from one object to another. He was fidgety, anxious, seemingly under a great deal of pressure.

"What you have to understand about this wreck we're working, it's in deeper water than most of the wrecks in the Keys. That's why it wasn't discovered sooner. The way it looks, this ship hit the reef and drifted out deeper before it went down. It drops off fast there, and the treasure's pretty well scattered. We've found stuff in 80 feet of water and some out in 120.

"With the sub, we can take core samples over a wide area and stay down a lot longer than a diver can. And we can go out with this on days you couldn't dive."

Devereaux closed the hatch, and now his eyes were looking straight into Dallas's.

"The other thing is we may not have much time. Normally, you'd wait until late spring when the weather calms down. But the feds are pushing through some new marine sanctuary laws that could shut us down or greatly restrict what we can do. The way it looks now, it's going to go into effect August first."

He paused and his gaze veered off into the distance.

"Mel Fisher's been working the Atocha for years, and he's still scoring. We may only have a few months to find the mother lode on this one."

Dallas was about to step down off the sub when he noticed something written on the hatch cover that didn't register until they were walking back to the front of the building. It was a name: Juergens Engineering.

#

The boat Keith called home could be considered a boat only in the sense that it was afloat, but not if you applied the more specific definition of a vessel for transportation. This one obviously hadn't transported anyone or anything in a long time, considering the vine growing along the rail of the companionway and draped over the gunwale. It looked about as sea kindly as an old washtub, which may have been the model for its lines— broad, angular and gawky.

It was evidently a homemade job with one of those ferro-cement hulls that seemed to defy the concept of buoyancy. Part trawler, part schooner. That is, only part of the masts remained, and their current function was to support a hammock and a clothesline. The latter, Keith pointed out, was not only useful for drying clothes but also provided shade. Keith confirmed the existence of an engine beneath a hatch cover with rusty edges but couldn't say what it would take to make it run.

"I'm not going nowhere, man," he said.

Just as well. Dallas couldn't imagine crossing open water in this thing. It would wallow like hell in any kind of a sea. As homely as it was, there was a hominess about it that was comforting. The name on the transom was appropriate: *Big Momma*.

"People say, 'What is it, man?' I say it's a junk. Not what the Chinese call a junk. Just junk. But it's my junk. It's home."

"I'm sure even the Chinese would agree," Dallas said as he crossed the companionway, which bowed and groaned under his weight.

The curious thing about *Big Momma* was that it was a whole lot more pleasant to be aboard than to look at. The broad lines that made it look like a hat box with masts afforded more roominess below deck than most boats. The dominant interior color scheme of green, red and yellow took some getting used to. But a huge tapestry of Bob Marley's face on one bulkhead in the main salon lent a personality and presence.

Dallas took it all in before sinking down in an overstuffed sofa that was also in conflict with typical nautical decor.

"So, you're Jamaican?"

"Surprise, no. Panamanian. But Marley's my main man. The beat was in his soul. His soul is the beat. The Caribbean heartbeat. He's gone, but it's still there. Still alive. I feel it pumping through my veins. BA-pu-BA. Marley's beat. Marley's soul."

"You still didn't tell me, what kind of a name is Keith Richards Sah-moan? Doesn't sound Panamanian. Or Jamaican. Or anything Caribbean."

"Yeah, so what kind of a cockamamie name is Dallas Huston? Sounds like a tale of two cities. And a pretty tall tale at that, no?"

Keith was laughing again, an infectious laugh. Dallas wasn't quick to bestow trust, but he already felt an odd simpatico with this man. He sensed strength of character. There was more than music in the man's soul — and music wasn't a bad foundation to build on.

"Just chill, man. I make you a drink. Then I tell you a story."

Keith was right about the coconut and rum. Sweet, yet refreshing. Best of all, liberating. By the third one, Dallas could feel the beat, throbbing from the stereo in the corner — Marley's beat — pulsing through his own veins. Or was that the rum talking? He surprised himself when he heard his own laughter; the timbre was the same as Keith's.

The story wasn't bad, either. Seems that Keith's father, ol' Jacob "Junkanoo" Salmon, played bass in a blues band that sometimes opened for the Rolling Stones. He did some sessions with the Stones, filling in on background instrumentals, and every now and then backed them up on stage. Guitarist Keith Richards was particularly helpful in getting gigs for J.J.'s band.

"Pops worshipped the man, and so did I. Still do. He's like Marley, a god. I went on the road with pop's band every chance I got, couple times when they went with the Stones. I'd just hang out and take it all in. Man, it was wild. That was the big time.

"Most of the time it was a lot of driving and playing in dives and joints, but I didn't care. I was having a ball. I was 5 when pop's band went to Woodstock. I had no idea what it was. It was just another trip, lotsa driving. And then we get there."

"You were at Woodstock?"

"You won't see pop's band in any of the movies: Rockin' Ronnie and the Mudcats, they were called. The front man was this dude Ronnie Chester, he could really wail. They played in the middle of the night. But what a time."

"You liked Woodstock?" Dallas asked, calling up his own memories.

"Oh, man, it was the wildest. I got separated from the band for almost a day. Like I was lost, but it was OK. All these people were looking out for me, taking care of me. I remember this white woman, naked above the waist, and man, she had some lanterns on her. She just wanted to hug me. She pulled me in and I buried my face between those beauties and never wanted to leave. I thought I was in heaven, man."

Dallas couldn't remember when he laughed so hard. He felt tears in the corners of his eyes. Keith filled his glass again from the pitcher on the table and spiked it liberally with the bottle of Ron Rico.

"So, you knew Keith Richards?"

"Knew him, he was like my godfather. The last time pop's band played with them, I was 10 or 11. I think they all knew it was the last time. Anyway, before we split, Richards comes over and says, 'Here, little bloke.' Just hands me this guitar and smiles that ghostly smile."

Keith disappeared for a minute and came back with a red Fender guitar that had obviously been down a few roads and had tales of its own to tell.

"This is the one. Been playing it ever since."

Keith plugged it in to a small amplifier and started playing the lead to "Jumpin' Jack Flash." Dallas grabbed a broom from the corner for a mike and began strutting around the salon, doing his best Mick while Keith shifted into "Midnight Rambler." The performance finally dissolved into laughter when Dallas stumbled over a stool and flopped onto the sofa.

"Oh, man, we're going to have to get you up on stage," Keith said. "Can you do Marley?"

Dallas put his feet over the arm of the sofa and stared up through the cloudy liquid in his glass.

"I don't know about Marley, but I sure could play Chico Salmon on my bicycle spokes."

Keith sank into a chair, still hugging the guitar. "I'll let you in on a secret, my friend. I used to do the same thing."

"Are you superstitious, Keith?"

"Of course. Can't go on stage without my lucky wristband. And always have to enter the stage from the left and leave to the right. Why do you ask that?"

"Because of Chico Salmon. The thing I remember about him as a ballplayer was his superstitions. I recall reading about how he was afraid of ghosts, so when the team was on the road he would spread flour on the floor of his hotel room around the bed. Said it kept ghosts away. Whoever he roomed with must have thought the guy was out of his mind."

Keith threw his head back and laughed so hard his whole body shook, along with the guitar.

"That sounds like my uncle. Quirky, but a great guy. You know a lot about baseball, huh?"

"Used to."

Keith rummaged through a black case of cassettes and put one in the player. Marley, naturally. Dallas stared though a window, across the canal where a cluster of seagulls were scrapping for morsels of something a woman in a yellow sundress was scattering for them.

"Here's another name for you," Dallas said. "Ever meet Behrent Juergens?"

"No, man, what band's he in?"

CHAPTER 12

His eyes were following a bead of sweat cascading down the glistening valley of Regina's cleavage. As she rocked, her breasts swung together, then apart and the bead slid through the narrow passage and descended onto her tanned, taut belly. That is what Ortega liked about this girl. She withheld nothing. He wanted to roll her onto her back, but that would have to wait until his elbow got better. So he laid back and stared up at her face, taking it all in: her heavy-lidded eyes watching him, the way she bit her lower lip. That did it for him, sent him over the edge.

Afterward, when he heard her in the shower, Ortega awkwardly managed to wrap a towel around his waist. He lit a cigarette and shuffled onto the balcony. The sun wasn't quite overhead, and he squinted through the glare reflecting off the water far below.

The Port of Miami was off to the left, the red stacks of two cruise ships poking above the trees and buildings. Virginia Key stretched out straight ahead, a broad green buffer from the ocean's wrath. He could see a pair of Jet Skis flitting like water bugs alongside Rickenbacker Causeway near the mouth of the old marine stadium. At the southeast corner of the balcony, he had a clear view of Luciano Pavarotti's domed penthouse a couple floors up atop the next building. Whenever Ortega hosted parties, someone would aim speakers in that direction to serenade Pavarotti. He smiled at the thought of Carlos, his navigator, waving a wine bottle, shouting, "Hey, opera boy, you like Gloria Estefan? Here's a free concert, just for you." And cranking it up.

Ortega wondered what Pavarotti thought of Madonna. He could see the red Spanish roof of her mansion on the other side of the causeway, just past Bruce Willis's and Demi Moore's place.

The portable phone on the table next to the chaise lounge rang. It was Hawke from his car phone, heading down Bayshore Drive. He frowned. Fucker thinks he can just drop in, like we're pals. Fuck him. Ortega went inside and poured a scotch. Returning to the balcony he rested a foot on the bottom rung of the railing and stared toward the ocean. A cruise ships was leaving port, another load of happy, happy people bound for a week of prepackaged hokey pokey and bingo. Ortega didn't watch its departure. His thoughts were somewhere over the horizon.

Hawke arrived wearing a black silk shirt buttoned halfway, two fat gold chains around his neck, more gold around each wrist — old fart trying to look like a young stud. And that damned cowboy hat. Ortega could barely be civil.

"Nice view you've got here, Ramon. Prime piece of real estate. What did this place set you back? One-point-five-mill or more, I'd guess. Nothing like waterfront property. This is the *el supremo* for a room with a view. Very impressive, *compadre.*"

"Is this a social call or is there a point to you being here? You'll have to excuse me for not having coffee ready. I wasn't expecting you."

"Oh, it's business, and it's social, too. I want to get to know you better, Ramon. You've got to have rapport with someone if you're going to do business with them. How's the elbow? That was a nasty spill you took. You gonna be back racing soon, or you gonna take up golf or canasta?"

"I'll be back, better than ever."

"Believe me, you'll live a lot longer if you stick to golf. I'm worried about you, Ramon."

"It's not for you to worry about me. Cut the crap. What did you come to say?"

The expression on Hawke's face suggested a smirk.

"Got any bourbon?"

"No."

"Okay, I'll have whatever you're having."

Hawke strolled onto the balcony and stood by the railing.

"Yeah, nothing like a waterfront view."

Ortega stared at him in disbelief for a long moment and shook his head. He poured two scotch on the rocks in matching glasses.

"Thanks. Cheers! Now, Ramon, the reason I came: I've got good news for you. My associate has agreed to take the job. He went and had another look. So, you come up with the cash, it's a go."

"When?"

"He'll be away for a few days, firming up the details, getting everything in place. He wants the 25 large one week from today. Then he'll set the wheels in motion, and it'll happen two weeks from today. At least, that'll be the target date, depending on weather and other factors. You just have to let us know the timing, the window of opportunity. He prefers to do it late in the day."

"Two weeks?" Ortega frowned. "That the soonest?

"Yeah. That's what he says. You can't dictate to this guy. You want the job done right, right?"

Ortega took a sip of his drink. His injured arm itched. He couldn't wait to get rid of the sling in another day or two. Hawke was facing the ocean.

"You're a lucky man to wake up every morning in a place like this. Look at all that water out there. Gorgeous. Simply, gor-ge-ous!" He turned toward Ortega. "Don't worry. This guy's the real deal. The best."

"He looks a little old to me."

Hawke had that expression again. Clearly a smirk.

"I'm only going to tell you this once, Ramon, so don't forget it. This guy's a pro. A-Number 1. *Numero Uno*. Genuine *El Supremo* — just like the view from your balcony. You don't ever want to underestimate him. And you don't ever want to cross him. *Capiche?*"

Ortega felt rage well up. He stared into Hawke's eyes and let him see the fire. He spoke in a measured tone.

"And I'm going to tell you this just once. If you ever bullshit me, you'll regret it. How you say, *capiche?*"

Hawke smiled and nodded.

"OK. Understood. You know, that's good. I think we're making real progress. I like you, Ramon. We're starting to build rapport."

"Time will tell, *amigo*. Tell me, what do you call your, ah, associate? What name does he go by?"

Hawke smiled.

"He's been known by many names. Who knows, maybe even he can't remember which is real. I just call him Chief."

"El Lagarto," Ortega said quietly.

"What?"

"Tell me another thing, is it true you've done business with Fidel?"

Now it was Hawke's turn to frown. "I see, I see. So that's where you're going with this."

"We need an intermediary if we're going to get into that second project with you. Because that's where it leads. Thing is, we can't very well just call him up."

"Right, I can see the problem there," Hawke said. He seemed suddenly nervous. "OK, well, we can get into that more next time. I'll call you to arrange to pick up that laundry, like we talked about."

"Not here. We'll pick another place."

"As you wish. We can meet for dinner. Italian place in the Grove, if you like."

Hawke held up his glass. "Here's to rapport."

Ortega took the last swallow of his drink, more water than Scotch by then. "*Salud!*"

#

Ortega stayed on the balcony after Hawke left, thinking. Two weeks. He smiled. Jorge wouldn't be happy about the wait. But it was just right for him.

Regina came out wearing white shorts and a tight, yellow bare-midriff tank top. He glanced at her and let his eyes make the tour of the tanned panorama. She had on dark sunglasses, hiding her eyes.

"Who was here?"

"Just business. It's done."

She put her hand on his shoulder and pressed her hip against his.

"Good," she said. "That means time for more pleasure. How 'bout we go have lunch on South Beach."

"There'll be lots of time for pleasure. Eventually. There's a lot of business to do first." He turned back toward the ocean, keeping an arm around her waist. He was talking, but she wasn't sure if he were really addressing her.

"Some people make money. Some people make history," Ortega said. "Before this is done, we're going to do both."

#

Another Saturday night and no beer in the fridge. Dallas looked at the clock and was surprised to see it was going on 1, which meant he'd been hammering for nearly three hours on the old Smith-Corona he'd bought at a second-hand shop in Tavernier. He could use a cold one. A burger, too, or conch fritters.

He had been working hard, trying to make a good impression with D'Arbonnell. He wanted to get a few stories in the can before he got busy on the salvage boat. Keith called and said Devereaux was ready to go as soon as the wind settled down.

Dallas had been in Miami on Friday night to do a story about shrimping under the full moon on Biscayne Bay. It was a perfect night for it. Clear. There were gas lanterns dangling all along MacArthur Causeway and people leaning over the railing with long-handled nets for an all-you-can-scoop seafood fest. Dallas was out in a boat with a couple of guys that Zack Tomlin knew. Shrimping from a boat was definitely an advantage over the bridges and jetties, although they had a couple of unpleasant confrontations with commercial boats whose operators thought they owned the waterway. Fists were shaken and curses exchanged in at least three languages.

Still, it was a productive and memorable night. The guys Dallas was with, Brady and an old cracker from Ocala known as Tim-Bo, were pleased with their haul of 175 pounds of shrimp. Back at the dock, they got a pot of water boiling on a gas stove. Three Cuban guys Brady knew came by with a couple of girls and a boombox. They were all eating shrimp, guzzling cheap light beer and carrying on until the sun came up. Dallas took about five pounds of shrimp in the cooler when he drove back to Islamorada. He slept till after dark, then got up and started writing the shrimping story.

D'Arbonnell was going to like this one, especially the part about the dockside party. Dallas even got some pictures with the Cuban girls eating shrimp as they danced. Dallas was getting into the spirit of the D'Arbonnell concept of outdoors journalism and thinking that *Florida Nautique* had a chance to catch on. It seemed a big improvement on the typical water-and-woods genre in which the fishing editor tells in painstaking detail how he tied his flies and rigged his tackle and caught his limit of grunts or whatever. This was real people doing their thing on the water with all the sweat, swearing and an occasional gut-wrenching bout of seasickness.

It was a world Dallas knew well, and he was enjoying putting it on paper. Feeling creative and fulfilled, even if the first paycheck hadn't come in yet. But right now he needed a mental break. He could cook up some of the shrimp he brought back, but he was shrimped out from the dockside feast. Besides, you can't eat shrimp without beer. It's almost a law.

So, he drove to one of the few places open at that time of night in Islamorada, a popular Keys redneck joint. Thankfully, too late for the laser karaoke sing-along. But the house band was still cranking out some rockin' oldies. Dallas took a big swig of cold Corona and glanced at the dozen or so revelers shaking it on the dance floor.

He couldn't take his eyes off one gangly couple, both of them over six feet and rail thin, all kneecaps and elbows waggling and whirling. They reminded Dallas of a line about a couple of goofy dance partners in a song on the latest John Prine album. Here they were on vacation, gyrating the night away. Song after song, lanky limbs flailing all over the dance floor like a couple of willows in a tornado.

Dallas ordered a basket of chicken wings and was immediately engaged in conversation by a guy on the next stool with spaghetti sauce on his shirt who had the lowdown on how the chicken industry was poisoning America with chickens pumped up with steroids and radiation. Funny thing was the guy looked like the Kentucky fried colonel himself.

John Prime was right, it is a goofy old world, and Dallas wasn't so sure it had been a good idea to venture into it for a late-night snack until a familiar figure appeared on the dance floor. He hadn't noticed Claire in the place and hadn't expected to see her. She was dancing with a young guy wearing a T-shirt that read: "I ate it" on the front, and "Raw" on the back. They weren't together. After the song she returned to a table she was sharing with a heavy-set, dark-haired woman. They were drinking wine, talking and laughing with gusto. Dallas sent a round to their table and held up his bottle as a toast when the waitress pointed out the source. Claire looked surprised but smiled and raised her glass in his direction.

He was finishing the last chicken wing when he heard a voice at his side: "Does the gentleman dance?" Usually he wasn't keen on it, but right about then he would have agreed to vacuum the carpet in order to escape the chicken conspiracy buff. And he would have gladly taken out the garbage, too, for a chance to get close to Claire. Dancing was a preferable means to both ends, even though it was a fast song and he nearly lost a couple of teeth to one of the goofy ol' gal's wayward elbows. Afterward, he accepted an invitation to join Claire and her friend, Margie, who turned out to be a desk clerk at the hotel next to the Leaky Tiki, the focal point of the resort complex.

"Margie dragged me out here."

"She needed cheering up. I said, 'C'mon girl, we're going out and get your attitude adjusted.' "

"Yeah, she made me take this nasty stuff."

Margie giggled. "It's not nasty, it's perfectly legal."

Dallas was incredulous. "You two doing uppers?"

Margie giggled louder and Claire smiled sheepishly.

"It's not really a drug, although they advertise it as the drug of the '90s," Margie said. "It's all natural ingredients, ginseng and a lot of other herbs and roots. Herbal Ecstasy is what it's called. They just started selling it down here."

"It's supposed to give you a lot of energy and make you want to dance all night. At least that's what she says," Claire said.

"And," said Margie, laughing so hard she could barely get her words out, "it makes you horny as hell, too."

Claire smacked her friend in the arm, and the two of them laughed uncontrollably.

Dallas feigned surprise. "You mean you need a pill for that?"

In the week since the boat race, he had spoken to Claire a couple of times at the Leaky Tiki and once, briefly, on the phone. She had seemed preoccupied or evasive each time. He studied her eyes as she wiped tears of laughter from the corners.

"Is everything OK with you?"

"I'm fine. It's just been a rough week. There was a situation I had to resolve."

"The crabber. I mean, the guy with the beard?" Dallas blurted out.

She just looked at him for a moment and he thought, oh, damn, I should just shut up.

"He's somebody I was doing some work with. He has a jewelry store that buys some of the Spanish coins we've salvaged. He was showing me how to put a gold bezel around a coin to make it into a pendant, and I was working part-time for him at the counter. But it turned out he had other things in mind for me. I was starting to get a lot of pressure. After everything I've been through, I couldn't handle that. So ..."

She paused and looked embarrassed. "So, hey, I hear you're going to be working on the boat with us. That's good."

"Yes, thanks for the recommendation."

She was looking into Dallas's eyes now. Something about his expression must have suggested what he was thinking. Her mouth curled into a wry smile, and she said, "Hey, now, I do feel like, ah, dancing. Come on, let's go."

"You damn well better dance with him," Margie said, "or I will."

CHAPTER 13

The unknowable soldier checked his watch. Thirteen hundred hours. Almost showtime. His time. He could feel it. All systems, mental and physical, switched to a heightened frequency, in sync, processing information, filing away procedures and responses until needed. This is what set him apart. In his vision he could see the mission through to conclusion as clearly as the gas station sign across the street from his motel window.

He had been over all the contingencies again and again, and he knew he would be able to select whatever course of action necessary to succeed. It was more than conceit. The mission was the maze, and he was the master at choosing the correct turns. On those occasions when he veered into a dead end, he knew his resourcefulness would set him back on course. That is what made him much more than a soldier. He didn't just execute, he improvised as the situation dictated. He never panicked, never lost sight of the objective.

He held out his right hand, checking himself. Unwavering, like the earth's rotation — around and around, through all the missions and all the years. At these moments he felt as in his 20s, vital. He still had it. There would be another test, another challenge. Not for any pleasure to be derived from the act. He was no sportsman. He was a professional, a mercenary. That had been his identity for so long he could recall no other. When he referred to himself as a soldier, it was an understatement. He meant commando. The battles he fought might be large or small, political or private. He had served in detachments of various sizes but preferred to operate as an elite force of one. The pay was better for a specialist in any field. In his field, he was on par with a neurosurgeon. He could do what few others would attempt. Even at his advanced age.

Was that his conceit? Yes. And the paradox of his life. Although he remained as anonymous as possible he coveted the renown his achievements brought. And so, his reputation loomed in clandestine circles, a legend of the underworld even while nobody knew his real name and almost no one alive could connect his face to his deeds. He was, at this point, more myth than man. Even the myth became less distinct as the past grew more distant and faceless. It was a testimonial to his enduring status that he retained his niche in the shadowy network and that fragile links of communication still found him when he consented to contact.

Events tend to blur with time, but not in his mind. That's how he maintained his edge. He remembered it all, every detail, momentous and ancillary, the triumphs and mistakes. Even after decades of missions, he could recall each one and replay them as if he were watching the events unfold in a vivid mental cyclorama played out in precise slow-motion. Maybe there was an element of sport to this, critiquing the action, analyzing why it succeeded, or in some cases, failed. Often the failures were the result of the inevitable involvement of others. That was the best aspect of this latest mission: It was virtually solo. That advantage, however, was more than offset by the audacity of the undertaking. There was no margin for error and too many variables that had to be left to chance. Wasn't that precisely why he had accepted the assignment? His whole career — yes, his legend — had been built on boldness. Wasn't that what this job was about, maintaining status, adding a notch? Those were questions he refused to entertain. His mind was focused entirely on the mechanics of the task.

As always, his modus operandi was methodical, almost ritualistic. Yesterday morning he stepped ashore at a nondescript boatyard in Islamorada carrying a sea bag and a medium-size metal case. He visited the Asian girl for an hour, then ate a hearty lunch alone in a quiet, cool corner of a mostly empty steakhouse, his last indulgences before switching into full operational mode.

In the afternoon he drove the gray, nondescript sedan that had been provided to him north along U.S. 1, through the unappealing congestion of Key Largo, the smattering of marinas, restaurants and schlock shops in the Upper Keys and finally the tedious two-lane stretch amid mangroves and marshes at the southern tip of the peninsula. At Florida City, he took the Homestead extension of the turnpike, skirting west of the sprawl of Miami and its suburbs. From the highway, remnants of the devastation of Hurricane Andrew, which burrowed its evil eye through southern Dade County the previous August, were evident. Large tracts of trees were either laid flat or locked in a permanent westward lean like a routed army trudging in retreat with heads bowed. Passing residential areas, workers atop houses were still a common sight repairing roofs wrenched away by winds that gusted to 200 mph. Many buildings were boarded up. Some had messages scrawled on walls and plywood-patched roofs in defiance or desperate. One read: "We shall overcome." Another: "Allstate, give us a hand." Still another: "Andrew, *pendejo!*"

The mercenary didn't notice any of it. He drove at a steady, purposeful speed, eyes on the road, thoughts on what he must do to complete the mission and slip back into his carefully guarded netherworld.

In the next 20 hours his focus rarely strayed from that purpose, unless it was to recall incidents from the past that might serve him now. It was his custom to be positioned close to the venue of an operation well in advance of zero hour. Preparation was paramount, and he made careful use of the hours leading up to an event, whether in setting up his cover, scouting an escape route or observing an aspect of topography or architecture that might give him an edge. He had a knack for blending inconspicuously into a setting, a skill that had enabled him to operate in very public places. It was what he termed creating an invisible presence, and he achieved it by making himself appear ordinary so as to leave no impression on witnesses, as well as in understanding how people behave in moments of confusion and chaos. In that respect he was as great an illusionist and escape artist as Houdini. The proof was in his enduring freedom and anonymity.

In this mission, which was predicated on stealth and surprise, an invisible presence was vital yet impossible. But delaying detection was essential. With that in mind, late on the afternoon of his arrival in the Miami area he drove west of Hialeah along a two-lane road, passing underneath the turnpike he had traveled earlier, for a final preparatory look at the Dade-West Correctional Institute nestled on the fringe of the Everglades. What a godforsaken spot to be caged, he thought, as he passed the turnoff to the prison, continued another half-mile to a dead end and turned around. If the system didn't beat you down, surely the mosquitoes and humidity would. Nitwit Hawke had mentioned that Gen. Manuel Noriega, the deposed Panamanian dictator, had been housed there while awaiting trial. The mercenary couldn't fathom why Noriega hadn't chosen the less agonizing alternative of a bullet strategically placed at the base of his skull when U.S. troops came knocking at his door, when the little despot knew full well that the American political guillotine would make sure he never again walked free. Better a lethal dose of hot lead than one stifling day in a dehumanizing place like this.

The mercenary didn't linger, nor did he plan to stay long when he returned the following afternoon. He spotted what he was seeking in a cluster of lanky pines and melaleuca trees beginning about 400 yards to the north of the prison and bending around the west side in a half-moon arc before thinning out to the south. Not perfect, he thought, but it just might buy him enough invisibility to make a difference. Confident in his plan, he'd returned to his first-floor room at the motel and slept for 10 hours undisturbed.

Now, with his appointment at the prison less than three hours away, he again envisioned that wooded area, his soon-to-be ally, as he opened the metal case on the bed.

#

"This Joanna's a real spitfire. And a sweetheart, too. You'll love her. And when it comes to fighting a big fish, she's the real deal. I've never worked with an angler who had better concentration or better technique. That's part of why she lands so many tough fish. The other is she's got amazing endurance, and you'd be surprised by how strong she is."

Dallas had already seen evidence to support Zack Tomlin's effusive endorsement of Joanna Zimmerman's angling artistry in a professionally produced video of her subduing a series of marlin off Costa Rica. Now he was going to meet the lady legend herself and, with luck, see her tangle with a tarpon or two. They were chugging through Miami on the 836 in the Great White bound for big game, or at least a big story. Kirby D'Arbonnell had been incredulous then ecstatic when Dallas called to say he had a fishing date set with Joanna Zimmerman.

"You gotta be kidding. She's turned down everybody, even *Sports Illustrated*. Says she doesn't do interviews for the same reason she doesn't enter fishing tournaments. She's not in it for glory or publicity."

At least she didn't court it. Didn't have to. Not since the *60 Minutes* piece a couple of years back that followed in the wake of her five blue marlin catches over 500 pounds in one remarkable day off Venezuela that made her the most recognizable angler in America, and since then the most elusive. Her angling feats still managed to find their way into the prominent fishing magazines, thanks to Jake Zimmerman, her husband and unabashed P.R. agent. Her fishing videos frequently appeared at odd hours on ESPN and other cable networks. The media fascination with Joanna was due largely to the fact that she was already well known as a figure skater before she wet a line and reeled in her first marlin. As Joanna Cannizzarro, she was set to succeed Dorothy Hamill as America's ice princess until a knee injury shattered the dream a month before the 1980 Olympics. A decade later she became the champion of women over 30 with her hugely popular exercise program, *Getting Fit For the Love of It*. The show, geared toward the mature woman, was laced with racy innuendo that not only made her female followers snicker while they sweated but earned her a voyeuristic male audience. She always opened the show by saying, "Remember, ladies, every muscle is a love muscle, so let's work them with passion."

It was no wonder that she could stand up to the roughest hombre at the end of her line. Even the high-roller sportfishing set, which hated the attention she received, had to concede that Joanna was a hell of an accomplished angler. While men were largely in quest of the biggest blue marlin, she had shown them all up by landing more than 100 blues in the Caribbean. What made her achievements impressive, she reeled them in standing up, using a short, high-leverage rod supported by only a belly harness and gimbal, rather than strapped into a fighting chair which turned the angler into little more than a glorified winch operator.

"It's amazing to see. That lady has got to have the strongest legs to be able to stand up to a fish like that," Tomlin said.

Dallas smiled. He knew that Zack frequently worked as a mate on the Zimmermans's boat on outings of a week or two in the Bahamas, St. Thomas, Costa Rico, Cayman Islands and elsewhere. He had, in fact, been aboard that watershed day off Venezuela, and his effusive commentary in the cockpit as Joanna fought the marlin had been a highlight of the *60 Minutes* segment. It was Tomlin who had persuaded her to do this rare interview with Dallas.

"I bet you've spent many hours admiring her technique and marveling at her endurance."

"Hey, hey, watch yourself with that stuff. Jake's a hell of a guy. But he's very protective of Joanna, and he doesn't miss a trick," Tomlin said. Then, with a wink, he added. "You're damn right."

Jake Zimmerman not only played eight seasons for the Washington Redskins, he was one of the last great white defensive backs, twice making All-Pro at strong safety. He was every bit as self-assured and impressive now as president of a company that installed and monitored home security systems. Jake loved being on the water and catching snapper and grouper on a spinning rod, but Tomlin had never seen him fight a big fish, preferring to rig baits and attend to support duties when Joanna dueled marlin. Tomlin often said, "I think he wants to save his energy for Joanna."

The Zimmermans were already aboard their open fisherman with the twin outboards idling when Dallas parked the Great White at a marina on Watson Island next to the Port of Miami.

"Hey, Zachary, you should've seen the big jack Joanna caught off the dock while we were waiting. Must've been 20 pounds. Bouncer Smith came by and said there's still loads of mullet out there in the channel. The tarpon are busting them all over the place. They caught a couple 100-pounders last night."

It quickly became apparent that this wiry man could talk as relentlessly as his wife fished. Dallas sensed there was little chance of any man moving on his wife as long as he was around. And Jake was rarely not around. He was no more than 6 feet tall but had forearms like sledgehammers and a handshake like a vise. Dallas wasn't sure he'd be able to hold a fishing rod after being welcomed aboard by Jake. He much preferred Joanna's handshake. Her hand felt warm and conveyed a sensuous strength that made Dallas blush. He felt envious when she greeted Tomlin with a kiss on the cheek. Jake did most of the talking as they motored past two freighters and a cruise ship docked in the port on the way to Government Cut. Joanna seemed reticent, but there was great depth to her dark eyes. Dallas hoped she would allow a glimpse inside.

#

The leaky vessel was typical of many Ensign Culver had seen wallowing precariously in the Gulf Stream with greater frequency the past few years, it's hull wooden and termite ridden. A sail constructed from a tarpaulin lashed to a makeshift mast reinforced with 2-by-4s. Culver could only guess at the despair that led people to pile onto such a floating death trap and trust their fate to the unlikely odds of the sea delivering them to the promised land and wonder at how many of them never made it this far. He had counted 26 faces aboard a craft that couldn't have been more than 25 feet long. Two of the women were pregnant. Eight children, all undernourished. An old man with one leg huddled on a bed of rags. Not a sight for the faint-hearted. They all had a look of hopefulness that was almost surreal, and it told Culver he wouldn't hesitate to undertake the same improbable voyage if he were in their situation.

Lately it seemed that the principal duty of the U.S. Coast Guard had evolved to operating an offshore shuttle service for refugees from Haiti and to a lesser extent Cuba. These freedom floaters had become so common off South Florida that their condition no longer shocked Culver. He recalled the first refugee detail he'd been on, an overloaded boat of hysterical people jabbering in Creole. And when it became clear that two of them had just died with the cutter in sight, the corpses still onboard, Culver had rushed to the rail and puked into the ocean.

That night, back on shore getting drunk on rum, he'd mused on the Janis Joplan line about freedom meaning nothing left to lose. To him, the description seemed more apt for desperation. Here it was in rawest form. Culver had seen it, smelled it. It drove him to drain the bottle, puke again and pray to never be reborn poor in Haiti, or any place that destitute.

This crew was in better shape than most, and with the sea calm the decision had been made to tow the rickety craft with the people still aboard into the Port of Miami. Culver looked not back at the vessel in tow but toward the buildings ahead on the horizon as they made slow progress toward Government Cut. It was pleasantly placid on the ocean for February, and his thoughts were on a hot meal and letters he needed to write after his duty was done.

CHAPTER 14

The mercenary found the helicopter in the designated spot behind a remote warehouse complex in western Dade County, resting like a disoriented albatross amid palmettos and weeds. He wore a black, rubberized diving suit and carried a metal case, which he set on the passenger seat. He had checked out the helicopter extensively the previous afternoon, but he repeated the examination of the engine and external systems before climbing into the cockpit.

For him, flying a Bell 47 was as routine as a milk run to the corner 7-Eleven. He'd flown variations of the same model since 1950, when he earned a chest full of medals and nearly an early grave as a chopper jockey in the X Corps in Korea. That was the first war that proved the potential of helicopters as a military tool, and he had been one of the early masters, shuttling men and supplies in and out of enemy territory.

He'd cemented his reputation in one incident in mountainous North Korea when he made a dozen daring flights to liberate a company of fellow marines pinned down near Funchilin Pass until machine gun fire forced him down on the 13th trip in. He spent the next five days in sub-zero weather dodging and occasionally engaging Chinese patrols before discovering that his unit had pushed on to the north. When he finally caught up to them at Hagaru-ri, he stormed into the command tent and raged at the officer he blamed for abandoning him in the mountains. The episode cost him two toes to frostbite and earned him a Silver Star, which he later hurled into the Changjin Reservoir. It didn't prevent him from climbing into the next Bell 47, but the incident left him embittered and aloof. Thereafter, he was regarded with a wary reverence. He also made it a point since then to fight his battles in warm regions and on his own terms, whenever possible.

This helicopter, painted Navy blue, had seen plenty of service but was in good shape mechanically, its engine recently overhauled. The mercenary had made it clear he would walk away from the job if the bird didn't meet his standards. When he was satisfied all systems were functional, he opened the metal case and removed a Glock 9mm pistol, securing it in easy reach to the side of his seat. He strapped a holstered .38-caliber revolver around his waist before stowing the metal case.

As marked on his chart, the Dade-West Correctional Institute was 2.8 miles to the southwest, indicated by a precise X in red ink. He studied the route one last time before twisting the throttle and pulling back on the collective-pitch lever. The steel albatross rose and hovered 100 feet off the ground for a moment as if trying to get its bearings. The direct compass course to the prison was 237 degrees. But the mercenary pointed the nose at 265 degrees, almost due west before easing the stick forward and beginning his journey. The late afternoon sun glinted off his mirrored sunglasses. The sun looked like a bright orange beach ball slowly descending. But this was no day at the beach.

#

Dallas was trying to get a read on Joanna Zimmerman. She'd seemed standoffish when he started asking innocuous questions about the gear she used that enabled her to fight large fish standing up for long periods of time. Jake had quickly jumped in to explain that it was all custom-made, offering more information than Dallas cared to digest about the tackle and the man who made it, a friend in St. Thomas, Virgin Islands. Was she a snob? Then it became clear: It was simply shyness. The realization surprised Dallas: Here was a very attractive woman who had begun performing before large crowds in international competition as a teenager and hosted a televised exercise show spiced with sexual innuendo, and yet she was nervous around Dallas Huston, apprentice journalist. Tomlin noticed the tension and pulled him aside to whisper, "She's gotta get to know you. You'll see."

Gradually the walls came down as she settled into her element aboard the fishing boat. Jake steered them through Government Cut, crossing the bow of an incoming freighter with containers stacked three high. Tomlin, standing with one foot on the gunwale and the other on a cooler for a better view of the water ahead, spotted what they were looking for. When he pointed it out, Dallas and Joanna rushed to the bow, and she actually giggled and made a little jump in her excitement.

It was a remarkable sight — the spectacle in the ocean, that is. At first Dallas could just see that something was disturbing a patch of water the size of a football field. The source of it became apparent as Jake brought them closer. Swarms of fish were coming to the surface, big fish feeding on little fish in a frenzied, all-you-can-eat, no-holds-barred smorgasbord. Jake shut down the engines, and the boat drifted into the middle of the massive school of mullet, the main course in this seafood fest.

Mullet migrate from the north in the fall and congregate off South Florida until late winter.

This was a common seasonal drama that goes unnoticed by the typical dweller in the beachfront condos, absorbed with watching pro wrestling and the Home Shopping Network. The star players were tarpon, some of them larger than 100 pounds. In their pursuit of a free meal, they came to the surface showing a flash of silver side and creating a swirl with tail and fins. Occasionally, one of the giant fish in its haste leaped completely out of the water, splashing down with a smack like a fat kid in a belly-flop contest.

The mullet were so thick they appeared as a massive floating ink spot, and tarpon were popping up everywhere in their midst, rolling and splashing. The fading sunlight cast a red-orange blanket that created a surreal impression of fireworks bursting on the surface.

Was it pure feed or part frolic? Dallas couldn't tell, but like everyone on the boat he felt the same childlike joy of being treated to such a spectacular display of the natural world. Dallas was hypnotized seeing fish this big coming so close he could have reached out and tickled them with the tip of a fishing rod. Joanna was the first to summon the presence of mind to fetch a rod, a light-tackle spinning outfit rigged with a white jig and feather made more enticing by a live shrimp. Even with all the commotion in the water, Dallas couldn't help admiring the grace with which she made her cast and began working the lure.

"They've got so much to eat, they probably won't pay any attention to this. But maybe one of them will go for it because it's something different," she said.

"Yeah, shrimp and lead on a string. That's always been one of my favorite treats to top off a big meal," Dallas said.

To his surprise, Joanna not only smiled, she handed the rod to him.

"Try casting just past the edge of the school. A lot of times you'll get a fish out there looking for a straggler."

It became apparent to Dallas that he would learn more about this woman by observation than from asking questions. Zack handed another rod to Joanna and rigged one for himself. Jake stood by, arms folded, watching the three of them at play.

"Remember that time Joanna had this tarpon on and it jumped right over the outboards? I had Zack's camera ready and got a great shot of it in the air as it went over the back of the boat. I shot a whole roll of film on that fish, or so I thought. Turned out Zack forgot to put film in the camera."

"Those were the best pictures you never took," Tomlin said. "For once, it didn't matter that you can never get a jumping fish in focus."

Dallas was less interested in trying to catch a tarpon than in watching them. Joanna was right about the fish showing little interest in shrimp on a barb. She was also right in her strategy of working the fringe of the school. She didn't say a word when she felt the fish pick up the bait, just kept feeding line until she felt the time was right to engage the reel and set the hook.

The first anyone realized she had a fish on was when the tarpon rocketed out of the water and did a reverse cartwheel. Dallas thought it was another free jumper until he saw the bend in Joanna's rod. Tarpon are one of the toughest game fish to hook because their mouth is 90 percent steely bone, so most succeed in spitting the hook on the first jump. Joanna's hook found a soft spot, and she was using her skills to ensure it stayed secure. This one clearly was a 100-pounder. On every jump she "bowed to the fish," as fishing captains instruct, to avoid pulling the hook free. She kept the pressure on during the runs and reclaimed line at every lull, so the fish got no rest.

Dallas had been enthralled by the spectacle of the tarpon frenzy, but now Joanna commanded his fascination, the combination of grace and strength with which she confronted the fish. The angle of her back, arched for maximum resistance, her knees slightly bent, the muscles in her calves and thighs powerfully defined. Dallas longed for a glimpse of her arms and shoulders hidden by the windbreaker. Tomlin was right. If this filly were a thoroughbred, they'd be draping garlands of roses around her neck at Churchill Downs and toasting her with mint juleps.

#

"Hor-hey, man, you wouldn't believe what they had on Sally Jessy, today. You shoulda watched it with us."

Jorge Ortega stood in the exercise yard of the Dade-West Correctional Institute, his gaze to the west, his thoughts to the south and east. He was of average height, but his bearing gave the impression of a taller man. Even in his prison blues he retained a presence that set him apart, as if he were wearing an Armani suit and everyone else rags. This was rare, to maintain that aura behind the steel doors and barbed wire. A lot of the big shots — underworld dons and defrocked white-collar kingpins — couldn't pull it off. Peel away the gold bling, designer clothes, the limos, lackeys and babes, hose them down and wrap them in the state's stark costume, and the masquerade ended. Prison shrank them to irrelevance.

Not Jorge Ortega. He was the same inside the system as outside. Unbowed.

Ortega didn't acknowledge the other man, Manny Lozada, striding up to him, keeping up his animated chatter.

"Hor-hey, you should've seen it. Fag bowlers and their lovers," Lozada said, recounting the latest installment of the "Sally Jessy Raphael" daily freak show. "Where the hell do they find these people? These pretty boys swishing their asses on the alleys. And their lovers complaining about them like housewives. Guy says, 'I wash his bowling shirts, go to a lot of trouble to get them all nice and white, get the stains out, and do I get so much as thanks?' Cracked me the fuck up.

"But the best part. They ask what they do to bring their lover good luck when he bowls for money in these big matches and stuff. This one guy goes, 'I shine his ball.' You should've seen Sally Jessy; her jaw dropped to her knees. The whole place was howling and hooting and shit. It was great."

Ortega's expression was unreadable, distant, giving no indication he was listening. Lozada even turned as if to follow the path of Ortega's brown eyes.

"Hor-hey, man, I'm telling you. Listen, you gotta lighten up in here."

"Fags, is that what they called them?"

"Huh?"

"Fags. Did they call them fags on TV?"

"No, man, course not. They said homosexuals. I think what they said at the beginning was: 'Homosexuals on the pro bowling tour, their lives and loves.' Or some such shit. But this one — it was funny, man — called himself the Queen of the Alley. Sally Jessy, she even cracked up at that. Man, I'm thinking that's gotta be the best job that she has. I could do that, you know, be a talk-show host."

For the first time Ortega revealed a trace of a smile, though he still did not look at Lozada.

"Like they're going to give a talk show to a spic con."

"Hey, I know this girl works for a station in Miami. She could help me get to the people you gotta talk to, listen to my idea. I'd gear it to our people. We'd do the show out on South Beach. Lotsa atmosphere on the set, sexy *chiquitas* and scenery all around. Call it, *He Says, She Says, By the Seashore*. You like? See, I could do that. I got personality. I'm a character. That's why I get along so good in here. I make people laugh. You should try it, Hor-hey."

"Sounds good. Need a sponsor, you call me when you get out and get it going."

Ortega was focused on the horizon. He heard what he sought before he saw it. Lozada became aware of the sound but it didn't register. Now he was the one transported in reverie, hair slicked back, microphone in hand, surrounded by neon and palms, interrogating Hispanic cross-dressers and cracking wise.

Ortega's fantasy future was closer at hand. He recognized it immediately, the rhythmic bleat of the engine and rotor, and scanned the sky over the Everglades until he picked it up, a black dot coming almost straight out of the sun. With the benefit of that blinding cover, the helicopter approached with elegant stealth, swooping into the prison's exercise yard before anyone grasped the drama unfolding. The other dozen inmates in the 50-by-200-foot yard were absorbed in a basketball game or lifting weights. The guard in the southwest tower heard the engine but couldn't immediately locate its source. The guard in the northwest tower had just turned to greet his relief, and the two men didn't react until too late.

Ortega caught a flash of light off the pilot's sunglasses as the chopper, angled forward, buzzed over the 12-foot fence and dropped into the yard. He crossed his hands above his head in the appointed signal and began moving away from Lozada, ducking low as he dashed toward the chopper. The skids didn't even make contact with the asphalt before Ortega found a foothold and leaped through the opening in the cockpit bubble onto the open seat. As if they'd practiced the maneuver together a hundred times, the pilot immediately whirled the helicopter around and began the escape in the direction from which he had come.

They were gaining lift, approaching the fence, when the 'copter suddenly lurched back and tilted toward Ortega's side. He looked out and was astonished to see Lozada clinging to the skid beneath the cockpit, eyes wide and a smile to match.

"No, man, no! You've got to let go. You can't come. Let go. ..."

His exhortation was quelled in mid utterance by a forearm across the chest knocking him back into the seat. Ortega saw the glint of steel pass in front of him as the pilot leaned across and fired a bullet into Lozada's forehead above the bridge of his nose. For an instant, Lozada appeared frozen in a mannequin's stare, his fingers still gripping the metal bar before gravity applied the *coup de grace* to an aspiring talk-show career. Ortega would be left with the image of the red dot appearing on Lozada's forehead, making him look like a fakir begging for salvation.

When he later reflected on the incident, the astonishing aspect was the stealth with which the pilot dealt with the crisis. The unexpected addition of weight and the distraction of dispensing with Lozada carried the helicopter into the perimeter fence, the undercarriage hooking on a loop of razor wire. Momentarily it teetered atop the fence, and Ortega feared it would pitch them forward into a heap of twisted metal just outside the prison or catapult them back into the yard. Either way, the exhilaration of freedom so near was giving way to the terror of impending doom.

The pilot never hesitated. No sooner had he fired the single shot than he dropped the gun onto Ortega's lap and began emergency manipulation of the controls. With one hand on the stick taming the throttle and altering the angle of the main rotor, the other on the lever feathering the blades, he coaxed the panic out of the bucking beast. Ortega saw the fence shake as the skids pulled free and he thought they were going down backwards. There was a horrible shriek of metal as the tip of the tail rotor grazed the ground, but then the front dipped and the 'copter leveled off, hovering briefly as it regained its bearing. In essence, what the pilot did was throw the contraption into reverse and back it away from the fence. Then they were up and away.

Ortega was incredulous when he saw the fence pass beneath him and the ground rushing past. Shots were being fired. A bullet pierced the cockpit bubble but to no effect. They were gaining speed though remaining close to the ground. Ortega could see trees coming up on the right and felt the helicopter bank steeply to that side as it began a wide, low arc to the north and east, using the woods as the final blanket of cover. Glancing back, Ortega caught a flash of light reflecting off the window at the top of a guard tower before the prison vanished from sight. Only then did he realize he was clutching a 9mm pistol as if it were a life preserver.

#

Ensign Culver heard the call on the radio dispatching the Coast Guard chopper to pursue a civilian helicopter that may be approaching the coast. He wondered what it was about. Drugs, probably. Culver was enjoying the colorful palette of the impending sunset. The cutter was still south of Port Miami, a couple miles east of Cape Florida Lighthouse at the tip of Key Biscayne. Lt. Laudermilk began scanning the sky to the west with a pair of binoculars. But Culver spotted it first with his naked eye, just a speck, moving erratically, like a bug.

A few miles away, Dallas Huston noticed it, too. He had been admiring the way the muscles stood out on Joanna's neck and the firm set of her jaw as she fought the tarpon. This was a determined woman. The fish was formidable and just as stubborn. On one occasion she had gotten it to within an arm's length of Tomlin being able to grab the leader before the tarpon, with a mighty twist of its head, turned away and ripped off 50 feet of line. The struggle was turning into a standoff. Dallas was fascinated by the war of wills. He was pretty sure Joanna wouldn't quit, the question was whether she would make a mistake the fish could capitalize on before it was too spent to resist.

They had drifted to the south opposite Virginia Key when Dallas's attention was diverted by the small helicopter, one of those bubble-type two-seaters, flying low almost directly toward the boat. Abruptly it banked to the south and dropped even lower, nearly skimming the waves. A couple of times it stopped to hover momentarily. Dallas asked Jake for binoculars and located the helicopter just as the Coast Guard's orange-and-white Sikorsky thundered overhead, heading southward.

Joanna had the tarpon close again. Tomlin was poised to make a lunge for the leader. Jake, at the helm, maneuvered the boat so the fish couldn't take the line into the props. Dallas stood apart watching the two helicopters. The small one, distant, appeared to circle. Then, to his surprise, it descended to the ocean.

"Hey, that helicopter's going down!"

"Zack, can you reach it?"

"Almost. ... Damn!"

The knot of the leader remained inches from Tomlin's outstretched fingers as he leaned over the side of the boat.

Aboard the cutter, Capt. Simon gave the order to release the tow on the refugee boat and nobody bothered to mutter the standard joke: "He didn't say Simon says."

They were gathering speed, no more than a half-mile away from the rogue helicopter when its main rotor slowed and it set down so gently there was barely a splash.

The tail of the Bell 47 was slipping beneath the waves as the Coast Guard helicopter arrived, too late to get a line on it, and began searching the surrounding water for the occupants. Joanna was still trying in vain to tame the toughest tarpon she'd ever tangled with. Jake turned to survey the distant scene that had Dallas pointing and shouting. The sun's denouement bathed the clouds in a brilliant burnt-orange, which cast a gauzy yellow glow on the ocean as they stared to the south. The Coast Guard chopper was hovering and a boat was converging from the opposite direction.

Dallas and Jake noticed the white hull at the same moment. The boat slowed to idle a couple of hundred yards from the Coast Guard helicopter. Then it erupted in a mushroom of fire and smoke.

CHAPTER 15

The bar at the Leaky Tiki wasn't officially open, and Dallas was on his second Bloody Mary at a stool across from the cooler where Claire was loading beer from cases. Even describing the events of the night before didn't quite validate them. Maybe it was lack of sleep or the alcohol. It still seemed unreal.

"That's a lot like what happened to your boat, huh."

"And my friend Zack, the fishing captain who was with us, he saw something like it out here the week after mine happened."

"Scary, huh. You know, I've heard they still find German torpedoes from World War II out there sometimes." She paused. "But I thought yours was a gas leak from the stove."

"That's what I thought. It's the only thing that makes sense. Hate to even think about other possibilities. Thought it was supposed to be carefree Margaritaville here."

"Don't be so sure. Can see you haven't been in South Florida very long. Not so sweet and innocent under the sun. Look at the daily news: home invasions, drug dealers with Uzis, lots of road rage. Sometimes I talk to people back home and they say, 'Aren't you scared to live there?' I say, 'What da hell, scarier than L.A. freeways?' At least the Keys are pretty laid back. But even here, things aren't always what they seem. Or the people. The friendly boat captain buying you a drink might be a smuggler."

Dallas couldn't get his mind off seeing the Coast Guard cutter engulfed by the explosion, an image out of a Stallone movie. Even from a mile away, he could feel the concussion and see the rain of debris. It was chilling, and it caused him to reassess recent events.

"Makes you wonder what's going on. Too many things to be random accidents," he said. "They send men to the moon and build superconductors — scientists can explain how that's possible. How do you explain a bunch of boats blowing up out here? There's got to be a connection."

"Do you think they really went to the moon or did they film that in the desert?" Claire said, looking up from the beer cooler with a deadpan expression. She smiled. "Seriously, I know what you mean. Some things make no sense at all. Like, Michael Bolton's popularity."

She surprised him. Her response didn't fit the moment, but he laughed anyway. It felt good.

"Yeah, and why people send money to TV preachers."

"And why lawyers can say the ridiculous stuff they say, and their noses don't grow."

"Same with politicians. 'I'm not a crook.' Yeah, right," he said, laughing again.

"I guess that's why more people watch *Unsolved Mysteries* than the Discovery Channel."

"Then there's the biggest mystery of all: Where do jokes originate? You know, there are certain jokes that circulate everywhere. People tell them at parties and places they work and in bars. I always wonder, where do they come from? I mean, somebody had to make it up originally. But how does that happen? Is there some place, a joke mint where they write jokes and put them into circulation?"

"I know, sometimes you'll hear the same basic joke in different forms. Except I always forget them before I can tell them."

Dallas realized he was giggling, his thoughts suddenly far from the horror he'd witnessed the night before. Another mystery: Why did this woman make his spirits soar, just being with her? He had barely eaten or slept in the previous 24 hours, yet as he shared his tale with her he felt oddly invigorated.

Still very hungry, though, or something like it. More like an emotion, but it was confusing. Usually he'd see a woman who was attractive and the response was primal, easy to trace. This was different, something from the distant past and barely recognizable, the uneasy afterglow of sensations unleashed on a dance floor in a high school gym. It didn't compute in the context of his present jaded perspective, so he refused to acknowledge it. Must be his brain playing tricks. He'd been through a traumatic experience. That was it. Better get some sleep soon. Self-analysis could wait.

Dallas looked up and was startled to see her studying him.

"The more I think about it, the stranger it seems. Surreal, actually," he said. "It was as if the Coast Guard boat ran into a mine, something floating out there."

"Maybe that's what it was. The guy was escaping from prison, right? Maybe they set a mine out in the water. Arms dealers could probably get one of those, right?"

"But the cutter hadn't even gotten to where they went down. The Coast Guard helicopter was right over the spot. That's the really crazy part. There was no sign of anyone there. They just vanished."

"Maybe they were unconscious and couldn't get out of the helicopter."

"I don't know, the way it went down; it didn't crash. It looked like they meant to, ah … to land on the water. I was thinking they might have had scuba gear. The cops were searching Key Biscayne all night in case they came ashore."

"What happened to the people on the Coast Guard boat?"

"By the time we got there they'd picked up all but one, those still alive in pretty bad shape. They were lifting the body of the captain in the basket. There was somebody in a raft calling out for somebody named Culver. We helped them search until well after dark. It was hopeless. They were supposed to send divers down this morning to look for the helicopter."

"Such a shame."

Dallas shrugged. "Bizarre. Never seen anything like it."

"So what happened to the fish?"

"The what?"

"You know, the one the woman had on when it happened."

"Oh, they were going to release it, anyway. It was a tarpon, so they weren't going to keep it. I guess you could say it got early parole. The funny thing, the rest of the night her husband, this guy Jake, kept saying, 'Damn, that was a hell of a fish. Now we can't even count it,' like he's keeping score or something. Here we're towing in this boatload of Haitians that was the reason the cutter was even out there. There's all these starving people in this god-awful boat that's practically sinking, and this guy's lamenting having to cut a fish loose."

"Sounds like a jerk. Some people have no perspective."

"But the best part was when we finally get back to the dock and this Joanna says to me: 'Well, you wanted a fish story to write about. Looks like you ended up with a real whopper.' She's right. If I hadn't seen it, I'd have never believed any of it."

CHAPTER 16

Keith Richards Salmon had a wonderful knack for indirect explanation, telling a story to illustrate a point. He was a master of allusion.

This is Keith explaining how Devereaux was able to find the wreck of *Nuestra Senora de Carmelita* in the world's busiest treasure-hunting area.

"I had a girlfriend who worked at the seabird care center in Tavernier. I used to go there and just hang around and watch her work — she was a slinky one; I loved that girl. She did a lot of work with the pelicans, and I spent a lot of time watching them. They're funny, man.

"This one time they're eating these fish she'd put out for them. They finished the fish and they're grubbin' around looking for more. This one pelican, who's off by himself, calmly walks from one end of the pen to the other where there's this pool of water that's so dark you couldn't see the bottom. This pelican's cool, man. He walks right into the pool, reaches down and snatches a fish and walks away. The other birds go crazy. They're like, 'How the fuck did he know that was there?'

"It's the same way with my man Skeeter. He can smell treasure. You've got people rooting around every inch of those reefs for years, and he comes in and finds this ship right under their noses. That's why I work for the man. Yeah, he's an odd cat. But he's the best at what he does."

"Better than Mel Fisher?"

Keith and Dallas were chilling with rum-and-coconut aboard *Big Momma* after helping Devereaux complete work on the airlift pump and prepare the salvage boat to resume the treasure quest. Dallas had been treated to one of Devereaux's famous foot-stompin', Cajun howlin' tantrums over a broken bolt and a banged knuckle. When the work was done and all systems were go for Dallas's debut as a treasure hunter the following day, he'd gotten his first glimpse of the gold-rush glint in the old captain's eyes. That convinced Dallas the endeavor would at least be interesting and could be highly entertaining.

"That's it, he gets the look. You're not sure what he's seeing, but it makes you want to follow along and find out," Keith said. "Let me tell you, you can't take anything away from Fisher. He found the *Atocha* when everyone else was looking for it 100 miles away. But nobody even knew to look for this one, and Devereaux comes in and finds it. It's like he has a sixth sense when it comes to shipwrecks and treasure.

"The big difference is, Fisher loves the notoriety and our man shies away from it. He hated it when we started bringing in treasure and TV crews and reporters were sticking cameras up our asses every time we turned around. One day we came in and he sees them on the dock waiting, and he turned the boat around and went to a different boatyard. Left them to interview each other. He's totally different out on the water, not so uptight. He's happiest when he's underwater getting that nitro buzz."

"I don't blame him for shying away from notoriety. You mean acclaim."

"What the fuck you talking about, man?"

"Notoriety. That's one of those words most people misuse. It means being famous for the wrong reasons. Like John Gotti or G. Gordon Liddy."

"G. Gordon who? The fuck, man, you talkin' like a college professor. Don't be talking to me about splittin' hairs with words. I ain't no man of letters, unless you're talking about chords. Only one thing I know how to spell."

With that, Keith picked up his guitar and started singing, "R-E-S-P-E-C-T, sock it to me, sock it to me, sock it to me. ..."

They ended up laughing and having another drink before crashing for the night. Dallas sacked out on the sofa because they had to be on the boat at dawn. He had a strange dream in which a guy kept coming to the door saying he was Chris Columbus. Not Christopher, he said, just Chris — and he was selling paintings of Indians that were really Chinese. Must have been tainted coconut, a real coco loco dream.

Thereafter, Keith often referred to Dallas as Professor. Meanwhile, Devereaux, for reasons less apparent, took to calling him Buck. So whenever he was on the boat he found himself answering to three different names. Of the three, he much preferred the way his real name rolled off Claire's tongue.

If he were honest, he'd have to admit she was the main reason he was getting involved in this enterprise, even though it was intriguing on its own merit. Dallas told himself, there could be a great story come out of this — D'Arbonnell said to get underwater pictures of the sub at the wreck site. Could be more than a story, he could be in on uncovering a fortune. Could turn into a television special hosted by Geraldo.

So Dallas started getting that glint in his eye, too, like Devereaux. But it wasn't gold-rush fever. He got it every time he stared at Claire in the blue wetsuit she wore on the boat. Even if they did hit the ol' Spanish lottery, he didn't figure to get rich. He was getting paid by the hour. Part-time, no health insurance. For now, being close to Claire was the main benefit.

There was no guarantee they'd find the so-called mother lode. Indications were this ship had scattered its contents when it went down, and it was in relatively deep water. They had found enough coins and artifacts to verify the date and identity of the wreck. The most notable find, late the previous summer, was a 200-pound mass of silver coins, apparently from a single chest, that had been fused together from 300 years of saltwater corrosion. Keith dug up several pie-shaped wedges of silver nearby. But just as it seemed they might be onto something big, it petered out.

Then, as Keith so eloquently put it, "The damn hurricane came and dumped shit all over what we'd uncovered."

So when Dallas joined the scavenger hunt in late February, Devereaux's Almiranta Explorations Inc. was more or less back to square one, bucking strong winter currents and facing the threat of new legislation that could turn them into just another sightseeing operation offering sunset cruises with watered-down rum punches. Presented with these dubious prospects, Dallas was delighted when Devereaux elected to take Keith with him in the submersible, leaving Dallas and Claire to mind the topside operation. She was the treasure on his mind.

His own fantasies about the barmaid-adventuress were often echoed by Keith, who was constantly teasing Claire with remarks such as, "You keep bending over like that, you're starting a revolution in my pants."

To which she'd respond, "Looks like a small uprising to me."

Dallas enjoyed their byplay but kept his own lusty thoughts to himself. In the exploration of HMS Claire, he was tiptoeing through the coral heads. He sensed that one false step could destroy the fragile chemistry he hoped would blossom into a healthy colony of symbiotic desire. Huh, who said that? Even he couldn't believe his mind was conjuring such metaphors. Must be the influence of the Bermuda Love Triangle.

As days passed together on the boat, it was surprising how easily their conversation flowed and the detours it took. When they talked, time seemed to shift into hyper step. More surprising the way she was able to draw him out, lead him away on tangents, serious as well as whimsical. Dallas wasn't the sort to tell the story of his life to every bus-stop acquaintance. He wasn't proud of much of it.

Claire was a revelation, the rarity in a self-absorbed society, someone who actually made an effort to listen, and didn't make it seem like an effort. Perhaps it stemmed from working behind a bar. She wanted to know all about his travels, his adventures and how they'd affected him. Her voice was 200-proof sodium pentothal to his inhibitions. She got him to talk about his brief marriage — the love lost its luster as soon as the lust wore off. She jokingly referred to her own ill-fated turn at matrimony as "a marriage of inconvenience," but he could see the hurt behind the chuckle.

As he got to know her better, Dallas could see that pain from the past ran deeper than the failed marriage. It would take a while to extricate it. As open as she was on some subjects, she maintained a shroud of mystery on others. Getting to know her was like exploring the catacombs under a castle.

Her background was diverse: Mexican mother, Irish father. In her late teens, it appeared Claire might make a career singing and playing the guitar. She performed on local television, mainly religious programs, and cut a record of Jesus rock songs, most of which she wrote. When her marriage was breaking up, she sold a $5,000 Gibson Super 400 guitar for three grand to help finance her getaway to Florida.

"I'd love to hear you sing," Dallas said, trying to imagine her singing voice.

"I don't sing much anymore, except bedtime songs for Lyle. And in the shower, of course."

"Maybe you'll make an exception and sing for me some time. If you're ever in the mood."

She didn't reply, and he tried to read her thoughts, fixated on her eyes. Therein lurked the greatest mystery. There was the morning a couple weeks into Dallas's time aboard *Levante* when she removed her sunglasses to clean them and the light on her face drew his gaze.

"What? You're staring?"

"It's your eyes. They look green today."

She laughed. "They're green every day, though I guess you couldn't tell. I've been wearing the blue-tinted contacts a lot lately. Part of my experimentation phase, I guess." She smiled. "I lost one of the blue ones last night. Decided to go back to the clear ones. Let the natural me show through."

She shrugged and slipped the sunglasses back on.

"OK?"

"Green's good. So's blue. They both go well with your hair," he said as a wave of it sweep across her face. He wondered what other mysteries she concealed.

Claire was a zephyr, flirtatious at times, but just as quickly retreated. Once she caught him staring and smiled slightly, but a minute later slipped on her windbreaker. He understood the unspoken message. She'd been through a lot, the wounds still fresh.

He thought of the cerebral crabber/jewelry maker. Guy wasn't that smart after all. Telegram to Dallas: Keep it light. Stop. Take it slow. Stop.

So he kept the focus on Devereaux's mission, trying to be as helpful as possible while enjoying her company. At this point, it was just the four of them. Once they began bringing up artifacts again, a state archaeologist would come down from Tallahassee to examine and inventory the booty, which would be placed into a vault until it was determined who got what. Like everything else that lawyers, the pirates of modern society, have gotten their hooks into, the glamour of treasure hunting was wrapped in red tape.

Out on the water the dream still felt as pure as child's play: Somebody lost something, let's go find it. But it wasn't a simple matter of finders keepers. The state wanted its cut, the feds and historians there's. And the lawyers, if they had their way, would grab it all. Now the environmentalists were conspiring to prevent anyone from taking any of it.

"It's like fighting an octopus every time I bring something up," said Devereaux, who became more irritable as he perceived more arms dragging him back. "The scum-sucking lawyers, they'd eat your goddamned lunch if they could get a court order to take the sandwich out of your hands."

The circumstances put Claire in an uncomfortable position on the crew. Although she was assisting Devereaux, the grant money she was working under came from the Department of Natural Resources, making her an agent of the state.

"It was pretty bad at first. I felt about as welcome as the flu," she confided to Dallas. "It wasn't Keith. He and the other guys who have worked on the boat have always been great to me. But the captain, he treated me like I was a spy or a traitor. It's been a whole lot better since I found the snuff box and spoons."

Officially, her duties were to maintain a daily log on the salvage efforts and itemize treasure that was recovered. But there is no glory in clerical work. The magazine ad Claire answered promised adventure, and she was determined to be more than a well-tanned bookkeeper. So she became adept at scuba diving that first summer and began participating on the dive team as often as possible.

Because the depth of the wreck severely limited the time divers could stay on the bottom, Devereaux didn't mind another set of hands rummaging around in the sand, though his instructions to Claire were explicit: "Keep the hell away from me down there."

One day the previous July, while Devereaux was turning up nothing but rocks, she was 100 yards away working in tandem with Keith. With crowbar in hand, she felt like a street punk in the Bronx armed to rip off hubcaps. Poking about in the sand, she had an unprompted vision of administering a two-handed Chris Evert backhand to her ex-husband's kneecap. At that moment, the crowbar dislodged something that was about the shape of a kneecap, only smaller. Although corroded beyond recognition, the object was clearly from the wreck, so she slipped it into her mesh treasure bag. Additional digging turned up a corroded silver spoon with a bent handle. With her air supply running low, Claire hammered a marker into the sand and returned triumphantly to the surface with her first genuine treasure.

The first item turned out to be a silver snuff box, not a monumental find, but it cleaned up well enough to reveal the inscription of its owner, Sanchez. More significantly, further exploration the following day of the area, which became known as the Sanchez Site, turned up a dozen silver coins, 4 and 8 reals, and a gold doubloon. It was nearby, south by Sanchez, that Keith found the mass of silver coins. But of more importance to Claire, her find earned acceptance as part of the crew.

"A couple of days later, we're getting ready to go down and the captain says, 'You stick with me, Miss Sanchez.' He still calls me that sometimes: 'Come on, Miss Sanchez, let's find the mother lode today.' I think he thinks I'm a good-luck charm now. He gave me the doubloon on a chain for my birthday. I'm supposed to let him rub it before every dive."

Dallas had admired the gold coin dangling in her cleavage and wondered if she would let him rub it, too. As she told her tale they were alone aboard the salvage boat, a wood-hulled 40-foot former lobster trap tender. Devereaux had converted it for his purposes and renamed it *Levante*, the Spanish term for a dangerous wind that ambushed many treasure ships traveling to and from Cadiz, once the primary port on the Spanish Main. Their job was to sift through the sandy glop and rocks the airlift brought from the bottom for any treasure that was sucked up.

It was a balmy afternoon at the end of Dallas's first week of salvaging. The sub had been down for more than an hour and had produced little of interest: one silver coin and several shards of ceramic from a shattered plate or cup. This was the dirty work of treasure hunting.

He noticed a smudge of seafloor muck on Claire's cheek. She smiled when he wiped it off with a towel that was not entirely clean. He felt like the announcer at Woodstock that damp, muddy morning, surveying the unwashed masses and blurting out, "We must be in heaven, man." The gold coin swinging between her breasts caught his eye, and he was hypnotized. Here it was, the mother lode.

It was too good to last, the reverie and the reality. On the fifth day, the sub surfaced after an unproductive dive and Dallas immediately sensed trouble. The first thing he heard when the hatch clanked open was Keith's voice, exasperated, saying, "You don't like the way I do it, you can kiss my black ass until your lips bleed."

There were a few more curses exchanged, and then neither Keith nor Devereaux spoke as they hauled the sub aboard with the winch and secured it in its cradle. On the way back to port, Keith offered insight on the problem in typical roundabout fashion.

"It's like when my father was making an effort to get along with my grand'mum — the one on my mama's side. They had one interest in common, and that was fishing. They both loved to fish. So, he takes her out in the rowboat. They're out there a while, and then here comes my father swimming back to shore.

"My uncle's laughing. He says, 'What happened, weren't the fish biting?' My father says, 'Oh, they're biting.' My uncle says, 'Then why'd you come in?' My father says, 'I couldn't take another minute in the boat with that woman. It's always the same: It's her way or the highway.' My father chose the highway."

On the trip back to port, with *Levante* wallowing in a quartering sea, Devereaux motioned Dallas to his side at the helm.

"Buck, you ever driven a submersible before?"

"Not since my last expedition with Jules Verne."

"Tomorrow you get your first lesson. Hope you ain't claustrophobic."

CHAPTER 17

Life in the chain of Bahamian out-islands known as the Exumas moves like a python with a freshly-swallowed rabbit in its throat. Palm fronds rustle gently, the hammock barely sways and then it's tomorrow, another day locked in a postcard pose. Island folk don't hustle, they amble. Because, what's the hurry, *mon*, there's always *mañana*.

Ordinarily, the fastest things on the flats around Staniel Cay are bonefish, which can strip a spinning reel in a heartbeat. The appearance of the speedboat, or whatever it was, on a nondescript early March morning so startled Capt. Monty Rolle that he lost his balance on the poling platform of his skiff and landed with a splash in the knee-deep water, likely eliciting a smirk from every bonefish between George Towne and Nassau.

Rolle hadn't seen anything like it since Carlos Lehder's cocaine coast guard was flitting around Norman's Cay in the northern Exumas during the early '80s. This was nothing like the go-fast boats of Lehder's fleet, though. None of them could have operated through such shallow water. That's what caught Rolle by surprise. He was able to navigate his flat-bottomed skiff through these waters only because he knew every sandbar and nuance of the bottom as well as he knew the crevices in his own weathered hands. This thing hurtled boldly across the bank, stirring hardly any wake and making very little sound.

Rolle didn't even notice it — a low-flying saucer? — until it was on him. Then, whoosh, it was gone. The only thing he could think, maybe they were making a sequel to *Thunderball*, the James Bond movie filmed in the area back in the '60s. Rolle was alert when the strange craft came through again and got a better look. Damned if it wasn't some kind of Bond contraption. Sure as hell wasn't a boat. God's sake, it wasn't even riding in the water.

Rolle, still dripping from his splashdown, stared as it passed and mouthed the words, "Holy, moly!"

#

Later that afternoon, over rum punch and conch salad in Thunderball's bar on Staniel Cay, Jorge Ortega expressed similar amazement.

"Very impressive. I expected Sean Connery to climb out of the boat. If you can even call it a boat."

"Skimmer. It's a skimmer, is what we call it," Edison Hawke said. "And that old coot couldn't handle it. None of those Hollywood Bond guys could. It'd even be a handful for a pro like your brother, right, Ramon?"

The man in the Stetson laughed like a hyena, and the rest of the group chuckled, except for Ramon Ortega, who glared from behind his dark Bolles. Ramon no longer carried his injured arm in a sling, but the elbow dislocated in the speedboat crash was tender and the pain flared with the flash of anger.

He still regarded Hawke as an insufferable asshole, but in his brother's eyes the S.O.B was a hero. Even Ramon had to concede grudging respect for the slick efficiency of the prison escape, even though Hawke's work was all behind the scenes. He was the facilitator, though. And it appeared his particular expertise would be needed again, so Ramon said nothing.

Besides, he enjoyed seeing his brother like this, more relaxed than he'd been since the escape and, in fact, for a considerable time before his indictment on racketeering and tax evasion charges. Watching him from behind the shades, a faint smile replaced the frown on Ramon's lips. The rum had something to do with it, but more so the bright flowered shirt his brother was wearing. What were they, hibiscus? Or was that the scent of the cologne? In his Panama hat, white cotton slacks and that ridiculous shirt, Jorge Ortega looked like a dapper Latino record company executive on holiday rather than a fugitive on the lam. The blonde with the mile-long legs and fingernails to match who was strumming the hairs on the back of Jorge's neck completed the illusion. God, he loved blondes, even if it was bottle blonde.

This was the first time Jorge had ventured out in any sort of public venue since his dramatic exit from the Everglades Hard Days Inn. His beard was filling in thick and black with scattered silver highlights. It didn't effectively mask his identity, but as long as he moved about discreetly he was reasonably safe on these islands out of the mainstream, where memories are short and curious questions go no deeper than, "Ready for a refill, *mon*?" Besides, he was starting to go bonkers in the secluded villa on the even more remote Exuma cay southeast of Staniel. The view of the ocean was terrific and the breezes intoxicating, but there was no point in hiding out if you had nothing to look forward to. Jorge Ortega was an operator. It was hard to operate without access to people.

"Tell me — I've been involved in the designing of some of Ramon's race boats — what keeps your, ah, skimmer, stable at those speeds? Why doesn't it flip over backwards?"

Now Ramon really had to smile. Jorge didn't know any more about aerodynamics and hydrodynamics than he did about composing a symphony, which was nada. Jorge had a tin ear. His involvement in the racing team was to write checks. Sure, he'd looked at the blueprints, but they made about as much sense to him as the Dead Sea Scrolls. What Jorge knew was wheeling and dealing, and in that capacity he shared a natural kinship with Edison Hawke. They spoke the same language, albeit with a different accent.

"Ah, what you're asking me is a look into the mind of the genius Behrent Juergens, who made it all possible. You've really got to meet him, and you will when we get going on production. He's an amazing man, and he can go on for hours about this. Especially if there's a bottle of Stoli nearby, if you know what I mean. What I can tell you is it has to do with the tubes that run through the, ah, you know, pontoons of the skimmer."

"Sponsons," Jorge said, showing he was hip to the lingo.

"Sponsors? We'll get into that later."

"No, sponsons."

"Ah, right, sponsons, very good. The tubes run through the sponsons and the air gets funneled through. When the skimmer takes off, it locks onto the airflow and it's like you're riding on rails of air. That's the way ol' Behrent explains it. His eyes get all wide and he says with that Kraut accent of his: 'Climb aboard, ve're goink for a ride on da vrails of da air.'

"But you ask how it does that? It's like asking how Michael Jordan hangs above the rim, defying gravity. That I can't answer. You're trying to define genius, whether you're talking about Jordan or the Juergens Principle. Only Behrent knows how to make the tubes just right. And believe me, they've got to be just right. I saw a few of the tests with the models that didn't work. Believe you me, it was not a pretty sight. He's got it dialed in to perfection now. It really is incredible to watch."

"Magical," Jorge said, raising his glass. "Here's to your friend, the magician of motion."

"Here, here! To the genius, Behrent Juergens."

"*Salud!*"

They swilled rum punch like Kool Aid, letting the sweet, potent nectar cool their throats and numb their brainstems. There were nine of them seated at the long table, six men including the two accompanying Hawke. Plates of fresh grouper lightly battered and set on a bed of beans and rice appeared and were assaulted with vigor as steel-drum music pulsed from tinny speakers. The women postured and laughed. Cigars were smoked. Ramon stared silently toward the water in the direction of Thunderball Grotto, snorkeling haven and primo movie prop, wondering when the conversation would get around to business. And like the Energizer Bunny on the run in bullshit alley, Edison Hawke kept talking and talking.

Finally, he lowered his voice to a confidential tone. Ramon could almost see the words coming out of the side of his mouth.

"You know, there are quite a few foreign governments that would love to get their hands on this thing. We've had discussions with several countries around the Persian Gulf and a couple in South America. The U.S. government, forget it. You know, Behrent isn't a young man. By the time they'd get through all the congressional hearings and quality-control mumbo-jumbo, he'd probably be up there designing chariots for St. Peter. Our thinking is the way to go is to work with a private concern that has the wherewithal to produce these things, and we sell them all over the world, whether for military use or transportation or recreation. What we're talking about is a partnership whereby we work together to produce a unique product, and we all share in the immense profits that would lead to. That is, if you share my vision."

"Not bad," Jorge said, holding his cigar out and watching the smoke curl and bend in the light breeze. "I'm not sure all the same letters on the chart are in focus, but I think we can both read the dollar signs."

Hawke laughed raucously, emitting a burst of cigar smoke that swirled and danced with the plume rising from Jorge's stogie, disrupting the tidy pattern. "I like that. That's deep. You are an intriguing fellow, Senor Ortega. I think we can do some very productive business."

"Come," Jorge said. "Take a walk with me. It's getting smoky in here. I need to smell the ocean and feel the sun on my face. It replenishes me."

Ramon started to get up with them, but Jorge stopped him with a glance and a shift of his eyebrows. The woman, Regina, took Ramon's arm and said, "C'mon, dance with me." Jorge led the way out of the pink building and down the path to the water, Hawke two paces back until they turned north along the beach.

"These are the things I missed most, the simple pleasures: walking on the shore."

"They had you dead to rights, huh?"

Jorge studied the other man's face for a minute, choosing his words, deciding what to reveal.

"Not exactly. A lot of it was nebulous. But they had a lot of witnesses looking to cut deals for themselves," Jorge said, spitting out the word witnesses with contempt. "They were trying to connect us with the white powder. We never dealt in that shit, but we had some associations that could have hurt our case. Look, I'm no saint. I'm a bold businessman. Sometimes I think the letter of the law is written so you can't help but step over the line. I could feel the deck being stacked." He paused. "Unfavorably."

"Glad we could help out. So, what did you think, ever seen a more dramatic exit?"

"Maybe in the movies. One of those with Arnold Schwartziewhatzis. But that's not real."

"I don't know much about making movies, but I know my man doesn't need no stunt double. He's the real-deal action hero. They don't make 'em like him anymore."

"Lagarto. His exploits have been known to my family for a very long time."

"What did you think of the sub?"

"Crowded. Not that I'm complaining. It was brilliant. I have to admit I was a little, how you say, panicky, when he put us down in the water. The Coast Guard's bearing down on us and he's telling me to climb down this hole in the water. What could I do? He shoved me in there. Then, boom, the Coast Guard boat's gone."

They walked in silence for a hundred yards, leather shoes crunching in the sugary sand. Jorge Ortega's were black, Hawke's brown. Both in character.

"I'm curious, wondering if you've thought about where you would put the factory, if we were to enter into an agreement to produce these vehicles. I don't think you're going to be doing business in the States any time soon. Am I right? Unless your brother would oversee the day-to-day operation and you would supervise in absentia. But you don't strike me as a hands-off kind of guy, Hor-hey. Am I right?"

Ortega's reply came after a dramatic pause, as succinct and penetrating as the quick, lethal thrust of a stiletto, punctuated with one eyebrow raised.

"Cuba."

Two short syllables but voluminous in implication, spoken with the lilt and intonation of Ortega's homeland — "Koo-bah" — so that they sprang from his lips and hung in the air thick and sweetly aromatic like steam from plantains on the grill. Hawke stumbled slightly, kicking up sand. He was momentarily speechless — but only momentarily.

"You are full of surprises, Senor Ortega. I must say I wasn't expecting that, and I'm very curious to know how you propose to accomplish it. Your brother did inquire about lines of communication with Fidel, and I can assure you those doors can be opened with the right lubrication, if you know what I mean. We've done some business in the past. Fidel's a tough nut to crack, unless you know the right buttons to push. But I'd be very interested to hear how you, an expatriate from his ideology, propose to break through Castro's protectionist web and set up a capitalist enterprise in his backyard. I mean, of all places. You must be joking."

Ortega had been looking forward to this moment and he intended to milk it. He stopped to pick up a stone, honed flat by waves and shifting tides, that had found its way onto the beach. It was shaped like a slightly rounded triangle and fit snuggly between the thumb and forefinger of his right hand. It felt smooth and cool against his skin.

"When I was very young I used to walk on the beach of my native country with my mama, and I'd look at the ocean and ask her what was out there. She said there was a big land, and one day we might have to go there. I'd look out at the horizon, and the edge of what I could see would be waves that looked like the teeth of a saw against the background of the sky. I'd find rocks like this one on the shore and imagine that if I could skip it from wave to wave out to those saw teeth and beyond, I'd see the big world on the other side: America. Of course, it never happened, but I got pretty good at skipping rocks."

Hawke, nodding respectfully, said, "That's very interesting, Hor-hey. Profound. I can relate to what you're saying. When I was a boy down round Mobile Bay, I'd look for rocks like that — the sharper the edges the better — and fling 'em at the seagulls. I imagined if you'd hit 'em just right you could slice their heads clean off. Never could hit those sumsabitches, though."

Ortega didn't hear a word of it. His mind was skipping across the saw teeth of the Gulf Stream.

He said: "Then it happened that there was so much craziness in my country, and I remember being put on a boat one night. The moon was full and I could see the light reflected on the faces of my family. For the first time I saw fear in my papa's eyes. My uncles, too, and they were proud, tough men. Papa and his brothers owned a textile factory; very profitable, until Fidel took it from them. The boat took us in the direction I had aimed my rocks, and I never again saw the fear on papa's face. But I never again saw him smile like I remembered. Instead, there was anger. And sadness.

"When I was a teenager I would stand on the beach in Miami and imagine that if I could skip the rock back to Cuba the anger would go away. But I couldn't, and it ate at my papa. I'm convinced, the anger killed him. Now I feel it, too. There's only one way to make it go away, once and for all."

Hawke, to his credit, fought off the compulsion to laugh. In a tone that exhibited more sensitivity than he seemed capable of, he said, gently, "There's a million Cubans in Miami who feel the same way. They haven't figured it out in over 30 years."

"They can't get past their emotions," Ortega said. "They don't comprehend Fidel's vanities. They don't understand you don't bully a bully. You got to finesse him. It took me a long time to get that through to my brother. I think he sees it now. It's not easy, he's like the rest of them. So macho. And his interests are different; he wasn't born there. The thing he understands is the money to be made. That drives him."

Hawke had been frowning. His ears perked up at the last part, like Pavlov's gangster: *Here's your treat, big boy, suitcase full of C-notes. Now roll over and say, "Greenback."*

"Look," Hawke said, "I've brokered simple transactions down there. And I have met the man face to face on more than one occasion. But as far as working within the bureaucracy down there, I don't know. That's very difficult, and very dangerous."

"Yes, but think of the profits: astronomical. Whoever liberates that place is going to walk into a fortune. That's the … the, I dunno the word for it. They're starving to death down there, and the whole time they're sitting on a gold mine. They don't realize it. Think of when Cuba opens up, the people that are going to want to go there, the investment money that's going to pour in."

"Constipation. That's the word," Hawke said, proudly offering the biggest one he knew the meaning of."

"No, that's not the one. But you get the picture. We're not talking about working within Castro's bureaucracy, we're talking about making it go away. It's like you build a house of dominoes — I did that when I was a child, too — you pull out the main tile in the foundation, it all comes down. That's Fidel. Believe me, the time has never been better. He no longer has the Soviet Union propping him up. He's the only tile holding it all up. He still has followers. A lot people still support his revolution. A lot are afraid to say they don't. The whole thing's wobbly now. He knows he needs help to keep it from crumbling down on him, even if it has to come from outside. That makes him vulnerable."

Hawke lost all restraint. He slapped Ortega on the back and left his hand on his shoulder as he tilted his head back and let out a belly laugh.

"You're a dreamer, Hor-hey. I never woulda thunk it, a shrewd businessman like you. But a dreamer at heart. You're like all the Cubans I know in Miami. All they can think about is getting rid of Castro. They dream up schemes in their sleep. You were in your jail cell doing the same damned thing. I'll give you this much: Castro is on shaky ground. But he's no pushover. He's still a force."

Ortega stepped in front of Hawke, faced him, his eyes as dark and as riveting as twin magnets. "You spoke before about being a man of vision. Open your eyes. The big fish will jump in our boat. Your invention … this … skimmer, is the bait. Even if he doesn't want the factory, Fidel can never resist the chance to show off. It's his weakness. He likes to think of himself as a great sportsman. He still brags about being a baseball pitcher before the revolution. My uncle was a shortstop, played against him. Fidel was no real pitcher. He couldn't be batboy."

Hawke took a step back and tried to evade Ortega's eyes. He was confused, trying to sort it all out. He slipped a hand under his hat from behind and scratched his scalp.

"Let me get this straight. We're going to play ball with Castro?"

"No, no, no. We're going to take him for a ride. On the skimmer. Let him drive. His guard is down. We use the element of surprise. Before he knows what's happening, it's bye, bye, Fidel. The skimmer's outta sight, and so is he."

Now Hawke's eyes were wide open, staring in disbelief, while Ortega's danced an evasive Ali Shuffle.

"We'll need your friend to pull it off. Lagarto. And your deadly sub. That's when I knew it could work, when the Coast Guard blew up — and when I mentioned Cuba to Lagarto and saw the rage in his eyes. I know of his past. He has unfinished business there. And he has ultimate ego. One more thing you can bank on. When this business is complete, there will be more than enough down there for all of us."

"It's going to take a lot of cash to get that far, to get the cooperation," Hawke said, regaining his sense as a capitalist. "Could take millions."

Ortega didn't blink. "Money's no problem. There are sources, investors who will jump at the opportunity, some of the same people that got me in trouble."

Ortega glanced at the stone in his hand as if he had forgotten he was still clutching it. He stepped to the water's edge, his shoes sinking slightly into the damp sand.

"You don't need an army, you need intelligence and determination. One thing I can assure you, I am not willing to spend the rest of my life in exile. Not here. Not in Miami."

Ortega drew his right arm back and with a smooth, sidearm motion sent the rock spinning out toward the Great Bahama Bank in a south-southwesterly direction. Given the benefit of a satellite guidance system, he couldn't have aimed a truer course toward the mouth of Havana Harbor some 120 miles away. The rock took two long hops and three short ones, leaving a trail of expanding circles to mark its path. For the record, it fell considerably short of the horizon, shorter still of Ortega's vision.

Returning to Thunderball's they encountered Capt. Monty Rolle walking with a client who appeared too wealthy for his ragged Topsiders. Rolle was recounting something odd he had seen on the flats that morning.

"No, no, faster than that. It was like something out of science fiction. All I can think is what a flats skiff you'd have with one of those, whatever it was. If the fish aren't here, you could pick up and run anywhere to find them. Hell, you could run all the frickin' way to Havana, in a heartbeat."

CHAPTER 18

"Let's go. Down the hatch!"

Keith had that damned Miami-to-Nassau grin. Dallas had that desperate God-almighty-isn't-the-governor-going-to-intervene expression. He took a long look around — his last? — breathed deeply and slid into the Navy-blue chamber of horrors, feeling like an aquatic Major Tom. David Bowie's daunting lyrics echoed in his psyche and he sought the muse of Alan Shepard, John Glenn, Gus Grissom, *et al*, the real-life tin-can space cowboys doing the "Beer Barrel Polka" on heaven's beltway.

Keith tossed in a playful parting shot before sealing the hatch.

"Have fun. Don't do anything I wouldn't do."

Clunk.

Now Dallas knew how the lobster felt when they put the lid on the pot, just before turning up the heat.

"Shit!"

Devereaux was already strapped in, going over a checklist. He handed Dallas a headset without looking up. Dallas eased into the left-hand seat and banged his kneecap on a metal crossbar.

"Fuckin' thing wasn't built for someone my size."

Devereaux reached over and pulled a lever. Dallas's seat slid back two inches.

"Thanks. That's a big help."

His eyes were adjusting to the dim light and he was surprised by the complexity of the controls in front of him, an array of handles, switches, colored lights and digital readouts.

"It's like the Starship Fucking Enterprise in here."

"Pay attention. You'll catch on."

Dallas looked up for the first time at the porthole on his side and was surprised to see Keith's face peering in, his features exaggerated as if by a fisheye lens. That grin stretched from New Orleans to Bermuda now. Keith wore a headset, too.

"You kids nice and cozy in there?"

"Bite me."

"Radio works. Dat's a start."

Devereaux snapped two switches on and growled. "Let's do it."

Dallas could see Keith hunched over something in front of the submersible. Claire appeared briefly in the porthole and disappeared. The sub tilted back in its cradle and moved slightly, then a bit more. More tilt, more movement, then a lengthy slide.

All Dallas could see of the world through his little spyglass was blue sky. He felt resistance behind and knew from working on the outside during the previous launches that the stern was now in the water. He realized he was hyperventilating.

"Shit!"

The sub lurched backward again and the bow dipped abruptly. The whole thing rocked left to right. They were afloat.

Devereaux's hands moved quickly and purposefully, like a pianist, punching this, tweaking that. Dallas felt a vibration behind him.

"We've got propulsion. ... We've got thrusters."

Waves were splashing against the porthole and slapping the hull, reverberating inside the capsule. Dallas saw *Levante* slide by to port, Claire and Keith at the rail watching as they passed. He concentrated on slowing his breathing, trying to fend off claustrophobia. He noticed another porthole low to his left that afforded a view of the seafloor, mainly sand and rocks.

"Lookin' good, little buddy. Ya read me in der?"

"Gotcha. How's that hose look? I'm about ready to take a dive."

It was slow going for the sub heading into 3- to 4-foot waves and dragging the fat airlift hose, which was clamped to the robot arm — Devereaux called it the claw.

"No kinks. You're clear to take 'er down."

Devereaux opened a valve and Dallas could hear water rushing into the ballast tanks. As the water level rose to the porthole and above, Devereaux glanced at him and laughed.

"You fixin' to hold your breath the whole damn time we're down? Can't have you passing out on me. Keep your eye on the claw. Keep it clear of the bottom. That's your job. Use that." He motioned toward a pair of joysticks on the console between them. "One on the left."

"Just like Pac Man."

"The other one works the claw. Don't monkey with that one. Just keep the arm up until we get set. We're coming up on the site I want to work."

They were 10 feet above and parallel to a fairly steep drop-off, bucking a substantial current. Devereaux adjusted the throttle until they hung steady in the current like a fat grouper waiting for a meal. He let more water into the ballast tanks and the sub dropped close to the bottom. Objects in Dallas's viewing port were moving forward, and he felt a bump behind him that rocked the sub slightly. He became disoriented and his breathing quickened again.

"Shit. This current is going to kick our ass today," Devereaux said, adding power to the main motor. He activated a side thruster.

Keith's voice echoed in their headsets: "You're coming up on it now."

The GPS doesn't work underwater, so they had to rely on support crew as their eyes to the wreck site.

"When we're set, I'll show you how to position the dredge."

It was a clumsy procedure — imagine fastening a vacuum cleaner hose to the bumper of a car to clean your driveway — but somehow it worked, at least most of the time, provided the current wasn't extreme. Mel Fisher's famous "mailbox" blowers, used to direct propeller wash from the salvage boat to blast holes in the seafloor, were crude by comparison. It was surprising that Devereaux would have such equipment because everything else about his operation was sparse. He appeared to be an old-fashioned dreamer-schemer like so many of the salty offshore prospectors who fueled Florida's sunken treasure rush in the '60s.

"How'd you get your hands on this thing? It must be worth a million bucks or more."

"The sub? It's experimental. The designer owes me some favors from way back. He lets me use it for my purposes; I give him feedback on how it performs. We're both happy."

"Behrent Juergens," Dallas said, matter-of-factly, like he knew him. Devereaux gave him a look, one eyebrow raised. Dallas shrugged. "Name on the hull. Sounds like a rocket scientist."

"I'm sure he could build one. All right, ease the claw down. Plant that sucker right here to start. Let's find that mother."

All at once, Devereaux's crusty exterior melted away and he turned into a child rummaging through a toy chest, though the frequent curses that spiced periodic bursts of laughter suggested a very delinquent child. When they heard Keith on the headset announce that the hose had spit up a fragment that looked like a shard of a porcelain plate or cup, the laughter — and the curses — intensified. Dallas began to feel as if he was locked in a tuna can with a madman, yet it was somehow non-threatening. Devereaux was simply, in his own peculiar way, having a blast, immersed in his private obsession. For Dallas, that helped enliven a chore that seemed about as exciting as waiting for a bus. At least aboard the salvage boat there was the constant hope of seeing something interesting emerge among the glop spewing from the airlift hose. There was fresh air, sunshine and, best of all, Claire. Down here they couldn't even tell when they might be sucking up something worthwhile.

Dallas wasn't sure what he'd expected, certainly not the ghostly hulk of a Spanish galleon, its figurehead draped in seaweed and barracuda peeking out of the gun ports. He had enough sense to know the wood worms would have consumed all the timber long ago. But somehow it stunned him to see nothing — only sand and rock. If there was a wreck, there should be *something*.

"How did you ever find this ship, ah, wreck? And how can you be sure you've even found it?"

Devereaux stared at him for a moment, then pulled the lever to raise the airlift off the bottom. He checked the compass, turned the sub slightly to the right and powered forward. He checked the compass again and another readout — Dallas wasn't sure what it was — then made another course adjustment before stabilizing the sub in the current. He lowered the claw and said, "There, see that?"

Dallas squinted through the silty murk outside his porthole. He could see a dark, bulbous shape protruding from the sand next to the head of the dredge.

"Ballast rock. Look, there's another. It's here, all right. You're now aboard *Nuestra Senora de Carmelita*," Devereaux said, dragging out the full Spanish name.

The look on his face was proud and at the same time defiant, Dallas thought — his ship now. Dallas turned back to the porthole and saw the second ballast rock, then a third. Devereaux was still beaming.

"Intuition. I got a nose for a wreck," he said. After a pause, he added, "Some good information. Bit of luck didn't hurt. Sometimes dead men leave a forwarding address."

He fell silent and began manipulating the thrusters to stabilize the sub again. Dallas could see it wasn't easy maintaining position and controlling the dredge hose.

"Is it worthwhile using the sub? Wouldn't it be better just to dive it?"

"We'll be diving plenty, soon as we find a site we know is worth working. Till then, we'd be pissing upstream and wasting bottom time. At these depths you can only stay down so long, and the amount of time you stay down today affects how long you can stay down tomorrow. You know that."

"Residual nitrogen."

"That's the difference between this wreck and the ones they found in shallower on the shelf. This is slow-going, but we can put in the time we want. Shit, I'd have never found this wreck without the sub. I spent a couple years out here dragging the magnetometer all over this drop-off. You'd never find it from the surface. Not in a thousand years. Good thing those poor sonsabitches didn't get farther to sea or there'd be no chance of getting any of this up. I knew they couldn't a got too far or none of them would've made it to shore in that storm."

Dallas didn't say anything, his eyes fixed on the various creases that exaggerated the older man's leathery features as he spoke animatedly.

"Fuckin'-A, I told you I got intuition about a wreck. I could feel its presence the whole time I was out here looking, some days stronger than others. That's how I knew I was getting close. I feel it so strongly right now, I can hear the friggin' masts creak. Those poor sonsabitches."

Dallas could picture Devereaux out here day after day solemnly combing the drop-off like some detached U-boat skipper who never got word World War II was over and was still intent on sinking the biggest enemy ship. Except Devereaux's *Bismarck* was already sunk. And even when he made the big strike, it still eluded him. So, the obsession intensified along with the frustration.

"You see that ballast rock there; we've already moved that by hand. Now we're trying to work a trench alongside, to see what settled down in there. We found some silver and porcelain and shit in this area, but it didn't lead to anything major. So far."

Dallas was scanning a partially unfolded chart Devereaux had on his lap showing a hand-drawn map of the wreck site with depths and notations in pencil about areas that had been worked so far. He saw "SANCHEZ!" — Claire's find — and not far from it an X where Keith found the mass of silver coins. There was a vague outline of the ghost ship with "bow" and "stern" designating the ends. Dallas noted the orientation on the map and realized the supposed stern was pointed toward deep water, though it was at about a 45-degree angle to the reef line.

"You figure they went down before they even got to the reef?"

"Fuck no," Devereaux said, looking at him incredulously, as if he'd speculated the earth really was flat back in those times and the ship had fallen off the edge. "They were on the reef, all right. The wind pushed 'em back out. Otherwise, they'd a gone down on the shelf and been found long ago. The eye of that storm went through and turned everything around. They dragged anchor until they were off the edge. They either holed the hull or got swamped. Maybe both. They damn well hit the reef."

Dallas couldn't resist a smile. "Your intuition tell you all that?"

"Weren't no one else knew where to look." Devereaux's own smile was smug, like there was something he wasn't telling.

Dallas studied the map of the site again, trying to envision the ship as it sank. "Any idea what part of the ship they stored their treasure?"

"It's not as easy as that. This stuff's been down here for 300 years. The ocean's always changing. It can be scattered over miles. We use the cannons and ballast rock as a starting point and work out from there."

If the supposition about the ship's position was correct, they were on the starboard side, roughly amidships. Dallas put a finger on the spot and traced a path to the port side and closer to the stern, slightly beyond the outline of the hull. "I think you should give it a try here." When Devereaux stared at him blankly, he added, "Just call it intuition."

The move didn't come for a while. Devereaux continued to fight the current while struggling to keep the airlift in the sand. Dallas stared through the porthole, daydreaming, his thoughts drifting across the barren sea floor. Occasionally, schools of fish would pass, but they were random, unlike the concentrations on the reefs. At one point he thought he spotted a shark, but it was quickly out of his field of view. Perhaps it was only a shadow. The mind plays tricks in a confined setting. He tried to concentrate on the task of steadying the dredge. His thoughts kept straying trance-like.

Every time he regained awareness, Claire was in the forefront of his daydreams. Could he really be that smitten? Then he realized, it was her voice in his headset.

"Having fun down there, guys? We're getting some more fragments. Nothing big. One looks like a nail. Lot of corrosion. Hard to tell."

Devereaux nudged him, offering a sandwich wrapped in waxed paper.

"Hope you like ham and cheese."

"Was hoping you didn't bring salami or sardines down here. I'd pass out for sure."

They ate in silence. Dallas was feeling closed in and creepy. He hoped they'd be surfacing soon. When Devereaux finished, he crumpled his sandwich wrapper and pointed at the lever controlling the claw, indicating he wanted it raised. Then he moved the sub in the direction Dallas had indicated on the chart.

"This the spot, hot shot?"

Dallas smiled. What if it's not? Maybe he wouldn't have to go down again in Das Bot with this Cajun Captain Queeg.

"Yeah, sure, right here. This is the place."

"We'll give it a half-hour."

Dallas was counting the minutes like a schoolboy anticipating the final-period bell. This was more monotonous than trolling for marlin, which averages about 80 hours of tedium for every strike. But at least there you have fresh air and sunshine. He once drank with a British sub crew in Nassau. Their world was a test-tank for the vagaries of mental health. They spent weeks at a time underwater, months without setting foot on land. Weird fucking guys, but not a bad lot. No weirder than this Devereaux. Dallas wondered about his story, his past.

"What's the most valuable thing you've found?"

"Here?"

"Anywhere."

Devereaux took a minute before answering. "Gold, silver, jewels on lotsa different wrecks. I helped dig up Port Royale, the city sunk in an earthquake in Jamaica. But that was known to be there. Lotsa stuff, all over the world."

"So, why aren't you rich and retired by now, living on some exotic island with native girls attending to your every whim?"

"You think that's what we're doing here? Let me tell you, nobody gets rich doing this. Hardly anyone. This is about solving mysteries. Finding something that has gotten away and bringing it back before anyone else can do it. It's like …"

"Like climbing a mountain?"

"Yeah, kind of, but it can be a hell of a lot more satisfying. Tell me, what's the point of going to the top if you don't come back with anything. This way you have something to show you accomplished something."

The first indication they were about to scale a significant peak was Keith's voice on the headset.

"We might be onto something now. Some chunks of pottery and bits of … Looks like glass from a bottle."

Dallas and Devereaux stared out the portholes at the spot where the nozzle of the hose was snorting lines of sea bottom like a cocaine-crazed eel. At least they were into something from the ship.

Devereaux was antsy, wanting more information. "Anything else?"

There was static on the headset, some indecipherable noise, then Claire's voice broke in shouting, so loudly they both recoiled.

"Emeralds! It's not glass, it's emeralds!"

Devereaux was nonplussed, not comprehending, shaking his head.

"No. Emeralds? You sure? Can't be. They weren't on this ship, only on the other one. You sure?"

Hearing the excitement in Claire's voice over the headset gave Dallas chills. He felt even more restricted knowing what might be buried out there just a few feet away. He wanted to swim through the porthole and dig with his hands until his fingers bled.

"I'm almost positive. I've seen uncut emeralds in Richard's store. This one's pretty big."

"I can't believe. Nothing on the manifest," Devereaux muttered. "It's either smuggled or belonged to a passenger. Probably just an isolated amount."

It took 10 minutes for Keith to don tank and fins and come down to stake out a grid on the site. They watched through the porthole as he disengaged the airlift from the claw and swept an area 10 by 15 feet, clearly struggling with the hose in the current, his dreadlocks waving like braided seaweed. They heard Claire announce another emerald.

"A tiny one; I almost missed it. Damn!"

#

Back aboard *Levante*, after the sub had been hastily secured in its cradle and a wild celebration ensued, they stared at the five stones laid out on a white towel. Even there they seemed insignificant in size, if not substance. The improbability of the find struck each of them. Devereaux hefted the largest emerald as if trying to gauge its value.

"You're looking at some of the rarest emeralds in the world. These had to be found twice in improbable conditions."

Claire said, "It's like finding a needle in a million haystacks."

"Only, the haystacks are all underwater," Keith said.

Dallas couldn't resist. "You sure they're not fragments of a Heineken bottle someone tossed overboard?"

Surprisingly, even Devereaux smiled. The man smiled!

"Not the right color, *mon*," Keith said. "I buy you a cold one when we get back, you'll see."

Of course, he was correct. Nothing synthetic quite matches the deep, dark green of an emerald. The shade of — he looked up and a sparkle of light reflected in Claire's eyes. There it was. From then on, that would always be Dallas's vision of emerald green, the matching hues of Claire's eyes, *au naturel*, and the emeralds of *Nuestra Senora de Carmelita*.

CHAPTER 19

The substance of the find, if not the significance, was confirmed at Overseas Jewel and Gem, ironic considering where the gems in question were found. The shop was run by Richard Ames, the one whose aim apparently was to please Claire.

Dallas's first assumption about him wasn't far off. Ames wasn't a crabber but had operated a dive boat until a brush with skin cancer dictated he take an inside job. He had an intensity about him that prompted Dallas to dislike him instantly.

"Arrogant fuck," Dallas confided to Keith.

"No, *mon*, he's OK. You just got the red ass about him because he's after the girl, too. You both want the same thing. It's natural."

"Aw, you don't know what the hell you're talking about," Dallas said, but knew there was truth in the admonition. So while the emeralds were being examined, he hung back in the room, arms folded, envisioning Ames' banishment to a remote observatory tracking the hole in the ozone layer over Antarctica.

Ames's assessment of the value of the emeralds echoed what Devereaux had said about their rarity. Because they came off a 300-year-old wreck of a Spanish galleon, these stones were worth several times as much as newly mined emeralds of comparable size and quality.

The largest they'd found was the size of Mike Tyson's knuckle. When Ames saw it he let out a whistle of admiration, as if he'd just walked in on the Playmate of the Year stepping out of the shower.

"Look at the depth of the color. Extraordinary! You're looking at over 20 carats here. It'll cut to roughly half that — maybe close to 12. At that size and quality, and considering where it came from, you're talking close to 100 grand a carat, maybe more."

The thought that they had churned up a $1 million nugget from the ocean floor staggered Dallas. That's a lot of Heinekens. The other stones were considerably smaller but would command a nice dollar.

The day's work had also turned up a half-dozen gold pieces of eight, common spoils on any Spanish shipwreck from the era. But the emeralds were the *piece de resistance* of this one so far. The unanswered question on all of their minds was, were there more out there?

"Legend has it that the Holy Grail was carved out of a huge emerald," Ames said. "Then again, it is possible the cup was made out of green fluorite. That was quite popular with the Romans." He shrugged. "Hard to know for sure about things from the past, unless you can get your hands on them."

"The fucking grail's out there, all right," Devereaux said. "If I live long enough to get back to it."

"Maybe you wrong about your Cuba boat," Keith said.

Wrong thing to say. Since they had returned to shore, the giddy Devereaux had given way to a pensive, almost melancholy one. Now the dour Devereaux returned, complete with frown and fiery eyes.

"The fuck do you know about it?" he snapped and headed for the door, nearly bumping into Dallas. Their eyes met and Devereaux paused for an instant, then he dipped his head and pushed past. Dallas watched him drive away in his dirty white Ford pickup.

#

"He acts like he just lost a million bucks, not found it," Dallas said as he and Keith drove down U.S. 1 in 5 o'clock traffic.

"He knows he's not gonna see much of it."

"You mean after the state takes its cut."

"That's not the half of it. The state, the feds, they both got to get theirs. A lot of it goes to his investors. Then a bunch of it goes to the damn lawyers fighting the state and the feds to let us keep going out there. What we found today just means we can fight a little harder and maybe keep going out there a little longer."

"He's got investors?"

"Damn right. How you think he got the sub and can afford to do 'dis 'ting at all?"

"He told me the inventor owed him a favor."

"I don't know about favors, but I know he got more debts 'dan Dunkin got doughnuts."

Dallas had to laugh. When Keith got excited his voice took on more of the Caribbean lilt he affected in his singing. They made an unlikely duo, the displaced Texan and the faux Rastaman.

"What did you mean about his Cuba boat?"

"You not hear him talk about it yet? That's his obsession. He's been trying to get back there since Castro came in. He say that's the one got all the emeralds. Calls it the green ghost ship. It's the sister ship to this one. Went down in the same storm trying to get back to Havana."

"Couldn't this one have had the same cargo?"

"He says no, these rocks were probably smuggled by passengers. No big stash of 'em. He's got the — what-da-ya-call-its?"

"The manifests?"

"Yeah, whatever. This that we found today, it's a tease. It just makes him want even more to be where he can't go. You maybe don't know it, but you can believe what I tell you because I don't lie. The one person struck it rich out there today was you, my friend."

Dallas looked as if Keith had declared himself Moses reincarnated and vowed to part the sea to Jamaica. "What the?"

"Listen, listen. I'm not talking about getting rich in the money sense. At least not yet. What I'm talking is, in the eyes of the man, you made it today. You OK with him now."

It had never occurred to Dallas to gauge his status by acceptance from a maniacal old treasure seeker. Given a choice, he'd rather have a cut of the emeralds than Devereaux's grudging endorsement.

Keith read his thoughts. "You gotta understand, you don't want to be on that man's bad side. This is a good thing. Like when you think the dessert's all gone and you go to the fridge and there's still a big old piece of key lime pie waiting with your name on it. Believe me, 'cause like I tell you — you know I don't lie. This how t'is. We're out there putting the sub back in the cradle and he turns to me and says, 'Your friend's got the knack.' His eyes were real wide. He says, 'You know, we worked that same spot before.' "

"So that's it, a key lime pie kind of day," Dallas said, and he thought that was about right: part sweet, part sour.

CHAPTER 20

The day's greatest irony didn't occur to Dallas until they got to the Leaky Tiki and walked into a St. Patrick's Day party. What better way to toast the Emerald Isle than with emeralds from the sea? Here the celebration was more conventional, a salty clientele already green around the gills. In the middle of it, the usual yahoos setting a predictable tone of the event with chants of, "Erin go braless, show us your tits!" directed at every passing female. Surprisingly, a few complied, including a waitress Dallas didn't recognize.

Keith ducked into the Parrothead. His band was playing later. Dallas wondered if they knew "Oh Danny Boy." He was pretty sure they weren't playing reggae in Dublin today. Picture that: Keith's crew in some pub over there, jammin'. Bloody hell, pour me a pint and pass the spliff.

Dallas found himself wandering with a bemused expression on the fringe of the mob at the outside bar. It was a pleasant Keys springtime late afternoon, a mild breeze blowing off the ocean. He ordered a burger at the bar and learned that Claire had gone to pick up her son at Margie's.

Scanning the faces, he was surprised to see Devereaux surrounded by a boatie-looking group. He recognized a few of them as guides and captains from the charter fishing fleet at the resort. Waiting for his food, he began to discern a buzz about the shipwreck, word spreading that something had been found out there today. Devereaux looked uneasy, and at the first opportunity slipped away to a bench beyond the thatch roof-covered stage where swaying revelers were slurring their way through "When Irish Eyes are Smiling" on a karoake machine. Dallas brought his sandwich and beer and took a seat at the other end of the bench next to the quart of dark rum and 2-liter Coke that Devereaux was using as mixer.

"Word's getting around," Devereaux said after a big swallow.

"How much more of it do you think is out there? These stones?"

"Can't say. It's not documented, from what I know."

He let the thought hang.

"What's the other ship called? Your Cuban wreck?"

Dallas watched his companion out of the corner of his eye. It took a few minutes to process the response. Devereaux looked over at him, then away, thoughts drifting to another place and time. He wasn't so much deciding what to reveal as he was revisiting it. By the time he spoke, Dallas was more than halfway through his food.

"I was so young and full of piss and vinegar back then," Devereaux said, and Dallas nearly choked, thinking what, compared to what you're full of now? But he said nothing, realizing that in an odd way he was almost becoming fond, or at least intrigued, by this old coot.

"I never would have believed that after all these years that damn wreck would still be down there and I'd still have no hope of getting to it. That cocksucker Castro came in and ruined everything, and that S.O.B. Kennedy didn't take him out when he had the chance."

Dallas couldn't tell which epithet carried the greater disdain. But by the time his burger and beer were gone he'd gotten a rambling, ragin' Cajun history lesson ranging from the Spanish Main to pre-Castro Cuba. As he talked, Devereaux picked up the bottle of dark rum, but instead of pouring he sat clutching it around the neck as if he had a stranglehold on … somebody.

He told about being an engine mechanic working on the yachts of casino owners in Cuba and their sleazy-rich clientele off and on between 1954 and '59, and of the craziness and corruption of the latter days of the Batista regime. Of machine guns and mayhem. Of revolutionaries and counter-revolutionaries. The waterfront was his refuge from the madness.

The day in March 1957 when 50 students stormed the Cuban presidential palace while another group seized a radio station, and they all died in a hail of machine-gun fire, Devereaux met a Dutchman in Havana harbor who would have a revolutionary effect on his own life. This man had been directing the excavation of the wreck of a Spanish galleon off Puerto Rico and was on his way back with supplies. His tales stirred Devereaux's imagination.

"I'll never forget what he told me. He says, 'Everybody's got gold fever, and there's nothing wrong with that.' And he smiles and shows me his gold tooth. 'But the greatest prize on these wrecks,' he says, 'is those big ol' chunks of green Colombian rock candy. Sometimes you get lucky and find them just sitting down there on the sandy bottom. So beautiful, it's enrapturing.' I said, 'What're you talking about?' He says, 'Emeralds, man. Emeralds!'"

Dallas mused about how the concept of Colombian rock had changed a few decades later, fueling the drug trade. But not for Devereaux. That green rock remained his obsession.

Before leaving, Devereaux's friend introduced him to scuba diving, then in its infancy. He took him to a known Cuban wreck site that had been picked clean of treasure but still had a couple of cannons along with a pile of ballast stones. More importantly, he let Devereaux in on a secret about a wreck off the Cuban coast that he referred to as the "Esmeralda Almiranta." This ship was said to carry a huge cache of emeralds from the Chivor Mine near Bogota, which the Spaniards worked until 1675. It was part of a fleet scattered by a hurricane in the Florida Straits. The flagship carrying the emeralds tried to make it back to Havana but ended up on a reef somewhere to the east.

"He got real close like he was afraid somebody would overhear, even though nobody else was there, and he says the name, almost in a whisper: *Magdalena*. Then he winks and smiles, and I can still see that gold tooth shine. He says he's coming back to look for it as soon as he's done with the one he's working."

Devereaux was speaking to Dallas in the same manner as he described the Dutchman, conspiratorially. Dallas recoiled slightly from B.O. and the liquor on his breath. After a pause for dramatic effect, Devereaux said, "He never got the chance. He got the bends six months later in Puerto Rico and croaked."

By then, Devereaux had already begun the search for *La Magdalena* on his own, venturing along the coast whenever spare time permitted, trading boxes of Petit Uppman cigars or bottles of Bacardi for local knowledge of possible wreck sites. He was directed to five or six that didn't pan out. One of them turned out to be a Spanish galleon that he worked for a couple of months before determining the ship was an earlier vintage than *La Magdalena*. It yielded Devereaux's first significant windfall in gold and silver coins, which only whetted his appetite for the grand prize.

He hit the jackpot one Sunday afternoon in a small coastal town; Dallas noted that Devereaux avoided revealing its name and was purposely vague about the location. He was looking for a bar when he noticed a sign for a maritime museum. Actually, it was part museum, part dress shop, run by a woman whose husband had been in the merchant marine. The husband had been lost at sea and his widow turned the downstairs of their home into the museum as a tribute to his memory. She didn't care for cigars or rum but was more than willing to regale Devereaux with Cuban seafaring lore while she hemmed a gown with a steady, precise stitch. The Esmerelda Almiranta? Oh, yes, she knew all about it. Turned out, she'd told the same tale to a certain Dutchman with a gold tooth who had visited a couple of years before.

The old woman was an entertaining storyteller, but Devereaux began to wonder how much was fact and how much embellishment. Perhaps sensing his skepticism, she produced a number of yellowed documents pertaining to the fleet of 1687 and its demise. Among them was a lyrical account of the tragedy and salvage effort written by a man named Osvaldo, who described himself with no false modesty as "a maker of the metals and the jewels of the highest regard in all of Habana."

Devereaux could barely decipher the handwriting let alone make sense of the archaic Spanish verse. With the aid of a huge magnifying glass the woman translated it for him and transcribed key passages.

Devereaux took a swig or rum and recited the verse:

> *"These stones delivered to me*
> *from the mountains beyond the sea,*
> *the fairest green brilliance I have yet to behold.*
> *In the year of our Lord 1687,*
> *I gave them life in jewels worthy of our king,*
> *dressed in gold and shaped with my blessed hands*
> *a great cross for his reverence and glory,*
> *a deep chalice to drink for his health,*
> *and for my friend the bearer of these gifts,*
> *a lizard of the esmerelda hills,*
> *to give him strength and God speed*
> *to his exulted destination."*

Dallas was incredulous. "You have that memorized?"

"I've still got the pages, she wrote it all down for me. Probably read them a million times. She had a whole journal about it. Wished I'd known Spanish better and could have read the whole thing for myself. She said the Spaniards salvaged what they could of the cargo. They used slaves to free-dive the wrecks in those days. Only got about a quarter of the gold and silver on the manifest. Never did find any of the emeralds. Was supposed to be a shitload of them. That's what got the Dutchman all fired up."

"And you."

Devereaux closed his eyes and thought for a moment, then recited Osvaldo's postmortem, obviously written with a heavy heart.

> *"Our valiant ship, tormented and torn*
> *by the heartless wind and waves,*
> *made its brave regress for safe keeping*
> *in our dear Habana harbor.*
> *Alas, too great the rage of the gale,*
> *nature's might snapped her masts like twigs*
> *and tossed her eastward of her mark.*
> *On that afternoon gray with death,*

with the sun choked away from hope,
our Almiranta crushed on the Diamond Point,
all lives we knew dashed in the foaming swill
and the most precious cargo,
our esmerelda dream."

"We can only hope this guy was a better jeweler than he was a poet," Dallas said.

Devereaux wasn't amused. "That's just the way it was translated. It was old Spanish. It was beautiful for its time. They didn't have no CNN back in those days. What they saw is what they knew. Those people were pioneers. They risked everything to come to this part of the world to civilize it and find treasure to bring back to Spain. There were no convenience stores. No conveniences at all. Damn few stores. It was a wretched life. Most of them died trying. But that's all they knew. The glory was in the trying. Sometimes I wonder if I lived back in them times in another life."

Dallas noticed that while still clutching the bottle of rum, Devereaux was bringing it to his lips at regular intervals as he became more animated in the telling of the tale. Or did the tale become more animated as the swigs became more frequent? Whatever, Dallas was finding it increasingly difficult to follow. Devereaux started rambling on about the routes of the Spanish treasure fleets and the rigors of life aboard the galleons, and Dallas's eyes began to glaze over.

More out of desire to reel him back into this century than out of real curiosity, Dallas said, "Did you ever meet Hemingway down there?"

It took a couple of more sentences of history lesson before Devereaux's eyes narrowed and he said, "What?"

"I said, did you ever run into Hemingway when you were in Cuba?"

"The fuck you asking about him for?"

Dallas shrugged. "Just wondered. You always hear how popular he was there, like a legend of some kind."

Devereaux snorted. "I knew people who worked on his boat. I met some of his favorite bartenders. I visited his favorite whorehouse. I know they all liked being around when he was spending his friggin' money."

"What about Castro, did you ever see him?"

Devereaux chuckled. "I sure as hell ran into some of his comrades in arms. More like, his henchmen."

Devereaux discovered the maritime museum/dress shop while the conflict in the Sierra Maestras was coming to a head between Castro's rebels and Batista's army. The woman at the museum was able to direct him to the so-called "Diamond Point," and within a few weeks he located the ballast pile of what he was certain was *La Magdalena.* By the time Castro marched into Havana in January 1959, Devereaux was living in a shack near the shore, diving on days the weather allowed, staying as distant as possible from the events transforming Cuba.

"When Castro came in, people were overjoyed at first. You got to understand, Batista was a real prick. Everyone lived in fear. So Fidel comes in and chases off the people everyone was scared of. He cuts their rent in half, lowers the price of a lot of things. Of course everyone's thrilled. Well, people who owned the apartments and the people I had worked for who ran the casinos and that sort of thing, they weren't happy. By then I was out of there, working my own angle.

"It's the same thing anytime someone gets power like that. People think he's a savior, at first. After a while you could see Castro had his own agenda, like they all do. He's as corrupt as the next bastard that gets a country by the balls — just another tyrant."

Devereaux didn't consider getting out just as his quest was starting to pay off. That summer he began finding gold and silver along with other artifacts from *La Magdalena*. He tried to keep it as quiet as possible. Then one day in August he was returning from a dive with a basket full of gold coins when he was met by a welcoming party dressed in khaki and brandishing machine guns.

"They say, 'All of this belongs to the Revolution.' I often wondered who put them onto me. I gave some of what I found to the old woman, so I doubt it was her. Maybe she said something to the wrong person. It was a small town where I was, hard to keep secrets."

Devereaux was thrown into prison and "thought I might rot there," but after about a month he was suddenly freed and put aboard a ship bound for Santo Domingo.

"Same place Batista fled, wasn't it?"

"I never saw him, either, in case you were wondering. And I never knew why they sprung me."

"Would you go back if the situation changed over there?"

"Never stopped thinking about it. Running out of time now. Hell, I'd a gone back a long time ago if Kennedy'd had the balls to follow through."

Dallas was gazing in the direction of the St. Paddy's revelry but not focusing on it, viewing it as an impressionist painting on a distant wall. Like Devereaux, his thoughts were drifting back a few decades but centered several states to the west.

"Did you know, before he died Kennedy was trying to repair relations with Cuba? Can't say how it would've played out, but the embargo would have been lifted. Everything would have changed. Things would have opened up down there a lot more by now than they have. Who knows, you might have worked something out with the government and gone back there."

"The fuck do you know about any of that?"

Dallas shrugged. "I've always been interested in Kennedy and the events of that time. I saw him get killed. Was just a kid — he got shot almost right in front of me."

He felt Devereaux's eyes on him, staring, but Dallas kept looking beyond, at the crowd. He shrugged again. "It's true, I've studied a lot about it. There were discussions going on behind the scenes. Castro was supposedly receptive. Who knows what would have happened. It's something I keep coming back to, about how everything would have changed if it had never happened, if he had lived. I don't know what kind of president he would have turned out to be, good or bad. A lot of things have come out about him since, a lot of it bad. So who knows what to believe? One thing I know, events would have happened differently. All of history since then would have unfolded in a different manner, for the world and for a lot of individual people. It's one of those things I can't help wondering about.

"I mean, we'll never know. Just like we'll never know for sure what happened there that day. I mean, I was there. A lot of people were there. But there's no agreement about what really happened. It's amazing, a president gets murdered in the middle of a major city in the middle of the day in front of scores of witnesses, and even now, all these years later, it's a dark mystery. I know what I saw. I know the government's version was a joke. So are a lot of the other theories. Funny, the truth can be harder to find than your sunken treasure. Maybe because a lot of people would rather bury it deeper than dig it up."

Devereaux remained silent. "Sorry, didn't mean to get philosophical," Dallas said. He took the final swig of his beer and stepped out of the time machine. Glancing in the direction of the bar, he noticed Claire had returned and was talking to Sami and a waitress. Even from a distance, something about her body language suggested something was wrong.

Without looking at Devereaux, he got up and said, "Don't drink too much. You know, we got more of that green rock candy to find."

"Hey! Wait."

Dallas was already a few strides away. He stopped and turned back. Devereaux was standing, fishing in his side pocket. He pulled out a small brown envelope and spilled something out into the palm of his hand. He held it out to Dallas.

"I think you should have this."

Even in the fading light, Dallas recognized the object. It was the smallest of the emeralds the airlift had snuffed off the ocean floor. He hesitated.

"Go ahead. Maybe you'll bring us some more luck," Devereaux said, thrusting his hand closer.

Then it dawned on Dallas that Ames had only examined four of the stones. He took this one, the fifth, between his thumb and forefinger and held it up to the light. Then he nodded and slipped it into his pocket. As he walked away, Dallas glanced back and saw the old captain in profile, both hands clamped around the bottle, staring at the ocean, off somewhere beyond the horizon.

CHAPTER 21

Claire wasn't upset as much as exasperated. The excitement of the day had taken a toll, leaving her light-headed as the adrenaline rush that followed the discovery of the emeralds faded. This was one St. Patrick's Day celebration she could pass up, which was unusual for her. The green T-shirt that hung untucked over her cutoffs was her concession to the occasion she often touted as her favorite holiday. But right now her hair was pinned up under a California Angels cap with a warped bill and her party spirit was overcome by weariness. Her skin still felt clammy from the salty air, and although she had hosed the silty, sandy airlift sludge off her hands and arms, there remained dark splatters on her legs. Her immediate priorities were a shower, a quick bite to eat and sleep, in that order. She didn't need this aggravation with Lyle, as she explained to Sami and the new waitress who was loading a tray with drinks at the end of the bar at the Leaky Tiki.

"He's just sitting up there. Not only won't he come down, he won't even talk to me about why he won't come down. He just shakes his head and won't look at me," she said, nearly surrendering to tears.

That was when Dallas walked up, the unsuspecting white knight in blue jeans. She turned to him and with a torrent of words related the situation: seven-year-old Lyle sitting disconsolate in a tree behind her friend Margie's house. Margie's son Cameron said it had something to do with some kids at school picking on him. Most perplexing to Claire, she couldn't get through to her son.

"We've always been so close; we've had to rely on each other so much. We tell each other all our secrets. Now the only thing he'd even say to me was, 'I want to go back to California.' That really hurt."

"How high up is he?" Dallas asked.

"I don't know, farther than I can reach."

"I watched Keith get coconuts down. Shouldn't be all that hard to get a little boy out of a tree."

"Lyle can be as hard-headed as a coconut sometimes. He's like me that way."

They drove to Margie's in the Great White, top down. When Claire called out the turns, Dallas glanced at her and wished her hair was down so he could see it blow in the wind.

When they arrived, Lyle was still adamantly aloft, jaw set like Brando, eyes distant like Eastwood. He tensed slightly when he saw them coming.

"Got any ideas?"

"Psychology," Dallas said with a shrug. "If that doesn't work, bribery."

He motioned her to stay back and strode purposefully across the yard but stopped short of the tree, directly in front of Lyle, and stood with his hands in his pockets. Instead of looking up, he looked past the tree, staring into the distance, like the boy but in the opposite direction.

"You really ought to turn around, you're missing a heck of a sunset. From up there it's got to be spectacular."

Lyle started to turn but resisted.

"What kind of tree is that anyway?"

The boy's right leg swung at the knee in a steady cadence.

"You know, I've climbed a lot of trees myself. That looks like a pretty good one. The best one I ever found was this big ol' willow I used to climb when I was about your age. It had branches as thick as an elephant's leg. This one spot where two of the branches came together, it was like a natural seat. I'd sit up there with a Pepsi. Do you like Pepsi?"

"No, Coke. Classic. It's better."

Dallas had his attention. He kept talking.

"I always preferred Pepsi. It's sweeter. You'd take a real cold one, and it always tasted better up in the tree. I'd sit up there on summer nights, and I could watch the baseball games this semipro team played on the field next to the tree. I'd be about even with where the right fielder played. I'd watch him waiting to catch a fly ball and I'd imagine throwing a ball out there at the same time to see if he could figure out which one to catch."

"Did you ever try it?"

"Naw. The tree wasn't that close to the field. I liked that you'd see the ball come off the bat before you heard the sound. Once in a while a foul ball would come over that way but they usually fell short. Except this one time, the big first baseman turned on a curveball — he was a lefty — and pulled a long one foul. It hit in the tree above me. I heard it rattle off three or four branches, and when I looked up it dropped right down to me.

"The right fielder came running over and I tried to throw the ball to him. Threw it way over his head, and he looked at me disgusted. That was kind of embarrassing. Distances are deceiving when you're trying to throw down to the ground like that."

"You shoulda just kept the ball."

"Naw, I couldn't. Everyone was yelling for the ball. When I was older, I played on that same field."

"Right field?"

"No, pitcher. I threw a no-hitter there once. It was all those hours sitting in that tree that I learned to love the game. That's when I knew that's what I wanted to do, be a pitcher."

"I want to be a pitcher next year when I play real baseball. We didn't have a pitcher in T-ball."

"You look strong for your age, like you might have a good arm. I could help you, teach you some pitches. What do you say, come on down and we'll talk about it?"

Dallas thought he had him. Piece o' cake. Fish in the boat. He was wrong. The boy thought a moment, then shook his head.

Claire, staying a discreet distance away in the shadow of another tree, couldn't hear the conversation. She watched their body language, trying to guess what they were talking about. Watching Dallas moving his hands animatedly, making some kind of throwing motion, it was more passion than she'd seen from him. Thinking, who was this man? What was his story, really? He seemed decent enough. Attractive, too — she couldn't deny it. She sensed he found her appealing, though he maintained an aloofness that intrigued her. He seemed different than men she'd known, so he was difficult to read. Was he someone she could trust? Could she allow herself to trust anyone, in that way, again?

Of more immediate concern, she just wanted to see him convince her son to come down from the tree so she could finally go home. Please! If he could do that, she would ... well, she would gladly offer to share whatever she had in her refrigerator, which probably wasn't much. At least Lyle was looking down, attentive. And all at once he was jumping down and they were headed her way.

"Come on," Dallas said. "We've got another stop to make before I take you both home."

"How did you get him to come down," Claire said, taking his arm and holding him back as Lyle walked ahead.

"I tried talking baseball, but that didn't work. So I told him about the leprechauns." She looked at him, bewildered. "I'll explain later," he said, his voice a loud whisper as he slipped something into her hand. "Hang onto this. When we get to my place, there's a big tree next to the house. While I distract him, you put this in a hole under the roots. It's from the leprechauns. You'll see."

As they reached the car, he looked back at her with a sly grin and shrugged. "Well, it is St. Patrick's Day. And the boy's part Irish, ain't he?"

#

Later, at the double-wide trailer that Claire always stressed was "just our temporary home," she was drying off from a shower when Dallas returned from the supermarket and began clattering around in the kitchen. An interesting aroma found its way into the bedroom as she slipped on a pair of white jeans and a yellow knit top that revealed a bit more cleavage than she felt comfortable with under the circumstances. She exchanged it for a light green number with a higher scoop-neck and smiled to herself in the mirror. Smile melted to frown when she noticed the redness of her eyes and realized how tired she was, though at the moment hunger took precedent. The scent of cooking drew her trance-like to the kitchen.

"Smells good."

"Yes, you do," Dallas said quietly as she came close to see what he was dishing out. "Sit," he said, steering her to a seat at the table and pouring two glasses of wine. He felt like Aunt Bea or Auntie M. or Aunt Jemima, which is to say completely out of character to be playing host on his first visit to someone else's home. Of course, everything that had transpired on this extraordinary day was without precedent in his experience.

"You are full of surprises," she said, weary eyes marveling at the setting. It felt enough like a date to make her slightly uneasy. There was red wine — corked bottle this time — and candles on the table. Lyle was already in bed dreaming about leprechauns when the main course was served.

"Irish stew," he said. "It was the best I could come up with on short notice, with a big assist from the miracle of modern microwave technology."

"Let's see, you uncover long lost emeralds on the ocean floor, you commune with leprechauns and you create a banquet in the time it takes me to take a shower and change. What other mysterious talents do you possess?"

"Believe it or not, I can cook a bit. Used to do it on the fishing boats I worked on. My homemade chili has earned raves and heartburn on three oceans."

Dallas glanced over when he heard a strange noise from Claire's side of the table. She had an odd look on her face. Her shoulders began to shake. She had a mouth full of food and was trying to keep from laughing, but it was no use.

"What is it, the food?"

It took fully 15 seconds for her to swallow and regain enough control to speak. "I'm sorry. No, the food's great. I'm touched, really. It just struck me." She laughed again. "Fool's gold? Leprechauns? How did you ever come up with that?"

Of all the unlikely images of the day, this was the one he would cherish most: Claire, overcome with laughter, her face crimson, tears of joy streaming down her cheeks. On an emerald day full of serendipity and revelations, this was the golden moment. And it was then that Dallas was sure beyond all doubt: He had to have this woman.

"Fantasy. Never fails. Did you see the look on Lyle's face when he found the stone? All kids want to believe in magic and pots of gold at the end of the rainbow. I know it got me through a lot of tough times. My old man took a hike when I was very young. I told you about seeing President Kennedy get shot. I was pretty much an emotional wreck after that for a long time. So, I'd retreat into my own world where nothing could hurt me and all things were possible.

"And along with my tendency to be accident prone, I did have a knack for finding things. Whether it would be something insignificant, like a penny or four-leaf clover, or a stray cat or dog, I'd find it. Or it would find me. One time I found this really fine stopwatch in the grass by the side of the road where I was walking. No idea how it got there, but I found it. My sister was always saying, 'You're so lucky.' My mom would say, 'No, it's Lucky O'Brien. The leprechaun left that for you.' Then it became anything unusual that happened that couldn't be explained, it was Lucky O'Brien who made it happen."

"Looks like you still have that knack. Is that how you found the emeralds? Lucky O'Brien down there in scuba tanks?"

"Could've been," he said, feeling the heat of a blush.

It surprised him how easily he revealed himself to her. He liked the way her eyes watched him. He liked the way she … listened. That was it. That was rare.

They had finished eating and moved to the living room, such as it were: a sofa, a well-worn rocker, a television. They sat at opposite ends of the sofa, Claire with one foot tucked under the other leg.

"I think you're right about kids. I know it's been tough for Lyle, the divorce and all the crap that led up to it. Then the uncertainty of coming here — it's been pretty scary. I know he still doesn't feel at home. He just needs some good things to happen in his life."

"Maybe I can loan him Lucky O'Brien."

"Maybe some of that luck could rub off on me, too. But there's one thing I want to know, Dallas Huston." She had that smile again that melted him, the one that crinkled the corners of her eyes. "Tell me, how did you just happen to have a piece of pyrite in your pocket?"

"Doesn't everyone?" Now it was his turn to laugh. "My minor league pitching coach gave that to me the day I got called up to the Bigs. He said it was to remind me not to get cocky, because just when you think you've got it made, it can all turn to … well, I won't say the word he used but you can probably guess. Of course he was right, as it turned out. I don't know why but I've carried that rock ever since — as if I've needed a reminder. Maybe it will bring Lyle more luck than it brought me. Do you think he bought the whole story?"

"It surprised me. He's pretty street-smart for his age. It's not easy to put anything over on him. What was that line you gave him?"

"I told him it was leprechaun gold, better than the real thing because there's magic in it. Like I said, everyone wants to believe that dreams can come true. Not just kids. Look at ol' Skeeter."

Claire nodded. Dallas wondered about her dreams. By the way her eyes were glazing over her dreams were very close at hand. He knew it was time to leave. But he'd promised her a special surprise dessert, so he returned to the kitchen to prepare it. Not much to prepare, really. Just a matter of retrieving the package he'd stowed in a cupboard, opening the cellophane and finding two plates. In the center of each plate he placed a Ring Ding. *Voila!*

It wouldn't supplant key lime pie as the prime treat in these parts, but he figured it would earn him another smile from Claire. He was wrong. By the time he rounded up the Ring Dings and the rest of the wine she was already out, her head back on the arm of the sofa. Dallas wasn't sure how long he stood there watching her in repose, the real test of a pretty woman. He studied her face, wondering how she'd looked on her prom night and how long ago that may have been. His gaze followed the flow of her hair in contrast to the soft skin of her neck and lingered on the swell of her breasts. A twinge of desire flared and he felt like a perv staring at her like that. *Time to go.* He found a light-weight blanket draped over the rocker and carefully covered her with it. Just before he turned away he leaned down and touched her lightly on the cheek. *Really time to go.*

Too bad about the Ring Dings. Dallas left them in the fridge along with a note: "From Lucky. Enjoy!"

#

Dallas had every reason to be exhausted, too, but he was still in that adrenaline pipeline, breezing along U.S. 1, reveling in having his hands on the wheel of a big car, feeling like the new Bogart, fresh prince of the Keys. Or maybe that was Bogey in the passenger seat, cupping a cigarette butt, giving him the look.

"Whatsamatter with ya, kid, when are you going to get these wheels aligned? Don't you feel that shimmy in the front end? How about laying out some dough for some new rubber on this baby? Whitewalls, man. And polish up that chrome. It's a disgrace to let a Caddy go to crap like this."

Dallas threw his head back, sucking in the balmy air and laughed loudly, simply because it felt good. He thought he spotted a shooting star or maybe a flying saucer. Too late to alert the media. Past deadline. But not too late for last call. The Great

White wheeled into the parking lot next to the Leaky Tiki as if by its own volition. Good idea, Dallas thought. He wasn't ready to go home yet, nor was Bogey. He gave the driver's door a good shove just to hear the resonance of metal slamming together.

The crowd had thinned, the party all but over. Dallas was getting used to stumbling through the residue of Keys debauchery. At least there were no casualties lying in the shrubbery. There was one of those green plastic bowler hats upside down in the walkway with a cigar perched on the flat underside of the brim as if on an ashtray. Passing the docks he heard music and laughter from a cabin cruiser and noticed a brassiere dangling from the outrigger of a fishing boat. Somewhere, Erin, braless.

Only a few stalwart patrons around the tiki bar still toasting Saint Paddy — that's right, not St. Patty; he'd partied with enough Irish to learn that much. Dallas ordered a gin-and-orange because he wanted something sweet to take the place of the missed dessert. Sami served it with a bemused expression and an opinion.

"You look like hell."

"No, hell, I feel great. I may stay up all night."

When his mind was revved up as it was at this moment he could go long stretches with little sleep. Sami left him alone with his thoughts until his drink was mostly melted ice. When she returned she rested her chin on a hand with an elbow on the bar and looked straight into his eyes.

"So sailor, are you looking for a party tonight? Is that why you're here?"

He stared into her dark eyes and felt the rapture of a moonless night. Even at the end of a long work shift she looked delicious. He thought of the Ring Dings and how he still hadn't had dessert. He looked down into his almost-empty cup to break the spell.

"Believe me, I'm tempted. I mean, that night we, you know, it was … I had a great time. But …"

She giggled, and it struck Dallas that he'd been getting that reaction a lot this night.

"I know, I understand. It's obvious what's up, and it's OK." She winked at him. "Don't worry, Sami never betray a secret of a friend."

Dallas looked into her eyes for a long minute and thought he saw the reflection of that shooting star again. He said, "I do want to show you something."

He pulled the brown envelope out of his pocket and carefully removed the emerald. Sami's eyes widened when she saw it. She rolled it around in the palm of her hand, examining it from every angle.

"It feels cool," she said. "So tiny, but so beautiful. I have studied all about the powers of jewels. There is much magic in this one."

He touched the stone with a fingertip feeling its cool radiance against the warmth of her skin. She placed it back in his hand and closed his fingers around it.

"You do what I say. Get this emerald set in gold as soon as you can and wear it on a chain close to your heart. It will bring you love."

She winked and added, "No charge for friendly advice."

CHAPTER 22

Sleep seized him as soon as his head hit the pillow. He felt the sensation of falling and momentarily tried to fight it off. Too late. It pulled him under like an anesthetic. He felt weighted down and wobbly. And where was all this water coming from? And, the noise?

"Don Diego! Don Diego!"

The shout was persistent, annoying. Dallas ignored it. He was riveted to a bizarre sight, a cow carrying a pig on its back. They were on some sort of stage. No, it was the deck of a boat. "*Levante?*" Larger. He looked up and saw a stout mast swaying with bits of shredded canvas flapping like agitated ghosts. Then he understood the noise, and the water. The rage of the wind was deafening, and immense waves were crashing over the side of the vessel, a ship of some sort.

Dallas thought he was watching the scene, as if in a movie. Then realized he was part of it, clutching the rail of a ladder affixed to a bulkhead. He felt terrified, but the sight of the piggybacked animals sliding by on the pitching deck was so incongruous, so ridiculous that he responded as people sometimes do in situations of extreme duress. Inappropriately, illogically: He laughed.

The next haymaker from the sea and lurch of the ship swept the cow across the deck into the starboard rail, and the pig did a swan dive into a great, green wall of water. The rail briefly kept the cow aboard as the wave crashed down on its back. When the water receded all that remained was wet wood and tangled lines. He wanted to applaud, but he couldn't let go of the ladder. He began to shake with hilarity and fear, and he kept hearing the persistent voice in the wind.

"Don Diego! Don Diego!"

He felt a hand on his arm and turned to see a face, vaguely familiar. The man was trying to tell him something, but the din of the storm made it difficult to hear. The

133

man shouted again, to no avail. Finally, on the third attempt, his words hit Dallas head-on, full force.

"Don Diego! Why are you laughing?"

Dallas stared at the man, bewildered. Not by the question, but by the mere fact that it came through so loud and clear.

"Don Diego, are you all right? Have you been hit on the head? It's me, Rodrico."

"Yes. I know."

Suddenly, this man, Rodrico, was struck by the same realization as Dallas. The wind, their relentless tormentor, had abruptly, inexplicably ceased, though the waves continued to pummel the ship. His face brightened.

"Don Diego! The storm, it's over. The pendulum of our luck has swung again. And just in time."

"Maybe."

The scene changed, and Dallas again had the sense of watching. A play? No, a movie. Then of physical presence in places at once foreign and familiar. There were mountains, a mining operation. He found himself leading a trek, and sweating. There was another mine, and the scurrying of men at work. Then jubilation, and one word being shouted over and over.

"Emeralds! Emeralds! Emeralds!"

Dallas found himself repeating a strange mantra: "Green rock candy, how sweet it is."

There followed a period of brightness. Dallas, in his subconscious felt at peace, at times euphoric. It was as if he were watching a slideshow of a strange journey over land and water that somehow all made sense. Through it all, this man Rodrico was almost always present.

They were in a noisy bodega, a group of men with goblets of wine raised in toast.

"Here's to our venture, and to our king, Charles the Second," Rodrico said.

"Here, here! To the king!"

"To our idiot king, Charles the Mad," Dallas said quietly.

"Wait till you hear Don Diego's plan to convince the king that the key to the future, the salvation of the crown, is in emerald mining. It's brilliant."

Dallas found himself standing and addressing the group.

"I don't know if you are aware, your majesty, (wink, wink, nod, nod) but the Chibcha Indians in New Granada worship *esmerelda* as the stone of love. They mix the powder in a potion that they drink as part of the marriage ritual and again at the beginning of every cycle of the woman. I know of one tribe (wink, wink) in which two of every three babies born are sons. They attribute this to the power of the stone."

The speech brought cheers and laughter. A man next to him said, "It's not so much what you say, it's how you say it." Someone poured wine into his cup until it overflowed and soaked his hand.

Dallas was aware of thinking this is a very strange dream, and briefly felt as if he were coming out of it. Instead, the surroundings brightened and he was standing in a harbor watching cargo being loaded onto old sailing ships moored in a harbor.

"Don Diego! Don Diego!"

He turned to see Rodrico walking briskly toward him along with another man he recognized from the table in the Bodega.

"Wait till you see Velasco's masterpiece. The king won't be able to resist."

The second man carried a dark, wooden box. When he opened it, resting on red velvet was an ornate gold cross nearly five inches long decorated with 10 emeralds. A trio of tiny emeralds added luster to each tip of the cross.

"Those are the stones you selected from the mine," Rodrico said. "Isn't it exquisite?"

"Incredible." Dallas said.

Dallas and Rodrico were about to step into a longboat when the man called Velasco grabbed his arm and placed something in his hand. It was a jeweled representation of a lizard made of gold, about four inches long with a row of gleaming emeralds set in its back.

"For you, my friend. For good luck and safe passage for *La Magdalena* and the other ships," He pointed to the emeralds. "See, same color as the lizards you described in New Granada."

Dallas found himself on a ship looking back at Velasco in a crowd cheering and waving from shore. Then they were at sea sailing in a group of similar ships. Light faded to darkness, and Dallas realized he was in a bed. Someone was shaking at him, and again he thought he was coming out of the dream. Instead there was Rodrico's face. He seemed very upset.

"Amigo, there's been a fire. We have to go."

"What?"

"The fire's out, but there's been damage. This ship must return to Havana. They're putting us on the *Carmelita*, sister ship of this one."

"No! We can't go without our cargo."

"Don't worry, they're transferring all the chests to the *Carmelita*. But we must hurry now."

Dallas found himself on deck again staring at huge seas, wondering how he was going to transfer to another ship. He scanned the sea and spotted another ship clearly aground on the reef, dismasted, its hull and every soul aboard now at the mercy of the battering waves.

"Is that?"

"I don't know which one that is. I keep thinking about *La Magdalena*. Turns out they're the lucky ones after all. If they made it back."

Dallas looked around the deck. The foremast had gone over the side. The anchor maintained its grip in the sandy shallows, but the waves still towered 20 feet. In nearly every trough the keel slammed against the bottom.

He looked at Rodrico, and all he could think to say was, "Did you see the pig and cow?"

Maybe that was it. Maybe that was as bizarre as it got. Then again, maybe they hadn't seen anything yet.

The answer came in the return of the wind, a devastating counter punch from the opposite direction from before. The ship began to swing on its anchor line, bringing more chaos and confusion as the waves seemed to pound them from all sides at once. Then came the first jolt from the coral reef. The ship seemed to bounce then hit again with greater impact. This time it stuck and held firm, knocking Dallas off his feet. He looked around frantically but couldn't find Rodrico.

There was a flurry of activity to launch the longboat. Dallas moved toward it, still desperately searching for his companion. His eyes stung from salt, and he could no longer see or think clearly. So much water. So much wind. So weak now. He felt a hand on his arm, another hand, someone pushing him. He realized he was in the longboat. Someone was trying to put something in his hands. He wiped his sleeve across his eyes and squinted.

There was Rodrico holding something out to him. Incredibly, it was the wooden box containing the emerald cross intended for the king. How had he been able to find it and fetch it? No time for questions. Got to help get his friend aboard. But there was someone else there, someone in a uniform pushing Rodrico away. Dallas had him by the wrist, then lost his grip. At the last instant, as the longboat was being lowered, he seized the lizard jewel he'd kept in his pocket since the voyage began and held it out. Rodrico, stretching over the rail, was barely able to take it by the tip of the tail before they lost contact.

Dallas never saw the wave that swamped the longboat. His eyes were on Rodrico's face at the side of the ship, black hair matted, his expression forlorn. Then a mountain of white water lowered the boom.

Dallas awoke in a sweat, hyperventilating. The sheets were soaked and the air was dank and heavy. He could hear rain pounding the roof, and something clacked against the window next to the bed. The clock by the bed was dark, telling him the electricity was off.

He found his way in the dark to the kitchen and gulped tepid water from the spigot. He located a candle on the table, lighted it and carried it into the next room to the chair by his typewriter. In the flickering light he scanned a page he had written about a terrible day in Dallas long ago. He removed it, inserted a blank sheet and began typing.

"When livestock ride piggyback and pigs do swan dives, either the apocalypse is close at hand or you shouldn't have stopped for that last cocktail."

CHAPTER 23

An unlikely gathering took place in the Bahamas on April 1, another faux holiday, or contrived occasion. Even Edison Hawke III was struck by the irony of the invitation, though amusement was not likely shared by the man who extended it.

"Frankly, I don't know if you boys know what a privilege this is. If I didn't know better, looking at the calendar I might've thought it was some kind of April Fools' joke. Couple of things I can tell you about the chief. He's no prankster, and he's not big on entertaining."

Hawke chuckled. "Matter of fact, I've only been out here two or three times myself, and we're business partners, so to speak. Just shows the regard he holds for you Cubanos. If the chief has a soft spot in that old porcupine heart of his, it's for Cubanos — at least for the ones who share his distaste for the bearded honcho in Havana.

"Even I didn't grasp the depth of those feelings. I guess the proof's in this little junket we're on. Must admit, I was leery about presenting your little scenario to him, Hor-hey. We had a meeting in Nassau and I waited till our other business fell into place and the planter's punch was flowing real good to lay it on him. His response floored me. He actually smiled. I've never seen him smile at a proposition before, only when something has turned out to his liking. He says, bring the *muchachos* to the island on the first of the month. I said, we'll be there with bells on. And let me tell you, you're in for a real treat. Because this place is like no place you've ever been, or like any place you're likely to go again."

They were standing at the bow of the *Mary Lou II*, the Ortega brothers flanking Hawke as he tried to pick out the island from the others across the shimmering shallows of the Bahama Bank in the Central Exumas. Gradually it took shape from a green mirage on the horizon to a distinct entity, rising higher than the island to the north of it and stretching farther than the one to the south.

"There it is, Gilligan's Island. Sure hope Ginger's out sunbathing again," Hawke cackled.

Current nautical charts label the island: "No Name (Private)." However, residents in the area still refer to it as Bent Guana Cay, named for the "tail" that curves sharply from the northwestern tip of the lizard-shaped island abruptly back toward the southeast.

An early edition of "Cruising the Exumas" carries the lizard illusion further with its description of limestone cliffs that rise to a height of 50 feet at the "head" of the island before tapering off around the "dewlap" at the southern corner to a sugar-white beach at the "belly." However, the name was only partly in recognition of topography. The reason so many islands, or cays, in the Bahamas have "guana" in their name is due to the populations of iguanas that once flourished there. Hunting, habitat destruction and the intrusion of non-native wildlife have wiped out the docile reptiles on most of the islands, aside from remote and protected outposts such as two large colonies in the Northern Exumas. That same out-of-print edition of the Exumas guide notes that the owner of Bent Guana Cay, in cooperation with the Bahamian government, has re-established a population of rock iguanas and that they can sometimes be seen sunning themselves on the cliffs and rocky outcroppings near the shore.

None of that information is found in the latest edition of the guide, which contains only the succinct entry: "This unnamed island is private and visits ashore are by invitation only." That is not unusual in the Bahamas, where privacy is prized and discretion a virtue, notwithstanding that pockets of hospitality and open fellowship abound in the islands. It is rare, though, for the identity of an island to be wiped off the charts, as this one has. However, with hundreds of tiny cays sprinkled like rock salt among larger islands comprising the various chains that make up the Bahamas, islands and aliases are readily interchangeable.

Or, as Hawke put it in terms that Jorge Ortega could relate to, "Where else can you find invisibility and paradise in the same place?"

Jorge concurred up to a point, though he was finding that the bargain of freedom with an ocean view and steady sea breeze in his Southern Exumas hideaway engendered the same disconcerting side effect he had experienced in his previous accommodation as guest of the United States government: boredom. A man of action can only sip rum and play pinochle so long. Even the women his brother ferried in for his amusement were beginning to depress him. As he put it, "I don't like being a charity fuck."

Brother Ramon had even less patience for the out-island lifestyle.

"You mean this guy lives out here all by himself? Not even a *chiquita* for his bed? I'd go stir crazy."

"You have to understand the chief," Hawke said. "He gets around plenty. When he needs solitude, he comes here. When he needs action, he goes away, any place he pleases. Monte Carlo, Vegas, Bangkok. Wherever business or pleasure calls, he up and goes. One thing I can tell you, he's a master poker player. He can bluff with the best of them. I shouldn't tell you this, but one of the aliases he once used was Jack Diamond."

"How many aliases this guy got? And how do we know what's real and what's bluff?" Ramon wondered. "I'd feel more comfortable doing business if we knew more about who we're doing business with."

"Rest assured you're not dealing with some Johnny-come-lately. I told you before, this gentleman is the real deal, and I think his actions speak for themselves. The proof is in your brother sitting here and not behind bars. In his world, names are a dime a dozen, reputation is everything. You can vouch for that, can't you Horhey?

The elder Ortega stared straight ahead, his gaze fixed on the island as the *Mary Lou II* neared the tip of the tail at the mouth of the natural harbor on the south side.

"Uncle Manny, he just say, Lagarto — the lizard man, cold-blooded, straight shooter. As long as he's your ally, you don't worry. If he's your enemy, you got big worry. That's good enough for me."

Hawke was nodding in agreement, his Stetson riding his head like a bucking bronco. "There you go. Your uncle should have been a poet. But I guess he was a freedom fighter. Whatever, he was a hell of a judge of character. You'll see.

"By the way," he added, his tone turning confidential, and head pivoting back and forth to address both Ortegas, "the chief doesn't exactly live alone on the island. I should warn you, his friends are a little unusual. But they grow on you."

#

At first, there seemed to be nobody to greet them. The *Mary Lou II* was moving along the channel at idle speed, approaching a weathered wooden dock that paralleled the shore. Two boats were moored there, a center-console open fisherman and a speedboat Ramon Ortega recognized as one of the Blue Thunder high-performance catamarans built in North Miami by legendary boat builder Don Aronow, which the DEA used to chase drug smugglers in the Florida Straits and George H.W. Bush used to cavort in the Florida Keys while vice president. One of the two crewmen was trying to figure out how they were going to land the old shrimp boat without crunching the two smaller boats when a man suddenly appeared on the dock to receive the bowline and direct the mooring operation while barking succinct orders. Ramon recognized him immediately, recalling their first meeting at Mariners Hospital the morning after his accident, remembering the piercing eyes and the arrogance, and he felt his back going up like an animal threatened. Thinking, just chill, Ramon, stay cool.

The reception was the same way, cool, mostly Hawke babbling as they stood awkwardly on the dock. Lagarto, dressed in khaki pants and camouflage T-shirt — they all took note of the sidearm on his hip, large caliber — said little but conveyed much with his eyes. He accepted Jorge's gift box of Cohiba Esplendido Cuban cigars, the genuine article, which had actually been procured by Hawke. Noting a glimmer of gratitude and respect in the man's expression, Ramon felt better.

Before they came face to face, something else caught Ramon's attention, a low-slung form on the beach moving out of the shadow of a small coconut palm.

"Hey-su Christo, the fuck is that?"

Startled, they all turned and stared until Hawke's laughter broke the tension. He laughed so hard the hat nearly bounced off his head.

"I told you the chief has some unusual friends. Boys, you've just met your first rock iguana. Handsome fellow, ain't he?"

The creature looked to be nearly four feet long, including tail. It walked with jerky strides on short, stocky legs that carried a thick, beefy body covered with a dark, rough hide. Its head, small in proportion to its body, gave the impression of a snub-nosed alligator, though its appearance was somewhat comical rather than menacing. That was due in part to the apparent absence of teeth as well as to the bib-like flap of skin dangling beneath its chin that swayed from side to side as it moved. Handsome? Hardly. The reptile's head was covered by leathery, reddish bumps.

"Looks like he's got a bad case of acne, eh? Hey, pizza face," Hawke said, and he laughed again. "He's got kind eyes, though. Looks like my junior high biology teacher. Ugly sucker, but a hell of a decent guy. Taught us all about re-pro-duction. That was one class I paid attention to."

The lizard's gait gave the impression of an elderly beachcomber out for a morning stroll. All that was missing was a metal detector.

"Cyclura Cychlura inornata," their host said, citing the scientific name. "There's three different types on the island, all imported from other parts of the Bahamas. All highly endangered. If they don't make it here, they probably won't make it anywhere."

That made Ramon think of a tune and he tapped his foot lightly on the dock. Strangely, once he got over his initial shock he found himself fascinated by the iguana. He was ordinarily attracted only to sleek and stylish forms, in boats, cars, women and animals. He loved to watch his pet cougar prowl around its large pen at the warehouse where his racing team was based. It was an animal he related to. This one — he couldn't quite pinpoint the appeal — was different. It was so primal, not a predator but clearly a survivor. That was another quality he saw in himself, the one which assured that when his predatory side failed him he could always fall back on survival instincts.

"Kinda reminds me of my throttleman. Not too bright looking, but lovable. I could see keeping one of these things around." Ramon said. He felt Lagarto's eyes on him, and it made him uneasy. For once he was relieved to hear Hawke's voice.

"Hey, you wanna go to an iguana's feast? You ain't seen nothing until you've seen these characters put on the feedbag."

The crew of the *Mary Lou II* unloaded two huge garbage bags bulging with whatever it was Hawke had brought along for a lizards' banquet. Ramon could only imagine what they eat. Miguel, the deck hand, hauled one of the bags while their enigmatic host shouldered the other and led the way, a mercenary Santa Claus in fatigues bearing gifts for the West Indies rock monsters. Following an inclined path that led to the interior of the island, Ramon had a feeling that could best be described as the opposite of déjà vu: *I have never been here before, and what the hell am I doing here now?*

He was thinking this was crazy dealing with someone you couldn't even address by a name. El Lagarto. Clearly it was the sort of nickname used in reference to someone, not to speak to him. On the other hand, Ramon had dealt with plenty of individuals with names and cover stories that couldn't be believed or trusted. At least with this one you knew what you were confronting. What was he, the last action anti-hero? What had Jorge said about the getaway in the prison yard: "He reached over with the gun and shot the guy as casually as swatting a fly. He never gave it a thought; it was all reflex."

They continued on a narrow path carpeted by needles from towering Australian pines that swayed and hummed a soothing tropical hymn with every gust of wind, then bore off on a less defined trail leading to the island's interior. The island was only one and three-quarter miles long and less than one-half mile wide at its broadest point, but all sense of proportion was lost once they passed out of sight of the sea. Footing became rockier and required looking at the ground to avoid stumbling. These boat shoes weren't made for hiking, Ramon thought, feeling sweat on his back as he trudged along behind Hawke. Lagarto was pulling away from the rest of the group.

"Watch out for the dildo cactus," Hawke said, pointing to the bulbous cacti that were abundant in this part of the island. "Wanna tickle your girlfriend's fancy? Take her back one of those. Don't forget the Vaseline."

The man in the Stetson cackled in his distinctive laugh, amusing himself if no one else. Ramon was feeling his impatience yielding to anger before they stepped into an open area, a limestone shelf that led to a shallow pond. Ahead, Lagarto was dumping the contents of the garbage bag on the ground: mostly green, leafy matter, apparently spinach and lettuce, along with carrots, squash, apples and tomatoes that had been chopped into chunks. The bag carried by Miguel contained more of the same.

"It's a giant chef's salad, my gift to the iguanas. I love watching these rascals eat," Hawke said, as the last of the contents hit the ground.

No sooner had those words been uttered and Lagarto and Miguel stepped away from the pile than a rustling was heard in the underbrush. Then came the charge of the lizard brigade. They scrambled out in a herky-jerky, exaggerated rumba gait like a conga line gone amok and plowed into the pile of food. At the peak there were nearly two dozen of them, ripping into the goodies in a frenzy to put a shark feeding to shame. Though it wasn't with ferocity as much as urgency, like a mob of shoppers unleashed at a Macy's bargain-basement lingerie sale. *Gimme that bra. Snap! Hey, I saw those bloomers first.* It was a tail-swinging, tongue-darting, jaw-grinding hoe-down of gluttony that was at the same time comical and astounding.

"Not bad for a bunch of critters with no teeth. Looks like a gang of old gummers at the nursing home tearing into their last meal," howled Hawke, thoroughly enjoying the show.

"My uncle tells of eating iguana when he trained for the invasion with you in Guatemala," Jorge said, turning to Lagarto, whose eyes were fixed on the ravenous reptiles.

"We called them *gallina de pallo* — chicken of the tree. I showed the others how to get them out of the tree and prepare them. It was a lesson in survival."

Jorge, studying the older man's face, was surprised to see the trace of a smile. Apparently, the memory was a fond one.

"Why is it all the weird shit always tastes 'just like chicken?' Why not just eat chicken?" Ramon said. "I think I'd pass on iguana as a main course, but I could see having one for a pet. Imagine taking one of these things for a stroll down South Beach."

"We had no choice in the exile camp. A lot of times iguana was all we had to eat. That was a different kind of iguana than the ones you see here. These don't live in trees. These are as old as the rocks, the closest living things you'll find to dinosaurs. They've survived a long time, but their days are numbered. Their demise, it's probably inevitable."

It was Ramon who noted the trace of wistfulness. He was surprised a man as obviously hardened as this one, someone so wary as to greet visitors wearing a large-caliber handgun, would reveal even that much. It was as if he identified with the iguanas. Ramon recalled what he had been told by a reliable underworld connection when he sought help in liberating Jorge: "The man I am going to refer you to is a hit man supreme. But he's more than that. He's a no-holds-barred warrior." The prison breakout had proved that, and though Ramon felt uncomfortable in the man's presence he had to acknowledge that Lagarto was as formidable and resourceful as advertised.

Jorge's laughter brought his brother back to the spectacle of the lizards fighting over the last scraps of the feast. Two stout males were squared off, one of them with a large piece of spinach in its mouth, the other trying to snatch it away. The defender of the spinach countered each time by jerking its head aside like a fencer parrying a thrust of the foil. After each rebuff it managed to take another chomp of the leaf. Finally, when just a scrap of it remained sticking out of the side of its jaws, which created the illusion of a smug grin, the iguana turned toward its audience and began bobbing its head rapidly up and down.

"*Mita, mita!*" Jorge said, "It looks like you, Mr. Hawke. All it needs is the cowboy hat."

#

They sent Miguel back to the boat and followed a better trail past the pond and through the interior toward the eastern end of the island, along the way passing Lagarto's black Bell Ranger helicopter poised on its pad.

"Too bad we don't have time for exploring," Hawke said. "There's a cove on the other shore where a boatload of Haitians wrecked in a storm. A few of them are buried right there. Nights when the moon's out you can hear voices chanting in Creole. Isn't that what you told me, chief?"

"I don't want nothing to do with no spooky voodoo crap," Ramon said.

Lagarto, walking ahead, said nothing. He stopped where the path leveled out atop an incline. When the others caught up the ocean came into view again. It was clear they were on a plateau of considerable elevation. What they didn't notice at first, until their eyes adjusted to the brighter light reflecting off the water, was the dome-shaped building nestled among the palms and pines near the edge of the cliff that formed the island's eastern shore.

"This is where I live."

Lagarto's house, painted olive drab to blend into the foliage, rose from a three-foot thick ring of rock. The rest of it was built of aluminum reinforced with steel beams. Power was derived from solar panels atop the house as well as a half-dozen windmills that churned on the northeast corner of the island. Although there were numerous windows, each had a roll-down shutter that could turn the house into a sealed pod. The dome shape was designed to withstand the most severe storm, or as Lagarto ominously put it, "Whatever forces may be brought to bear against it."

It was an intriguing and imposing structure, unlike any house Jorge had seen before. He wished his own hideaway afforded sanctuary as secure.

"You built this?"

"With some help."

Curiosity about the interior went unrequited as Lagarto led them around to a deck that provided a breathtaking view of the ocean. Jorge whistled through his teeth when he saw it. There would be no guided tour, but of greater interest to the Ortegas was whether this visit would include lunch. Watching the lizard feast had made them aware of their own hunger.

They were pleasantly surprised when Lagarto disappeared into his house and returned carrying a tray containing salami, cheese, a basket of Bahama bread and a large pitcher of mango juice. He even showed he was not devoid of humor, saying, "Sorry, no iguana today." Hawke winked at the Ortegas as if to say, "See, this guy's human."

Lagarto sliced the salami with a large hunting knife, and they ate with little conversation. Afterward they smoked Cohiba Esplendidos and sipped cognac while enjoying the view.

Lagarto was wiping the knife with a cloth when he suddenly fixed his gaze on Jorge and said, "This thing you propose is insane, you know."

Jorge tensed and searched the other man's face for a clue to what might follow.

"So insane, it has a probability of success."

The tension abated but Jorge wasn't sure if he should speak yet. Hawke, never one to let dead air space go unfilled, seized the opening.

"The response to our preliminary inquiries through contacts in Cuba were, let's just say, encouraging. Fidel is desperate to generate industry and revenue. He's also feeling very isolated and is anxious to possess something of strategic importance on the rest of the world. And we were also able to get the sense that you are correct in your assessment of his ego."

"You think he could be persuaded to test drive your skimmer?"

"Indications are he would insist on it. He's well aware of the boats the DEA uses and his friend, or shall we say nemesis, the ex-Prez, gallivants around in. We let it be known this vessel can run rings around any of those ordinary go-fast boats, because, of course, this isn't technically a boat."

"So you're saying you are willing to ...?"

"If you can provide proof of the financial resources you claim, to grease the skids into Cuba, to meet our, ah, professional fee, and ultimately to set up the production facility, then I can foresee a lucrative, and I might add, historic, partnership."

Ramon, again recalling his first meeting with Lagarto, said, "Do you intend to let us in on how you plan to pull off this coup or is that your, ah, professional secret?"

He was looking at Hawke when he posed the question, but it was clearly directed to his partner. Hawke smiled and turned toward Lagarto, drawing the attention of both Ortegas to their host, who was standing, arms folded, with his back to the ocean.

The response stunned all of them. Lagarto smiled.

"Oh, you will need to know all about it, my young macho friend. You're going to be driving the skimmer."

Ramon was shocked into speechlessness, so his brother asked the obvious question.

"You're saying Fidel is going to consent to letting the son of an expatriate enemy of his take him for a boat ride, or whatever you want to call it?"

"That's not really a problem," Hawke said. "Ramon can pass for Colombian as easily as Cuban. We have highly placed allies in Colombia who have credibility with Fidel and can provide genuine papers to create an authentic identity. That's the beauty of this thing. It's the perfect ruse. Fidel won't suspect a thing."

Ramon still didn't speak. His eyes were locked on Lagarto's, feeling their heat but conceding nothing, summoning all the force of his Latin machismo.

Finally, Lagarto spoke. "It'll have to be done this way. I can't drive the thing and take him out alone. He'll certainly insist on having a bodyguard along. We'll limit it to one. There are two hidden compartments built into this craft, one on either side of the turbine. I can fit inside one, with an oxygen supply. You will have a microphone and transmitter inside your helmet; I'll have a receiver. When you give a code word, I come out and take the bodyguard. The rocket launcher will be stored in the other compartment. If they have helicopters over us, I can bring down one or two.

"We will also have the sub, which you are familiar with, on station to create a diversion. We are getting good results with the torpedoes Juergens has been developing, as you saw for yourself," Lagarto said, nodding toward Jorge. "The sub will fire on the nearest patrol vessels they have out there. Before they can react, we'll be gone."

The Ortegas were flabbergasted, especially Jorge. The plan was much as he'd fantasized, except it had been refined into a sophisticated commando operation. When he heard it described in a detailed, clinical monologue, it was at once exciting and frightening.

"How will you contend with Fidel's air force? You can't expect to outrun them," he said.

"You'd be surprised," Hawke said. "Remember, this thing gets up off the water. I'll let you in on a secret: We've gotten it up to 350 miles an hour, no sweat, over relatively calm seas, and we won't go out there if it's rough. So you see, Ramon, why it was foolish for you to think you could keep up with us in your racing boat."

They sat quietly, smoking for several minutes trying to comprehend this grandiose vision that if undertaken could either get at least two of them killed or alter the course of history in the Caribbean. Ramon, whose head was spinning with the implications, broke the silence by asking the biggest question.

"What do you intend to do with the man?"

"You don't need to be concerned with that. All you need to know is I'm not in awe of who he is. He's just a man. He's nothing to me."

More silence, this time interrupted by Jorge, who showed no deference to this man — this warrior — whom he had seen kill without conscience.

"Why do you feel motivated to take on a job like this? It's not the money, is it?"

For the second time, Lagarto surprised them with a smile.

"It's all a treasure hunt. Everything. Everybody's life. Most of the time it's money they're after. Sometimes it's something else." He paused to take a drag on his cigar, then blew a perfect smoke ring. "Maybe this is my destiny."

The final word and the smoke ring hung in the air like the resonance of the final note of a symphony before the sea breeze caught it and scattered it above the cliff that gave substance to an otherwise insignificant island.

There was a sense that the meeting was over, that is was time to go. Jorge rose to his feet. Ramon, already standing, began to move toward his brother. Hawke, who had his hat in hand, positioned it back on his head. Without a word, Lagarto led the way back to the boat, this time via a different path overlooking the south shore of the island.

The twin diesels of the *Mary Lou II* were idling when the group reached the dock. Just before he stepped onto the boarding ramp, Jorge turned toward their host. He shuffled uneasily.

"I know discretion is necessary. Who would know that better than I do? The thing is, if you're involved in an enterprise with someone, you should be able to ..."

Once again a smile appeared as an incongruity on the other man's face.

"Why don't you just call me by the same name as your uncle and his compatriots used, behind my back. El Lagarto. What, you thought I didn't know?"

The gangway was pulled up, lines were cast off. Ramon glanced toward the little coconut palm, searching for the rock iguana he had seen earlier. It was gone. When he turned back toward the dock, so was Lagarto.

CHAPTER 24

How many days in one's life start out with high expectations and exceed them? Dallas could count them on one hand. There was his first appearance in the major leagues, when he strode confidently out of the bullpen in Baltimore and struck out all three White Sox batters he faced. Magical. There was that night with Laura Shively at the senior picnic in high school. Unforgettable. There was the shutout he pitched for UT in the College World Series in Omaha. Extraordinary.

Two about baseball, one with a girl. A good sign. Dallas was thinking, maybe this could turn out to be one of those too-good-to-be-true days. Never mind all the Charlie Brown days he'd had in baseball and too many romances gone sour. This was a day for fresh starts, a day when everyone is 0-0 in the standings and hopes are beyond reason. Indeed, Opening Day. For South Florida, Grand Opening Day. April 5, 1993, the coming out of the debutante Florida Marlins. For Dallas Huston, a day alive with possibilities.

The kind of day when a brand-new baseball team can win its inaugural game with a 45-year-old knuckleballer outdueling a World Series hero? Highly unlikely. The kind of day that an over-the-hill Romeo can rediscover puppy love and more? Preposterous. Yet, for reasons he couldn't pinpoint, Dallas felt overcome with a butterfly flittering wave of optimism he had misplaced long ago in a minor league bullpen or the backseat of a '64 Plymouth at a drive-in movie.

He was behind the wheel of the Great White with Claire riding shotgun, top down — the car's, not hers. Dallas humming the tune of *In A Gadda Da Vida*, becoming increasingly animated. Zack Tomlin, in the back with Claire's son, Lyle, drumming on the back of the front seat and the side panels of the big Caddy. Lyle, looking incredulous, covering his ears. Claire, in light-blue halter and white shorts, head thrown back in laughter, long hair cascading from under a Dodgers cap. Dallas thinking, oh, yeah, baby, ain't life sometimes grand. *Doo wah!*

They were inching along in a massive traffic jam outside Joe Robbie Stadium in northwestern Dade County, trying to merge into the same lane that everyone else in the damn state seemed intent on occupying at that moment. A black Lexus full of lawyers wouldn't budge an inch to let them in. And still Dallas couldn't let go of the smile he'd been relishing since Jake Zimmerman passed along his four tickets to Zack.

"I can't believe they're starting ol' Charlie Hough. If I'd known a guy like that could be the ace for this team I'd have gone for a tryout. I'm younger than he is, and even now I can throw harder than he does."

It was that moment when Dallas noticed the lady cop giving him the finger. Not the nasty one. Rather, an index finger waggling toward the sky. Dallas looked up. Helicopters bearing the channel number of every TV station in a 200-mile radius were buzzing about, planes were towing banners that stood out against a sky washed the purest blue by an early-morning rain. The Marlins blimp hung over the stadium looking fat and happy like the ghost of Babe Ruth after a burrito binge. What's she saying? Yeah, I can see, it's a beautiful day for a ballgame, so? The cop's finger was waving more emphatically and coming closer until Dallas nearly had to cross his eyes to keep it in focus.

"Don't you see me here telling you to stop? Don't you see those people crossing there?

Dallas glanced at a group just now entering the crosswalk on the opposite side of the street. They were in greater danger of being injured by the cop's frantic finger than the creeping traffic.

"I wasn't sure what — I thought you were pointing at something."

"I was pointing at those people so you wouldn't run them over. Those are Marlins fans. We want them to not only get to this game safely but to come back again and again. Got it?"

Dallas glanced at Claire who was staring expressionless, trying to look invisible.

"I wasn't sure what you were trying to say. Usually, they put their hand up and there's no doubt."

"There's no doubt if you're paying attention. You're talking to your friends and looking up at the sky."

Dallas opened his mouth but no words came out. He rolled his eyes.

"Hey, don't make a face at me. You could get yourself in big trouble."

On and on she scolded, sounding like a parochial school nun whose bloomers were uncomfortably snug, until Dallas interrupted.

"Can I just tell you one thing?"

"What?"

"Your fly is open."

Finally, the cop was speechless. Horns were blaring behind them. The pedestrians were past. Dallas eased off the brake and the Great White surged ahead in the traffic flow. Dallas looked at the car full of lawyers and they were all staring at him, laughing, the one behind the driver waving his finger as if to say, "Tsk, tsk, naughty boy."

Not a good omen for a supposedly perfect day. For the moment the spell was broken, Dallas's smile was gone. Everyone in the car was quiet until Zack said, "Do you call it a fly if a woman is wearing the pants?"

Suddenly the car shook with laughter. Dallas had to squint through tears to keep from rear-ending the lawyers. Claire slapped his arm and said, "I thought there for a minute the lady was going to lock you up."

"That was no lady," Dallas said, "that was the Iron Maiden."

"She had a mustache," said Lyle, and they all laughed so hard the lawyers in the backseat turned around. One of them had a liquor flask. He raised it in their direction.

#

This was a carnival-like crowd converging on the stadium as if it were the last Ferris Wheel. They formed a plodding, jabbering sea of teal-blue, cresting over the walkways, flooding through the gates, surging up the ramps. Teal, teal everywhere. Teal caps, teal T-shirts, even a couple of way-cool teens with droopy drawers and spiked hair dyed — *ta da* — teal. When Dallas bumped into two pot-bellied fans with foam-rubber marlins on their heads asking directions from an usher with "Alice" on her name tag, he was glad his own hallucinogenic phase was a distant memory. Especially when a sheriff's deputy with a fresh mustard stain on his white uniform shirt addressed one of the men as "Your honor," and remarked to the other, "Sure beats an afternoon at the courthouse, eh counselor?" Clearly, the wheels of justice were as whimsical as a Charlie Hough knuckleball this day in South Florida.

The birth of Major League Baseball in the subtropics had sprouted as a cottage industry with vendors at every turn hawking mementos to preserve the occasion, shamelessly justifying jacked-up prices with the day's rallying cry, "Hey, the first game only comes along once." Dallas recoiled at the price on the team mug: $20. Zack picked up the best buy in the park, the Marlins cigarette lighter for $2. Claire got Lyle his program ($3) and pennant ($3), and Dallas bought him the obligatory Marlins cap ($18), teal, naturally, with black bill. He couldn't talk Claire into trading in her Dodgers cap — "They've always been my team" — so he got her the Marlins troll with the Don King hair.

"I haven't had one of these since I was a little girl."

"Bet it didn't have teal hair."

"No, actually it was chartreuse."

As with much in South Florida, baseball came with a Latin flavor. The competing aromas of arepas, jalapeno sausage and a Cuban sandwich called medianoche beckoned like the intoxicating fumes from an opium den. Zack went directly for the Italian-Polish sausage with a Busch chaser. Dallas wanted no part of the exotic fare and was stunned to learn that the Marlins didn't offer the most basic of baseball foods.

"Sorry, we don't have Cracker Jacks."

"You're sold out of it already?"

"No, sir, we don't sell it. We have Crunch 'n' Munch instead."

"What, no Cracker Jacks?"

"No, sir, Crunch 'n' Munch."

"You gotta be kidding. That's unthinkable. That's un-American. You can't have baseball without Cracker Jacks."

"Sorry."

Strike two for the concept of the perfect Opening Day.

Game time was drawing near, 78-year-old icon Joe DiMaggio warming up for the ceremonial first pitch. Lyle was insisting on a stop at the Fun Zone, an area with assorted games and tests of skill. He wanted to get a radar reading on his fastball at the pitching booth. He wound up slowly, kicked his left leg high and threw a strike off the buttock of a slack-jawed batter painted on a plastic screen.

"That'll teach him to crowd the plate," Zack said.

The electronic readout flashed "39 mph."

"Is that good?"

"Pretty good heater for 7," Dallas said. "When we get back home — I mean, to the Keys, I'll help you work on your control."

"Let's see yours."

"What?"

"How hard you throw."

"Yeah," said Zack, "show the kid *your* heater."

Dallas glanced at Claire. She smiled and shrugged. The guy running the booth handed him a baseball. It had been so long it felt oddly foreign in his hand. He studied it for a moment, hefted it and laid his first two fingers across the seams. He sensed Lyle looking at his hand and knew there would be a question later about the crooked finger. Ah, what the hell? He reared back and fired it into the gut of the painted catcher with a solid thud. A couple of muscles in his forearm and another near his shoulder cried out in protest, but his motion was surprisingly smooth, considering no warm-up. The velocity was more surprising: 81 mph. In his prime he threw just over 90. Could it be too late for a comeback? Is it ever too late to dream?

"That ties our top speed today. We don't see many readings in the 80s on this thing."

"Cool," Lyle said.

"Not too bad for an old codger," Zack said.

"Come on," said Dallas, "we'd better get to our seats."

#

The most breathtaking moment in baseball may be stepping into the sunlight and seeing the field for the first time. All that grass, mown in a perfect checkerboard pattern, somehow seemed greener than anywhere else on earth. Unless, of course, the turf was artificial, as it was when Dallas attended his first major league game, in Houston's Astrodome, which was nothing but an oversized rumpus room. Joe Robbie Stadium, just outside Miami, had been built for football, but at least it had real grass, and it unleashed more dormant images for Dallas: the sound his cleats used to make as he clomped down the tunnel, up the dugout steps and onto the dirt, the smell of fertilizer, the whiteness of the chalk lines, the noises of the crowd — even the hecklers.

Dallas thought of all that as he watched the great DiMaggio appear in a dark blue suit, striding as gracefully as ever, to throw out the ceremonial first pitch, wondering what went through the old Yankee Clipper's mind when he stepped onto a baseball field.

Zack and Lyle were joking about the physique of Dodgers manager Tommy Lasorda when he came out with the lineup card, calling him Tommy Lasagna. Claire was watching Dallas taking it all in.

"Bring back memories for you?"

"Oh, I was just thinking. This was always where I was, ah, happiest."

Weeks later Dallas would see a photo taken at the moment Charlie Hough delivered the first pitch for the Florida Marlins. Someone who had been there was showing a copy of it around the bar at the Leaky Tiki. The shot, taken with a special camera positioned near the top of the lower stands directly behind home plate, showed a panoramic view that encompassed the entire field and perhaps two-thirds of the crowd of 46,115 in the stadium that day. Hough was caught an instant before he released the ball as he stepped toward the plate, his right arm extended away from his body shoulder high. The Dodgers' hitter, Jose Offerman, waited in the batter's box. Fielders crouched at their positions, probably more attentive than they would be for any other pitch of the season. The sign on the jumbo scoreboard atop the stadium in right field read, "Play ball."

Dallas studied the crowd, most of which was facing away from the camera except for two vendors with their backs toward the field counting change. Dallas scanned the mass of teal caps midway up the lower level along the right-field line until he spotted one darker blue like Claire's next to a red shirt like the one he wore that day.

It occurred to him, this was the third instance that he had been captured on film as an onlooker in a public moment of historic significance. The first time, of course, was in Dealey Plaza when he was shown in numerous photos taken during and after the Kennedy assassination. The second was at Woodstock when he appeared among a group of bystanders watching a belly-flop contest in a mud bog in a photo that appeared in several magazines including *Time* and *Rolling Stone*.

The shutter opens and closes in the blink of an eye, forever preserving a moment of living or dying, joy or sorrow, or more often, something mundane. In each of these instances it projected the true story of Dallas's life, a voyeur of events beyond his control. His mother kept the scrapbook with the news photos from his baseball career, evidence that on occasion he had stepped into the spotlight and filled the frame.

On the rare occasions that he looked at those photos they seemed surreal, as if the face pictured belonged to someone else. He kept coming back to the others as a more accurate depiction of his life, of the life that most of us lead: a face in the crowd.

For the record, that first pitch was a strike, a prelude to the first strikeout in the first victory of the Florida Marlins. To Dallas, it was memorable less for the historical impact than for the whimsical flight Hough's knuckleball took.

"That pitch was about the same speed as the one you threw before the game," Dallas said to Lyle.

"What do you mean? He's a big-leaguer, I'm a kid."

"That's a knuckleball, and it makes big-league hitters look like Little Leaguers. He just floats it up there, and it dances all over the place. It's very hard to hit, not to mention catch."

That led to a discussion of baseball's most fickle pitch.

"They call it the butterfly ball. It's like third-class mail, it takes forever to get there and the anticipation drives you crazy. It sticks its tongue out and dares you to try to hit it. Most of the time you can't."

"Can you teach me to throw it?"

"I never could throw it effectively. Most people can't. The trick is you throw the ball so it doesn't spin at all. The air currents catch the seams and make it jump around. I had a pitching coach that said it was like throwing a hand grenade. I always thought of it as throwing a rotten tomato. You don't want your fingers to bust through into the mushy stuff, so you kind of push it out of your hand."

"Speaking of tomatoes, anyone ready for pizza?" Zack said.

It went on like that the rest of the afternoon with Dallas supplying baseball insight and Zack adding comic relief with shouts of *"gesundheit!"* every time Dodgers pitcher Orel Hershiser's name was announced on the P.A. The two of them goaded Claire about her allegiance to the Dodgers as the upstart Marlins took an early lead and kept the old guard at bay. Finally, in the seventh inning, when a rookie center fielder named Scott Pose made a leaping, twisting over-the-shoulder catch in front of the 434-foot sign in the most distant point of the outfield to quell any glint of a comeback, Claire yanked off her cap and flung it, exclaiming, "To hell with L.A." That quickly became the rallying cry of a growing faction of the crowd along the right-field line.

"To hell with L.A.!"

"Yeah, and to hell with Tommy Lasagna and Orel Hershiser."

"*Gesundheit!*"

When Dallas recalled it, the day became a panorama of mental images. The lady cop's finger. *Click*. Lyle's pitch off the imaginary batter's butt. *Click*. Charlie Hough's first knuckleball. *Click*. Scott Pose's catch. *Click*. Claire's hell-bent fling of the hat. *Click*. But the most extraordinary byproduct of the day, aside from the final score — Marlins 6, Dodgers 3 — was the unaccustomed sensation that crept into Dallas's consciousness.

He didn't identify it until the next day when he replayed the mental slideshow. An unseen hand changed the channel and there he was, Dallas Huston, starring in an episode of *Ozzie and Harriet*: Mom, dad, the kid and wise-cracking uncle go to the ballgame. It was crazy. He hadn't foreseen it that way. He hadn't even had an official date with Claire, for god's sake. But for one blissful three-hour plunge into the middle-American experience, he was dad. And most surprising, he rather liked the role. Maybe because he had never been a part of that before, even as a kid.

Oh, there was one final snapshot worth laminating and framing along with the ticket stub from the Florida Marlins' first game. As they were making their way from the stadium parking lot to the turnpike entrance, Claire pointed to a black Lexus sedan pulled over on the berm. A female officer of the law was busy scribbling on some sort of pad while an occupant of the car stood nearby appearing agitated as he spoke rapidly into a cellular phone.

As they passed, Zack leaned out of the Great White and yelled, "Hey, y'all, need the number for The Ticket Clinic?"

CHAPTER 25

He heard her footsteps coming from the hallway in the back of the trailer. She had changed into a casual dress, floral print on a cream-colored background. His eyes followed, his mind contemplated.

"He's asleep already. Guess we wore him out today."

Claire was placing candles around the small living room, moving gracefully on bare feet. He liked the way the material of the dress seemed to dance on her body. She cued a tape on a small stereo unit, a Spanish guitar instrumental with a Caribbean flavor, then disappeared into the kitchen, returning with two glasses and a bottle of Beaujolais. Her eyes sparkled in the flickering candlelight. They really were green.

"Wait."

One more trip, this time returning with a plate.

"Dessert is served. Specialty of the Islamorada French pastry shop, *aka* Quick Stop. Bon appetit."

Never have two Ring Dings on a plate seemed so romantic.

"This is the topper to the whole day," Dallas said, smiling.

"It was an exciting day, wasn't it? I'll never cheer for the Dodgers again. The Marlins are my team now."

"Hope everyone enjoyed it because that isn't going to happen every day. A new team is going to lose a lot more than it wins. And the good feeling you get from winning never lasts as long as the ache you get from losing."

"How could that be? Shouldn't the feelings be comparable?"

"That's the strange thing about baseball. It's a game of failure. Even the best hitters make an out seven out of ten times. Look at the pitchers, it seems like the majority have losing records. You have a few guys who win big, but most are lucky to break even. I think that's why baseball endures. Some other sports may be more

155

fun to watch, routinely more exciting. But baseball gets into your soul because the day-to-day struggles are so much like regular life — except these days the pay's a hell of a lot better. Most people spend most of their time just trying get by and are grateful for any little triumphs along the way. But the thrill doesn't last."

"You miss playing, don't you? I could see it today, in your face and in the way you watched the game."

"Yes and no. When I was playing, it gave me a focus."

"That you haven't had since?"

"What about you? You left a bad situation; are you happy with what you're doing now? Is it an improvement?"

"Living in a trailer? Working at a bar? Yeah, it beats being miserable. Look, I've had better jobs. I worked in a bank. Before I had Lyle, I was a big deal in the finance department of a large aerospace firm."

"Good with numbers, huh."

"Yeah, now I make change for drunks." She laughed. "Really, it's not bad. I do enjoy the people, at least most of the time. Except for some days when I'm not in the mood for the asinine questions and comments."

"Yeah, like what?"

"All the pickup lines. Or the things they'll say just to try to shock you or get a reaction. Like, they'll wave me over and say, 'Claire, can you explain something that we've been debating here?' Then they'll lean close and say, 'Why do they call it a blow job when you don't really blow?' "

Dallas nearly choked on his wine.

"Seriously, that's the No. 1 philosophical bar question. I hear it quite a lot, and not just from the men. Just the other night, there were these two teachers on vacation from Pennsylvania. Both women. They were pretty much zotzed."

They had been sitting close together. Dallas may have backed away slightly or maybe it was the expression on his face. Claire suddenly blushed and covered her face with her hands.

"Sorry. I can't believe I said that."

"No, it's OK. It just caught me by ..."

Now what? She must have read his mind.

"Oh, come here."

Just like that, he felt her hands on him and her lips were close behind, sweetened from the wine and plump with urgency. Talk about unlikely ice-breakers and mood-setters. No major barrier had fallen this abruptly or completely since the Berlin Wall. Dallas wasn't complaining if she wasn't retreating. He had the sensation of their bodies spinning, pressed tight by centripetal force, melting together, her breasts firm against his chest forcing their breaths to come in short gasps. She felt as right in his arms as he'd imagined. Just right. As she leaned into him her dress rode up and his hands drifted down naturally.

She broke the embrace and he feared he'd blown it. Instead she led him to her bedroom, which was bathed in the light of more candles. In one quick motion she slipped the dress over her head. She held out a hand and they settled down on red satin sheets.

"I have a confession," he said.

"Hmm?"

"I'm not all that crazy about Ring Dings. I'd much rather have you for dessert."

He was intent on tasting every inch of her. She spurred him on with appreciative sighs. He was a connoisseur on a mission, as if to find the perfect wine, and he was determined to uncork the best bottle at every vineyard in the valley, if that's what it took. He took his time, sipping and savoring until her words came in an unintelligible torrent, and he realized he had found the prize of the vine.

"Grand cru," he said as his mouth found hers again.

She bit his lower lip, playfully. "What?"

"I said, 'great vintage,' " he whispered, close to her ear. His lips tugged lightly on the lobe and she melted again.

When he finally sank into her, the air heady with their combined scents, their eyes locked and her body rose to welcome him, both intent on utilizing all of their senses to preserve every sensation to memory. They had each passed too many boarded up storefronts on too many faceless boulevards to take anything for granted or hold anything back. Not when a cop on every corner is bowing and waving you through, even the one with the waggling finger.

Claire saw herself on a stage in a great hall, seated at a piano so white it radiated its own light, her fingers flying over the keys, striking each note with more purity than they had ever been played. He saw himself dashing across a field so green and vibrant that the life force in the roots of the grass seemed to propel him into the next stride faster than the one before, until he leaped to snatch a ball careening like a comet out of the sky. He waved his cap above his head until the cheers of the crowd gave way to the roar of an immense waterfall. Somehow, from worlds in a divergent universe, they came together in the pipeline of a rogue wave, a dynamic confluence of water and air that sent them sprawling, breathless on a sandy shore.

Just before it crested, Dallas was struck with the realization that though he didn't know what she was thinking, he was sure of precisely what she was feeling. That he had somehow touched the very center of her soul. At that instant a surge of warmth passed though him. He could tell she felt it too, because as the moment passed to blissful history her eyes were probing as deeply into his being as he had ever allowed.

They didn't speak for minutes or maybe mere seconds, lying with thighs gently touching, feeling the dampness on their backs cooled by the sheets, until she said, "I knew that was going to happen."

"You did?"

"I didn't know when. Or if it should, just that it would."

"Are you glad?"

"Do I look regretful?"

"You look … radiant."

They returned to the couch to finish the wine and turned on the television news at 11 just in time to see a film clip of the rookie prez throwing out the first ball at Camden Yards, the new ballpark in Baltimore.

"He doesn't have the flare of DiMaggio, but at least he got it to the plate," Dallas said. "Last year Bush threw it in the dirt. Pretty damned embarrassing. He used to be a ballplayer, but his arm is shot. He couldn't get it there."

"Looks like this one can get it there, and get it up, too," Claire said, with a devilish grin.

"So they say." He laughed. "You don't have first-hand information, do you?"

"Maybe he won't be a great president, but he's a randy one. By all accounts."

They both laughed, and he kissed her on the laugh lines on the side of her face. He liked her playfulness. She didn't seem the least regretful.

"Maybe there's something to be said for that. He's the first one in a long time you could even imagine getting it on. I mean, it's not a good idea to have someone with their finger on the button who's all pent up."

"Can only imagine what button he's got his finger on — or whose."

"You mean, like this one?"

She giggled and grabbed his wrists and held them over his head. He pulled her down to him and nibbled her lower lip.

"I don't care what anyone says, it's good for the country's self-esteem to have a horn-dog as president," he said. "Think about it: The way the government is set up with all the checks and balances, nobody in that office ever really accomplishes anything. So you don't want to compound the problem by having a limp dick in office."

"I was just thinking, like Nixon. Can you imagine?"

"Probably hasn't been anyone who really assumed the position, so to speak, since Kennedy."

"With Marilyn Monroe, no less. What a thought, those two in the White House."

"That was the real Came-a-lot. I guess when somebody said the president is in the Monroe bedroom, they weren't referring to James Monroe."

"I read where there are theories about how that may have had something to do with why he got shot, his relationship with women the Mafia got for him, including maybe Marilyn."

Dallas was thinking some people might say a woman like that was worth getting shot over. He didn't agree. He was lying in a trailer with a noisy air-conditioner that couldn't quite cool the room. It wasn't the Ritz. It wasn't even Howard Johnson. He wasn't complaining. He felt like a king.

"To hell with the White House and the Monroe bedroom. I'd rather be here. With you."

"Smart guy." She smiled. "But what if you could be there with Marilyn?"

"Naw, I prefer brunettes to dead blondes any day."

She smacked him in the shoulder. Hard. He grabbed her wrists and rolled her onto her back. He demonstrated how sincere he was about that preference.

Later, she put on a thin robe, and they sat outside on a bench under a palm tree and stared at a nearly full moon.

"Do you see the man in the moon? I mean, do you see the face when you look at it?"

"Of course. Do you?"

She was quiet for a moment before answering. "I see reflections of the past, and sometimes glimpses of the future. I see faces of people I've known."

"Do you see anything about the future now?"

"No. I was thinking about what you said about the hurt of losing being a stronger sensation than the joy of winning. I think you're right about the good feelings being harder to hold onto. But I like to look at the moon a lot; it helps me remember things from my life. I look up and I see them so clearly. And I always see the good times, never the bad. I may not be able to bring them back, but I know they're always there. It's like with that kid that made that catch for the Marlins today."

"Scott, ah, Scott Pose."

"He may never make another catch that great again. But he'll always have that one. You can't take it away."

Claire leaned back against him and he encircled her with his arms, feeling her body through the gauzy material. He loved the softness of her hair against his face and the scent of their lovemaking on her skin. He stared at the moon and saw Scott Pose leaping and reaching back over his head to make the catch in front of the 434-foot sign — always making the catch. The robe had slipped off one of Claire's shoulders, and he kissed the back of it lightly. He didn't notice the lizard tattoo beneath his lips. His thoughts were soaring, painting eternal images on the moonscape. Thinking, what a day. All this, and a ballgame, too.

CHAPTER 26

"They damn well do exist. I've seen them myself from time to time," Devereaux said.

He and Dallas were at the open-air bar at the Lorelai, an Islamorada restaurant named for the mythical temptresses whose twisted gig was to lure sailors onto the rocks with an enchanting melody and a flash of bosom. As if that's a myth. Just ask the next poor sap stumbling listless and wan from divorce court to the Empty Pockets Saloon.

"First time it happened was on the Cuban wreck. I'm working something promising and I start hearing the music, all harps and flutes. Damned spooky but not unpleasant. Know what I mean?

"I look around and see something moving in the current. I go to get a closer look and there's this figure with lots of long, blonde hair flowing, seductive like. You know, everything kind of swaying like sea fans. I can't really make out the face because the hair's covering it, but I see these tits like cantaloupes with nipples that stand out as round and red as maraschino cherries. I start following, trying to get closer, but I never could. Almost forgot to come up from the dive."

"Ah, a little starved for female companionship, were you, chief? I've known the feeling," Dallas said with a laugh.

"Fuck, that wasn't it. There were *chiquitas* around, even where I was. I had other things on my mind then. This was a real vision."

"You know what Odysseus did to keep his ship from falling victim to the Sirens' song in the 'Odyssey'? He had his crew stuff their ears with wax, and he had them tie him to the mast so he could hear the song and still resist it."

"That don't work. See, these things can't be blocked out with wax or ropes. You cover your eyes, you still see them. Plug up your ears, you still hear them. It's like a spell that overcomes you, gets inside. It's not about being horny. It's about forces that you don't understand but can't ignore. It's like a strong magnet tugging at you, and when it grabs your soul you see the vision. You can't help but follow it. Because the Lorelei are in your head."

Devereaux was tapping the side of his head hard enough to make an audible thump, thump, thump. He had the wild-eyed look that had become more prevalent in the weeks since the discovery of the emeralds, as an unusually windy April brought the salvage operation to a virtual standstill. On days they were able to get out at all, contrary currents and minimal visibility severely hampered the work in the sub. Grappling with the claw to keep the airlift hose in position, Dallas felt like a drunk in a dark bathroom rummaging through a cluttered medicine cabinet in search of an aspirin. With each passing day, Devereaux became more irritable, cursing the elements and "those bastards" who were conspiring to put him out of business.

When he failed to show up at the boatyard for two full days and going on a third, Dallas went looking and found him at home staring out of the window while absently spinning the chamber of a snub-nosed .38. Thankfully, it was empty, and there weren't any cartridges in sight in Devereaux's spartan abode.

He lived in a one-room efficiency above a dry cleaner on A1A. Heat rising from the pressing machines and dryers was more than the undersized air-conditioning unit in the room could handle, even this early in the year. The ceiling fan did little more than stir the oppressive atmosphere that hung thick and pungent with the aroma of half-smoked Lucky Strikes that filled an ashtray the size of a salad bowl which shared a tiny table with a bottle of cheap rum less than half full.

Devereaux sat in front of the window to get some benefit of the wind that was keeping him off the ocean. Curtains old and yellowed danced like a well-past prime Lorelei taunting the land-locked treasure hunter. Each time he took a drag on his cigarette and exhaled toward the screen, the breeze carried the smoke back until he sat amid a ghostly shroud of his own spent breath.

Satisfied the gun was unloaded, Dallas stood in the center of the room with hands on hips.

"You planning on shooting something or did you misplace your yo-yo? You're not thinking of doing anything stupid, are you?"

Devereaux snapped the chamber closed and set the revolver on the table between the ashtray and the rum.

"You know, Ponce de Leon was the first white man to set foot on the Keys," he said, pronouncing the explorer's name Pon-sa. "He called them *Los Martires*. Good name for this place: The Martyred. So many lives wrecked here. You know, those reefs out there have claimed more ships than any place in the world. The reason this place was settled in the first place was for salvaging wrecks.

"Now the bastards want to chase us out, turn the whole thing into a time-share sunset cruise with pink cocktails that give you a headache. That's the trouble with everything anymore: They suck the spirit right out of every paradise, or what could be paradise. Sure as hell ain't no fucking paradise now."

Dallas, still shaken by seeing the gun, shifted uneasily. Thinking, funny how one man's misfortune becomes another's treasure. It was that way the previous summer when Hurricane Andrew walloped the south side of Miami. Someone had to clean it up, rebuild the roofs. Red-necked opportunists swooped in, shoveled up the mess and raked in a windfall born of heartache.

Dallas's own spirits had rarely been as high as in the past few weeks. The girl with the raven hair and emerald eyes had taken the tarnish off his soul. He'd even been inspired to wax the Great White and purchase some sporty duds at the nearby high-end fishing and sportswear outfitter in preparation for a Saturday night jaunt to Coconut Grove. They planned to see a play, hit the club scene, maybe stay over in one of the deco hotels on South Beach. He was even looking forward to Claire's vow to get him on in-line skates.

Right now he was feeling creepy, and the surroundings had a lot to do with it. Ordinarily, Devereaux spent little time in his room. He could usually be found at the boatyard or in any of a half-dozen watering holes, where he was the king handicapper of the Saturday night crab races.

Dallas looked around the dimly lighted room. The so-called kitchenette consisted of a hot plate, mini-fridge and sink. No bathroom facilities — toilet and shower were in a decrepit alcove down the hall. Devereaux wasn't big on decorating. The only wall hangings were a photograph of a stormy waterfront Dallas recognized as Havana Harbor by the distinctive Il Morro castle in the background, and one of those folksy homily plaques they sell in roadside schlock shops. This one read: "After all is said and done, a lot more is said than ever gets done."

Devereaux followed Dallas's eyes to the rum bottle and said, "I ain't drunk, if that's what you're wondering. I don't drink near as much as y'all think. I've been known to binge when shit's piling up. But not when I'm going to be diving. The juice cuts down your bottom time. Soon as this wind changes, we gotta put on the tanks and get to digging down there. The sub's not getting it done right now and we're running out of time."

Dallas took that as a good sign. The old fart wasn't giving up. So he talked him into leaving the room for lunch and called Claire to meet them at the Lorelei. But first Devereaux wanted to show him something. Dallas watched him root around in an old trunk and pull out an album with a black cover and pages brown at the edges. Devereaux's hands shook slightly as he flipped past pages of black-and-white photos until he came to a place with several loose, hand-written pages that looked like they may have been inscribed the day the Declaration of Independence was signed.

"These are Valentina's translations from the Spanish documents about the wreck of the *Magdalena* and the others."

The ink was faded and Dallas had trouble making out many of the words, but he could appreciate the steady hand that produced a flowery cursive as artful as calligraphy. He imagined the Cuban woman's writing was even more beautiful in Spanish. Devereaux pointed to a reference to the sister ship, *Carmelita*, in a description of the departure of the fleet from Havana. Dallas came to the passage referring to the jewels — a giant cross and chalice fashioned for the king and the "lizard of the esmerelda hills" — and noted that this page was more worn than the rest. It bore evidence of a gridwork of creases, as if it had been folded so as to be carried in a pocket or wallet.

"Valentina read each line out loud in Spanish and then in English before she wrote it down."

It occurred to Dallas that Devereaux hadn't spoken of the woman by name when he first told the story. He wondered how old this woman actually was when he knew her.

#

They had been at the Lorelei more than an hour and still no sign of Claire. They had plundered a mountain of steamers and conch fritters, and Devereaux was scanning the menu again. He ordered ice tea at first, but when Dallas returned from a trip to the men's room the captain was drinking a beer. That led to a second and a third.

"So, what are you saying, that there really are voices and visions of mermaids that lead ships onto these reefs? That this explains why there've been so many wrecks here?"

"Maybe yes, maybe no. There's all different factors involved. In many cases it's bad weather. Some, it's bad seamanship. Some, you can't explain at all."

"Yeah, like sometimes you're sailing along on a calm, sunny day and your boat just blows up under you."

"The sea's the great unsolved mystery, and there's forces out there that play tricks on a man's mind," Devereaux said. "You hear all the stories about the Bermuda Triangle, but it's baloney. There's just more traffic there than anywhere else. This stuff happens in all the oceans. Let me tell you how the Spanish used to sail through these waters. They'd leave Havana and sail straight at the Bahama Bank until they saw the white water on the shoals, then they'd turn and sail across the straits until they saw Florida. They felt better if they could actually see the danger they had to avoid. And still there's documented cases of ships sighting the reefs and sailing right onto the rocks like they're in some kind of trance. Crazy."

Dallas thought about this a moment, then said, "I've heard about instances where people are stopped at a railroad track with no gate when a train's going by, and the motion of the train draws them in. They ease their foot off the brake without realizing it and drift into the train like they're hypnotized by it."

"There you go. There's powers at work on the mind that you can't understand. They lead you to places you know you shouldn't go. Still, you can't help but go there. It's irresistible forces that take us down the wrong roads."

Dallas was amazed this madness was actually making sense to him and that he was contributing to it. At that moment he spotted Claire in the parking lot, hair blowing wild in the wind, which buffeted the palms in the parking lot, making a sound that was sort of spooky but not unpleasant. He smiled, thinking, if she were a vision on a rocky shore his ship was destined to be kindling wood, and he'd gladly use it to build her a cabin on the beach. Wherever this course was leading, fuck it, he wasn't altering it now.

#

Even before she reached the bar, before he got a clear look at her face, Dallas could tell something was wrong. There was indignation in her stride. They barely exchanged hellos before Claire launched into a rapid-fire account of her past hour, the reason she was so long in joining them. She'd been on her way when a hysterical woman practically threw herself in front of Claire's car on U.S. 1.

"She's eight months pregnant, for crying out loud. And this bastard just stops the car and tells her, 'Get out. Get the hell out!' Doesn't even pull off the road. Just stops with traffic backed up, reaches across, opens the door and damn near shoves her out on the pavement. Slings her purse out the door and drives off. She's only got about five bucks on her.

"And you know what she tells me when I get her calmed down? She says, it's not that big a deal, he's done this before. He's just got a bad temper. Damn it, she's eight months pregnant! That son of a bitch. A guy like that, I'd like to see him with a rope tied to his nuts and lowered into the sewer."

Claire's face was crimson with rage. Dallas shifted uneasily in his seat. Devereaux lit a cigarette and nodded absently.

"You know who this bastard is? He's a hot-shot sportscaster in Miami. The one they call Slick Nick."

"Nick O'Farrell?" Dallas said, trying to picture the impeccably groomed TV face peering up from a sewer.

"More like Nick the Prick. If I were her, I'd cut if off, like that Bobbitt woman did."

"Ouch!" Devereaux took another puff.

O'Farrell was a New York-Irishman married to a Hispanic woman named Ileana, who was a former Miami Heat dancer. Claire had driven her to Mariners Hospital.

After giving her whirlwind account of the sordid event, which drew the attention of everyone seated at the bar, she was headed back to check on Ileana. Dallas got up to walk her to the car, but she pulled away and was gone, leaving him with the vision of Slick Nick O'Farrell holding his severed dick like a microphone, bellowing with a barely discernible Irish lilt his familiar intro to every report of a Miami Heat victory, "*Aye Carumba!* Was the Heat ever hot tonight!"

Dallas turned back helplessly to Devereaux, who stubbed out his cigarette, shrugged and said, "You want to order more clams?"

CHAPTER 27

That night Claire was distant in bed, and for the first time their lovemaking seemed wooden, lacking the usual urgency of exploratory intimacy. Until then, they had been archaeologists of passion, uncovering sensual burial grounds each had long abandoned, pioneers of shared sensations neither had attained before. Inhibitions had peeled away like layers of varnish on an old barn until, in one unabashed moment a few nights before, Dallas had blurted out his initial rear-view attraction to her.

"Join the club," Claire said. "I once broke a guy's nose when he grabbed my ass in a bar." Turning to a provocative pose, she added, "There are exceptions to the hands-off policy."

But this night, they revealed little and felt nothing special. Dallas had trouble falling asleep. Can it be, less than a month and the emotional honeymoon is over? Was he doomed to end up as the pathetic figure in a country song that his sleep-deprived mind had somehow concocted and which kept twanging in his ear as he drifted into a dusty tumbleweed dreamland:

"Where do you go when you're out of luck in love, off the diamond, into the rough."

Cripes, no wonder he couldn't stomach country music.

When he awoke, Claire had already dressed and left to pick up the beleaguered Ileana O'Farrell at a nearby motel with plans to drive her to her mother's house in Hialeah. She called the next day, Friday, to say their weekend in Miami was off; Lyle had the flu. They didn't see each other again until Monday when the great treasure hunt resumed.

Claire nearly missed the boat, arriving moments after Devereaux declared, "We're leaving without her." She had to leap aboard as the impatient Cajun began easing *Levante* away from the dock. She smiled sheepishly as Keith gave her a hand aboard.

"Don't worry, now, dat sheet's been out dar 300 years. Another few minutes not gonna matter, now is it?" Keith said, grinning and laying on his faux Rasta rap.

"No worries, no hurries. That's why all you rhymin' banana republic bozos ever make is babies," Devereaux said.

"Now, now, listen to da mon be talkin' us down. My, my. Tell me, what good ever come out of your bayou hellhole but sauce so hot it eats a hole in a mon's stomach," Keith said with a wink at Dallas. "Whole damn place only fit for snakes and gators."

Devereaux didn't smile or respond. Keith shrugged and gave his hearty diaphragm-jiggling Eddie Murphy laugh, doing his best to disperse the tension that was making everyone on the boat uncomfortable. There were two additions to the group, though the newcomers were in no way members of the team.

Earle S. Culpepper was an underwater archaeologist working for the Florida Department of Natural Resources, Dr. Thomas McPeak a marine biologist with the National Oceanic and Atmospheric Administration, known as NOAA. The government agencies had taken renewed interest in the salvage of the *Camelita* since the discovery of the emeralds. With May bringing milder weather more conducive to offshore activities, the two scientists came to look out for their respective interests.

Culpepper was a lanky fellow nearly 6½ feet tall who carried himself in a permanent slouch indicative either of self-consciousness about his height or a bad back. He was known to everyone but Dallas, having spent time with the project the previous summer. He had been present the day Claire discovered the Sanchez Site and was so ecstatic about the find of the monogrammed snuff box he took the whole crew to dinner that night. His down-home manner and reddish beard interspersed with gray made him appear professorial except in moments of wild-eyed exuberance that Keith referred to as his Indiana Jones look.

"This is history! This is history! This is history!" he liked to say, always blurting out excited declarations three times as if to underscore his point, and at the same time making himself an easy target for mimicry.

"This is lunch! This is lunch! This is lunch!" Keith would declare as he passed out sandwiches.

Culpepper's interest in the many shipwrecks off the Florida coast was naturally at odds with people like Devereaux. Where they saw the potential for treasure, he saw a national treasure to be preserved. He could talk for hours about what artifacts salvaged from the sea floor revealed about the people and the cultures they came from.

"These wrecks are time capsules. They're time capsules! Time capsules, you see?" he said. "When we uncover them, we open a door to the past. We must take care in how we excavate them or that door will be shut forever and a part of our heritage will be lost."

To Devereaux, he said, "You're like a bull in a china shop, knocking all the plates off the shelves in search of the key to the cash register."

"Oh, bull," Devereaux said. "Like this stuff was put out here with care. Hell no, the sea dumped it on the bottom and has been kicking it around ever since. It we don't dig it up and bring it in, nobody's ever going to see it."

McPeak was a different breed altogether, a stocky, no-nonsense New Englander with a bug-eyed expression that prompted Keith to dub him "McPeeping Tom." If he had his way, not only would salvage of shipwrecks cease, so would most other public activities in the fragile marine environment of the Keys. Like-minded bureaucrats had authored the controversial Florida Keys National Marine Sanctuary Act as a 2,600-square mile safety net around the Keys with the admirable aim of preserving the only living barrier reef in the United States. But to many of those who found recreation and scratched out a living from that unique environment, the sanctuary was a conspiracy to turn an aquatic fantasyland into a no-fun zone, a look-but-no-touch marine biology lab.

Devereaux was able to continue poking around the sea floor because he was working outside the coral reef and had a permit obtained before the sanctuary became law in late 1990, and then only by the grace of a court injunction that was due to expire later in the summer. Grumbling could be heard in local bars among those who had already been put out of business by the sanctuary act that shady maneuverings by influential backers had gotten Devereaux his waiver. The mini bonanza spawned by the emeralds notwithstanding, Dallas couldn't help but wonder why these mysterious benefactors had invested such confidence in this eccentric old prospector.

Devereaux was well aware time was against him, a fact McPeak seemed to delight in reminding him.

"You're a dinosaur, Devereaux," he said. "Come the first of August, you'll be just another Triceratops. Extinct!"

Devereaux spat out something in pigeon Spanish that elicited a chuckle from Keith, who later confided to Dallas that the remark translated roughly to, "You are nothing but snot on my loafers."

This, then, was the strained environment in which began a new phase of the *Carmelita* excavation, very possibly the final push of the project. As promised, the sub remained in its cradle while Dallas, Keith, Devereaux and Culpepper donned scuba tanks. Claire and McPeak stayed aboard *Levante* during the initial dive. Culpepper was paired with Keith, who was operating the airlift hose. Devereaux stationed them on the same side of the wreck that the emeralds were found but well away from that site. He motioned Dallas to follow him to an area where several ballast stones were clustered, and they spent the duration of the initial 25-minute dive digging trenches perpendicular to the supposed position of the keel of the ship.

Through the years, Dallas had dived some of the most spectacular sites in the Caribbean, including Monk's Haven off Bonaire, St. Thomas's French Cap Cay and Grand Cayman's Stingray City, where rays congregate around dive boats like New York commuters rushing to the subway. Compared to those spots, digging haphazardly on the mostly barren drop-off beyond the Keys reefs was as stimulating as cleaning someone else's basement. Dallas found his mind wandering to his own visions of Lorelei, seeing the image of Claire frolicking in a string bikini in every flash of movement from a passing fish or shadow. Devereaux caught him idly daydreaming and brought him back to the task with a sharp poke in the ribs.

Dallas redeemed himself just before the end of the dive by unearthing two silver coins and an encrusted object Culpepper identified as a brass buckle. When they surfaced, the archaeologist was exuding over his own discovery of a nearly whole Chinese teacup.

"This is significant! This is significant! Really significant! It's one of the most intact specimens I've seen of K'ang Hsi porcelain."

Devereaux shrugged at Dallas. "This fuckin' guy gets his rocks off finding old plates and shit. So, I put him in the galley."

The hectic nature of the morning, with the arrival of the scientists and the preparation of the gear for the dive had prevented Dallas from doing more than exchange greetings with Claire and making occasional eye contact, which he sensed she was avoiding. The afternoon dive paired them on the airlift, working at the shallow end of the wreck site to maximize bottom time. As they positioned the snuffling maw to scarf up massive snootfuls of sand, Dallas stretched himself out, belly to the bottom, so he could gaze up directly into Claire's facemask until she sensed his stare. When her eyes, which had been focused intently on the nozzle of the dredge, began darting up to meet his with greater frequency, he reeled her in by making a motion as if spraying her goggles and polishing them with the palm of his hand. He could see the smile curl around her mouthpiece and the crinkling around the corners of her eyes, which appeared dark inside the mask. She shook a fist at him and made a motion as if to slice his air hose.

"You bastard," she said when they surfaced, socking him in the shoulder. "You made me laugh underwater. I thought I was going to inhale the whole ocean down there."

She was laughing when she said it, and again when she offered him a hand onto the boat that turned into a shove back into the water. They continued to banter in mock indignation as they helped each other off with their tanks until he grabbed her arm and, with his face close to hers, said, "I like when you laugh. I missed that. I missed you."

"I'm here."

"Are you?"

Back on shore, they helped Keith clean the boat while Culpepper and Devereaux took the day's haul to the bank, where it would remain in a vault pending dispersal. Hosing off the deck spawned the inevitable water fight that left the three of them dripping and breathless. When Keith shuffled off to his boat to change, Claire's playfulness quickly faded.

"I'm sorry if I've been distant," she said, toweling the water off her face and then doing the same for him. "This thing with Ileana brought back a lot of bad stuff and got me thinking."

"None of that bad stuff has anything to do with us. That's in the past. It's best to leave it there."

"I can't help but think about the future sometimes, wondering where things are going to go."

Dallas shifted uneasily, unsure of what he should say or what he wanted to say. "I guess it's always been my policy not to think too far ahead, to deal with the cards as they fall. I mean, we've been having fun, haven't we?"

"I told myself when I left California that was what I was going to do, just let it happen, try to enjoy life for once. Maybe it's my nature to worry. I don't know, I can't help but get insecure. I start thinking, what happens when this project ends, do I stay here, keep working at the bar? What if you decide to move on? Maybe it was OK before, drifting along. You start to get involved, it's hard not to look ahead to all the different ways it can go. Plus, I've got Lyle to think about."

"Just remember, everyone's not Slick Nick. Or the one you left."

Dallas was watching her face, somber in thought. Suddenly, she brightened.

"When I took Ileana home, there was a neighbor woman who's into voodoo or something. Santeria, I think it's called."

"You mean the ones that cut the heads off chickens?"

"Yeah, you don't want to cross those people. Spooky stuff. This woman was making it sound like she was going to cast some kind of spell on Nick O'Farrell. Ileana wasn't saying anything at first. Then she says, 'I keep imagining that he's on TV giving the sports news and all of a sudden he feels like ants are crawling all over him and he's going nuts, and he's still on camera.' And she kind of winked at the neighbor."

Dallas felt something land on the back of his neck. When he started scratching she laughed. He went home with her that afternoon. He had promised to help Lyle with his pitching. Dinner naturally followed. Later, her body answered the question: Yes, she was back, but he wondered for how long.

"What would you do if you got rich, if you won the lottery or something?"

They were quietly savoring the afterglow, spinning separate tendrils of thought, her head on his chest. She shifted to look into his face before answering.

"I don't know, probably travel. See all the places worth seeing. Have a nice place to live. Not a mansion, but nice. Comfortable. Maybe up in the mountains, or by the beach."

"That's it: a beach house. That's all I'd need. Don't need to travel. Already done too much of that. Just give me a beach house, where every day the sounds of the ocean would be the first thing I hear in the morning and lull me to sleep at night."

"Are you going to share that beach house with anyone? Or are you going to live there alone?"

"I'm going to share it, of course. That's what would make it special. That's what would make me rich. Would you be my beach house baby?"

She smiled and nuzzled into his chest.

"Mmmm, I like the sound of that. Yes, I'll be your beach house baby. But you've got to let me have my dogs. A couple of dogs to romp with on the beach."

He thought for a minute. "Yeah, OK. I'm not big on dogs, but they would fit in a place like that. I could throw the Frisbee for them, romp in the surf with them. They'd hang out on the deck in the afternoon while we drank rum punch and I grilled the fish I caught off the beach in the morning."

"I'm there. But where would it be?"

"Don't know. Could be here, could be California, could be in the islands. Wouldn't matter, as long as all the ingredients were right. Live like that, time stands still. You never get old."

"Now all we need is to win the lottery."

"Maybe not even that. You might be surprised."

He could envision it clearly, days unfolding like matching jewels that you polished in the daytime, then set on a shelf in a row side by side, glowing in the moonlight arcing through the window. It must have been some western coast in his head because the sun was crouched over the water when they took their afternoon walks along the shore, hand in hand. The house was an A-frame with big windows. He imagined falling asleep to the whir of ceiling fans and the distant whoosh of the surf while holding her, as he was now, lulled by the rhythmic sounds of her breathing.

A pleasant vision, but was it pure fantasy? He closed his eyes and tried to steal a glimpse into the future as reverie blurred into a dream. He found himself at the end of a bridge with water on both sides, like the many bridges that connect the Keys, but the sun was in his eyes preventing him from seeing the other shore.

Gradually he became aware, the light shining in his eyes was real. The lamp next to the bed beaming, Claire already up and the shower running. It was still dark outside. The alarm clock sounded. The future came shockingly early in Devereaux's navy.

CHAPTER 28

Day after day, dawn summoned them to the Snapper Cove Boatworks. The morning scene varied little: Devereaux hunched over some piece of equipment — the airlift pump was constantly acting up and the boat's engine was in dire need of an overhaul — and cursing through teeth clenched around a cigarette as he hurried to make repairs necessary to get them through the day. It was a mystery how he avoided getting smoke in his eyes or wasn't bothered by it.

Meanwhile, Keith would be loading scuba tanks aboard while McPeak stood on the dock with a cup of coffee, looking ridiculous in a floppy sun hat, lecturing about impending environmental ruin.

"We're standing in the middle of an eco-cesspool," he railed. "They've already killed Florida Bay with pollution and cutting off the freshwater flowing through the Everglades. We've got rich assholes building condominiums and flushing crap into the ocean, killing the reefs. We've got you lunatics rooting around in the sea floor like gophers searching for a pot of gold. And all the people who could fix the problem are too busy on their own ego trips."

One morning Culpepper arrived looking disheveled, carrying a thick book littered with scraps of paper marking various pages of interest. He immediately flipped it open to show Keith a picture of a piece of crockery that resembled one unearthed from the *Carmelita* site the previous day.

"See, an olive jar. Just as I said. And ours is in better condition. It's quite remarkable."

"Let me know when you find the liquor cabinet down there, my man, and we'll all have martinis for lunch," Keith said with a wink.

Culpepper had an area of the wreck site staked out in a grid. He photographed each item as it was uncovered and later recorded its location and position on a map with a precise hand that was as much art as science.

"Your pictures are pretty, Doc," Keith said, "but what are you going to do with them, wallpaper your office?"

"This is history come to life, don't you see? A looking glass into centuries past. We're talking centuries. Centuries, centuries ago! Let me tell you about the oldest shipwreck ever found. It's in the Mediterranean off the Turkish coast, and it dates to the 14th Century B.C.! That's B.C.! Before Christ! Thirty-four centuries ago, back to the time of the pharaohs Akhenaten and Tutankhamun. On that one ship, they've found items that can be tied to seven different Bronze Age cultures. The wealth of knowledge revealed is staggering. You see?"

He paused to catch his breath. Keith stood on the dock blinking in the glare of the morning sun. From a distance, Dallas could see the archaeologist was perspiring.

"Now, we already know a great deal about these Spanish naos. But to be able to accurately depict the minute detail of their commerce and the lives of the people who traveled here and sailed these ships, well, I've been working on a docu-drawing of the cross-section of an almiranta, such as this one we're excavating, drawn to one-twentieth scale, showing all the various compartments and cargo. It's extremely detailed and quite large. So you see, this work is invaluable."

Keith didn't say a word though he glanced in Dallas's direction and suppressed a smile. The rest of the day, whenever their paths crossed Keith would reprise Steve Martin's "Funky Tut" routine and do a comical Egyptian shuffle. Henceforth, anytime Culpepper began an archaeological rant, Keith would lean close to Dallas and mutter, "Tut, Tut, Tut."

#

The interplay was amusing but Dallas had a serious issue on his mind late one morning when he arrived at Snapper Cove. It was the second day in a row that high winds had kept *Levante* at the dock after a hectic couple weeks of underwater work that had yielded an impressive array of artifacts and coins, some silver, some gold. The sub was getting plenty of use, but increasingly the emphasis was on scuba diving. Devereaux and Culpepper were immersed in their respective agendas, and Dallas had taken on the vital task of logging the bottom time of each diver out of concern for the welfare of everyone. He was spending so much time pouring over the NAUI dive tables he felt like an accountant, although he was charting the ebb and flow of nitrogen rather than cash flow. Increasingly, the numbers were coming up in the red in relation to safety.

When a diver breathes compressed air under water, his body accumulates nitrogen like a sponge soaking up spilled orange juice. The deeper you go, the faster the nitrogen builds up. Stay down too long, you get bent, as they say, which in the mildest form means you're only doubled over in agony. At worst, your wetsuit can turn into a body bag.

The dive tables show the amount of time the average person can safely remain underwater at specific depths. It gets complicated, and more dangerous, when an additional dive is made in the same day. Compensation must be made for nitrogen remaining in the body from the first dive, and the bottom time has to be shortened accordingly for the subsequent dive. Although nitrogen supposedly passes out of the body after 24 hours, Dallas became alarmed when after five or six consecutive days of diving he felt some lightheadedness and slight tingling in one shoulder.

The project was beginning to spin out of control. It stemmed from a growing recklessness on the part of Devereaux as the would-be date of no return loomed larger in everyone's consciousness.

"If you think you're going to get that injunction extended, you're pissing into a gale," McPeak would say with obvious delight. "Come August first, your golden goose turns into a pumpkin."

"There you go mixing metaphors again," Dallas said as Devereaux glared daggers at the scientist.

"Not to mention fairy tales," Claire said.

Culpepper scowled. "It really would be a shame to let this historical and archaeological opportunity pass unrequited. With the proper controls and procedures, this work can be completed in harmony with the environment."

But he, too, understood that the feds held the hammer in this matter and the State of Florida was limited in its ability to control the fate of its own coastal interests.

At the same time, Devereaux was cursing his investors as much as the government for not pressing the issue more aggressively in the courts. It was clear he needed a significant find, and he needed it soon, to rekindle interest before his cause was deep-sixed for good. With that aim, he had announced a strategy revision and begun devoting more effort to searching in deeper water away from the main wreck site, reasoning that objects from the ship may have settled farther down the drop-off. He was testing the limits of the dive tables, stretching the bottom times like a watch wound to the breaking point.

" 'Deeper,' he says. 'Longer! Deeper!' You'd think he was directing a porno flick." Keith said, plopping down wearily on a seat next to Dallas late one afternoon after his second dive of the day.

Dallas glanced around the boat. Everyone looked exhausted. Except Devereaux, who appeared oddly energized. His expression on the trip back to the boatyard seemed diabolical, almost frightening.

Later, Dallas pulled Keith aside.

"What's the deal with Skeets? It's like he's on something. Is he taking speed?"

"I told you, the dude's pretty amazing for an old fart. He's on a mission, and once he gets zoned in there's no knocking him off it."

"I know. I'm totally wiped. If we keep up like this, someone's going to get hurt."

"You want to know what's with him today, I'll tell you. He found something down there. I don't know what, but I've never seen him react like that. I was digging this spot and he kind of disappeared on me. He's been doing that. I look around and find him farther down the drop-off — quite a ways down — and he's looking at something. I couldn't tell what it was, but he fumbled it and got frantic, searching before he picked it up again. He sees me coming then and slips this thing into his glove. He didn't know I saw. Anyway, next thing I know he's heading for the surface. I had to go after him and grab him to make his decompression stop. Crazy bastard.

"We get to the boat and I say, 'Hey, you OK?' He looks at me like he doesn't recognize me, like he's looking right through me. Never seen him like that. Scared the crap out of me. I left him alone after that. Whatever he found, looks like he's keeping it to himself."

"Another emerald, maybe — some big, friggin' hunk of green rock candy?" Dallas said. "Maybe he figures if the project gets shut down, he'll have one nice chip to cash in."

"No, man, this was no rock. I could tell that much. It was something else, some object that must've come from the ship. And the way his face looked, I can tell you it was no damn belt buckle."

CHAPTER 29

The flare-up in the weather that started that same evening came as a relief, although Devereaux insisted on going out the following morning.

"You gotta be nuts," McPeak said as he watched the boatyard flag flapping hard enough to loosen its stripes. He and Culpepper begged off. The others endured at Devereux's insistence, with almost disastrous consequences as they nearly Humpty-Dumptyed the sub while launching it. One side of the hull got scraped up badly, and it proved to be a wasted effort. The airlift was unmanageable under the conditions. They couldn't keep *Levante* anchored on station.

Devereaux relented after a foul hour and a half marked by considerable shouting and cursing. Nobody was speaking by the time they reached shore, and they were all relieved to go their separate ways. Even Dallas and Claire took the night off from each other.

So Dallas's mission when he went to the boatyard two days later in search of Devereaux was to try to restore sanity to the project. He still had a bandage covering battered knuckles on one hand and bruises on both forearms from the struggle with the sub. His thoughts were on what he wanted to say as the wheels of the Great White rumbled across the gravel entrance to the boatyard. The wind was starting to lose its teeth. Today was the only opportunity for a powwow. Tomorrow they'd be back on the water.

He waved absently to the two lesbians who were perpetually sanding the hull of a boxy sailboat, not really seeing them. His vision was focused inward, so what he saw in the boat basin didn't immediately register: a black hull sliding quietly past the mangroves, easing into the turn to the channel leading to the ocean. He gave the door of the Caddy a solid shove and started toward the building at a brisk pace.

Jesus H. Roosevelt Christ!

He spun on his heels, scattering gravel, and stared at the departing *Mary Lou II*.

What the ...?

Dallas dashed to the dock and jumped onto a piling to get a clear view over the bow of a Striker sportfishing cruiser. The *Mary Lou II* was completing its turn, already partly obscured by the mangroves lining the shore. But there was no mistaking the converted shrimp boat. Dallas watched — nobody visible on deck, nor was the *P-BJ-003* in its cradle — as it moved into the channel and quickly out of sight.

He rushed into the boatyard office where Sylvia Jernigan, the receptionist, bookkeeper, kicker-of-any-ass-that-needed-it with biceps like a longshoreman, was hanging up the phone.

"That boat that just left — old shrimp boat, I think — do you know what it was doing here?"

Sylvia was basically big-hearted and harmless unless riled, but she had a way of looking at you that could scare the scales off a bluefish. He instantly regretted barging in. She shrugged, "Ask your buddy, the ravin' Cajun. Those assholes are his friends, I guess."

"Guy in a cowboy hat?"

She rolled her eyes.

#

Devereaux was smoking, seated on a bench in the rear of the warehouse near the sub, staring absently. He had been sanding parts of the hull damaged on the previous outing. He offered no greeting when Dallas walked up. Just took a drag on his cigarette and said, "Wind's laying down."

"Yeah, thought it might be a good idea to go over a few things before we go back out."

Devereaux dropped the butt, ground it into the concrete with his heel, picked up a sanding block and resumed his work.

"The thing is, I'm concerned we're starting to get a little careless. Keith had to slow you down on your decompression stop the other day. The amount of diving we're doing, someone could get bent. I was thinking, maybe we should throttle back. If we dive two days in a row, the next day we just work the sub."

Devereaux turned toward Dallas, waving the sanding block to punctuate his words. His fingers were covered with dark powder.

"If you're scared, you want out, don't let the door hit you in the ass. Go ahead, take your girlfriend with you. I don't give a shit. Not that it's going to fucking matter, one way or t'other. It's all coming down. Soon. Very soon."

Dallas was looking past the block, straight into Devereaux's eyes. Ravin'? Yeah, he had the knack.

"I heard you tied one on at Woody's night before last. Couple people said they never saw you in a better mood. Like you were celebrating something."

"Celebrating, my ass. Nothing to fucking celebrate. How can I be fucking celebrating? Trying to keep my head out of the cesspool. Trying to keep the bastards…"

He stopped raving and went back to sanding. Dallas sat on the bench and watched. Sweat soaked through the older man's T-shirt. Devereaux was skinny, but by the looks of the sinewy muscles in his arms, pretty damn strong.

Dallas waited before saying, "You had visitors just now, didn't you?"

No response.

"Let's see, let me guess: There was a fast-talking, B.S.-out-of-both-sides-of-his-ass guy. What's his name? Oh, yeah, something like, Edison Hawke — the Third."

Dallas thought he saw hair on the back of Devereaux's neck bristle.

"What's your involvement with Hawke? Who's Behrent Juergens? And what do you know about their so-called skimmer that flies over the water?"

Devereaux turned, eyes wild, veins on his neck bulging. He tried to speak, but nothing came out but spittle and a twisted expletive that sounded something like "frooch," with a lot of spray. The punch that followed was out of frustration from being unable to get his words out. It surprised them both.

Dallas was getting up off the bench when he saw it coming and swung his forearm with leverage such that he not only deflected the blow but caught Devereaux across the chest with enough force to knock him off his feet. The sanding block banged off the side of the sub and landed at Dallas's feet. Before Devereaux could scramble up, Dallas immobilized him, lodging a knee across his chest and grabbing both wrists. With their faces inches apart, Dallas let fly with some spittle of his own.

"You salty son of a bitch, I ought to kick your ass right now. Nobody's quitting on you. We're out there day after day risking our necks for you and your cause, whatever the hell it is, for reasons I can't even explain. I sure as hell ain't cashing any checks to retire on. And you're pulling shit like this, acting like some deranged Captain Blye from the bayou. Near as I can tell, this crew is all you got in your corner. Without us, you might as well be farting out of your ear."

Claire had a good laugh about that one when Dallas related the incident. "Now there's an image to ponder over oysters and beer."

Odd combination of words can pour out in a heated moment, but Dallas wasn't going for laughs. He yanked Devereaux off the floor and set him down hard on the bench. No more ravin'. The subdued Cajun took out a cigarette misshapen from the tussle and searched his pockets for a light, grumbling to himself. Dallas spotted a book of matches on the floor near the sub and lit the crooked stick in Devereaux's teeth. Suddenly Devereaux looked like an old prospector whose last claim turned out to be an empty hole in the ground.

"Now you better fuckin' level with me. What's your connection with Hawke, and what was he doing here just now?"

"One of my investors. He's the one I deal with."

"No shit. You're working for Hawke, then. We're all working for Hawke. Son of a bitch."

Devereaux didn't like that. He started to get up, riled again. Dallas shoved him back down.

"The hell you saying — I don't work for nobody."

"But he holds the cards, and he's dealing you out. Is that it?"

"I ain't done yet."

"What do you know about this other thing, this high-speed skimmer? What's he up to with that?"

Devereaux shrugged. "Guess it's his new treasure ship."

Dallas studied him. The old coot was a chameleon. The color was back in his face, and with it the fire in his eyes. A spark still burned. Something in there, a scheme fomenting? Dallas couldn't grasp what intrigued him about Devereaux. Something mysterious he didn't yet understand. Just a feeling that told him not to dismiss this crazy bastard yet. He gave Devereaux a chuck in the shoulder and said, "Aw right, we'll see you tomorrow."

He started to walk away, maybe five or six paces before turning back.

"Hey."

Devereaux looked up.

"By the way, you saw it again, didn't you?"

"What?" Eyes narrowing.

"Last time we were out. The Lorelei. You saw it again."

Devereaux's expression changed again. Not quite a smile, but a softening.

"Maybe." More softening. Suddenly, he looked younger, the creases in his face losing their sharpness. He took a puff on the cigarette. The edge was gone from the voice, too, as he said it again. "Maybe."

CHAPTER 30

"You gotta try it. You've got to. You owe it to yourself. The first time I went diving, man, that was it for me. I was hooked, reeled in. Throw away the drugs. No more need for stimulants. That's it, no fooling. The man tells it like it is. Diving sets your soul free. It's the best. The best!"

Keith in the act of persuasion was a sight to behold. He could bring a lump to the throat of an Amway salesman — especially when he was talking about one of his passions, music or scuba diving, and had a sweet, young audience.

This attentive blonde was obviously interested.

"I tell you it's like free-fall without the landing. A space walk without the rocket. OK, maybe not better than sex, but if you combine it with sex, there's nothing better. Follow what I'm saying?"

Dallas had heard Keith's scuba spiel before. It was always amusing, and often effective. Something about his voice — not quite the deep resonance of Barry White's but it had an intriguing, seductive lilt — combined with his smile and enthusiasm was captivating to women. Keith preferred the term irresistible.

"What you've got," Dallas reminded him often, "is good bullshit."

"Yeah, man, but it's in the delivery. Give me credit, give me some damn credit. It's a knack. It's an art."

"Yeah, title it 'Brown spots on the wall,' bullshit on canvas. I'll give you this, you're a piece of work."

Standing a discreet distance away but hearing it all, Dallas caught Keith's eye and forced him to suppress a smile. The expression of the girl — she had one of those end-in-i names, Tami or Brandi, something like that — told a different story. She was the catch of the day, jumping in the boat.

She was a guest on the day's outing aboard *Levante*. She'd catch some sun, see what a real treasure hunt was all about; the private scuba lesson was to come later.

Dallas was surprised Devereaux didn't nix the idea. Uncharacteristically, he didn't react at all.

Later, Dallas wondered if the girl's presence may have contributed to the events of the day. Or was Devereaux's lack of reaction more indicative of a distracted state of mind that made inevitable the incident that brought the salvage of the *Carmelita* to an abrupt halt?

It was a confusing roller-coaster of a day. Refreshed by the three-day break, the *esprit de corps* was unusually high at the onset. Even McPeak showed up with a bag of doughnuts to share. He slapped Culpepper on the back and, bastardizing Mel Fisher's trademark line, declared, "Like the *Atocha* guy says, 'This is the day.' I can feel it."

"No, 'Today's the day.' That's the way he says it," Culpepper corrected.

"Yeah, today's the day we throw your sorry ass in the drink," Keith muttered. "But toss me a doughnut and I might let it slide. And it better be jelly — lots of jelly."

Claire took a look at the blonde in the day-glo orange string bikini and rolled her eyes at Dallas, who, no B.S., genuinely preferred the brunette in the sky-blue wetsuit. But he did give the string bikini a second look, and it reminded him that if he had taken the extra minute to floss he could have gotten rid of that bit of summer sausage lodged between upper molars. Damn, how do they wear those things?

"What?"

Claire was giving him a crinkled smile.

"I was just following your eyes. The way they're dancing around it looks like you're watching a ping-pong match."

"I was just thinking."

"I bet you were."

"I was just thinking that when she grows up she has a chance to be half as sexy as you."

"You're so full of crap."

Dallas shrugged and walked away.

On the way to the wreck site, he pulled Keith aside and gave him his theory on older women.

"My mother always had a little vegetable garden in her backyard. My favorite thing was the tomato plants. I'd watch them all summer waiting for them to grow and ripen. Once they turned red you could pick them — even if they were still a little green. But if you could wait a while longer, they'd get softer and juicier. That's when they're the best. It's the same with women."

"Damn, you're making me hungry." They both glanced at Miss Garden Fresh. Keith shook his head, "Man, I just don't know about the waiting." They both cracked up.

The mood remained light and irreverent as they reached the site, set the anchors and prepared for the first dive. At one point, McPeak poked Culpepper in the ribs and, nodding toward the girl, said on the sly, "I knew all along that sooner or later this crew would find a treasure chest."

It was all in stark contrast to the grim mood of a few days before. Even Devereaux was lacking his usual edge. He was oddly quiet, aloof. Later, when Dallas tried to reconstruct the day, the word that came to mind was detached. Yes, Devereaux had seemed detached. The man truly was an enigma.

#

Flippers in place, Dallas waddled to the gunwale and let himself spill backwards into the sea. Immediately, the scuba tank ceased to be a burden and the clumsy appendages on his feet became an asset. The scuba diver is like the pelican, comically awkward until taking flight — or in this case, taking the plunge. He cleared his mask and waited on the surface for the others. He was to be paired with Devereaux while Claire and Keith worked the airlift. The scientists were staying on board to monitor the outfall from the dredge and ogle Suzi Sunshine.

Fifteen feet below the surface Dallas was momentarily startled by a mass of cigar-shaped bodies to his left. When he got a better look he relaxed and pointed out the welcoming party to Claire. The divers were converging with a pack of barracuda cruising in the current like a gang of mobsters in gray silk suits sauntering into a casino.

Immediately, Dallas was reminded of a similar encounter during his introduction to scuba diving years before in Cozumel. He had been working as a mate on the sportfishing tournament circuit and anesthetizing the sadness over the abrupt end of his baseball career with a steady slosh of tequila and rum. Keith was right about the heady allure of scuba diving. It proved to be the tonic that finally dragged Dallas out of a self-destructive spiral, and the day of the barracuda was the turning point.

Rounding a massive coral formation and coming face-to-face with the sinister-looking predators, he nearly swam out of his wetsuit in panic. Two dive buddies had to literally tackle him to prevent a hasty ascent that posed greater peril than the fish. Barracuda are like the typical Italian *maitre d'*, frightening in demeanor but harmless, provided you don't make a dash for the door without paying the check. Once his companions got him calmed, they swam amid the barracuda until diminishing air supply dictated they bid adieu.

This school was smaller than the one in Cozumel, but Dallas wanted to adopt it as his entourage for the afternoon. Thinking, with these characters at my side I could breeze into any unseemly-looking joint without a worry. Tip a few with some biker dudes, then sashay into Mike Tyson's favorite roost and send over a round for Mikey and the boyz.

Leave it to Devereaux to spoil a macho reverie with a poke in the ribs and an impatient gesture toward the bottom — another descent to cavort with the ghosts in Devereaux's den. At this point, Dallas preferred the company of the 'cudas. He was bored with the tedious task of unearthing history — perhaps old disasters were best left concealed under the sediment of time, particularly those in his own life — and of the bleak landscape along the drop-off, a relatively barren underwater badland between the coral reefs and the dark abyss of deep water. Vegetation was sparse and fish generally just passing through, save for a docile Warsaw grouper, affectionately dubbed Lech Walesa, that bivouacked in a rock formation not far from the wreck site. Dallas stopped to visit whenever bottom time allowed. Occasionally sharks were spotted lurking ominously like pirate ships on the horizon, but only on rare occasions had the threat seemed sufficient to prompt retreat to the surface.

For some reason Dallas felt happier in the water this particular day than at any time since he joined the project. The sound of his rhythmic breathing was relaxing and the lightness of being adrift in the currents had him feeling playful. He would have preferred to spend the rest of the day on the reefs chasing quirky, colorful parrotfish and saluting striped sergeant majors over a carpet of swaying sea fans while Spanish guitar riffs played in his head. Instead, he was 80 feet down babysitting this mad Cajun Aqualung, the anti-Cousteau.

That essentially was Dallas's assignment for the day's second dive, ensuring that Devereaux stuck to his prescribed depth and down time. The morning dive had turned up some coins in an area Keith and Claire were going to delve into at a deeper depth with the airlift. Devereaux had been intent on returning to a rocky trough farther down the slope, but Dallas convinced him to work a shallower site near some ballast rocks that had shown promise.

Even with gloves, the work was rough on the hands. Though increasingly callused, Dallas's were usually raw and sore from constant contact with rocks and shells. He had taken to wearing a glove on his left hand for clawing into the bottom and keeping his right hand uncovered for better dexterity. It was easy to mistake small encrusted objects from the ship for rocks, especially if visibility was clouded by digging. That was the case with a softball-size chunk Dallas dislodged and nearly cast aside before his thumb slid over a smooth surface. On closer examination it turned out to be a clump of coins heavily encrusted. He couldn't immediately determine whether they were gold or silver, but in either case it was a nice chunk of change.

He slipped the conglomerate into a mesh goodie bag and continued probing the same area until his knuckles banged against something hard. Using both hands to scrape away loose material revealed an elongated shape that clearly was not the work of nature. He brushed away more sand and leaned in close until his facemask was inches away from what appeared to be a metallic tongue protruding from a gaping mouth in the ocean floor. Though still lodged, there was no apparent corrosion. Dallas's breathing quickened.

Silver hidden in the sand is easier to spot, its location often betrayed by tell-tale black spots from the oxidizing metal. Gold, on the other hand, refuses to bow to time or the elements. It remains as pure as the ace of hearts, a beacon of good fortune waiting to be dealt to a lucky hand.

This bar from the *Camelita's* deck — be it ace or joker — wasn't easily dislodged. But as Dallas scraped and poked, he could see that it wasn't the only one. The ends of at least two others were evident deeper in the sediment. Almost hyperventilating and beginning to feel light-headed, his mind raced with a rousing melody of an orchestra on a careening crescendo. He could see the bows of the violinists madly sawing strings, horns swaying violently, the cheeks of the players puffed out, and he nearly blacked out.

Dallas was familiar with so-called rapture of the deep, or nitrogen narcosis, the dangerously euphoric underwater high resulting from the intoxicating effect of breathing nitrogen under pressure. Had he been deeper he could have been in real danger, but at 85 feet his symptoms were more emotional than physiological. He retained the presence of mind to calm his breathing and regain his wits.

The gold bar wasn't going anywhere, so Dallas backed off. It was then that he realized Devereaux was no longer with him. Panic began to return until he spotted him moving away down the drop-off. With strong, steady strokes of his flippers, Dallas caught up quickly and spun Devereaux around with a yank on the arm. Later, he would recall the look in the man's eyes. It was one of confusion. If not for the discovery, anger would have compelled Dallas to haul the S.O.B. back to the boat right then.

Instead, he motioned for Devereaux to follow and pointed in the direction where the tongue of gold remained a taunting relic of the past. They were approaching the site when Dallas became aware of a noise emanating from above, the horn that was sounded from Levante any time the dredge spat out something important. He grabbed Devereaux's arm again and began scanning in the direction Claire and Keith had planned to work. Visibility was good and he spotted the arc of the airlift hose through the indigo column of water.

When they reached the spot, Keith had set aside the airlift, and he and Claire were carefully working on something in the sand. Claire looked up and gave a signal with her thumb and forefinger that divers often use to indicate everything is OK. Except that instead of touching the tip of the finger to her thumb, the finger was curled tighter so that the resulting 'O' was the size of the pupil of one of her green eyes. Dallas didn't immediately grasp what she was trying to convey, but one thing he could affirm with certainty later was that at that moment Devereaux was at his side. He would recall bumping his elbow against Devereaux's air tank as they both attempted to get a look at what Claire and Keith had uncovered.

It didn't look like much at first, a scattering of irregularly shaped fragments. Oh, crap, Dallas thought as he grabbed the corner of a jagged boulder to steady himself in the current, more busted pottery for Culpepper to salivate over. Just then Claire turned over the largest piece, a diaphragm-shaped shard the size of a saucer. When Keith started to reach for a nearby piece, she pushed his hand away and pointed to the spot that had been covered by the larger shard.

At first all Dallas saw were several dark spots on the sand, and he thought, silver sulfide stains, probably a buried trove of silver coins, likely pieces of eight. Then Claire reached down and picked up one of the spots, and it wasn't a spot at all. For a moment it didn't register. Then Devereaux's declaration came back to him: "Colombian rock candy, the greatest prize on these wrecks."

Dallas recalled the fire in the old treasure hunter's eyes the first time he'd said it. This time those eyes appeared blank, simply staring, not projecting any emotion when Dallas peered at them through the mask. But expressions, aside from panic, are difficult to read 100 feet below the surface.

Claire was picking up Colombian rock candy like spilled M&M's. Dallas wasn't sure how many — eight, maybe 10. He helped her contain them in a cloth sack they carried for objects that were too small for the mesh bags. When all the emeralds in sight were safely tucked away, they spent several minutes digging with their hands and turned up one more. They were all giddy, pawing in the sand amid a cacophony of bubbles from four scuba tanks — there were four of them, weren't there? It was like the ultimate grab bag conducted inside a giant champagne glass. And when all the loot was gone, they joined hands — Claire, Dallas and Keith — and did an underwater flapper dance, with flippers flailing and regulators spurting exhortations of joy like cartoon thought bubbles of Braille. Dallas caught a glimpse of Devereaux lurking nearby, watching. Dallas gave him a thumbs-up and he returned it, just before they headed for the surface.

#

Claire held up the sack and kept shouting, "Emeralds, emeralds, we found a shitload of emeralds!" Culpepper sounded long blasts of the horn. Keith scrambled aboard *Levante* shedding tank and fins and began dancing with the bikini girl. Dallas and Claire helped each other remove their tanks and joined the dance.

The dancing stopped abruptly when they were all struck by the same realization at about the same time McPeak voiced it.

"Hey, where's Captain Queeg?"

Dallas looked at Keith. They all looked at the water.

"Shit!"

As quickly as they could strap on tanks, Dallas and Keith were back over the side. Culpepper and Claire quickly followed.

Dallas felt as if a hand had been thrust down his throat and had his guts in a death grip. Would they find him in time? Would they even find him? Scuba diving is best approached deliberately with a clear head. In this situation haste took precedence over rationality. Success would depend in large part on luck. Thinking of the emeralds and the gold bar, Dallas could only hope the day's run of good fortune had a third strike remaining.

There had been no time to discuss even a cursory search plan, so Dallas devised his own during the descent: Find the wreck first, then look for Devereaux. Easier conceived than achieved in a frantic state. Dallas and Keith might as well have been descending to the surface of the moon, the bottom there all faceless sand and rock. The slope of the drop-off provided the only orientation of direction. Then they received their first break in the form of a distinctive rock formation.

Lech Walesa!

Dallas pointed it out to Keith, eliciting a nod. Both knew that from the home of the friendly grouper the upper reaches of the wreck could be found by swimming at about a 45-degree angle to the drop-off. They made the course correction and soon spotted one of the grids that Culpepper had staked out.

They separated and headed straight down the slope, Keith taking the right flank. Dallas checked his depth gauge. Eighty feet. That was about the depth where they found the emeralds. What were the odds of that discovery, one in a million? One in 10 million? About the same as finding a drinking fountain in the desert. The chance of locating a wayward treasure diver had to be considerably better. But would there be any life left in him? The odds grew steeper with each passing minute and additional foot of depth, now passing 100 feet.

They nearly missed him. The drop-off from the outer Keys reefs to the deep ocean is scored by numerous trenches carved by the unseen hand of the tidal flow. There was one between Dallas and Keith, and it was deeper than most. Keith had looked into it earlier. Now Dallas glanced at his partner. When he turned back, something caught his eye. It didn't register right away but it caused him to look again. He was about to turn away when it came again: a short burst of bubbles.

Devereaux was face-down in the crevice, hands on the bottom as if he were doing pushups. But he was motionless, the intermittent flurry of bubbles the only evidence of life. At least he still had air. Keith fumbled at the fastening of Devereaux's weight belt as Dallas hoisted him by the shoulders to an upright position. Just before they started for the surface, Devereaux's eyes opened slowly and he did something surprising. He winked. Then his eyes rolled back.

Dallas combed the memory banks from his diver training. All that came to mind was the ridiculous robot from the '60s sci-fi drama *Lost in Space*, arms flailing as it croaked, "Warning, warning, danger, extreme danger!" Got to keep a clear head. All three of them were in extreme danger. Dallas was exhausted from the work underwater and the frantic search. But he knew he must muster the energy and retain presence of mind.

Normally, ascending to the surface should be done at a controlled, deliberate rate of 60 feet per minute to enable gradual release of nitrogen absorbed during a dive. At that speed, a sightseeing pace, it would take them nearly two minutes to reach the surface. They needed to get there in seconds, not minutes. Very few bubbles were now gurgling from Devereaux's regulator. Suddenly the strident words of Dallas's former dive instructor, an ex-marine turned boat bum, came to him as loud and clear as if bellowed through the water with a bullhorn:

"If your air gauge is on empty and you're sucking fumes or your buddy is unconscious, there's one thing you've got to keep in mind: You don't have gills. You've got to have air, and sometimes the only way to get it is to go where the supply is unlimited. And you've got to get there *tout suite*, Buster!" Yes, the message was clear, because the instructor had said it not with the soft, fluid manner of the French, but with the sharp, attention-getting cadence of a marine drill sergeant. He roared: "Toot sweet, Buster!!"

Keith was giving him an urgent thumb's up, like Siskel or Ebert offering a ringing endorsement to a sequel of *The Deep*. Right, toot sweet. Dallas seized Devereaux's air tank and looked up at the faintly glowing picture window to the promised land. Damn, it appeared worlds away. He began kicking toward it, thinking, exhale, exhale, expecting at any moment to feel the explosion in his chest that would be his lungs bursting.

The light was getting brighter, the window larger and he felt incredibly light, even with the burden of the weight he was toting. It was as if they were ascending all the way to the clouds. The thought occurred to him, maybe this is how it felt to be a soul released from the restraints of the flesh. Maybe we're already dead.

CHAPTER 31

Dallas and Devereaux burst into daylight like a pair of Polaris missiles powered by AA batteries, but not the one with the bunny. They rose above the surface to chest level amid a flurry of spray and settled back. Keith popped up a moment later. Dallas and Keith looked at Devereaux, then at each other. Now what?

"Don't you know how?"

A voice from the boat was followed by a splash. It was the girl swimming toward them. *Tami? Sandi? Bambi? What?*

"Steady him while I get him in a do-si-do," she said, slipping her left arm under Devereaux's left arm to support his neck in the classic rescue embrace.

Do-si-do she did, this bathing beauty turned Wonder Woman cutting in on the dance of death. She went immediately to work performing mouth-to-mouth resuscitation while Dallas and Keith could do little more than watch in amazement. *Cindi, Barbi, Candi? What the hell's her name?*

Difficult to say how long it took. Seconds seemed like minutes. Claire and Culpepper returned to the surface and joined the vigil. Doubt began to creep in. *Too late? Damn, were we too late?* Then, like a flooded outboard motor, Devereaux began to sputter to life. A twitch. A cough. A gag. Then he puked. It was simultaneously a disgusting and beautiful sight. Dallas felt elation laced with nausea.

At least the mess was in the water. At least the bastard was alive!

"Amber, that was incredible? How did you learn that?" Keith said, after they lifted Devereaux aboard *Levante*.

"Actually — God, believe it or not, I learned it in Girl Scouts. But I worked as a lifeguard a couple summers ago."

Dallas sat on the gunwale, dazed and suddenly enlightened. So it wasn't an end-in-i name after all. It was fossilized sap, neither of which applied to this young woman.

Sometimes, you just can't tell about people.

#

Dallas was in a fortuitous spot when he recognized the symptoms of the bends, in the waiting room outside the multi-unit recompression chamber at Miami's Mercy Hospital where Devereaux was being treated for a severe case of decompression sickness and complications from the rapid ascent. Dallas had flown with him in the giant condor of a Coast Guard chopper that swooped down to pluck Devereaux like a water-logged rat from the cockpit of *Levante*. Devereaux was conscious though in distress as they flew at low altitude to avoid stoking the nitrogen bubbles that numbed his extremities. His expression remained mostly blank, but at one point in the journey his eyes locked on Dallas's for a moment, then looked away.

Keith took *Levante* back to Snapper Cove and drove with Claire to Miami. Only when the three of them were reunited and there was nothing left to do did Dallas acknowledge that what he'd been feeling since the rescue was more than exhaustion. His ears resounded with a bumblebee symphony. He'd been flexing his fingers for the past hour, trying to chase away a tingling sensation that made them seem detached from his hands. He'd been pacing nonstop until his knees felt like celery left on the table overnight, and he plunked down hard on the nearest chair.

"You OK?"

He looked at Claire, and her words seemed to come through an echo chamber, her face appeared distorted as if he were viewing it through a wide-angle lens. His heart was pounding. He looked at Keith. If a black man can appear wan, Keith was a Michael Jackson shade of pale. Dallas tried to speak; his throat felt so dry.

"Y-you look like I feel, and I feel like shit."

"Man, it's the deep. Deep Mother Ocean got its grip on us. I think we're bent."

#

In the solitude of the chamber the only sound was his own breathing, long and labored as if being drawn through a garden hose. The source seemed so far away and the tendency was to hyperventilate. *Stay calm, you'll be all right.* Four hours in the chamber, how much time remaining? The Doc said 285 minutes. What's that — four times 60, ah, yeah, another 45 minutes?

Dallas felt like the Kafka character in *Metamorphosis*, a man morphing into a bug. Was it noticeable yet? His mind playing tricks on him, sucking on that hose, trying to maintain his wits. Drifting, fading, into a gauzy state of consciousness, seeing himself transformed into a butterfly, bright yellow with black spots, flitting up and out of the chamber, into the bright sunlight. Feeling liberated, more free than he'd ever imagined. Savoring the warmth of the sun and the soothing sound of the birds. Then a harsh sound, alarming, drowning out the birds just as something massive, moving fast, eclipsed the sunlight. Then — spat ! — he was flattened against the blunt face of a Peterbilt.

CHAPTER 32

In the shroud of darkness before dawn, a figure dressed in black strode quickly from an executive jet to a waiting Mercedes limo. Ramon Ortega nodded toward the driver but didn't utter a word on the 20-minute ride to a luxury apartment on the outskirts of Caracas, Venezuela. The limo stopped outside a rear entrance where a tight-lipped man with a firm handshake led him to a service elevator, which took them to a 16th-floor apartment where they were greeted by another serious-looking man. The door clicked shut and the three of them stood for a tense moment before another door until it opened and a man in a red silk bathrobe entered the room.

Ramon usually wasn't any more forthcoming with his smiles than with his innermost thoughts. When he did offer one, it was an event to behold, transforming his face into a beacon of joy. It was enough to soften the expressions of his two silent escorts, who exchanged a glance as they watched the visitor embrace the man in the robe.

"Bro!"

"Nene!"

For a moment it appeared the two men might dance. They kissed each other on the cheek.

"You haven't called me that in a long time. I used to hate it."

"I know; it made you want to kick my ass. I stopped saying it once I knew you could."

"It's music to my ears right now. But don't make a habit of it."

Jorge Ortega laughed more heartily than perhaps at any moment since before his internment and hugged his brother again. His two bodyguards grinned then looked away.

"Come on, you must be hungry. Breakfast is waiting on the balcony."

They sat at a table set for two with a view of Venezuela's largest city as it tossed off the blanket of slumber. The distant buzz of traffic was not unpleasant, rather like background music. A young woman with finely-chiseled features and light coffee-colored skin poured orange juice for each of them from a glass pitcher and topped it off with champagne from a bottle she uncorked at tableside.

"I know it's early, but this is special. The juice makes it acceptable," Jorge said with a smile, raising his glass to toast his brother.

"It's good to see you happy again. The Caymans might have been more fun for you, but this is less conspicuous."

"This is paradise after what I was going through. I had to get off that island. I felt like a castaway. Here, I feel the pulse of life again. I look out, I see a city. It's vibrant. On the island, all I heard were the sounds of my own thoughts. It was deafening. I was going crazy."

The girl returned with a tray loaded with steaming food — piles of sausages, eggs scrambled and wrapped in soft tortillas, plantains and the obligatory refried beans alongside bowls of fresh berries and sliced melons. Ramon was starved, and he plowed through his food so quickly it made his brother grin.

"Do you feel safe here?" Ramon asked, finally giving his fork a rest.

"It's worth the risk. I go to the casino. It's not glitzy, but it's private, very exclusive. It's perfect."

"Have fun but don't blow a fortune."

"No, man, I'm winning. Last night, *mucho dinero*. You should have seen me at the craps table. The dice must have been named Ortega. I'd look at them in my hand and it was like an animal with eyes peering up at me, saying, 'You name it, we roll it for you.' It was crazy fun. People started crowding around. I decided I better leave before I attracted too much attention."

"Just be careful."

Jorge nodded. "It's OK. I got people looking out for me here."

"Maybe you should just stay here. Forget about this other thing."

Jorge frowned and stared out at the city. Finally, he said, "No, this is to give me my sanity back. But it's not forever. The other, that is something to live for. To be able to go home again. To be one of the ones to make it happen. To break the stranglehold. No, my brother, I have thought about it long and hard. God knows I've had time to think, and I am certain this is my purpose. I feel it in my blood."

Ramon had finished eating and was sipping his mimosa. He set the glass down and leaned forward, elbows on the table.

"Then I should tell you, we've gotten a response from Havana. Sounds positive. That Hawke, he's a turd, but his connections are genuine."

"You can't speak of him without letting your feelings surface."

"I hate him. But he's necessary."

"I know about feelings you can't discard. I hate the bearded devil like that."

"Maybe you'll get to tell him that yourself."

"Can it happen?"

"Hawke had a face-to-face meeting with certain key liaisons in Mexico City. They flew in to meet him. I'm not talking about intermediaries, this is a direct link to the top. It's the first sign they're taking the bait. Like we suspected, he's desperate for *dinero*."

"So much for the socialist ideal. So what's next?"

"We wait. Wait for him to swallow the hook. No way to rush it. We wait for the next response. You keep going to the casino."

"I'll take you there later. It's been too long since we played together, like brothers. You'll bring me more luck."

The girl returned to freshen their drinks. They waited until she walked away, their eyes following the fluid sway of her hips. Jorge winked at Ramon.

"See, it's nice here."

Ramon set his glass down and looked away. "I can't stay. I wish I could. It's like when we were younger. I always wanted to play. You always had to go. Now I have to go. Got to be in Key West tonight. We're running the new boat in the morning. The race is Saturday."

"Are you feeling up to it?"

"I'm aching for it. We tested the boat last week. It's killer. The best one yet. I can't wait to get out there and blow everyone away."

Jorge toasted his brother again. "You make me proud, Nene. Just promise me that one day you will slow down long enough for us to play together again. Like brothers."

#

"I still can't get over the way that girl jumped in the water and got Skeeter breathing again. I'm not sure he would have made it otherwise."

"He wouldn't have made it if you hadn't brought him up. You and Keith."

Dallas was stretched out on the bed in his duplex, Claire giving him the backrub she had promised on the ride home from Miami.

"You thought she was just a bimbo in a bikini," he said.

She slapped him on the shoulder.

"So did you."

"People are full of surprises."

"Are you disappointed she wasn't just a bimbo?"

He laughed.

"Course not, I'm happy. I've been to the abyss in the shadow of death and now I'm back here with you. How could I be anything but happy."

"You must be, you're whistling. I never heard you whistle before."

He whistled louder.

"Singing in the Rain?"

He whistled the tune slower, dragging out the end of each phrase of the melody while tapping out the beat on the mattress with his fingers.

"Why that?"

"It's been in my head ever since I got out of the chamber. The Doc examined me and said, 'Looks like you won't need any further treatment. You're cured.' All I could think of was Alex at the end of 'A Clockwork Orange.' It's a great relief to go through something traumatic like that and be told you're cured."

"You gave us a scare for a while."

"Scared the hell out of me."

He began whistling again, playfully.

"Glad you're back to yourself again, my little Alex. Just don't be coming after me with a giant alabaster penis."

He rolled over onto his side and took her hand into his.

"How about this one?"

"Hmmm. Pretty scary."

She began to whistle the tune.

"You don't have to whistle," he said. "If you want, you can hum."

CHAPTER 33

Dallas wheeled into Key West late Saturday morning, parked the Great White on a side street and hiked over to Duval, America's most forlorn main thoroughfare on any weekend morning, where even the T-shirts in the schlock shops droop like hangovers from the night before. At Sloppy Joe's bar, a shirtless employee wearing rubber boots was washing away the residue of Friday night with a hose and push broom. The stench wafting through the open doors was enough to gag a junkyard cat, and it wouldn't have been surprising to see a couple of leftover drunks swept out along with the cigarette butts, plastic cups and one jumbo pair of panties. The guy with the broom, clenching the stub of a cheroot in his teeth, shrugged at the quizzical expression Dallas gave the panties and kept sweeping. In Key West, you learn not to question the absurd. In most cases the sordid details of a no-tell night are best left to fade in the sobering sunlight and head-clearing ocean breeze.

Dallas kept walking toward the waterfront. The only vibrant signs of life were the clipboard-toting men and women already out hawking time-share resorts and sunset cruises, and a smattering of polyester tourists from the day's first cruise ship arrival. However, this was not to be a typical groggy Key West Saturday, given to gradual nursing of headaches in preparation to another full-bore, all-night assault on brain cells. The rude awakening for the night people would come at noon when a fleet of offshore powerboat racers were due to roar through the harbor to start the Hog's Breath Last Resort 100. Dallas was there to document it for *Florida Nautique*, whose publisher, Kirby D'Arbonnell, was coming in for the race.

"They're comping me at Casa Marina," D'Arbonnell said on the phone. "Might as well show up and act like a publisher. You got it covered, dude. You're the man. You do the wordsmithing. I'll be there — what do they say? — networking. That's it, networking."

By 11 the stupor of the morning was broken by the clatter of helicopters and distant thunder of high-performance engines revving in the former Navy submarine basin at the western tip of the island that was being used as a pit area for the race boats. Dallas went directly to the Pier House to pick up his media credential in the press room. His morning brightened considerably when he was issued his I.D. badge and a complimentary Bloody Mary by Maureen, a perky public relations assistant in white open-collar Izod shirt and shorts, who appeared relieved to break away from a serious-looking Italian journalist.

"He's asking me questions about carburetion and prop torque, and I'm thinking, 'What the hell is he torquing about?' I don't know carburetion from crab claws, but I do know we're going to have a boatload of those at the after-race party," Maureen said with a conspiratorial wink, which was her ingratiating habit.

She pointed out the room where the party would be held while leading Dallas outside to a second-story deck overlooking the harbor that had been set aside as a media and VIP viewing platform.

"There's a yacht anchored out in the harbor that you can go out on if you want. If you ask me, you're better off staying right here. At least, if you're like me. I get woozy on the water and it makes me just want to go to sleep. That's why I like when they race here: You can see just fine from shore."

Key West was the offshore racing circuit's most viewer-friendly stop, which included this early-season race and the world championships in November. The broad channel of Key West Harbor was the crossing point of a figure-eight shaped course that would be traversed four times. The boats would zoom past within 100 yards of the seawall at the end of each loop.

Dallas established his command post at the corner of the rail closest to the portable bar and made the key decision of the morning, switching from Bloody Mary to rum-and-orange. Ah, the grueling life of a motorsports writer. He took a sip and scribbled an entry in his notebook: "High-octane fuel is *de rigeur* to compete in this crowd, and the boats consume a small part of it."

"Hey, I see you're wasting no time sampling the flavor of the event."

Dallas felt a hearty slap on the back and turned to find a beaming Kirby D'Arbonnell, wearing a Hawaiian shirt, Ray-Bans and a grin as wide as the harbor. And why not, Kirby had an arm around a raven-haired beauty half a head taller than himself, which made her a little over 6 feet, heel-aided.

"Dallas, my man, this is Loaiza, our genuine girl from Ipanema. Well, close enough, anyway. From Rio, but she's strutted her stuff on all the beaches there, haven't you, darlin'? Loaiza's going to be our September cover. We shot a killer spread of her for the bonefish feature you're doing for us. Wait'll you see the cover shot. She's got a fish on the line and the shot is from behind; all she's wearing is a thong, no top — but of course you don't see anything up front. The headline says: 'The big bone rises.' "

D'Arbonnell laughed loudly. The woman looked bemused and slightly embarrassed.

"I'm not sure my story can measure up to that. Maybe you should just run the pictures," Dallas said.

"No, man, no. We're a legitimate outdoors magazine. But if the pictures enhance the appeal of the words, more the better. Our competitors and the bluenoses are the only ones who don't like it. But I've noticed, more bikinis are starting to show up in prominent places in some of the more traditional boat and fish mags. So, we must be doing something right."

As different as they were in personality, Dallas and Kirby shared at least one thing in common: Neither was a stranger to failure. The difference was D'Arbonnell didn't acknowledge his as setbacks, but rather as jumping off points to the next grand scheme. In a sense, that was an admirable trait. Being a realist was a curse, Dallas concluded. Maybe it was better to sail along as a happy idiot.

D'Arbonnell was set to sail out to the VIP boat with Loaiza to bask in his role as yachtsman publisher. But first he had some words to offer as editor.

"Look, we want you to build this piece around Ramon Ortega. The whole macho Latin brother of the infamous fugitive escape artist thing, and the bold comeback from the near-fatal accident angle. All that sexy stuff," he said, with a wink. "Our photog has an in with Ortega's crew and got some really bitchin' stuff around the new boat. He was there when Ortega blew in yesterday to test it. You should see his entourage. A scary bunch, that is."

Bitchin'. Dallas hadn't heard that since he roomed with a shortstop/surfer dude in Class A ball.

"So you're not looking so much for a story on the race as an expose on Ortega."

"That's it, man. You can even work in some flashback stuff of the brother's escape: the Coast Guard cutter blowing up, the brother's mysterious disappearance. What a break you were a witness to that."

"I didn't see it all that well. It was pretty far away."

"Whatever, you were there. You saw the explosion. Play it up. Milk it, man. Listen, the newspapers are going to tell everyone tomorrow about who won the race. And really, who outside of a small circle of motorheads gives a crap who wins a boat race, anyway. We're talking about intrigue on the high seas. Crashes, explosions, bad guys busting out and vanishing. And right here you've got the suave, sexy link to it all on display. We want you to bore in on Ortega. See if you can get under his skin, so to speak. The feds are supposedly all over the place watching him, trying to get a lead on his brother. There's even a rumor the boat called *Black Sabbath* is an FBI entry. Talk about putting a tail on someone."

"More like a roostertail," Dallas said. "If the crew is a couple fat guys armed with a box of doughnuts and smoking cigarettes, we'll know they're on stakeout."

"That's funny. That's good. See, that's why you're the writer. I know you'll come through, 'cause you're the man. Seeing as how you've got everything under control at this end, me and Loaiza are going to go mingle with the beautiful folks, assess the quality of the daiquiris and slurp a few oysters. Who knows where that will lead." Another wink.

"Keep your eyes open," Dallas called after him. "Maybe you'll run into Ortega's brother disguised as a waiter."

If only the race were as entertaining as D'Arbonnell. The most noteworthy scene on the water would actually occur a few minutes before the start when a Boston Whaler piloted by someone who was a ringer for singer Jimmy Buffett dashed through the harbor with two young women passengers, and all three peeled down their shorts and mooned the wharf. Probably another FBI plant.

As usual, the race was 30 seconds of spectacular commotion followed by two hours of boredom until the post-race party. When the fleet blasted by at the start, Dallas got a glimpse of the flashy new *Muy Caliente*, vivid red with gold trim, on the far side of the Superboat pack. Sure enough, the ominous-looking *Black Sabbath* was close behind. When they returned after the first 25-mile loop, *Muy Caliente* was comfortably ahead, its sleek hull carving a compact arc of spray. When Ortega passed the waterfront, a raucous cheer resounded from several packed balconies on the top floor of the adjacent waterfront resort.

"The Cuban contingent," said a television reporter standing near Dallas as his cameraman tried to zoom in on Ortega's cheering section.

Dallas opened his notebook and made a notation that *Black Sabbath* was following a discreet quarter-mile behind.

"I see you're actually hard at work. I'm impressed." It was Maureen carrying a tray with several frozen drinks. "Have one. It'll help get the creative process flowing. Or maybe not. But they're good, so have one anyway."

Dallas accepted a pina colada and chatted for a few minutes until a fellow with more hair showing around a too-tight tank top than on his head, mistaking Maureen for a waitress, said, "Hey sweetie, how about some liquor?"

Without hesitation, Maureen said, "I don't even know her," and went off looking for other accredited media members to dispense the remaining drinks.

An hour into the race, Dallas was engaged in a conversation about the differences in sporting interests between Europe and the United States with a Belgian woman who wrote for a French magazine. She asserted that Americans were unsophisticated because they didn't appreciate the subtleties of a sport like soccer. He argued that Americans had more interesting games to occupy them and that soccer was simply a Third World pastime. She became quite agitated at that point, and Dallas was certain he was being cursed but couldn't determine in which language.

Her male companion interjected that Europeans follow auto races for the skill and strategies involved while Americans only watch in the hope of seeing a crash. Dallas decided it was best not to mention his own experience at the Indy 500, spent in a drunken haze on the infield. He had paid about as much attention to that race as he was paying to this one. He had ceased looking up each time a boat passed in what had deteriorated into a high-decibel parade. He had the balcony crowd to draw his attention to the comings and goings of *Muy Caliente*, which by mid-race was no longer being tailed by *Black Sabbath*. Eventually, there was a radio report that the black boat had broken down off Sand Key — another setback for the pursuit of justice.

After Ortega crossed the finish line and completed a victory lap of the harbor, Dallas followed the crowd a block down Front Street to the yacht basin next to the Galleon Resort where the racers would dock. There were loud cheers and whistles as *Muy Caliente* eased into its slip. The three crew members emerged from their enclosed cockpit capsules like astronauts returning from a mission of genuine consequence. A race official hopped aboard and presented Ortega with a checkered flag the size of a beach towel. He promptly draped it around the shoulders of the first member of his bikini brigade to reach his side on the deck of the race boat and plant a ruby-red stamp of her lips on his cheek. Two of her cohorts quickly followed, and they staged a mock tug-of-war over the flag until a member of their support crew herded the three of them into a tight triad and blanketed them with the sacred cloth of the motor sports world, to the delight of dockside photographers.

Ortega, now bearing the complete set of lipstick prints, stood close and beamed like a conquering hero. To the victor go the spoils — red-haired, blonde and brunette. Dallas scribbled in his notebook, "Hail, Pseudo Caesar, the fastest fucker afloat." He noticed that Ortega had his thumbs hooked inside the back of the bikini bottoms of the women who had maneuvered into position on his flanks — the dark-haired one whose Latin features and coloring matched Ortega's and the blonde who provided a pleasing contrast. Dallas glanced around and noted looks of envy on faces in the crowd, men and women alike. The throttleman and the navigator were left to share the attention of the redhead in the silver bikini. All of this cozy affection made Dallas think of Claire, stirring a sensation of emptiness and longing that surprised him. How does the rootless soul resolve, let alone recognize, the symptoms of homesickness?

A dockside news conference ensued, though it was less an interrogation than a paying of homage. The small media contingent had to compete with the questions and compliments shouted by the adoring throng that had come to praise the

Twentieth Century conquistador. Ortega was impossibly smug about the performance of himself and crew, and the wonders of his new boat.

The victory was, in his words, "The logical step in an evolution, like when a baby goes from walking to running."

"When did you know you had it won?"

"Once we saw how the boat was running: yesterday during testing." The crowd whooped and chortled. Ortega shrugged. "It's what we expected. Believe me, the best is still to come."

Someone asked if he was at all concerned about "that black boat, *Black Sabbath*." Ortega flashed a wicked smile and rolled his eyes, suggesting he'd heard the rumors, too.

"They were of no consequence. All we were looking at out there was open water. Really, this was just a joy ride for us, a good, fast pleasure cruise."

More hoots of approval. More shouts of "Ortega rules!"

Dallas felt uncomfortable standing on a floating pier that swayed under the weight of more people than it was intended to support. It would have been justice if they all spilled into the water, and Dallas would have gladly taken the plunge if it put an end to the nonsense he was hearing. He waited until even Ortega became bored by the adoration before blurting out his question.

"Ramon, in light of how well your new boat ran, would you like a rematch with the experimental boat that gave you trouble at Islamorada? I think it's called a skimmer."

Ortega leveled him a look of such malevolence that it stunned and silenced the mob on the pier. His eyes were so dark, the stare so intense that Dallas rocked back slightly on his heels. For an instant he felt as if he were looking into the center of evil itself. For Dallas, it struck a distant chord, an unsettling sensation that was somehow familiar but elusive. He forced himself to hold the pose of the cocky reporter, but he wouldn't forget the impact of that stare.

Ortega regained his composure enough to mutter, "There's nobody on this circuit that we fear. All we have to do is take care of business. We don't have to prove nothing to nobody." He gave a slight nod and stepped from the boat onto the floating dock as his entourage formed a wedge through the mob. Dallas found himself backed precariously to the edge of the narrow passageway. There was a splash and a shout. He recognized the victim as the baldish gent with the hairy chest who had tried to bum a drink from Maureen. Hey buddy, how about some liquor?

#

The procession of the powerboat prince wended its way through a gantlet of handshakes and kisses to the Galleon, an exclusive waterfront resort, where one wing of the third floor had been set aside as his lair for the weekend. Several burly, serious-looking men in black T-shirts stood sentinel to sift those who were welcome to join the party from those who were not.

Ortega went to the main hospitality room, where he accepted a gin-and-tonic and met briefly with his inner circle. More hugs, more handshakes. When everyone who required his immediate attention was appeased, he took the blonde in the yellow bikini by the hand and slipped away to his private suite. Seeing them depart, Regina, the dark-haired woman, stormed out to the balcony, where she smoked a cigarette and was consoled by a gaggle of young women, most of them head-turning attractive in their own right.

Ortega emerged 45 minutes later and went to another suite at the end of the hall, where Edison Hawke III had just finished working over a bowl of steamers and was lighting a cigar.

"Have a Cohiba," Hawke said, "to celebrate your victory. A shame your brother couldn't be here to enjoy it, too." Ortega took the cigar but didn't light it.

"I saw him Thursday. He's happy to hear of the progress."

Ortega stopped, startled by the sudden appearance of another figure in the room. "I didn't expect . . ."

"I know, I know, I probably should have told you. But I didn't know myself until a couple days ago," Hawke said. "Things are happening fast. We've got a little situation up in Islamorada. The boss thought it best if he looked into it himself."

"A problem with the sub?"

"It's not a big deal, really."

"Did you work it out?"

"We delivered a message that should make everything a lot clearer."

Ortega turned to the other man, who had not yet spoken. He recalled the smoke ring hovering over that little island in the Bahamas the last time they met Lagarto.

"Any further developments I should know about? Anything clearer on the timetable?"

"What you need to know is to be ready, to be flexible. There is no timetable when you're dealing with this type of hierarchy. Based on indications, we're moving at the speed of light. Which means it still could take weeks, months, or not happen at all. We may not know for sure until the last minute. The window of opportunity, when it comes, won't be wide. And it likely will only open once."

"Are you still committed to this?"

The temperature seemed to rise in the room from the intensity of Lagarto's glare. "Are you?"

"Without question," Ortega said, coolly, his jaw set firm.

"Then be ready."

Ortega held the other man's gaze for several seconds, staring into those cold, bottomless eyes. Recalling the first time he saw them, in the hospital, and how they unnerved him. This time he sensed some sort of mutual understanding pass between them. This time he didn't blink.

#

Dallas had his fill of cold shrimp and crab claws at the after-race party. The friend of the Belgian journalist cornered him and was filling his ears with some dreadful motorhead rap, something about how the European champion's diesel-powered boat would ultimately prove superior to the faster American boats because of its greater reliability and endurance. Dallas's eyes began to glass over.

"It's like the old story. You know, the tortoise always beats the hare. You come back here for the World Championships in November and you'll see. The rabbit never learns."

Dallas leaned close to the chap's face — *ugh, nice breath!* — and said, "I'll tell you what I'd like to see, I'd like to see them all sink."

How to deal with a bore, rule No. 1: Leave him speechless. Exit quickly. Dallas paused only for a quick goodbye and thanks to Maureen. She gave him a wink and a pat on the shoulder.

He walked out the door and nearly headlong into Kirby D'Arbonnell and the lovely Loaiza.

"Dallas, my man, how'd it go? Did you get your interview with Ortega? New boat's impressive, huh?"

"I got to ask him what I wanted to. How was the VIP boat?"

D'Arbonnell was slightly red-faced. The woman appeared more animated than before. When Dallas caught her eye she giggled and clutched D'Arbonnell's arm tighter.

"A publisher's work never ends," D'Arbonnell said with a shrug. "It never hurts to spread the gospel about your publication when there's money around. Maybe it'll pay off in ad revenue." He shrugged again. "Hey, don't forget, I've got to have this story by Wednesday. Deadline's bearing down on us. By the way, here's something else you can check out while you're here — as long as I'm already paying expenses. Might turn into another story. Sounds kinky." He winked and handed Dallas a folded slip of paper.

Whole lot of winking going on here, he thought. Must be the influence of noisy boats and full-fuel boat drinks.

#

Dallas found a phone booth, rang Claire's number and got her recorded voice saying, "Sorry you missed me. Leave a message and I'll try to make it up to you." Could mean she and Keith had gone to Miami to bring Devereaux home. Hearing her voice brightened his mood.

"You're right, I miss you, from head to toe and all stops in between," he said into the phone. "Soon as I get back, I'll make it up to *you*."

Key West was in full Saturday afternoon clamor. Dallas nearly stepped off the curb into the path of the Conch Train, the ubiquitous sightseeing tram. The driver tinkled the bell and waggled his finger as Dallas jumped back. Another cruise ship was in and tourists were swarming the shops on Duval like ants crashing a bake sale. Amped-up music blared from all the bars packed with cookie-cutter patrons, the anonymous alcoholic army, every soldier clad in standard issue T-shirt, shorts and armed with a plastic cup filled with amber liquid. Many of them raised their cups in salute as a trio of motorcycles rumbled past.

Dallas looped back to the Galleon and took the elevator to the top floor, thinking he'd drop in on Ortega's party, pay his respects to the victorious crew. First he had to get past the welcoming party stationed in the hallway leading to the block of suites leased to the so-called Cuban contingent. They were a couple of cheery Latino fellows in tight, black shirts, impeccably polite with well-groomed mustaches, well-pumped muscles and fully-contrived smiles.

Bouncer 1: "How ya doing, friend?"

Dallas: "Fine, thanks."

He took a half step, then realized he'd be whistled for charging if he took another.

Bouncer 1: "Sorry, this is a private party."

Dallas: "No problem. I just wanted to offer my congratulations to Ramon — Mr. Ortega."

Bouncer 1: "Who can I say stopped by?"

Dallas hesitated. He glanced at the other tough guy, who was bigger than the first. Until a muscle in his jaw twitched, he could have passed for a mannequin. What the hell, it was a long shot anyway.

Dallas: "Actually, I'm from *Florida Nautique* magazine. I was hoping to talk to Mr. Ortega about his new boat. That was a very impressive performance out there today."

Bouncer 1: "You're with the press?"

His smile turned to incredulity. His partner's smile vanished instantly as he piped in with a variation of a classic movie line. It wasn't original, but Dallas had to admit it got the point across.

Bouncer 2: "Press? Ramon don't need no stinking press. He already made his statement today."

Dallas: "Guess it would be out of the question to ask for some *hors d'oeuvre* then, huh."

#

The only glimpse of Ortega's party would come from the seawall outside the building. Dallas peered up at the row of balconies along the third floor cluttered with people, Ortega's gang having a high time on a high-octane Key West Saturday afternoon. Lots of laughter and swaying to loud Latin music.

Dallas stood for several minutes staring up at the celebration, vaguely aware of a feeling of emptiness that comes from being excluded. Not that this was a crowd he could have blended in with, nor wanted to. No, there was something else. Suddenly, he felt extremely uncomfortable. His ears were ringing and it gradually dawned on him that he wasn't the only one spying. There was another set of eyes peering intently, and they were focused on him.

Dallas hadn't paid attention to the top-floor balcony closest to him because of all the commotion on the others. This one was empty except for a solitary figure glaring down. The man was older, heavyset. It wasn't so much his expression that was daunting, it was the weight of his gaze. Certain people are difficult to look in the eyes. Even from this distance Dallas could tell this was one of them. In the moment their eyes met, Dallas experienced the sort of lightheadedness that can be triggered by craning one's neck to look upward at a sharp angle. But it was more than simple vertigo.

The man removed a cigar butt from his lips, and with a quick flick of two fingers flipped it off the balcony. The butt hit the concrete with an audible thump, bounced and rolled into a small puddle a few feet in front of Dallas, where it died with a hiss that released an acrid blend of smoke and steam. When Dallas glanced up at the balcony again, the man was gone. He turned and walked briskly away as a chill passed along his spine.

CHAPTER 34

Dallas had spent many lonely Saturday nights in more ports than he could recall on a bet. Occasionally he'd found company for pleasure. Often he found company in a bottle. As hazy as some of the memories were, he could say without a doubt he'd never before found company with a gay fishing club. Where else but Key West? Damn that D'Arbonnell.

He'd thought about driving back to Islamorada, less than 90 minutes away. But then what? If Claire was back from Miami, he knew she was supposed to work late. So what the hell, he had a room that was paid for the night. And there was the possibility of another Ortega encounter in the morning. So he unfolded the paper that D'Arbonnell had given him. On it was printed: Martin Mayfair, Rainbow Ventures Fishing Club. He shrugged and dialed the number.

#

Sunset in Key West. Party time. Camera-toting tourists jamming the pier at Mallory Square for the nightly rocky picture show of local color. Red sky merely a background mural for a discordant troupe of three-quarter-time players who collect their pay in upside-down top hats and guitar cases. Sassy jugglers. Card tricksters. Esoteric musicians playing a concerto on homemade-looking instruments; some kind of washboard thing with about 80 strings. A Frenchman exhorting common housecats to jump through flaming hoops and walk tightropes. Career hippies selling leather goods and weaving floppy hats out of palm fronds. And always the cookie lady on her bicycle pedaling "Key West sweets, Key West treats, buy one and we both can eat."

Dallas had done sundown Key West style years before when it was a spontaneous, funky celebration of the end of the day. It had evolved into something contrived, a happening turned into a scheduled event. If a cruise ship was at the pier, you were hard-pressed to even get a glimpse of the sun kissing the horizon.

Just as well that while most visitors to the island were ushering the day out — Ortega's crowd raised glasses in salute from their balconies — Dallas was several blocks away in the quaint lobby of a guest house sampling another Key West Saturday sundown tradition. A group of men, some lounging on a couple of sofas, others sitting Indian style on a finely polished hardwood floor, was listening intently while Martin Mayfair's companion Daniel (never Dan or Danny) played and sang at an elegant white piano. Lots of Sinatra and show tunes interspersed with classical standards, some Elton John hits and a just-for-grins Buffett medley played with exaggerated lounge-lizard panache. Not much of it Dallas's taste, but there was no denying the guy could play.

"I'm the practical one, he's the talented one," Mayfair said, explaining his partnership with Daniel, which included the operation of the guesthouse. "I keep everything running, he keeps everyone coming back. He's got a real knack with the rod, too. I mean, you'll see."

Dallas raised an eyebrow, grateful he'd been given a seat of honor in a soft, overstuffed chair, alone. That, along with a skull-numbing rosy-red rum punch, helped ease the awkwardness of the setting. He had to admit, the hospitality sure beat what Ortega's henchmen were offering. No limit to the *hors d'oeuvres* here, a tasty assortment of cheeses, crepes and crackers. The little cocktail weenies made Dallas squeamish, though.

This was all designed to put the boys in the mood for ... fishing?

"It makes it more social," Mayfair explained. "Gives us a place to meet and get an attitude adjustment before we go."

After the music there was a short ceremony recognizing the outstanding catches of the past month. Among them, Mayfair had taken a 30-pound permit on fly that was leading the Key West Fishing Tournament, a serious competition contested in six-month increments. "I've been dreaming of that fish for months," Mayfair confided. Afterward, they all headed to the harbor, Dallas bouncing around in the back of a pickup with three other fellows.

Three hours later, as he reeled in another vermilion snapper, it dawned on Dallas that the trepidation he had started the outing with was gone. And why not? What could be more relaxing way to spend a sultry Florida summer night than drift-fishing over the reefs with a couple boatloads of fishing buddies? He might have preferred more of a mixed crowd. But, hey, these guys were pleasant and engaging.

"Is this a typical night out for you guys?"

"Yeah," Mayfair said, sarcastically, "what did you expect we did out here all night, slap the mackerel in unison? We're fishermen who just happen to share a certain lifestyle. But we're dedicated to the sport."

"We're just a bunch of guys who enjoy cutting bait together," Daniel said with a snicker.

It dawned on Dallas that it may have been the first fishing trip he'd been on that was void of overt sex talk, save for an occasional wry innuendo.

"It shouldn't surprise you that a bunch of Key West queens would be good at bottom fishing," Daniel said, evoking more snickers.

"You must come back in the winter when the big tarpon are in the harbor," said a guy with short-cropped blond hair named Phil. "That's our favorite time. Those fish are such brutes."

What set an outing with the Rainbow Ventures Fishing Club apart from other fishing groups? Non-stop jazz on the boat's stereo, for one thing. Perhaps a bit more laughter. And it was the first time Dallas had attended a wine-and-cheese party on an all-night fishing trip. This crew didn't shy away from serious snacking.

There was an uncomfortable moment on the way back to the harbor. The two boats were cruising single-file in Southwest Channel when Daniel suddenly grabbed the wheel away from Mayfair and wrenched it hard to the right.

"I see him, I see him."

"It looks like our friend. I'm not in the mood to tangle with them again."

Dallas didn't see the boat until it was almost abeam, a dark force bound for the open sea. As it swept past, the moonlight illuminated a familiar profile of a hull, and Dallas was overtaken by the same ominous feeling he'd experienced when the man on the balcony of the Galleon flipped the cigar butt in his direction.

"You know that boat?"

"Afraid so," Mayfair said. "We've had a couple brushes with them out here before. They tried to run us down one time."

"*Mary Lou II?* Is that the name?"

"That's it," Daniel said. "Not sure what their deal is. But strange things happen when they're around — like, gunfire and explosions."

"Really? You've seen that?"

"It's best to keep certain things you see out here to yourself," Mayfair said. "We just try to stay away from them. It's safer that way."

#

Before leaving Key West on Sunday morning, Dallas stopped for breakfast at Shorties, a cozy Duval Street diner that was like a fast-food theater with the grill as the stage. A couple of middle-aged American gothic cooks performed there, slinging hash and flipping flapjacks with the proud and practiced hands of master craftsmen. These guys looked like they could feed a battleship crew with shell fragments peppering the deck and never break an egg yolk. Probably did in their day. Not that they'd lost their touch. The hash was damn good and over-easy was just right, not runny. Coffee cut through the thick crust of too-little sleep. The waitresses were brassy but endearingly so. Dallas felt like applauding as he slapped down the tip and strolled out into the steamy morning feeling better than he could justify.

Just outside the door, squinting into the morning glare, he encountered one last Key West oddity. A little girl and her younger brother were studying with curiosity and trepidation a pair of 3½-foot long iguanas lounging on the saddle baskets of an otherwise nondescript Schwinn parked outside the restaurant.

"They're so ugly," the boy said.

"I think they're kind of cute. But weird," the girl said. "What are they?"

At that moment an elderly black man was passing by.

"Those belong to the Iguana Man, and you don't know what you're talking about, child," he said, stooping down next to the bicycle and stroking the head of one of the lizards. "They not weird, they wise. Because unlike little boys and girls, they don't make a sound. They just watch and learn from everything they see.

"These creatures have been on this earth millions of years. They've seen all the mysteries and know all the secrets. You could learn a lot from an iguana. Except he's not talking. Granddaddy iguana, he keeps everything he knows to hisself."

"These are a million years old? Even Gramps isn't that old," the boy said, incredulously.

"Of course not, you Dodo. Nothing can live a million years," his sister scolded.

The man chuckled, catching Dallas's eye. "These guys here haven't lived that long, but their kind has. Their ancestors passed down everything they knew. And each generation adds more because they're always watching. They've seen it all. Anytime I see them I say, 'Hi, professor, what you know?' But they never make a sound. No, sir, not a secret do they ever reveal."

The girl had moved closer and was gingerly stroking the head of the other iguana. The boy reached out and tentatively touched the back on one of the animals as if expecting an electric shock to leap from the rough hide.

"I still think they're ugly," the boy said.

"I wish they could talk," the girl said. "Maybe if I lean close he'll whisper a secret to me."

"I wouldn't get too close, he might bite your ear off."

"Lord no, son, he's got no teeth. The thing you gots to worry about with an iguana ain't his bite, it's his tail. That's his weapon of offense and defense. He can strike a nasty blow with the tail, knock a man right off his feet. And if you try to grab him by the tail, he'll drop it. You be left with the tail and he be gone. Don't matter to him, he just grows another one. Ain't that the damnedest thing?"

The boy backed away, regarding the animals more warily than before. As he spoke to the children, the old man was looking at Dallas. But not in the eyes. Somehow his gaze found its way to the crooked index finger on Dallas' right hand.

"Ain't that a beauty," he said.

Dallas shrugged. "Hedge trimmer."

"Shouldn't feel bad. That's like a signature. That makes you special."

"I was a pitcher."

The old man tipped his cap and held up a right hand with three fingers.

"Me, I play the sax," he said.

CHAPTER 35

Her breath was coming faster now. He could feel it tickling his face in waves from no more than six inches away. So many luscious sensations, at each junction of their skin and passion, competed for his attention. But all of his concentration was on that sweet air filling his head, on breathing her in, savoring her. It spurred him to coax even greater exertion from her lungs. He was awash in the intoxicating haze of her essence, not even conscious of the barely audible mantra he repeated with the numbing rhythm of train wheels clacking across the cracks between rails: "More, more, more, more, more."

She answered each call with a reply that was more melodic than lyrical, a siren's song that evoked tears from both of them until her breathing paused in a rapturous moment and a crimson smile swept across her face, giving new meaning to the famous collegiate exhortation, "Roll, tide!"

Then her breath returned in a gasp and she called out his name. That was the magic word for him.

Even as the rise and fall of her chest subsided to normal and her eyes twinkled at him from under half-open lids, he hovered close, inhaling her, a shameless drunkard intent on extracting that last drop from the bottle. Until finally, unnerved, she giggled.

"I guess you missed me a little, then."

"Well, after you've spent a night in a boat with a bunch of gay fishermen."

Dallas rolled onto his side, pulling Claire with him.

"Hmm, I'm not sure if I should take that as a compliment or as something to be worried about," she said.

"Don't worry, all I could think about all night was you. But I must say, there was an odd tension out there that I never experienced on a fishing boat before. It made me a little uneasy, but it helped put a lot of thoughts in my head about what I wanted to do when I got back to you."

She was smiling, and that was always the greatest gift to him. He kissed her and inhaled deeply again, understanding how a paroled convict must feel stepping into the daylight and taking his first breath of freedom.

"You definitely had a better night than I did," she said, reflecting on Skeeter Devereaux's traumatic homecoming.

"Yeah, it doesn't sound like much fun. Sorry you had to deal with that. I feel kind of guilty about not being there. How's the old buzzard doing?"

"Pretty upset, as you'd imagine after he found his place was broken into. The thing that finally calmed him down, I left Keith and Lyle with him and went and got some food. He wanted a pork sandwich and pea soup, of all things. I've hardly ever seen that man eat before; he scarfed it right down. Then, after the police left and we helped him clean up the mess at his place, he said he was still hungry. So we all went out and he ate almost a whole chicken and a big piece of blueberry pie. Keith said, 'Who do you think you are, George Foreman?'"

"A lot of people react to adversity by going on an eating binge."

"I think it had more to do with being in the hospital for five days."

"Good point. When you've been locked away from the finer things in life, it makes you crazy for them. I know all about that."

With that he rolled on top of her again and began peppering her neck with kisses. She giggled but didn't protest.

Afterward, her expression was incredulous.

"What's gotten into you? How am I supposed to go to work? I'll be lucky if I can walk."

"Can't help it, I love the scent of poontang in the morning."

Smack!

"You're so bad. What are you trying to do to me? I felt like I was going to, ah, explode." She was breathless again and laughing at the same time. "That reminds me, July Fourth is coming up, and Lyle is on his fireworks kick. He asked me, 'What if you filled a paper towel tube with gunpowder and lit it, would it blast off to the moon?' I told him he'd feel the biggest explosion on his butt if he even thought about trying something like that. Would you talk to him? He needs to hear these things from someone other than me, and he looks up to you."

Dallas nodded. He kept staring into her eyes. "The Fourth of July never was my favorite time."

"Lyle takes after me; I've always loved fireworks. When I was a little girl my dad would come home with a big shopping bag full of fun stuff for the Fourth — bottle rockets, firecrackers, Roman candles, sparklers. I loved all of it, especially the ones that went up in the air and made a loud whistling noise, the screamers. It always excited me. You're going to think I'm strange, but the smell of gunpowder kind of turns me on."

"Oh, how Freudian. Nothing like a big bang to get the juices flowing."

She smacked him again, on the shoulder. "Yeah, yeah, and nothing like a screamer. It's just fun. The noise, the colors; it's exciting. And for some reason, that smell sets something off in me."

"People start setting off firecrackers and cherry bombs and stuff, it makes me real jumpy. The big ones, like M-80s, I just about jump out of my skin."

She eyed him quizzically, uncomprehending.

"You've got to understand, I was a pitcher. A lot of places, they shoot off fireworks after a guy hits a home run off you. So it's not a good association."

"It's not only that, is it?"

He thought a moment before answering. "No. The sound of explosions, it brings back Dealey Plaza. That whole thing, you know."

Now there was compassion in her eyes.

"It's hard for me to realize that you were really there and saw that. I kind of forget about it. But it must always be there for you, when you've witnessed something like that."

"It's not like I think about it every day. Certain things trigger the memories, so to speak."

"Have you done any more work on your book?"

"A little. Not a lot. Haven't had much time."

"Funny, last night Skeeter made some reference to the Kennedy thing. About you having been there."

"He said something?"

"Yeah, it was kind of weird. On the way back from Miami, kind of out of nowhere he mentioned it."

Stranger was the scene that had greeted Claire, Keith and Devereaux when they arrived back in Islamorada. Seems an anonymous welcoming committee had taken the liberty to rearrange Devereaux's furniture. Emptied the drawers and cupboards, too.

"It looked like Hurricane Andrew came back," Claire said. "It's not like Skeeter has a lot, but what he has was dumped all over the floor. The thing that upset him most was they smashed the one chair he likes to sit in."

"The time I was up in his room, he showed me some stuff he kept in a trunk, documents and records about the wreck he found in Cuba."

"The trunk was dumped over. I didn't see too much in the way of papers on the floor. He probably has a secret hiding place. He made us all go outside for a while and closed the door. He was a lot calmer after that."

"Nobody around there saw or heard anything?"

"The police couldn't find any witnesses. The laundromat downstairs was probably closed when they broke in."

Dallas was on his side, playing with some raven strands of her hair. "Do you think he has any idea who tossed his place?"

"He kept repeating to the police, 'Probably just vandals.' I had a feeling he had some suspicions. I kept thinking, rival treasure hunters? Gambling debts? I don't have a clue. He's pretty much an enigma. As cantankerous as he can be, I've never really seen him get into a hassle with anyone."

"You know, he has a gun. A handgun. I wonder if that was in his secret hiding place, too."

CHAPTER 36

Dallas drove to Snapper Cove, unsure of what to expect. Devereaux hadn't been cleared by the doctors to resume diving, but Dallas knew that wouldn't stop him. Dallas wasn't in the mood for treasure hunting. He had the piece on Ortega and the boat race to finish for *Florida Nautique*, and he was on a roll at the typewriter that morning. He described Ortega's cheering section as the "minions on the balcony awash in hi-octane hero worship," and quoted an anonymous female spectator on the dock after the race confiding to a companion about Ortega, "That guy's probably a bastard who'd break your heart, but he makes my panties dewy." He smiled, wondering if Kirby D'Arbonnell would leave that in.

He was having fun, turning phrases, painting impressions with prose. A lot more fun than being stuffed into a sardine can with Captain Tuna and rooting around the bottom of the sea with metal lobster claws searching for doubloons. Life, for the moment, felt pretty damned grand. He'd started the day making love to the woman who'd put the back-beat into his heart until more than their lips were sore. Now the writing was transferring stimulation to the most neglected part of his body.

When had he felt so alive? Certainly not since first getting called up to the big leagues. But even then he'd been a soul adrift, feeding off physical conquests, on more than just the ball field. Funny the quirks of fate: Just when he'd about abandoned hope of attaching purpose to his haphazard odyssey through life, an explosion dumps him into the Gulf Stream, and out of nowhere this heaven-sent survivor of her own shipwreck of a past throws a lifeline around his heart. Even now, he couldn't foresee what lay ahead, especially with D'Arbonnell dropping hints that all was not well financially with *Florida Nautique*, and the salvage of *Nuestra Senora de Carmelita* in limbo. But at this moment he felt energized, aglow with creativity and contentment. Hadn't that always been his latent ambition? Seize the moment and go with it, because life can kick you in the ass tomorrow. He'd even typed out a few more thoughts for the JFK book. He thought he might spend the whole day writing.

Then the phone rang, a cryptic Devereaux on the other end saying, "Meet me at the boatyard in 20 minutes. Got something to talk about." Dallas was already feeling guilty about not rushing over to visit him. This would be less unpleasant than going to his room.

When Dallas pulled up, Devereaux was aboard *Levante*, moored at the fuel dock, engine idling. He was standing near the stern smoking a cigarette, tempting fate as usual. His face appeared gaunt, his skin pasty but his eyes were as keen as ever.

Devereaux reached up to release the stern line, barking, "Get the bow."

The submarine was not in its cradle. That was a relief. No scuba gear was visible on the deck. Dallas tried to read Devereaux's mood but didn't speak. He freed the line and stepped aboard.

The boat ride was short. Out the cut through the mangroves, bearing left, then right before passing the limestone bulkhead of the mainland to emerge into Hawk's Channel, the broad band of water between the Keys and barrier reefs that is a threshold to open water rather than a channel. The water was a dull shade of guacamole under an overcast sky. Dallas could see a waterspout miles out on the ocean, while dark bulbous clouds behind them over the Gulf of Mexico foretold the coming of the predictable summertime afternoon squall.

Dallas could feel vibrations through the souls of his well-worn boat shoes from the diesel, rumbling comfortably at a moderate cruising speed. He kept a hand lightly on a handle affixed to a bulkhead and the corner of his eye on Devereaux. He noted they were on the approximate course to the wreck site, but less than halfway there Devereaux suddenly cut the throttle and shut down the engine.

That moment, when the clatter of machinery yields to the subtle symphony of the sea, settles in like a deep sigh. Dallas sat on the port gunwale watching the pattern of Lilliputian waves climb to modest peaks and slide back down with muffled cries of "whee." In the distance he could hear the drone of a dive boat outbound on its noon trip to the reefs. The light breeze felt good on his brow even with the humid heaviness of the air, or perhaps in spite of it. Devereaux stood amidships facing astern, drawing the last carcinogens from another cigarette. They were drifting, miles from nowhere in their thoughts.

Devereaux finally flicked the butt into the water and exhaled through his nose a long, double-barreled smoker's salute to the god of tobacco. Dallas watched it sputter and dissipate. Devereaux was still facing his dissolved vapor trail when he spoke.

"Something you should ... ah, I wanted you to know. I was there that day."

Dallas looked over, confused. He was expecting something about Devereaux's accident and rescue. He was there which day? Where? Something about Cuba? The explosions — Dallas's accident, the Coast Guard cutter? What day?

Dallas was totally unprepared for the answer. It came after a dramatic pause, while Devereaux dug another smoke out of a crinkled pack of Lucky Strikes, lit it and turned to face him.

"In Dallas. You know, when it happened. I saw it, too."

Dallas's eyes widened as he grasped at comprehension. Did he mean?

"You did say it happened right in front of you. I was there, too, when they shot him."

The words rushed out, the reference clear now. The two men stared at each other, Dallas searching for the significance of this revelation. He felt lightheaded.

"You brought me out here to tell me that?"

"It's all I can really do. For whatever it's worth. It don't change nothing. But you were there. There are some things you should at least know. I owe you that much."

Then it dawned on him. Devereaux, in his awkward way, was trying to thank him for saving his life. What exactly was he saying? That their paths had crossed before at one of the monumental events of the century. What was the correlation between the murder of a president and the near-death experience of a half-mad treasure hunter, and what was the significance of sharing this information under the cloak of secrecy? Then a phrase flashed like neon in Dallas's brain, and his eyes grew wider. Devereaux turned away and took another drag on his cigarette as an ash that had grown to nearly an inch dropped onto the deck.

"Where exactly were you when *they* shot him?"

"I was up that little hill, leaning against this low wall next to some steps. Drinking a Coke."

Devereaux looked at him and their eyes locked again until Dallas blinked. Devereaux looked away. Dallas's mind was racing back through the years, to a boy in a Navy blue sweater with a little American flag on a stick standing on the sidewalk between his mother and sister, waiting for the president. Hearing the echoes of the motorcycles, seeing the big car, famous faces coming into focus, hands waving, the boy literally jumping with excitement. Then seeing it all dissolve into chaos and indelible horror. Piecing the images back together now, thinking, up that little hill — *He was behind me*. Feeling a chill schuss the back of his neck.

"That's it? You brought me out here to tell me you were there, drinking a Coke?"

Devereaux shifted uneasily. He took another puff and exhaled deeply, again through his nose. He looked past Dallas, avoiding eye contact.

"It's complicated. A lot of things were happening there. I'm not saying I know all about it, but I know some things." He paused again, deep-sunken eyes staring in the direction of a pair of frigate birds surveying something in the water. "It wouldn't do

216

no good for anyone to ever try to bring it out in the open. It's all distorted beyond what could ever be proved. You were there. You might as well know, for your own sake. I can tell you, it wasn't like they made it out to be, some nut just acting on his own. It was a hit, pure and simple. There are people in certain circles who've always known that. It was all very professional."

Dallas rose to his feet, aghast. He could feel a surge of anger, his face reddening. It was all he could do to suppress the impulse to lunge at this man and clamp his hands around his throat. *Certain circles?*

"You're saying you knew about this? You ... you were ... involved in it?'

The force of Dallas's reaction caused Devereaux to take a couple steps back. But he didn't seem concerned about defending himself. His arms hung at his sides. He remained calm, matter-of-fact. Dallas looked at his face and saw sadness.

"Look, I'm not proud of much in my life. I can tell you this much, I never killed nobody. Sometimes circumstances get you sucked into things you can't control. You find yourself in situations you don't want to be in."

Dallas was speechless. He could feel a vein in his neck pulsing, a ringing in his ears as loud as a waterfall. The two men stood swaying slightly with the motion of the boat, looking through each other. Thunder rumbled in the distance over the Gulf of Mexico.

"You do want to know, don't you?"

Dallas stepped back and sat again on the gunwale. He ran his fingers through his hair. "It was the most exciting day I'd ever known. I got to stay home from school. I was going to see the president. It rained, and then it turned sunny. So beautiful. And then it turned so dark. What were you doing there?"

Devereaux shifted uneasily, his T-shirt soaked with perspiration under both arms. Dallas could feel salty moisture on his own forehead, a bead of sweat cascading down one temple.

"There were some people I worked for. They helped me out when I was in Cuba. They were responsible for getting me out of there and getting me back on my feet. So the thing was, they'd come up with little jobs, and I was — it was understood — I was obligated to do them. Not that I really minded. It wasn't bad stuff. Mostly courier-type work — pick something up, drop something off. And they paid well. I was glad to do what they said and ask no questions. That was understood, too. I was living in New Orleans. It was mostly little things around there. I was trying to figure out what I wanted to do next. It paid the rent. And sometimes I'd get to travel. They'd say, go to Dallas, go to Miami, go to San Antonio. Couple times Mexico City. This time it was Dallas again."

"Right, go to Dallas and help murder the president."

Devereaux didn't respond for more than a minute. Dallas could see his mind retracing steps through dark alleys of memory, excavating images long concealed, but even under the weight of years, irrevocable. Everyone has a distinct history that glows with a tungsten intensity that can scorch the cornea if viewed directly. So each of us comes equipped with a self-contained filter to temper the burn and diffuse the images to palpable levels. What did this man see when he looked back? Did the filter leave only the barren landscape or was it littered with remorse and regret? Dallas searched the face for clues. Lines were imbedded like scars, the eyes reflective of pain. But whose?

"They said to go to this place downtown at a certain time. There was going to be a parade, and afterwards pick up this vehicle at a certain place and drop it off at a certain place." Devereaux looked down at his feet. "I gotta tell you — you gotta understand — I didn't know what was going to happen. I didn't even know about Kennedy coming there until I got there. I figured something pretty important had to be going on. They were paying a lot more than I'd gotten before, and there was the promise of a bonus when I got back. So I went to the parade and waited."

Now the other man's eyes bore the faint flicker of a film projector lens. It occurred to Dallas that the images playing there now were similar to ones he was so familiar with. The perspective virtually the same — the street, the lighting — only the angle slightly different. Millions of others know the scene from the herky-jerky 8mm images recorded by a man standing on a four-foot high concrete pedestal, the famous Zapruder film.

The camera captures whatever it sees, within the limits of the lens, film and lighting. The mind's videotape is more selective. It often registers only what it wants to retain. Sometimes it is fooled and records a distorted picture. Sometimes the passing of time alters the image. Dallas knew that was probably true with many incidents in his past. But not this one. Even after nearly 30 years, it remained the same blinding panorama, a mental horror show he always viewed in slow-motion, frame by excruciating frame: From the first realization that something wasn't as it should be in this postcard setting to the unfathomable reality of the famous man's head erupting in a red haze; the horrified expression of the pretty woman in pink; the chaotic blur of mass panic; his own sensation of falling, turning to search for his mother; his eyes somehow drawn to a spot atop the fence on that hill, lured by a glint of light, the reflection of something shiny. Suddenly becoming aware he was clutching something, an ankle, yes, his mother's, the two of them prone on the ground; feeling a tug on his sleeve, seeing his sister's hand, then her face, hysterical. It was always at that point in the replay that he stopped and wondered, had he really seen what he thought he saw above the fence?

The answer was always revealed in a snatch of clear focus, a single but distinct mental freeze-frame on the outline of a face and the reflection of light off something silvery. Sunglasses, mirrored, the same type as the policeman wore that time he came to their door looking for his father, who by then was already long gone. Yes, there was a face, if only for a moment. For in that instant of recognition it was looking directly at him. Or so it seemed, because it ignited a surge of fright that jabbed at his scalp like a thousand needles causing him to hide his face in the grass. When he'd dared to look again the face was gone, but the aftershock of fright remained along with the bitter taste of vomit in the back of his throat.

Later, when they were in a dreary office where his mother was supposed to give a statement, he told her he'd seen a ghost behind the fence and she grabbed his arm firmly and brought her face close to his and said, "Don't say a word about that. Not ever. Keep that to yourself. Forget you saw it." And when a curt, official-looking man came to the house to question his mother, Dallas understood what she meant because the wave of fright struck again, the same as when he'd spied the man behind the fence. The same as it would many times since.

It all seemed surreal recalling that day, yet it was as clear as the dawn breaking over the ocean. You squint, but the light is still bright. Close your eyes, but the camera's flash still jabs at the brain. This was like that. It never went away completely.

He understood what it must be like for soldiers who return from war, haunted by scenes of death and mayhem they can never suppress. There was something different about this. Suddenly he understood, maybe fully for the first time, that it was more than the image he retained of the violent act. It was the mystery that remained all these years later.

Dallas's eyes widened and he looked at Devereaux again. There they were, two very different men with perhaps only one thing in common: tortured souls.

"You were supposed to pick up a vehicle? Like a getaway car?"

"It was more of a truck. With a compartment on back. Like a shed or a camper. Had the name of a plumbing company on the side. When all hell broke loose, I got out of there, away from the hill. People were running everywhere. Sirens and cops all over the place. I remembered what I was supposed to do. I came back around and found the truck where it was supposed to be. I slipped in with the traffic and drove away from there."

Each detail shook Dallas like a trumpet blast in a pup tent. Chills racing up the back of his neck caused his shoulders to jerk. What he was hearing was no errand to help a plumber with a transportation problem. This was a distinct corner of the much-theorized conspiracy that millions accept but nobody has proved. And Devereaux apparently was a player in it, albeit unwittingly. Or so he said. Dallas shook his head in disbelief.

"You're saying someone was in the truck?"

"I didn't know. That's a fact. They didn't say I was picking anyone up. They said, pick up the vehicle."

Another pause. Another puff. Then, "I had my suspicions. I had a feeling. I could sense it."

The rumble of thunder in the direction of the Keys, probably over the Gulf of Mexico, interrupted. Dallas was locked on Devereaux's face, trying to look inside of him. Devereaux's gaze was out to sea.

"I drove to another part of the city. A warehouse district. That's where I was supposed to drop it off. Had to walk a few blocks to catch a bus. But first I went around the other side of this building where I could watch the truck."

Dallas became aware that his own jaw was hanging open. He wiped a ridge of saliva off his lower lip. Another clap of thunder, this one closer, startled him. He kept his eyes on Devereaux, who gave a quick glance at the storm clouds but kept talking. The confession was pouring out, words coming faster like water through a spillway that was being cranked open wider and wider. Then abruptly it clanked shut.

Devereaux looked over. Dallas raised an eyebrow as if to say, well?

"I saw him get out the back. He took a jacket out of a case he was carrying, put it on and walked away."

Devereaux shrugged, as if to say, end of story.

"You think he was carrying the gun, a rifle in the case?"

"Couldn't have been a rifle, unless it was disassembled. Case wasn't long enough. It was like a soft suitcase. Or more like a doctor's satchel. Who knows, someone else may have picked up the gun. More likely he left it in the truck and it was picked up later."

"So you're saying this guy was the assassin? How can you be sure of that?"

Devereaux shrugged again.

"He was one of them. You can take that to the bank. Judging from where I picked up the vehicle, I'd say he was the one behind the fence. Judging from his reputation, I'd say he was the one got the job done."

The tingling on the back of Dallas's scalp was almost unbearable. His heart was pounding with the intensity of the thunder, which was getting closer. He shook his head in disbelief.

"You mean, you know who this man was? You recognized him?"

Devereaux took another mental journey back across the decades. When he returned, the wind was whipping whitecaps across olive-drab waves, rocking *Levante* like a cradle. He reached for a handhold to steady himself.

"I told you about how I got out of Cuba. I wasn't the only one. There were a few of us on that freighter freed at the same time from prison. There was this one that the rest stayed away from. He kept to himself."

"This was the same man you saw?"

"He's not one you'd forget. Just the same, you hardly knew he was around most of the time. Right before we got to Santo Domingo he came up to me and asked for a cigarette. Surprised the hell out of me. I rolled him one while he waited. He left an impression."

"You know anything about him? A name?"

"In that situation, you made small talk. You played cards. You talked about broads. You didn't pry into people's business." He paused to explore another memory. "I remember, someone asked a question. This other old boy — I think he was called Nunez — kind of nodded in the direction of the one we're talking about. Said, 'You want to find yourself a war, he's the one to follow. Otherwise, best to stay away.' "

Devereaux seemed to be working something out in his mind. Dallas waited, studying him with a sidelong glance, not staring, letting him sort it out.

"We were on that freighter a couple days waiting for it to leave. This fellow Nunez, he was the only one had contact with that one. They played cribbage in the shade next to the cargo hold to pass the time. He came back to eat with us. Said, 'You should see the cribbage board. Hand carved. Beautiful work.' Carried it in a special case, lizard skin. That's what Nunez said. Called him the Lizard Man. Thought he was a big deal to be accepted by that one. The rest of us kept our distance."

Revulsion had given way to fascination, Dallas assuming the role of special investigator for the Committee Overseeing Pandora's box. Each question ratcheted the lid off another can crammed full of worms with jagged teeth and stiletto horns. A few miles farther to sea, a gray ghost masquerading as a waterspout cut a menacing swath across the Gulf Stream. Above the fragile continental tail that comprises the Keys, unseen hands pounded a thunderous timpani solo inside a tower of black clouds. Between this convergence of nature's show of force, two men in a nondescript workboat were discussing the possible perpetrator of one of the nation's most notorious murders as matter-of-factly as if trying to pinpoint a mutual acquaintance.

The scene had taken on a surreal aura for Dallas. But his curiosity spurred him to peel away the veneer of a mystery that had tormented him and so many others for three decades.

"You ever seen this man again? I mean, after Dallas?"

Another pause, a look that was difficult to read. Then Devereaux looked away and said, "I didn't stick around after Dallas. Didn't want to see anyone I knew or knew me for a long time. Collected my bonus, gathered up the resources I had and went as far away as I could. I'd read about this Dutch ship they were salvaging off Western Australia. Went down there and worked on that. Didn't come back to the States for years."

Dallas's mind was racing, trying to remember it all and figure what to ask next. How much did Devereaux really know? Was he telling the truth? Thinking, damn, Mike Wallace is never around when you need him.

"These people you worked for, what are we talking about? American or foreign? Organized crime? Big business or people connected to the government itself?

"You're asking for a distinction? Shit, it'd be like looking out at the ocean and asking, OK, where's the horizon? It depends on where you're standing. You see water and you see sky, and somewhere they run together. But where? Can't say for sure. See what I mean? Where do you draw the line between the government and organized crime? All through history the government's been the muscle behind more break-ins, killings, overthrows, holdups than you can shake a stick at. You've got Watergate, Iran-Contra. Those are just the big ones that are well known. Go way back and look at what they did to the Indians. All very organized. All very criminal.

"Look at Kennedy. The Chicago mob got him elected. When he wanted to get rid of Castro, he asked the mob to do the job for him. He had a bimbo taking cash to Sam Giancana and Johnny Roselli, two of the biggest mob guys of all time. So you tell me, where's the distinction between the government and organized crime? Why do you think they wanted to pin the assassination on that Oswald right away and look no further? I mean, that guy'd done work for the CIA, and he certainly had ties to the mob. It was in a lot of people's best interests for the thing to die right there."

"So you're saying you don't know who you were working for?"

"I'm saying everyone's in business of some sort and nothing's what it seems from the outside looking in. It's the same with the mob, the government and any other industry. It's the same with you and me. The best you can do is look after your own business and not dig too deep into anyone else's. I always figured that's what happened with Kennedy. I know he pissed off a lot of people."

Pebble-sized raindrops began splattering the deck of *Levante*, a tentative volley turning into a full-blown torrent. Dallas and Devereaux ducked inside the open cabin that provided shelter amidships. Devereaux noticed his half-smoked cigarette had been extinguished by the rain, tried to relight it but the matches were soggy too.

"Got a match?"

Dallas thought of the blue-collar workers' pat retort — *Yeah, my ass and your face* — but didn't say it.

"Sorry."

Devereaux cursed and flipped the cigarette overboard. Dallas smiled to himself. Strange the things the mind dredges up at the most inappropriate moments.

The wind piped up to 30 knots or more, kicking up a good froth. Devereaux started the engine and pointed the bow into the wind. Like a typical summer squall in South Florida, the storm came and went with the brief intensity of a stubbed toe, leaving behind a gentler patter of rain as the wind simmered back to a breeze with a pleasantly cool tail. Dallas was watching individual drops pop up off the worn fiberglass deck before settling into a flow racing for the scuppers at the transom and back to the sea where they might be gathered up to fuel tomorrow's tropical outburst. The rain machine, Dallas thought, was a lot like Devereaux, mostly bluster. It pitched a fit almost every afternoon, and the net result was to make life tolerable during the sultry season. Occasionally, it cranked up a tantrum that made life in its path a living hell, as Hurricane Andrew did the previous year.

Such has always been the dynamic of operating in these waters. The key to survival was knowing which flare-ups to ride out and which ones to run like hell from. Dallas was reminded of the luckless crew of *Nuestra Senora de Carmelita*. Doomed by their own ignorance and bad timing, the poor bastards didn't know they'd walked into a haymaker until it was too late to duck. Funny, even in the modern world, with all its technology and foresight, fate still deals the cards in the same ruthless way. So, in many ways, we're as clueless as ever, our guard lowered by a false sense of security.

Dallas moved back into the open, into the rain, not caring if it soaked him. He turned his face to the sky and closed his eyes. The drops felt therapeutic, tasted tangy but pure. He wished they could penetrate inside of him, do for the soul what a good shower does for the body. He heard a rumble from the retreating storm and tried to reorient himself — was it over the land or the water? Like the shifting horizon, the path of sound can be deceptive.

Eyes still closed, water dripping off his nose and chin, Dallas sensed a change in the rain: suddenly more bitter tasting. Or was it a change in his perception?

"You saw it, like I did," Dallas said, his voice rising above the engine noise. "A man gunned down in front of his wife, in front of the world. It wasn't like in the movies. It was real. It was shocking. I know I've never forgotten it. I can't believe you have either. I can't help but wonder, considering you're telling me all this now, if you maybe feel some regret about whatever you were involved in."

As he spoke, Dallas turned his head toward Devereaux, squinting through the rain. The old Cajun pulled the lever to neutral and shut the engine, then looked back over his shoulder at Dallas.

"I know what you probably think, and you can think whatever you want. I don't give a damn. But you better understand, it was going to happen one way or another. You don't stand in front of a fuckin' hurricane. I was just part of the tide, and it was the same way for others, I'm sure. I couldn't say who all was involved, but I knew people who knew a lot more about it than I did. A few of them are still around. I can say that most of us didn't have a choice of being involved or not. At least, nobody would want to choose the alternative. As to whether I felt regret or whatever that it happened, the answer is no. Hell, no. People make their beds to sleep in, and that man chose how he laid his out, sure as shit. The whole Cuba thing, Bay of Pigs, left a pretty sour taste for a lot of people. I know it did for me, and the wound was still fresh. I mean, I couldn't have pulled the trigger. I don't have the guts. All I did was pick up a truck and drop it off. And like I told you, I didn't know what was coming. But there was reason enough not to shed any tears once it all played out like it did.

"Now you wonder why I'm telling you all this? Maybe in time it'll make sense. At least you'll know it when the time comes."

Devereaux turned the key, the engine sputtering to life signaling the end of the discussion. Not a word was spoken on the trip back to port, the diesel's drone providing a shroud for thought. Dallas felt mentally overwhelmed trying to digest it all, to separate feelings from facts. There was no doubt he had been privy to something remarkable. But what could he do with it?

Devereaux was right, this information didn't change anything for the rest of the world, but it altered his perspective forever. Not necessarily in a bad way. Surprisingly, the more he thought about it the better he actually felt, despite the fact that he was now an acquaintance and cohort of a conspirator in the murder of John F. Kennedy. Devereaux had done for him what no congressional committee or private investigator had been able to achieve in 30 years, which was to validate his own experience that fateful day in Dallas.

They might as well have been two fishermen coming back from a fruitless trip. Devereaux eased *Levante* into the basin at Snapper Cove, spun it slowly around and backed it into its slip. Dallas secured and adjusted lines from the bow to mooring pylons on both sides. By the time he finished, Devereaux was on the dock doing the same with the stern lines. There was no catch to unload. The big ones had all gotten away. Or had they?

Devereaux unfurled the hose and began spraying the deck, more out of habit than necessity, his eyes riveted to the simple chore. Dallas sensed that the free flow of information was over, and still so many questions were unanswered. How much was Devereaux not revealing? What did he know about Lee Harvey Oswald and Jack Ruby? Even in his confession, he was cleverly evasive. Who was the man in the plumbing truck; what was his reputation? And who or what was behind it all?

Dallas glanced around the dock, and seeing nobody around, said, "You know, I always knew that last shot came from up on the hill. I was just a little kid, but I couldn't believe it when the police came out and said it was one man in the window. I wanted to run up and shout, 'No, there were more of them.' It was hard to understand why they didn't want to hear it."

Devereaux took his thumb off the trigger of the hose nozzle and turned around. His eyes were clearer than Dallas had ever seen them. His voice was calm.

"I told you about the woman in Cuba that showed me the papers about the wreck. She had these little glass prisms that she sold in her shop. She hung them in her windows and they made the light dance on the walls and ceiling. It always felt different in there than anywhere else. Even a dull day seemed brighter in her place. It was … enchanting.

"Truth is like a prism. It's a matter of how you look at it and how you change the angle of the light you shine on it. No two people view it the same. So it's all a distortion. You can shape it any way you want if you put your mind to it, shout it loud enough, convince enough people. That's what dictators do. That's what people with the power in this country do. Look at the way the courts work. Look at the political system. Look at the TV news. Truth is nothing more than a consensus, that's how it comes out in the end. Shit, all powerful people understand that."

Dallas stared, taken aback. Devereaux was a man of many surprises, himself a prism. Cajun philosopher? That was the most unlikely twist of all.

Devereaux started to turn back to finish hosing the deck. As he did, Dallas blurted out one more thought.

"I saw the man you drove in the truck. Just for a second, but I saw him. Behind the fence. I've always thought about him being out there somewhere, living with that secret. I can't help wondering, is he still alive? And, what it'd be like if I ever saw him again?"

Devereaux turned back. His eyes narrowed. He didn't say a word. His expression was answer enough.

CHAPTER 37

"The French, you know, have a term for it. It means 'Little Death,' " Margie said, one eyebrow raised conspiratorially.

"Oh, the French are so morose. With me, it's more like temporary insanity," Claire blurted. An instant later her face reddened, and she clamped both hands over it to hide embarrassment and stifle laughter. Margie laughed so hard her whole body shook.

"My gawd, you snorted," Claire said, and she laughed until tears formed in the corners of her eyes. "I can't believe I tell you these things. We sound like a couple of sophomores."

"I think you're crazy in love, girl."

"I don't know what it is, but I must be crazy. I tell myself, 'Be careful, don't get too involved.' Then, next thing you know, it happens again."

"You know what they say, if it feels good, do it. ... again. ... and again. Why do you think I go through vibrators like my Eddy goes through whiskey? If I had to wait for him, I'd be dead first. Damn, I should've married a Frenchman."

This time Claire snorted. Her cheeks became a river of tears of laughter. She looked down the bar of the Leaky Tiki and saw two middle-aged men, just in from a charter fishing trip, watching them with amusement. One of the men raised a cup of beer and nodded in their direction. The other shouted, "Whatever you girls are drinking, I'll have a double."

Claire walked over and served them each a shot of their choice on her, trying with little success to suppress a sheepish grin. Returning to where Margie was sitting, Claire cracked up again.

"I don't know what I'm going to do. The last thing I need to do now is fall for anyone. I've got my hands full with Lyle. I've got to think about what's best for him. I just wanted to come here, get my head together, prove to myself I can make it on

226

my own. You know, Claire's Big Adventure. I told myself I wasn't going to get caught up in another situation I might regret later."

"Are you having fun?"

"At first it was like I had an itch. I thought why not, you know, take care of it? We all have, you know. I mean, I figured, what's the harm? I knew Dallas is not the type to, ah, latch on. Then it became not so easy to keep it casual. He triggers something in me, I guess."

"I guess he must have a good trigger finger. Little death: It's more than coming, it's the feeling you're coming apart."

Claire blushed again. "Gawd," she said when her laughter subsided. "OK, so it's fun. The thing is, fun leads to complications. It's like, you start to think, now what? Where do we go from here? This guy isn't exactly settled in his life. He doesn't even have a regular job. I mean, one with any security. He's here today, who knows where he'll be tomorrow. It's kind of romantic, but it's so uncertain. That's what worries me, the thought of getting hurt again. It's fun right now, but ... I mean, Dallas is a great guy. Not like the last one. I can't imagine this turning into something like that. He's not the type. He has a good soul. I know he wouldn't mean to hurt me."

Claire covered her eyes with a hand, and peeked through two fingers. "Oh, brother, I'm talking like you're my shrink or something."

Margie did have big, empathetic eyes, like Oprah. She could have been one of those schlock talk hostesses who everyone confesses to. They were eyes that had seen a lot of pain, much of it her own. Nonetheless, they were eyes that cared. Really cared.

"I just don't know," Claire said. "Pain of the heart can be as bad as the physical kind, maybe worse. Even though he'd never admit it, Dallas is a dreamer. He's just lost touch with his dreams. He's got his demons, too. I guess maybe that's part of the attraction. We're alike in a lot of ways."

"I think maybe sometimes you — I don't mean just you but anyone — can analyze too much," Margie said. "You can spend so much time worrying about the regrets you might have that you end up regretting that you let something good slip away. No matter what choices you make, most lead to regrets anyway. Might as well grab the goodies while you can — that's what I think."

Seeing a heaviness in Claire's eyes, Margie gave her a sisterly smile, touched her arm. "And don't worry, you'll get my bill at the end of the month. What are shrinks getting an hour these days, anyway?"

Claire smiled and squeezed her friend's hand. "Obviously, I've gone a few gazillion miles past caution already," she said. "It's not like I've been holding much back. It's just that sometimes, like, ah, afterward, I look at his face and he's the boy with the faraway eyes. I wonder, where is he off to? Will he let me go there with him?"

#

The meeting took place at sea, 10 miles off San Salvador, the island that may or may not have been the first landfall of Christopher Columbus. Like the unwitting Lucayans who awoke to find Europeans on their beach, eyes peering through binoculars beheld a virgin sight. The appearance of the helicopter in the distance drew them to the spot where something hurtled across the surface of the ocean, a shape not yet recognizable and without point of reference.

The shimmer of sunlight off the waves cast the object in a surreal glow. To one squinting observer on the top deck of a motor yacht, an impeccably groomed man with slicked-back hair that gleamed like velvet, it appeared as a giant skimming stone flung by a playful Neptune. Standing next to him, an older man with deeply tanned features and bushy white mustache, witnessed what looked like a ghostly skier, each foot on the back of a supersonic dolphin. Simultaneously, the two men pulled away from their binoculars, blinked and looked at each other. A third man, distinguished by a brown Stetson and ebullient demeanor, stepped into the void between them and pointed.

"Look, he's cranking it now. Look at that bugger go," Edison Hawke said, slapping the back of each man.

The object was approaching at a surprising rate, a low-slung blur that resembled some sort of boat but didn't act like one. There was no rhythmic smack of the hull over the waves, no rooster-tail wake. Occasionally there was a slight wobble and burst of spray. Any sound it may have made was blotted out by the clamor of the helicopter yapping along behind like a range dog on the heels of a wayward bull. It whooshed by no more than 100 yards off the bow of the observation yacht, a low-flying comet leaving a trail of vapor that painted but barely disturbed the water it traversed.

"It's a hydroplane. Like the, what do ya call it, *Miss Budweiser.* I saw them race in Miami once," the dark-haired man said.

"No, there's a big difference, Mr. G," Hawke said. "The way it was explained to me, your basic hydroplane skates along right on the top of the water. It always has contact with the water. If it gets up off the water, it'll flip over backward like a plane doing the loop-de-loop. This thing you see out here, it's revo-lu-tionary. I call it a skimmer, but that ain't really right, either. This baby actually rides above the water, like it's sitting on a pillow of air. Or, what does Behrent say? A what-da-you-call-it, envelope. That's right, old Behrent, he's the mastermind of this beauty. He says it rides on an envelope of air. All I know, it sure can bring home the mail. But you can see that for yourself."

As they waited for the *P-BJ-003* to return for another pass, Hawke stood between the two men with the binoculars. Both Latinos, a generation apart, they reminded Hawke of the Ortega brothers, although the younger, Mr. G., was closer in age to Jorge Ortega. The older one, whom Hawke addressed almost reverently as Senor Figueroa, had a grandfatherly appearance that only partially obscured the bearing of a pitbull. Several other men watched from various vantage points on the 90-foot yacht. Five minutes later the remarkable craft returned from the opposite direction, helicopter still in tow.

"See, you could never run a hydroplane through this kind of water. What's the chop out here, three or four feet? With this thing, it's no problem. You can run over a lot rougher shit than this, though it can get a little squirrelly, so you got to tone it down a bit. But one thing's for damned sure, you don't have to worry about anyone keeping up with you when the going gets rough."

This time, after the strange craft that was neither boat nor plane flashed past the motor yacht, the pilot eased the power of the jet turbine until it settled onto the water in a flurry of spray and came to rest near a squatty, converted shrimp boat, which steamed over to pluck it from the water with a harness lowered from a compact crane. The helicopter hovered low above the shrimp boat like a giant dragonfly over a flower. Hawke and his companions watched intently through binoculars while a ladder was lowered and two men ascended in turn into the helicopter, which quickly crossed a half-mile of open water to settle neatly onto a pad atop the yacht.

"Bravo, bravo," Hawke said, clapping his hands as the men who had climbed the ladder stepped out of the helicopter. He removed his Stetson and bowed at the waist. One of the men, Ramon Ortega, snickered to himself at the sight of the pale dome framed by a rusty, gray fringe.

"Splendid. A simply splendid display, Ramon. You have shown yourself to be a master of any craft. In the pantheon of great pilots, you're right up there with the best of them: John Glenn, Chuck Yeager and King Richard Petty himself. That's the highest praise I can give, my friend."

"*Payaso. Bufon!*" Ortega muttered to himself. *What a clown!*

Ortega carried a video tape which he handed to Hawke, who presented it ceremoniously with both hands extended to Mr. G.

"Let's hope our little audio-visual display captures the imagination of the exulted Maximum Leader, ol' El Maximo himself."

"I can assure you, he is intrigued," Mr. G said, drumming his fingernails on the plastic of the tape case before handing it to an aid who slipped it into a briefcase.

Hawke turned to say something to Senor Figueroa and saw that his attention was elsewhere, directed toward the other man who had disembarked from the helicopter, trailing a few paces behind Ortega. He was not Latino. His ethnic origin was difficult to pinpoint. Features suggested Eastern European as part of the mix. The rest was elusive. Something in the cheekbones contained a hint of American Indian. But it was the eyes that dominated the face and those who beheld it. Riveting eyes. Cold. Lethal.

Senor Figueroa stepped forward, ignoring Hawke.

"Lagarto," he said, drawing the syllables out. "Somehow I knew it was you."

Hawke spun around, aghast. No one addressed his partner by that name. Not to his face. Ever. He'd dealt with the man for many years. Their association had been mutually beneficial. Still, his own salutation was always Boss, Chief or No. 1, even though their relationship was, more or less, on equal footing.

This could be ugly. Hawke sensed the whole objective on the brink of blowing up in their faces. His mind raced, grasping at strategies to defuse the delicate moment. Instead, the crisis was averted by an unexpected source. It started as a sound, a sort of deep-throated wheeze that grew into a chuckle and ended with a word.

"Paco!"

This from the man Hawke knew as an enigma wrapped in a dynamite fuse. What followed left Hawke wide-eyed and for a rare moment speechless as he watched two unlikely comrades renew acquaintances. They stopped short of a warm embrace, yet there was a measured grace in their coming together. Lagarto extended his hand and pumped Figueroa's once. Hawke's attention was drawn to their hands, a quick intense clench that lingered for a single beat at the end of the downstroke, then a mutual release and quick withdrawal. At the same time, the eyes of each man never left the face of the other, as if both were gauging the effects of the years.

Figueroa said, "How long has it been, *mi compadre?*" Both were well aware of the occasion of their last parting. He muttered, "Bahia de Cochinos."

"When was it, the clusterfuck?" Lagarto said. "Sixty-two … Sixty-one?"

"Sixty-one."

"Of course, sixty-one."

"I can never forget."

"Kennedy's clusterfuck." Lagarto spat the words out bitterly.

The ill-fated scene on the Cuban shore flashed back to both men. Chaos on the beach, Bay of Pigs. The chattering of gunfire intensifying. Behind them, smoke billowing from one of the foundering invasion ships, a portent of disaster. In front of them, beyond a line of vegetation, one of Fidel Castro's tanks silhouetted in the morning light, searching them out. Above, one of his planes boring in again to hammer their position. Fingers dug into the sand, faces pressed to the ground, grit mixing with sweat. Looking into the face of the other, two men sharing the same realization, reading at the same time as feelings of betrayal turn to rage.

"Motherfucker!!"

The Cuban thinking it — or an equivalent in his native tongue — as his mercenary comrade shouted it, both grasping the grim reality. The air support this operation hinged on wasn't coming. Without it they were doomed.

Another explosion, this one too close. Gunfire whistling overhead. Survival instinct clicking into overdrive; scrambling to another position to crouch behind some type of grass along a ridge in the sand. A respite only, no place really to make a stand.

"Motherfucker!! Motherfucker!!"

The shout renewed and punctuated with fire from an automatic weapon. The Cuban looked at the mercenary and almost smiled. The S.O.B. venting and giving them hell at the same time. If you had to be in a hopeless situation, this was the sort of bloody bastard you'd want at your side. The Cuban aimed his rifle at a shape in motion, aware of the futility even as he fired. The response came with more vengeance than before.

Once again the eyes of the two men locked. They had attained a mutual respect during the months of training in Guatemala. That is not to say they knew or understood one another. Their only common ground was the cause, though even on that their motives diverged. The mercenary was the subject of much speculation, a daunting figure with a past no one could seem to trace. Not given to interaction except within the context of the objective, he showed interest only in the tropical lizards that he befriended with a Pied Piper's virtuosity.

To the men of the camp, including the other Americans, he remained a mystery that approached mythical proportions. Was he even American? He was believed to speak six languages and known to employ dozens of aliases. Who was he really? No one was certain of his actual name or origin. Rumors of his deeds spanned wars and continents. The CIA ran the operation. Everyone knew that. Yet he stood apart from the outfit, the ultimate freelancer of freedom fighters. Who brought him in? Who did he answer to?

The Cuban always wondered why the mercenary chose him as liaison, his link of essential communication. Perhaps it was his own earnestness, his no-nonsense dedication to the cause and the way the others seemed to instinctively defer to him in serious situations. He assumed the role with trepidation until he realized it was out of respect that the mercenary bestowed the nickname of Paco for reasons that were never clear. He grew to cherish it as a macho badge of honor, even when others mocked him with taunts such as, "Paco, your pal, *el loco* Lagarto, is looking for you. I think he has a new iguana for you to meet, or maybe to eat."

The situation on the beach deteriorated rapidly. The Cuban looked out at the transport ships on the bay and at the sky. With air support they had a chance. Without it their options boiled down to surrender or die.

The mercenary was the last of the non-Cuban commandos to pull out, or make it out, leaving the exile force to its fate. Before he left, the Cuban caught his eye again, and with a forlorn expression posed the simple, essential question. "Why?"

The reply cut through the din with the bluntness of a machete hacking through sugar cane.

"Mother-FUCKER!!!"

Looking into that face again for the first time in 32 years, Figueroa finally understood what was implicit in that declaration. The intonation was the same as now: "Kennedy's clusterfuck."

"I guess that one got what was coming to him." Figueroa was looking into the mercenary's eyes when he said it. There was an awkward pause. Neither looked away.

Finally, Largarto said, "Your objective remains. This one still has his grip on it."

"That's why we meet again, why we're both here, is it not?"

They moved farther from the others, to the starboard rail of the yacht — Hawke was talking to Mr. G but showing more interest in this curious reunion. The discussion was not about old times, of regrets or opportunities lost. They spoke as they had more than three decades before in Guatemala when they and the cause were young.

"You know how they say you can't catch a lizard by the tail," the mercenary said. "You want to kill it, you got to get the head. That's why the tail is so ridiculously long and the head so small. It's a diversion. The old bait and switch. You try to grab it, you always get the tail. In the end, you've got nothing. The only way is to use your head: Lead it into a trap."

#

Claire found Dallas where Keith said he'd be, fishing at the mouth of the inlet in the channel that led to Snapper Cove Marina. She parked her car behind the Great White on the edge of a vacant lot. Still dressed for work in dark skirt and scoop-necked T-shirt, she stumbled over rocks several times and cursed under her breath as she made her way along the path to the shore. Despite the darkness, she was able to spot him in moonlight silhouette, a solitary figure hunkered down on a cooler staring at the ocean.

"Looks like the big ones have all gotten away," she said from a discreet distance so as not to startle him. Her unsteady approach had already achieved that.

"Haven't shown up yet."

He continued staring at the ocean but slid to one side to give her room to perch on the cooler. She accepted the invitation and immediately leaned into him with an arm around his back. His scent was a blend of salt and Speed Stick, cool spice on a hot summer night.

"Hiding out?"

"Not from you. Came out to think and maybe catch a snook — if I'm lucky."

He had a live shrimp on a spinning rig drifting in the incoming tide passing through the inlet. Another rod with a bucktail jig dangling from the tip was propped against the bait bucket. Obviously, he wasn't working hard at it.

"Kind of romantic out here."

"Now it is."

He put an arm around her, but she didn't get the kiss she craved. Her skirt riding up left most of her legs exposed, and she was aware of his denim shorts and leg fur against her bare skin. It sparked teenage memories of summer makeout nights with boys on the sand at Huntington Beach. Once again her recurring randiness surprised her.

Dallas stood to retrieve his bait and cast it out for another drift through the inlet. Instead of returning to his seat he handed the rod to Claire and picked up the other one, sending the lure to the corner of the opposite seawall with a flick of the wrist. He worked it with a herky-jerky retrieve, then duplicated the cast. She watched him in the darkness, thinking that fishing was like smoking, an adult pacifier, only healthier. Dallas seemed to be concentrating on outwitting prey that may or may not be lurking in the dark water, but she sensed his focus was elsewhere. She waited for him to return, but even then he caught her off-guard.

"Where were you when President Kennedy was killed?"

"Kindergarten."

"I know it's a cliché to ask."

She frowned. He kept coming back to this. It brought to mind her shrink cautioning about obsessions with the regrettable events in her own past: "If you spend more time thinking about what has already happened than about what is happening now, you become a slave to your past. You don't have to suppress the past. Learn from it and move ahead."

Nice shrink logic. Not so easy for the tortured soul, and Dallas was that all right. She'd been attracted by the image of carefree strength. These inner demons of his were a concern.

"I was very young when that happened. It was so long ago. I just remember my parents being very upset, my mother crying a lot. It was on TV for days, and my mother was constantly wiping her eyes with a Kleenex. I felt bad because of the way it affected everyone else, and I liked his face. They kept showing his face. I said, 'Why would they want to hurt him?' Made my mother cry even more."

Dallas thought he had a strike, but it was a snag. He freed the jig, reeled it in and inspected it before making another cast, this one into the channel beyond the inlet.

"Had an interesting visit with Skeeter today. He took me out in the boat to tell me where he was when Kennedy was killed."

Dallas turned toward her, sensing the look of puzzlement that he couldn't see it in the darkness. He braced the butt of the spinning rod against his leg, letting the line sink as he related Devereaux's remarkable confession, everything except his impression that Devereaux may have had recent contact with the mysterious figure from the plumbing truck or had some knowledge of his whereabouts. When he finished the tale, Dallas started to reel in the jig. Almost immediately something struck it.

"Pretty big fight for such a little jack," Dallas said when he brought the oblong-shaped fish to the edge of rocks and unhooked it. Claire stooped at the edge of the seawall, peering through darkness for a glimpse of the jack crevalle that Dallas cradled in both hands. He was right, it wasn't very big but its face was somehow distinctive with a jutting jaw that looked as if it should have been dangling a cigar butt. And just before Dallas set the fish back in the water, the eye that seemed to Claire to be looking directly at her appeared to blink. Or was it a wink?

Got her thinking about the way the mind perceives what the eyes observe. As soon as the fish was gone she wondered if she remembered it as it was or the way she wanted it to be.

"My ex always insisted that Oswald alone was the killer. He used to argue with a neighbor who read a lot of books about it and was convinced it was a conspiracy. He had all kinds of theories but could never say for sure which was right. My husband would get furious and say, 'You want to believe that anyone but Oswald did it, even though he was there and everything pointed to him.' Our neighbor, Sherm — my husband called him Sherm the Worm — would say, 'Ah ha, that was the conspiracy. It was set up for Oswald to take the blame.' And, ah, you better get off of those rocks before you fall in."

Dallas was still crouched at the water's edge where he'd released the fish. One slip or shift of balance and he'd be bathing with the jack and whatever else was prowling the dark water of the inlet. She gave him a hand up and they hugged in the darkness on the seawall next to the inlet where the tide sought its ebb and a jack crevalle nursed a sore lip.

"I hope you don't think I'm just another conspiracy nut like Sherm the Worm. You have to understand, this was something I experienced, and it left a mark that I can't wipe away. There've been periods of time when I didn't think about it much at all. But lately a lot of things have been happening to bring it all back and stir up the feelings again.

"Then with Skeeter today, it's like getting hit with a sucker punch. It's confirmation of what I believed all along. The thing I've never gotten over in all these years is the way something as major as the murder of a president can be railroaded to suit somebody's hidden agenda, and truth be damned. And the media and people in high places who could do something about it just follow along blindly. I mean, Oswald never went to trial or even had a hearing. And yet, if you read any history book or newspaper article that refers to it, they always write that John F. Kennedy was assassinated by Lee Harvey Oswald who fired three shots from the Texas School Book Depository, like it's the freakin' gospel. That, despite the fact that the last official investigation concluded that Kennedy probably was the victim of a conspiracy. And even that was a copout."

"I never gave it much thought," Claire said, "probably because I was taught what it said in the history books. As far as I knew, that's all there was to it. But then one time when I was older I read a magazine article that claimed the Mafia did it because they thought Kennedy double-crossed them or something. I brought that up one time when Sherm was over, and he said the Mafia was pissed because they helped him get elected and sent him women, and Bobby Kennedy was giving them a hard time, targeting them for prosecution. I don't know, it's too bizarre but kind of interesting in a gossipy way. That whole idea really pissed off my husband, which I thought was funny. The thing that stands out is Sherm saying they could never have convicted Oswald because the case was so full of holes and they couldn't have proved it beyond a reasonable doubt. He said, 'Look, they couldn't even convict the L.A. cops in the Rodney King case and they had that on videotape.' "

"I've often wondered how everything would be different if the same thing happened today," Dallas said. "For one thing, the media is a lot more skeptical and competitive now. So maybe they would have dug up a lot of stuff right away and wouldn't have been so quick to accept the official version.

"But the biggest difference that strikes me is that if it happened today, every other person in Dealey Plaza would have had their own video camera to film the president. Even if some TV station didn't have a camera on him at that moment, someone would have gotten good footage of what happened on tape, and it would have been on the air within an hour being broadcast all over the world. Back then, the few people with cameras were shooting film that had to be processed, and the technology was pretty crude. The only one that really showed it, taken by that Zapruder guy, was bought by *Life* magazine and locked away in their vaults. It wasn't shown publicly for something like 10 years. If that film had been on television the day of the assassination there would have been such an outcry that they could have never made anyone believe it was Oswald acting alone and concocted the ridiculous idea that one bullet went through Kennedy and caused all of Connally's wounds. If you've seen that film, well, you'd have a hard time believing the shot that killed him didn't come from in front. And if you'd been there ..."

"Funny name."

"What?"

"Zapruder. I mean, I've never heard of anyone else with that name."

Claire turned quiet trying to recall what she'd read and heard about the assassination. She hadn't gotten around to seeing Oliver Stone's twist on history, but she thought she had seen a clip from the Zapruder film as part of a story about the movie. Her thoughts were interrupted by a clatter on the ground and the thump of something solid against her ankle that caused her knee to buckle. It was the spinning rod she had set on the ground while Dallas was fighting the jack. The line was still in the water.

Dallas got a hand on the rod before it reached the seawall and gave it to Claire, who was stunned by the blow to her ankle and flustered by the ferocity of the tug on the line.

"Oh my god, oh my god!"

"Just hang on, don't let him get to the rocks on the other side."

To anyone who may have heard the commotion in the darkness, it must have sounded like someone with a scorpion in their clothes or a game of Twister gone awry. Despite her incoherent shrieks, Claire regained enough composure to halt the retreat of the fish and was beginning to reclaim line. She had enjoyed fishing with her father as a kid, and since moving to the so-called sportfishing capital of the world had become a competent and determined angler. The worst thing about losing a big fish is never finding out what it was. She was intent on seeing what had bopped her on the leg and was trying to drag her to Havana.

"That's the biggest snook I've seen out here," Dallas said after Claire brought the exhausted fish within reach and he had a firm grip on the gill plate. "Gotta be over 20 pounds."

Regardless of its size, the snook was much more majestic than the feisty little jack, its body sleek and as powerful as a Ferrari.

"How about grilled snook for breakfast? Tough to beat."

Claire saw cunning in the eyes and firm lower jaw. She reached out and traced the distinctive racing stripe along the length of its flank, and the fish squirmed in Dallas hands.

"Put it back," she said and shivered at the thought that the fish's fate was her whim. "Let it go."

After Dallas removed the hook and released the snook, they sat close together again on the cooler, her head on his shoulder, his arms a protective shell tight around her body.

"What are you thinking?"

"Wondering who wrote the Final Jeopardy tune, and if they get royalties every time it's played on the show."

It was so out of left field, she nearly fell off the cooler. It was vintage Dallas, and she took it as a good sign.

"Look, I don't want you to think I'm some kind of nut who keeps bringing up the Kennedy thing," he said. "I know, it's damn near ancient history."

"It's OK, I understand. It is a big thing. I can't imagine how I'd feel if I'd witnessed something like that."

"Hey, I know it doesn't matter all that much now," he said. "The world doesn't care anymore. A large segment of the population wasn't even alive then. They know Kennedy as a myth, a martyr, like Davey Crockett or General Custer. All they know is he bluffed the Russians in the Cuban missile crisis and boffed Marilyn Monroe. The assassination is just another movie-of-the-week melodrama in our twisted, spin-doctored history. Who really cares about what really happened, how it happened and how it altered the course of the last 30 years?

"Most people are more interested in whether Elvis is really dead. Maybe I'm no different about most things. But I was there, and it's a canker sore that won't go away, that keeps getting bitten and swollen up and throbbing just when I think it's all healed and forgotten. It's like an orphan who goes through life, becomes successful and rich but can't ever quite find peace because the question nags about who his parents were. It's the same for me, like an itch that never goes away no matter how much I scratch. I don't even want to think about it, but I can't suppress the urge that just wants to know."

If you can't find peace, you can at least seek comfort. Claire understood that. It was what they could be for each other, certainly on this night. They spent the remainder of it in the cramped quarters of Dallas's rental unit — Lyle was sleeping over with Margie's son — ending the day the way they began it, making love until both were teary from the flood of pleasure.

"Little did I know I'd land two big snook in one night," she said, playfully.

"You call this a snook, huh? I used to fish with a guy, he'd have a bit to drink and he'd go up to women in bars and say, 'Ever catch a trouser trout?' "

They were still laughing when the phone rang. The call abruptly soured their slice of joy and comfort. Dallas appeared shell-shocked when he hung up the phone.

"It was my sister. Mom had a heart attack."

CHAPTER 38

It was a summer of high water in the Midwest and high heat in the South. It was a summer of love and tears. The onset of July found Dallas Huston in his hometown closer to tears than love, marking time in a waiting room of Parkland Memorial Hospital, fingertips grimy from newsprint, tongue bitter with the aftertaste of cafeteria coffee and eyes gravelly from lack of sleep. Somewhere on the next floor Mom was undergoing the latest battery of cardiac tests.

Think you've got worries, pal? The morning paper brought more bad news about the sodden watershed of the upper Mississippi River. Another drenching pushed flooding in Davenport, Iowa, close to record level. Winds up to 83 mph slammed Waterloo, Iowa, which seemed appropriately named. Navigation was at a virtual standstill across 500 miles of the mighty, muddy waterway with locks closed, leaving barges and their towboats literally up a creek without a port in the storm. The dubious good news was that one of the riverboat casinos had managed to stay open at dockside, presuming that people losing everything couldn't resist the opportunity to risk adding their last cent to the casualty list. Perhaps, that was the best time to go for it, although even a lightning strike of good fortune at the craps table couldn't be counted on for salvation.

Dallas read about a former carnival ride operator in Pennsylvania who'd won $16.2 million in the state lottery five years earlier and now was broke, his mansion in shambles and his brother in jail for plotting to kill him. So much for the premise of a (lottery) ticket to happiness.

Other news items that caught Dallas's eye pertained to recent deaths of people of varying degrees of prominence, including Pat Nixon and Roy Campanella. Dallas native Spanky McFarland, of Little Rascals fame, had died the day before in Fort Worth of a heart attack. He was 64, same as Mom.

There was also a story about the controversy simmering in the wake of John Connally's death a couple of weeks earlier. The JFK assassination conspiracy camp had been seeking the removal of bullet fragments from the body of the former Texas governor who was wounded along with Kennedy. It was Connally's reaction to being shot that first clued young Dallas Huston that what he was watching in Dealey Plaza wasn't a happy parade. Any additional clues Connally may have provided in death were buried with him, but the embers of controversy were stoked again.

Dallas stared without focusing, threading old film through the cortex, doing his own mental Zapruder in the same hospital where JFK was pronounced dead and the so-called magic bullet was "discovered" on a stretcher, just as the door to the waiting room swung open. He looked up expecting to see his sister, Linda, returning with news or a soda. Instead, he witnessed the entrance of a stocky, balding, animated fellow in a pumpkin-orange Hawaiian shirt with a tall, tight-lipped companion in tow. Mr. Personality was delivering a monologue in a conspiratorial tone calculated to ensure that every word would be overheard, including the frequent mention of his own name, by anyone in the vicinity, which meant Dallas and a middle-aged woman watching *Days of Our Lives* on a fuzzy TV screen.

"Now, if you said to me, 'Wayne Glick, how can I be sure this'll go over big?' You can take my word, it can't miss. I know because I've been involved in this thing in one way or another for almost 20 years. It's one of those things that never dies, if you pardon the pun. Thing is, nobody can resist a good mystery. Look at how long *Murder, She Wrote* has been on the tube. This is a hell of a lot better mystery than that. It's real, and it's never been solved. It's the ultimate mystery. And there's a hook for it now with the 30th anniversary coming up. So we've got to move fast. I just need a boost of cash to put it in motion. Already got a lot of the photos in the can."

The woman frowned and turned up the television, so Glick homed in on Dallas, delighted to have doubled his audience. With arm extended and a slight bow, he presented his card, which had an ink drawing of a 35mm camera and the inscription, "Wayne Glick, Pictures for Posterity."

"That's Glick, rhymes with click, the sound a camera's shutter makes. Get it?"

He introduced his companion as Haygood, "one of my main men." It was unclear if that was a first or last name and where he fit in this get-rich conspiracy. Dallas smiled weakly and glanced at the door, hoping Linda would show up to rescue him. Glick pressed the opportunity, detailing his grand plan to produce a glossy "coffee table picture book" of sites relating to the Kennedy assassination.

"Understand, most of my business is weddings and portraits — boring studio stuff. This is my fun. Think about it. You're a photographer around Dallas, what're you going to shoot? Cowboys or Kennedy — so to speak," he said with a chuckle.

239

"I don't mean to sound irreverent. This is all history that we're talking about, and around here, history is industry. What I want to do is present it in a little different light."

Glick's idea was to take scenes that people are familiar with and add his own special effects, capitalizing on the mythology surrounding the assassination.

"I've got a guy who owns a gun store who's going to pose at the house on Neely where the pictures of Oswald were taken with his guns. You've seen them, the famous Backyard Photos, right? Oswald said somebody superimposed his head on someone else's body, and a lot of people believed him. What I'm going to do is take a picture of this guy in the same pose with the same kind of guns and superimpose a clown's head in place of the guy's head. You see? It makes a point. It's different. It's avant-garde. It's cutting edge."

Dallas looked for a reaction from Glick's silent partner, who stood with arms folded and occasionally nodded but remained expressionless. He reminded Dallas of Dan Akroyd's Elwood Blues character. Dallas wasn't sure if Haygood was a potential investor or an actor for some macabre set-up shot. Glick explained that they were at Parkland plotting the best way to portray the discovery of the bullet on the stretcher that the Warren Commission determined had passed through Kennedy and Connally and emerged virtually intact.

"There's a couple ways to work it. I can show someone dressed like a magician —tuxedo, top hat, magic wand, white gloves — picking up a real bullet off a stretcher." Glick pulled an actual bullet out of his pocket and held it up for Dallas to see. "Or I could create a huge, cartoonish bullet painted with the Superman logo and have it lying on the stretcher like it was a patient." He shrugged. "Problem is, the people I've spoken to with the hospital aren't too cooperative. So it may end up we've got to come in like we're visiting someone, find an unoccupied gurney in a hallway and snap a couple quick shots when nobody's looking."

Such was the plight of the avant-garde historian. Glick explained he'd met resistance from some of the other people he'd approached who had various connections to aspects of the assassination.

"I do have a shot of the fella who was working the candy counter in the Texas Theatre when Oswald came in that day. I put him out front wearing big dark glasses and eating popcorn," Glick said. "It adds authenticity when you get someone who was there at the time. But not everyone wants to be involved. Say, you from around here?"

Dallas stared at the photographer, not knowing what to say. He looked at Haygood, still in undertaker pose. Mercifully, the door opened and Linda entered the waiting room.

"Used to be," Dallas said, excusing himself. "But not for a long time."

#

"I hate when they do that."

"What?"

Dallas turned away from the window and nodded toward the clock-radio on the table next to the bed, where "Brown Eyed Girl" was crackling through the static on a tinny, overtaxed speaker. He was still trying to comprehend being here with Linda in her one-room apartment above the lobby of the venerable Texas Theatre when familiar lyrics completed the '60s time warp.

"I hate when radio stations play the censored version of that song," he said. "You know, when they take out the part about getting it on behind the stadium. What's the big deal? There're songs out now a lot more explicit than that."

"You mean," Linda said with a laugh that sent a jagged blast of cigarette smoke through her nose, it's not like he's saying, 'Going down on you, baby, behind the stadium.' "

"Well, yeah, that's one way to put it," he said, his laughter echoing hers. Considering the circumstance, laughter was a welcome tonic and he milked it. That he was sharing it with his sister made it more satisfying. It was hard to recall them laughing together often in the past.

"The real point is, nobody has any right to be editing Van Morrison," she said. "The man's a master, the Leprechaun Bard."

"That's it, don't mess with Van the Man."

"Of course, that's maybe his most popish song. Probably why he stopped writing them like that. Got too much soul for the vanilla hell of Top 40."

Dallas studied her perched on a wicker swivel chair, smoking, one elbow on a rickety bar, one leg tucked under, the other dangling, bare foot keeping time with the music. Thinking, if he were an artist he would sketch her in charcoal, a real moody scene. If he were Van Morrison, he'd capture her in blues. Even in the pale light of a 40-watt bulb, the toll of the years was evident on her face. He had to squint to visualize the former second-runner-up high school homecoming queen. He wondered if she could still see that in herself, or if she even bothered looking, after two bum marriages, a car wreck and too many breaks in life that turned out sour. Second runner-up, pretty much the story of her life. And yet, the edge was still there.

"You know, you haven't changed. Still got a way with words," he said.

She took the last drag of her cigarette and stubbed it out. Now she was studying him, and he was bracing for a sharp volley.

"You look … Something about you … Something's different. Better. Living in Florida must agree with you."

"Whew," he said, exaggerating the exhale. "Guess that's a compliment. I'll take it. Maybe turning 40 isn't the end of the world after all. Maybe I'm one of those late bloomers."

"Well, let's hope so. You still haven't done shit with your life."

They laughed again and he held up his can of Lone Star in a mock toast. The beer was tepid and tinny, fitting for the occasion. Lone Star should be frosty cold in a long-necked bottle. This was a warm-beer-in-a-can night.

Dallas surveyed the surroundings, and the true weirdness of everything overcame him again. Mom awaiting her fate in the hospital where JFK died, and here he was with Linda in the god-damned Texas Theatre, where Lee Harvey Oswald was captured. Downstairs the Friday night feature — some art film about a power struggle in a South American banana republic — was over and the meager crowd had dispersed. Still plenty of traffic passing out front on Jefferson, with the occasional horn and squeal of tires providing background noise.

"I still can't believe you're actually living here. In my wildest imagination, if someone called and said, 'Guess what your sister's up to,' I'd never come close. I mean, the fucking Texas Theatre, where they arrested Oswald. I wouldn't have figured this place was even open. I remember it being boarded up years ago."

"It was. They were going to turn it into a warehouse or tear it down, until Senior Henriquez rescued it and poured a lot of money into fixing it up. He's trying to turn it into a cultural center for the people around here. Provide a place where musicians and dancers, anyone who has talent and the urge to perform, can come and have a stage. And to show alternative films, all for a price people around here can afford."

"Mostly Latinos."

"Right, that's who lives here."

"So, how did you end up here?"

"Cesar doesn't care if you're Latino or not. He's interested in talent and ambition. When he bought the theater, it came with all this film-making equipment. He decided to make it available to people who come to him with a project but no other way to get it done. I had this idea for a documentary I wanted to do on women and AIDS. We saw so much of that at the hospital. Girls as young as 15, wives who got it from errant husbands. Those are the two biggest groups. I wanted to help get the word out."

Linda was a RN, a good one. She had held a supervisory position at a hospital in Brownsville, Texas, where she lived with second husband, Larry, who had a foreman's job with an oil company. The last time Dallas visited her they were living in a big house — five bedrooms, pool — and she was driving a hot, red Mustang convertible. V8, 5.0-liter. Then Larry took a hike with a young senorita. Somehow Linda got the shaft twice. Ended up with just enough alimony to send Karen, the daughter she had too young, to college in Houston. Now she was driving a Chevy

Cavalier with bad shocks and living in a room with a bed and a bar in the Texas Theatre, working part time at a women's clinic and making a documentary about AIDS.

Dallas shifted uneasily. The fan in the corner was just stirring the cigarette smoke into lifeless air. There was no relief outside the window. Summer had Texas in a bear hug, and the bear never took a siesta. Dallas noticed a bird outside on the pedestal that supported the S in Texas on the façade of the theatre. The bird was hopping on one leg, the other hanging limp and useless. It seemed appropriate for this haven of wounded birds and dream seekers.

"How long you been here?"

"Couple months. It's perfect, for now. I mean, there was no point in staying in Brownsville. The place is a hole. And with Karen gone." She shrugged. "This way I'm close to Mom. I mean, I couldn't live with her, but I'm close by when she needs me. This is all I need right now. There's just me and my Beatles collection. And I've got the run of this place. I get a lot of editing done late at night. Film's almost finished. Want to see some of it?"

#

Dawn found Dallas watching his sister's documentary about women and AIDS from the same seat Lee Harvey Oswald occupied when police barged into the theater and arrested him. The seat — three rows from the rear of the lower level, center section — still bore an inscription noting that event. As Linda went to shut down the projector, Dallas tried to imagine Oswald awaiting his fate. Was he merely a fugitive hiding out, a desperate man without a clue about his next move, or was he there with a specific purpose, keeping an appointment with a contact, a player in something large and sinister.

The projector stopped and the house lights came up, just as they did when the police began searching for their suspect. Dallas wondered what was going through his mind at that moment. "It's all over now," Oswald had said before punching and attempting to shoot the first cop that approached him.

The sudden silence in the big auditorium echoed in Dallas's ears. But it was welcome after 45 minutes of watching broken women talking about their plights. The air was stuffy. Despite the vast space around him, he felt closed in.

"So what did you think?"

"Huh?"

"The film, knucklehead."

"Well, when they grabbed him, Lee H. was watching a movie called *War is Hell*. I'd say, so is AIDS. It's pretty poignant. You've done a lot of good work," he said, trying to make sure to say enough.

"Forget about Oswald. This place isn't about Oswald. That's ancient history. This is about now. It's about trying to do something for the community, for the people living here. Now."

"It's just that being here in this place I can't help but think about those events. We were so close to it. I'm sure it's not an issue with people living around here. But for me, it keeps coming back, especially now."

Linda was kneeling on the chair in front of his, facing him. He knew he must look a wreck, feeling quivers of exhaustion in his shoulders and neck. His reddened eyes felt as if they'd been pried open with screwdrivers. Hers were full of intensity. Still earnest after all she'd been through.

"What do you want out of life, Dallas? What do you plan to do with the rest of it?"

He blinked, brain screaming with the need for sleep. "Just trying to get through the night. And the next few days."

"Don't you ever think about the larger picture of what we're doing here? You can only be on the planet taking up space for so long. I certainly wasted a lot of years. Screwed around, sowed my wild oats. Now I want to try to make a difference, to somebody. Don't you ever get the urge to do something significant?"

Dallas rubbed the back of his neck. He noticed his hand was trembling.

"Well, yeah. Sure I do."

CHAPTER 39

Reality makes no consolation for sleep schedules, especially irregular ones. Out of a mid-day nightmare, Dallas and Linda found themselves back at the hospital listening to a trio of doctors giving the grim assessment of Mom's beleaguered heart. To Dallas, it sounded like a medical journal overflowing, the words all packing four or five syllables. None of them struck a chord of understanding until the doctor doing the most talking, a young Pakistani, laid out the bottom line in a sing-song lilt. "We must operate immediately. We cannot delay."

Linda asked all the questions while Dallas sat alongside feeling the knot in his stomach growing tighter and larger. Underscoring how critical the situation was, the operation was scheduled for the following morning, Saturday, July 3. This couldn't wait until after the holiday weekend. Dr. So-and-so was flying back from some golf resort to preside. Surely he'd be in fine spirits after sacrificing a prime tee time.

They were given assurances that "she'll get the best care we can provide," but no guarantees. As they were ushered out, Dallas noticed the tears in Linda's eyes. Before they entered Mom's room in ICU, she dabbed them with a tissue and reset her resolve.

Addie Huston was always a robust, formidable woman. Rosy cheeks, ready smile, a bit of the devil in her heart. She was quick witted and sharp of mind. Worked the crossword puzzle in the newspaper every day, down to the last square. Loved to bet the horses and always was up for a game of gin rummy. Kept her penny-ante gambling stash in a felt pouch with "Addie" stitched in gold. If you beat her, you had reason to feel satisfied. Mom gave no quarter. It wasn't in her makeup to back off.

She approached life the same way. Smoked too much. When she cooked, she cooked up a storm. And if you crossed her, you had a tempest on your hands. It didn't pay to mess with Mom. No one understood that better than erstwhile husband Fred Huston, who after leaving her with two kids to raise never again set foot in Texas. She'd warned him that if he did, "I'll kick your sorry ass all the way to the Gulf of Mexico and feed it to the sharks."

Dallas had his mother's no-holds-barred spirit when he pitched. Never back off. Never give in to the hitter. Here's my best, hit it if you can, you son of a bitch. That, and a nasty sinking curve, got him to the major leagues. Unfortunately, he had been unable to transfer the philosophy to other aspects of his life.

That's what made it so tough seeing her lying in bed, IV in one hand, breathing oxygen through a tube in her nose. She looked smaller, incomprehensibly vulnerable. So unlike Mom. But the sparkle was still evident in her pale blue eyes. Dallas was looking for it, and it was the only thing that kept him from melting into a pile of blubbery goo.

He reached for the hand without the IV and it was clutching a television remote control. She had hit the mute button when they came in. He kissed her on the cheek. He saw her eyes studying his face, then dart to Linda's.

"Did you hear who died?"

Her question startled Dallas. "Ah, oh, Spanky, from the Little Rascals. The guy who played him."

"George McFarland," Linda said, glancing at Dallas with similar surprise. "Didn't he live in Fort Worth?"

"No, not him. That was a couple days ago. I'm talking about the latest."

Dallas and Linda looked at each again, clueless.

"Fred Gwynne."

"Really, Herman Munster?" Dallas said, more out of a need to say something than genuine interest. He was more concerned with the crisis inside this room.

"Cancer, they said. McFarland, that was a heart attack. They were both young, 66 and 64. Too young." She pursed her lips and closed her eyes. Dallas felt the wave of emotion transfer to his own throat.

"Fred Gwynne, he was such a big, lovable oaf," Addie said. "You know he was six-five? Seemed even taller than that. I liked him best when he played in the cop show with that fat fellow who always said, 'Ooh, ooh.' I couldn't stomach the Munster thing. Such nonsense. He was better than that part."

This was so Mom. Everyone's concerns were hers. Neighbors, relatives, but especially people she saw on TV. She spoke about them as if they were members of the family. She was a monger for celebrity gossip. Read all the supermarket tabloids. Always right on top of who was sleeping with whom and who was getting dumped.

When she was home the TV was always tuned to the soaps or some talk show. The talk show hosts were her friends, called them all by their first name. Used to be Merv. Later Phil. She watched Dinah. Adored Johnny. Lately it was Oprah. She didn't like them all. Mike Douglas didn't have enough spunk. She watched Regis and Kathy Lee just to pick them apart.

"You should have seen Jerry Springer this morning. They had a 16-year-old girl who gave birth to triplets. The father was her brother."

Dallas cringed. "Where do they get these people?"

"Arkansas! No joke," Addie said, laughing heartily at the favorite brunt of Texans' barbs. It was Mom's familiar laugh, a gravelly smoker's laugh. But this one ended in a wince of pain despite her best attempt to conceal it.

Linda missed it in her disgust about daytime television. "Fortunately, I have better things to do than watch that garbage. Like sleep," she said, before leaving the room to grab a snack and no doubt a cigarette of her own.

Dallas sat through *The Newlywed Game* with Mom, gripping her hand. She muted the TV when a nurse came in to change the IV and give her several pills. Afterward, they sat in silence, both staring at the image on the screen but not really watching it.

"Scared?" Dallas said, finally.

"Not so much. More so angry. You always think you'll have more time. You think of all the things that still need to be done. You and Linda are long gone from the house, but there's still little ones around. Your cousin Penny's daughter Carolyn, my brother's grandkids." She paused, fighting for composure. "Hell, it's all my own damn fault, anyway. That's what I'm most angry about."

He felt her eyes on his face. It was another habit of Mom's. When she had a probing question to ask or advice to dispense, she'd look at you intently, locked on like radar. It was discomforting but effective. You couldn't avoid her. Dallas knew what was coming.

"When are you going to find someone special for your life?"

"Ah, I'm kind of seeing someone. She's pretty special."

The inevitable pause followed. She always did this, froze you with the arc of her eyebrows. All you could do was wait for the next bit of wisdom, thinking, *What? What? Come on, just say it.*

"I don't make a habit of quoting your father, but he had this thing he used to say: 'Leave no chips on the table, sing till you're hoarse, dance till you're breathless, love till it hurts.' Course, you know that tune: He danced off with the next partner and left the hurt behind, but that's not the point."

She winked. Dallas smiled.

"You're not getting any younger. But you know what, it's never too late. Don't let it slip away. The years go by so fast."

Now it was his turn to study her. The frailty of her appearance belied what was left inside. It was easy to look past the wrinkles and pain to the mom he stood next to in Dealey Plaza. She wore red that day to make her stand out, hoping to catch the young president's eye. She was mid-30s then, mother of two, and still an eye-catcher.

Addie Huston never did remarry, never went back to her maiden name. But she never lacked for male companionship. Dallas smiled to himself, recalling the men who used to come around and how she kept them at bay, always clearly in control. The smile faded as his mind drifted back to the question he'd wanted to ask for so long. Thinking maybe it wasn't the time to bring it up, in her condition. She looked so tired. But what if he never got another chance?

"Mom."

"What?"

"This probably seems like a strange question to ask now. If it upsets you, forget about it, we don't have to talk about it."

She stared back at him, her eyes curious. He waited until she nodded.

"The day Kennedy was shot, when we went to that office to talk to the FBI or whatever, what did you tell them about what happened?"

Addie Huston's eyes narrowed slightly. She wasn't used to being the one put on the spot. He felt her hand tighten on his and her gaze turn distant. Then she closed her eyes. Dallas waited until she returned, her eyes again clear and focused.

"At first, I told them the truth. Right away you could tell, that's not what they wanted. I'm probably a damned fool, but it made me mad. Kept thinking, what's going on here? Stuck to my guns for a while — until I started seeing them sitting out there in their cars, watching the house. They started knocking on the door, saying they wanted to go over the testimony and get everything straight. All they really wanted to do was scare me. They did a good job of it. I had you and your sister to think about. So, finally, I just told them what they wanted to hear."

Dallas could see the pain that accompanied these memories, bigger than the pain that now gripped her chest. He felt guilty about bringing it up at all. But through all these years they had never talked about it, never reconciled their feelings about the event.

"Remember, I told you I saw a man behind that fence on the hill, where the shot came from. Did you see him, too?"

Her eyelids were heavy now and she turned her face away from his.

"Dallas, let it go. The whole thing was bigger than the president of the United States. It's bigger than you and me."

This time when Addie Huston closed her eyes she didn't reopen them. Dallas sat there for a long time holding her hand, listening to the peaceful rhythm of her gentle snoring.

CHAPTER 40

The operation lasted five hours. The doctors emerged looking weary and grim. There were complications, they said. Aren't there always through the course of anyone's day? When the day revolves around open-heart surgery, complications can be catastrophic.

In this case, the biggest one was that Addie Huston never woke up. She passed directly from anesthesia to a coma. She clung to life through Saturday night, which was longer than Don Drysdale lasted. The great Dodgers pitcher checked out quickly that same afternoon in a Montreal hotel room. Heart attack. He was 56. Much too young. Dallas was in a waiting room at Parkland Memorial Hospital when Drysdale's death was reported on the 11 o'clock news. That was a shock. Always is when the gods of sports turn out to be as mortal as the rest of us.

Mom slipped away just before noon the following day. Sunday, the Fourth of July. Another reason for Dallas to dread that holiday. He and Linda got the news just after hearing about the death of Curly Joe DeRita, the last of the Three Stooges. Complications from pneumonia. He was 83. Not so young.

Geez, Curly Joe. Mom would have preferred to go out with Drysdale. She hated the Stooges. Called them the Three Stupids. Mom loved baseball, and Drysdale was one of her favorites, tall and handsome with the great fastball that he never hesitated to stick under a hitter's chin. His style was like her own: right at you.

Mom used to tell Dallas, "Pitch like that big Dodger, Drysdale. Don't be afraid to knock them down. You've got to earn their respect before you can get them out."

Addie Huston had a knack for boiling life down to the simple truths. She was usually right. Not that Dallas always paid attention. He'd been away from home for more than half his life. But there was something comforting in knowing she was there. Now she was gone, and a feeling of emptiness was setting in.

He wasn't even in the room when she died. After pacing around ICU all morning he left to get a Coke. When he came back, she had passed on. The doctor — not the head surgeon, the young Pakistani — offered his condolences along with an assessment of what went wrong. Dallas excused himself in the middle of it, leaving Linda to the postmortem. She found him later outside the hospital sitting under a tree, shirt soaked with sweat. The Fourth of July in Dallas is a sizzler, even without the gunpowder.

"You know, ever since I got here all I've been hearing about are people dying. John Connally, Pat Nixon, Roy Campanella, Spanky, Fred Gwynne, Don Drysdale, Curly Joe. Mom."

"Who doesn't belong on this list? Who shouldn't be on it?"

Linda's face reflected more anger than anguish. We all confront grief like building a jigsaw puzzle that never quite fits together. There is no distinct place to start. Reach into the pile, grab a piece and try to match it with the next thought or emotion. Linda started with denial. Dallas was struck by the emptiness. He kept grabbing into the darkness and coming up with nothing.

"Life shouldn't be this full of death," he said.

Dallas sat on the ground, picking at the grass like the child he wished he could return to, before he was old enough to have a worry. Could he even remember that far back? When had it ended, blissful innocence? When dad left? When Kennedy was killed? When his baseball career self-destructed? Had he merely taken the shortcut from childhood to numbing ignorance without ever bothering to give a damn?

He kept trying to replay it all, every retrievable memory from the past, the whole catalogue of images of Mom. This is what you do when someone close to you dies, as if the memories will revive the person and transport you back to a preferred time. It is healthy, if futile. At that moment, it is all you have.

Dallas lost track of how long they sat under the tree outside the hospital where John F. Kennedy, Lee Harvey Oswald and Addie Huston died. He was aware of Linda smoking more than one cigarette. Maybe the whole damned pack. He heard sirens racing to and from someone else's emergencies. He watched pigeons poking around for morsels of food, heads bobbing rhythmically like windup toys. He forgot about the heat and felt a slight cool dampness from the ground. Finally, Linda broke the spell.

"You know, this would have pissed her off."

"What, dying?"

"Having it be on a holiday. You know how she loved every holiday. It was an excuse to bring a bunch of people together and feed them until they couldn't walk."

"Never had much trouble rounding up takers. That potato salad she made was enough to bring them from miles away. I remember once we went to a picnic and some woman tried to serve me someone else's potato salad. I pointed to Mom's bowl and said, 'No, thanks, I want that one.' You know what she'd say if she could talk to us now: 'Come on, eat. Eat!' "

"She'd say, 'Is anyone having fun yet?' "

So that's what Dallas and Linda decided to do late in the afternoon on the Fourth of July. They set out on a mission that would have pleased Mom. They went to salvage the holiday. They made the short jaunt down the Stemmons Freeway in Linda's Chevy Cavalier with the bad shocks to the edge of downtown and parked in a pay lot near historic West End Market Place — "Where the fun never ends." Mom's kind of place.

First stop was Dick's Last Resort, which glibly bills itself as "The Shame of the West End — no cover charge, no dress code and certainly no class." The place had the ambiance of a crowded picnic pavilion with patrons packed along either side of long tables spanning the length of the dining area. The tables were covered with butcher's paper, all the better to contain the inevitable mess. Dallas understood why when the barbecue ribs arrived in metal buckets swimming in sauce.

"It's like they're slopping the hogs."

He was about to plunge in when the hands of a waiter appeared from behind and tied a plastic bib around his neck.

"As they say in France, *bone appa-teet*," the waiter said with a Texas drawl, "And you better not leave anything on the bones. Ya hear?"

"Mom would have loved this place," Dallas said.

"She did. I brought her here for brunch last month. They kept refilling her coffee and she kept emptying it. She didn't want to leave."

Now she was gone. They couldn't have picked a better place to summon her spirit. Dick's renders service with a wry smile, though you can never be sure if they're laughing with you or at you. Dallas discovered that when he returned from the restroom and found Linda smirking at him.

"What's funny?"

"Check your back."

He reached behind and discovered a handwritten note taped to his shirt that read: "I think, therefore I am confused."

"How long has that been there?"

"Long enough for everyone in the place to read it. Don't worry, you're not the only one," she said, pointing to a sunburned man passing their table who had a barbecue stain on the front of his shirt and a silly note on his back. It read, "My baloney has a first name."

Sometimes nonsense makes the best sense. It was the perfect defense for this day. Dallas kept glancing at Linda, feeling the compulsion to talk. About what? Their feelings? They both felt like crap but were concealing it well, masking it with revelry, picnic food, loud music and beer — Lone Star, cold out of the bottle — long-necked, naturally. The din of the crowd and the rockin' blues-and-gospel house band made conversation a lost cause anyway.

So, Dallas ordered another beer for each of them. When it came, he took firm hold of the neck and reached across the table to clink the base of the bottle against the one his sister offered in return. She gave him a nod and a wink before pouring the cool liquid down her throat with the gusto of the cowgirl she would always be at heart. In this manner they threw a lasso around grief and told it to wait outside with the horses, for a few hours anyway.

But once, when the band played a rousing rendition of "What a Wonderful World," the singer nailing Satchmo's bullfrog timbre with chilling accuracy, Dallas caught Linda with a tear in her eye.

They stood outside and watched a fireworks display over the city before taking the party around the block to Dallas Alley where seven nightclubs were engaging in a duel of decibels. They found adjoining stools in the back of a funky piano bar, where the volume was lower than inhibitions. The entertainment was strictly PC: pretty crude and plenty comical, with a pair of piano players singing bawdy ballads and vying to outdo one another in embarrassing the patrons, particularly women. A second duo took the stage and turned out to be raunchier than the first act. Dallas and Linda stayed long enough to hear the infamous "Pussycat Song," in which every verse ends with the word "pussy," preceded by adjectives such as pink, wet, deep, furry, itchy, etc., all of which were repeated with each succeeding verse. Strictly good-ol'-boy formula humor, but what struck Dallas was that the biggest guffaws seemed to be coming from women in the crowd. Linda gave him a mock-disapproving expression before breaking out into a wide grin.

"I don't think Mom would have liked this place," he said.

"Oh, she would have liked it. She just wouldn't have let on that she did."

One of the piano players brought a mousy, middle-aged court clerk from Iowa on stage and was instructing her in an outrageous pantomime of another risque song. The payoff was that when he sang the word nuts, she was supposed to grab his crotch. It took four or five aborted attempts and the crowd egging her on before she grabbed it with a force that crossed his eyes. When the laughter subsided, Dallas and Linda exchanged a glance that both interpreted as time to leave.

It was nearly midnight, but Dallas Alley was still rocking. With the holiday extending through Monday, nobody was in a hurry to let go of the night. They passed the karaoke bar where a bald fellow with eyes like a St. Bernard's was striking out with his mock Frankie Valli falsetto on "Walk Like a Man." Sounded like another victim of the mousy court clerk, Dallas thought, as the audience grimaced. They passed a seductive cowgirl selling cans of light beer out of a tub in the corridor near the juncture of four bars. Dallas wished he'd taken one for the road after they stumbled out into the blast-furnace of the Dallas night. Still it was preferable to the smoke-conditioned barroom atmosphere, at least for him. Linda was still conditioning a Benson & Hedges Light as they approached the parking lot where they'd left the Cavalier near the corner of Ross Avenue and Record.

Dallas would have been hard-pressed to explain the compulsion that came over him then. Blame it on the Lone Star and the strangeness of the circumstances. For whatever reason, he suddenly was overcome by a need to run.

"Come on. Race you to the next traffic light."

They did this all the time when they were kids. Usually Linda was the instigator and the victor. By the time he could outrun her, she was a teenager and too cool to race her kid brother. Her expression said that hadn't changed.

"I don't run anymore," she said, sucking the last lungful from her cigarette and flicking it past Dallas.

He watched the butt dance across the sidewalk, scattering sparks in the darkness like a silent firecracker. It wasn't until he looked back that he realized he'd been had. She was gone, leaving behind a puff of smoke, already 15 yards ahead as he began the chase.

"You bitch!"

"Sucker!"

He might have caught her if not for his own laughter interfering with his breathing, and if he'd been wearing shoes more conducive to running. Topsiders are meant to grip the slick deck of a boat but don't provide the bounce needed for a sprint. He could hear the hollow slap of his own footsteps as he followed the bend of the road to the left between two parking lots, across the Dallas Area Rapid Transit tracks and down a dark straightaway flanked by buildings toward a traffic light that bathed the pavement ahead in a red glow. For a moment, as the gap between them diminished, he thought he had a chance to overtake her. But with half a block to go his legs were seized by that strange sensation of trying to run in a dream and getting nowhere, as if slogging through wet cement.

Dallas was still two or three strides behind when Linda reached the intersection giggling and gasping, stopping at the edge of the sidewalk just as the light turned to green. They stood a few feet apart bent over, attempting to regain their breath. At least a minute passed before he stood up and began to get his bearings.

"Holy shit. Do you realize?"

Linda's face was flushed but triumphant, sweat glistening on her cheeks in the dim light. Her expression shifted from smug to incredulous. "You mean, you didn't know where you were? Hel-lo!"

"I knew we were near here. I just wasn't thinking that's where we were headed. I was too busy trying to catch your scrawny ass."

They were standing at the southeast corner of a nondescript red brick building at the intersection of Infamy and Atrocity, better known as Houston and Elm. The name on the facade above the entrance to the building identified it as the Dallas County Administration Building, but the world remembers it by its previous name: the Texas School Book Depository. For anyone just emerging from a 30-year siesta in a cave, a plaque verified the building's place in history:

"On November 22, 1963, the building gained national notoriety when Lee Harvey Oswald allegedly shot and killed President John F. Kennedy from a sixth floor window as the presidential motorcade passed the site."

"Look," Dallas said, "Somebody scratched an underline under the word allegedly. I'm surprised that word's even on here. Most of the history books don't even bother with it."

The window where Oswald *allegedly* fired was directly above where they stood.

Dallas and Linda moved toward the entrance and sat side by side on the front steps — the same steps that police dashed up to enter the building after the shots echoed through the plaza. The same steps where a newsman asked a man leaving the building for directions to a pay phone. That man was later identified as Oswald.

Even at this hour there was a steady stream of traffic moving west on Elm toward the Stemmons, bearing slightly left then right down the same little hill where John F. Kennedy met his destiny. The noise of the cars somehow was comforting.

"It's not like I haven't been here since then. But it's been a long time, and never at night. It feels … spooky? I don't know, maybe more like … surreal."

"You know, it's about damn time you quit dwelling on this thing. It's macabre. It's not healthy. It's pathetic, really."

"You mean, you don't feel anything at all being here, having seen what happened? That didn't have any effect on you?"

"Of course it did. It was terrible. But it's in the past. Way in the past. Horrible things happen all the time in the world. Sometimes they happen close to you; sometimes they happen to people close to you. If you're a survivor, you have to consider yourself lucky. You put it aside and go on. You owe it to yourself, and to those close to you. It doesn't help to wallow in bad stuff you can't do anything about. I learned that from the work I do, especially now with the AIDS women."

"I don't think I'm wallowing in anything. What happened here left a strong impression, some deep scars. It's not like I think about it every day. But when something reminds me, it all comes back like a stomach ache. So being here, especially now, it stirs up a lot of unsettling feelings."

"You're going to think this is terrible, but being here, the first thing I think about is being in high school and almost getting laid in a car in that parking lot," Linda said, pointing toward the lot behind the Grassy Knoll.

"What? Almost?"

"Yeah, well, a police car came."

"And you didn't."

"Something like that. At least, not then." She was smiling mischievously.

"Who was it?"

"Jimmy Kersey."

"Really? You gotta be kidding. Your best friend's brother? You little slut."

"Thank you for that. Hey, no one's life is pretty if you examine it under a microscope. We all make choices maybe we wish we didn't make. You see your father walk out and not come back, it's easy to quit caring about a lot of things. So, I probably compensated with sex and booze. Booze and drugs. Drugs and sex. Not to make excuses. It was just immaturity. Maybe that's why I'm doing the work I'm doing now. The women I work with have bigger problems than I can even imagine. Maybe it's too late for them. But the film, maybe telling their stories will help someone else before it's too late. What the hell, at some point you've got to try or you end up going through life numb and never giving a damn."

"I've spent a lot of my life trying to remove myself from feeling too much. Since dad, since what happened here — not wanting to ever feel that bad again. So, when my baseball career came apart like it did, all I remember feeling was numb. It was like, 'Yeah, that figures. It was too good to be true, anyway. Fuck it.' It was almost like I expected it to fall apart, maybe willed it. So, I just shrugged and walked away. Numb. Strange, but the one thing I can never quite do that with is what happened here. It still hits me with the same force, and I can't tell you why."

He was staring at the cars, their lights a duel of yellow and red streaks, seeing the world pass in slow motion.

"We're sitting here and these cars are going down that street, and most of the people in them probably aren't giving a second thought to what they're passing. And I'm thinking, why is this street even open? They should have closed it off and rerouted traffic around another way."

"I can only offer one reason: You're fucked up." She was smiling when she said it, and he couldn't help but laugh. He grabbed her around the waist and pulled her against his side, and they sat there like that for a moment on the steps of the former Texas School Book Depository laughing at the absurdity of their lives.

She said, "For me, the whole thing's a blur. It's like that all happened to somebody else. It did happen to somebody else. You read about it in the history books and it's like any other event — Pearl Harbor, the Civil War. It's a historic event that you know happened but doesn't quite seem real. It doesn't seem possible that I could have been there."

"I read about it in the history books and I want to tell the people who wrote them, 'You're telling a fairy tale. A lie.'"

"And you're the one that's going to set them straight?"

Dallas moved away from her and stared in surprise. "Are you saying, you believe Oswald or whoever was up there was the only one? You mean, you weren't aware of the shot that came from behind us?"

"I'm saying it was all a jumble of confusion. There was so much noise and commotion. I could barely comprehend what I was even seeing, let alone where the shots were coming from."

He kept staring into her eyes and realized she was telling the truth. It took a while to sink in. It had never occurred to him before that she could have been right next to him and not had the same perception. After 30 years, that was a bit of a shock. It gave him pause. Then he thought of Devereaux.

"You may think I'm crazy, but there is a reason why this is so much on my mind lately."

Still sitting on the steps of the most infamous building in Texas, Dallas related the story about the rube on the hill and the mystery man in the plumbing truck. Afterward, Linda said, "Do you believe him? You could fill the Cotton Bowl with everyone who's claimed to have been involved in the assassination or knows what happened."

"I believe he knows more than he's saying."

Traffic was thinning as Dallas and Linda strolled along the north side of Elm at midnight on one of the two nights of the year that cause the most anxiety for police departments across the country. It is a distinctly American phenomenon that every New Year's Eve and Fourth of July urban cowboys feel compelled to grab their precious handguns out from under mattresses or the back of bureau drawers, step into the backyard or onto a balcony and fire them blindly into the sky with little thought to Newton's premise that what goes up must come down. Dallas and Linda had been hearing the periodic pops throughout the night, some of it fireworks, some of it live ammo. Coincidentally, they were passing the concrete pedestal where Abraham Zapruder stood with his camera at the same moment that one or more gunners felt the inspiration for a grand finale: three rapid blasts — or was it four? — echoing through the Dallas night.

As the last report of the burst reverberated through Dealey Plaza a strange thing happened. Dallas became aware of it as a peculiar rustling overhead that prompted him to look up to the sight of hundreds, maybe thousands of blackbirds rising together from the trees lining the Grassy Knoll, wings pounding the air on a hell-bent flight to God knows where.

Without thinking, Dallas grabbed Linda's hand, and for the second time on this night they ran, up the concrete steps past Zapruder's perch to the top of the knoll, through the opening between the pergola and the picket fence leading into the parking lot by the railroad yard. It was the same inclination many people had after the assassination, to just run, without knowing why or where they were going.

There were few cars in the lot, but the first one Dallas passed was a 1960's-vintage Chevy Corvair parked near the base of the railroad switching tower, the same tower from which a railroad worker reported observing suspicious activity behind the picket fence when JFK was shot.

Seeing the car momentarily disoriented Dallas. He looked at Linda wide-eyed for an instant before dragging her along again. They ran to the other end of the parking lot, skirted a chain, crossed the railroad tracks and didn't stop until they reached Linda's Cavalier in the lot across from Dick's Last Resort. While Linda caught her breath, Dallas collapsed on the hood of the car and bawled his eyes out.

She just stood there, a hand resting lightly on his back until he regained composure. "You going to be OK?"

When he looked up, her eyes were glassy with tears.

"Just thinking about Mom. It's hitting me now."

"Me, too."

"I feel really crappy."

"Better that than feeling numb. Better than feeling nothing at all."

CHAPTER 41

Dallas was lucky to get on the plane at all, so it was difficult to complain about being stuck with the last middle seat between Bad Breath and Body Odor. Each of them had already staked a claim to the armrests of his seat. A sidelong glance each way told him a battle for elbow supremacy would only add to discomfort in the unfriendly skies. Instead, he settled in, trying to make himself as compact as possible, knees doubled up like a Swiss Army knife. Praying, dear God, deliver us a kick-ass tail wind. He reached up and adjusted the nozzle of the air-conditioning vent to direct a stream of lukewarm air onto his face, slipped headphones on and cued Bryan Adams's anthem of adolescent awakening on the Walkman. All it took was to press a button and close his eyes to be transported back to his own Summer of '69, slinging shutouts in American Legion ball, pounding drums with his buddies in the short-lived garage band Tres Jocks and skinny dipping under the stars with saucy Janine Hooker.

The jets kicked in on the second verse. Gravity grabbed, cargo shifted and seats creaked. He felt Body Odor grate against his shoulder. They were airborne, but he was still firmly rooted in sweet reverie. Huey Lewis once crooned in quest of a new drug. He already had the best one: No more exhilarating escape than rock & roll.

Now Bryan Adams was singing from the heart, soulful musings about the madness that goes with being in love. Dallas used to skip right past these kinds of songs, gravitating to the pulse-quickeners for emotional caffeine. Anything by ZZ Top. The Stones, vintage Zeppelin, Seger, Petty, Steve Miller, Van Halen. Van Morrison was the exception. When he felt pensive and drawn to gaze at the moon, he found tonic in the Van man's musings. Normally when he wanted to be transported out of discomforting reality he went with the rockers. This hellish flight certainly fit that profile. But here he was in the trance of a love song, weighing the impact of every word. And feeling tightness in his throat.

It had little to do with the emotional flood of the past few days. It had everything to do with the reason he was on the plane, why he'd pleaded with the ticket agent to find him a seat and paid the walk-up price. He missed Claire like a surfer in traction misses waves. He finally fully understood that and no longer attempted to pretend otherwise.

This was Friday, two days after Mom's funeral. Still plenty that needed to be done in Dallas to help Linda sort through Mom's stuff and figure out what to do with the house. None of it was going anywhere. He told Linda he had to go to Florida to tie up loose ends on a couple of writing assignments and would return in a week or so. This was partially true, but his thoughts were all on Claire and how she sounded when they talked on the phone the night of the funeral.

That had been every bit the heart-wrenching day he'd foreseen. Grieving relatives, some he barely remembered, rolled in like handkerchief-toting tumbleweeds. There were former neighbors he hadn't seen in more than 20 years and friends of Mom's he had never met, all combined in a stunning gathering of mass anguish. Dallas half-expected one of her favorite talk show hosts to pull up in a limo, all in black and teary-eyed. One of Mom's brother's granddaughters, whom she was close to, clung to the handle of the casket, repeating, "Auntie Addie, don't go." It broke everyone up.

Dallas had no intention of speaking at the funeral, figuring he wouldn't have been able to maintain composure. But after the rent-a-minister, who didn't know Addie Huston from Marie Antoinette, praised her as a "fine Christian woman" before taking advantage of the opportunity to proffer his own agenda on the subject of sin and salvation, Dallas felt compelled to set the record straight.

Mom had quit going to church after Dad left, though she still saw to it that Dallas and Linda attended Sunday school. That, too, ended abruptly after Kennedy was assassinated. That Sunday morning, the day Jack Ruby shot Lee Harvey Oswald, came and went without any mention of spiritual obligation. The subject never came up again. To Dallas's knowledge, Addie Huston never again set foot in a church. Although she never discussed her feelings on religion with him, he did once overhear her tell a Jehovah's Witness who knocked on their door, "I put my faith in those close to me. I believe in the here and now rather than the hereafter."

Dallas was thinking about that as the minister, a bespectacled, cherub-faced man with capped teeth, went on about how the only path to heaven was through Jesus Christ, our savior, blah, blah, blah. By the time he mercifully finished, his face was beet-red and his collar sweat-soaked. As the man wiped his brow and waited for the organist to strike up "Onward Christian Soldiers" or whatever they play at such moments, Dallas surprised everyone by stepping out of the first row and indicating a desire to speak.

Several times he had to pause to stem the flow of tears as he related memories that those who knew Addie Huston could relate to. His voice remained steady when he said, "My mother wasn't a religious person. By that I mean she didn't attend church, didn't read the Bible and didn't pray in the conventional sense. I'm not saying people shouldn't do those things, but rather that those are personal choices. Her choice was to direct spiritual energy toward those she cared about. I believe that's why there are so many of you here today."

Dallas' speech must have sounded like a rebuttal — actually, it was — because afterward the minister shook his hand and said, "You expressed some interesting thoughts up there, son, I wish we could sit down and discuss them some time."

Others were grateful for his perspective. Always blunt Chuck Robison, Dallas's former varsity baseball coach and a one-time suitor of Mom's, thumped him on the back and said, "Glad to see you can still bring the heat. I came here to say goodbye to your ma, not listen to a damned sermon."

As they were leaving the cemetery, Linda took his arm and said, "You really are a piece of work. I couldn't have said it better myself."

That was just the beginning of an exhausting afternoon. Most everyone who attended the ceremony came back to Mom's house to share memories and devour a bountiful hot and cold buffet provided by a bevy of neighbors. It was nearly dark by the time Dallas had summarized his life for the 87th time and said thanks and so long to the last of them.

He and Linda finished the last half of a bottle of wine before she kissed him on the forehead and drove away in a cloud of blue smoke, leaving him alone in the same red-brick, three-bedroom bungalow in which he was reared. Suddenly it was so … quiet. Just an empty house, no longer a home. He peeled off his shirt and sat on the front porch listening to the drone of crickets while beads of sweat formed on his chest. When he could no longer bear the silence, he fetched the cordless phone and dialed Claire's number.

Trying to reconstruct the conversation now in the equally stifling atmosphere of the airliner, Dallas felt dampness forming again inside his sport shirt. He turned the volume down on the Walkman so he could better recall the way Claire sounded and what she'd said. Right away he'd detected a trace of urgency in her voice. Actually, more than a trace.

"Lyle disappeared on me again. I was getting frantic. He finally came back on his bike and was all secretive. Said he was doing a favor for Skeeter but wouldn't say what it was. Skeeter actually has a soft spot for Lyle, so I don't really mind. But more and more I can't get through to him. He gets more distant, and I wonder what it's going to be like as he gets older. I wonder if I'm doing right by him, and the affect me being so unsettled is having on him. Sometimes it's all so confusing."

"Reminds me of something I heard the other day," Dallas said: "I think, therefore I am confused."

Her reply was silence. He pressed the receiver to his ear. All he could hear was the empty hum of the long-distance connection and the background buzz of crickets.

"What I mean is — I know what you mean. A lot about life is confusing."

What exactly was she feeling? Was it the simple frustration of daily annoyances or something larger? Dallas felt the weight of distance and absence through the phone line. How long had they been apart? Less than a week but it seemed much longer. He tried to visualize her face, so familiar, but he couldn't pinpoint the expression. He concentrated on her voice because it was the only direct link at that moment. Usually the sound of it was joy, but now it made him uneasy. Something present, an undertone. But what was behind it?

The same obstacle swelled in his own throat and he swallowed hard but couldn't dislodge it. He'd been fighting it all week. Unexpectedly, the image flashed through his mind of the explosion catapulting him into the ocean, but this time he couldn't keep his head up. Something was pulling him down, closing in. He squinted, trying to clear his mind, but thoughts were disjointed, his ears ringing. *Damn those crickets!*

"You still there?"

"Sorry. You have enough to deal with, you don't need my angst on top of it."

"No, it's OK."

He started talking fast, a rambling discourse, trying to override the silence, anything to ease the hammerlock of emotions fighting him for every breath. That's it, come out swinging, try to overwhelm it, suppress it with bluster. He told her about his impromptu speech at the funeral and tried to convey the scene, describing quirky relatives and homespun neighbors.

"These people were really great. They brought in all this food and afterward cleaned it all up. We didn't have to do anything."

Claire was sympathetic but obviously detached from what he was experiencing. She didn't know Mom, didn't really know much about his past. The night Linda called him in Islamorada was the first time he'd mentioned his sister by name. He gave a quick rundown on her and the strange circumstances of her living at the Texas Theatre. He recounted their race in Dealey Plaza and the spooky flight of the blackbirds. When he talked about the task that remained of sorting through Mom's things and putting the house up for sale, he realized he was thinking out loud rather than engaging in a conversation. When he finally paused, he was out of breath and awash in sweat.

For a moment, there was more silence. Then she spoke, a faint quiver in her voice.

"Dallas, what are your dreams? When you look into the future, what do you see? Do you still have dreams, aspirations?

The question unnerved him. It was so similar to the one Linda asked that first morning while he sat in Oswald's seat in the movie theater. When an answer didn't come readily to mind, he did what men usually do when women ask big-picture questions, he groped for a thread of the answer she was seeking. All he could come up with was a stopgap.

"Gee, right now I'm dreaming about dropping in on you unexpectedly at work while you're having a rough day. You can tell them something personal came up. We'll stop somewhere and get food to take out. Maybe foot-long subs. Bag of chips and some fruit. Six-pack of cold Coronas and a couple limes. We'll find an out-of-the-way place on the beach, sit in the sun and eat our food, listen to the ocean. Dig our toes in the sand. We'll stay there all afternoon, never leave the blanket. I'll pull you down with me and we'll lay on our sides and kiss … and kiss … and kiss. The rest of the world will disappear. It'll just be us kissing. I'll want that kiss to never end."

It was a damn fine reverie to come up with off the cuff. Quieted the crickets right down. For the first time all week the lump in his throat dissolved.

He heard her sigh.

"It's a nice daydream. It's not what I'm talking about. You can't always just look for the easy escape. That's just a way of putting off what you still have to face tomorrow. Sooner or later you have to decide to make a stand, take control of life before it gets away from you."

The crickets returned louder than before. It was the first time Dallas had heard her talk like this.

"I thought that's why you came to Florida. You made a stand by escaping the things that were making you unhappy."

"That was first-aid. I'm a survivor. I did what I had to do to survive that situation. But now what? Do I keep serving pina coladas to people who don't even have the sense to care that their sunburn is going to hurt tomorrow. All that matters for most of them is today. So, every day's the same. It lulls you until you don't even realize that you don't stay the same. All I have to do is look at Lyle and how fast he's growing up to see that. And the older you are, the faster it all changes. You can rot in paradise before you realize it."

The lump was back in his throat, and it brought a steel safe to rest on his chest and a drill to twist in his gut. "Just my opinion, but you don't look like you're rotting at all. Still ripening on the vine, if you ask me."

It was the classic male defense. When the going gets heavy, reach for a mood-softening agent. Nothing works better than a compliment. This one didn't even slow her down.

"I'm 35, Dallas. Five, 10 years can get behind you if you're not paying attention. I've got to start thinking about where I'm going to be when it does — where I want to be. Who's going to be there to check the clock when I'm late coming home from work? Who's going to watch my body grow old and my hair fade to gray? Who's going to care?"

No mistaking it, this was the Heartbreak Express chugging through the terminal, the conductor leaning out and shouting, "Buddy, either hop aboard or get the hell out of the way because we ain't slowing down."

Dallas wasn't sure what was behind this sudden sense of urgency. Maybe she feared that now that he was immersed in concerns at home he might not come back. Or perhaps she glimpsed the future and saw that he didn't fit with hers. Whatever, it was more than he could deal with at that moment on top of all the other heavy baggage of the day. So weary, he could barely hold the phone to his ear, let alone chase after that train. But the next day he jumped on one of those old hand cars and started pumping away in desperate pursuit, though he wasn't exactly sure what to do when he caught up.

He tried to project himself into her vision of the future, but the picture wasn't very damn clear. It was scary to try to look years ahead.

The tape was over. Dallas still sat with the headphones on and eyes closed, mesmerized by the rumble of the engines. He sensed movement on the aisle side and glanced over to see Body Odor hoist himself up and shuffle off to the lavatory. Hopefully there was a long line.

Still more than an hour remaining in this flying fun house. Dallas turned to the newspaper to pass time. He read that four Cubans had been killed in the past month while attempting to swim to the U.S. naval base in Guantanamo Bay. A State Department official said the Cuban military was using hand grenades and machine gun fire to thwart such acts of desperation. He learned that hate crimes were up in this country. Good and ominous news on the weather front: The latest hurricane under surveillance was taking an arc to oblivion, but storm watchers had their eyes on another tropical disturbance on the verge of making a name for itself. More bad news in the Midwest, where Old Man River was kicking over levees like Tinkertoys. Every turn of the page yielded more mayhem and misery, even in the departments of fun and games. Mets pitcher Anthony Young was on a record 24-game losing streak. NBC was taking a stand to keep Larry "Bud" Melman from accompanying David Letterman to CBS. Generalissimo Francisco Franco, still dead.

Oh, what a summer. Oh, what a wonderful world.

CHAPTER 42

Dallas slipped the newspaper into his carry-on bag and pulled out a book he'd found in mom's bookcase, a pictorial record of the Kennedy assassination. He had flipped through it quickly the day before while sitting cross-legged on the living room floor. Now he focused on a photo of JFK, relaxed and smiling in the limousine, moments away from tragic destiny, the youthful vigor and charisma he was known for on display. It is the ironic legacy of the assassination: Had he lived, John F. Kennedy would be 76, a venerable statesman, but in death he remains frozen in time. Forever young.

Is it better to fade away or to plummet from the pinnacle, suddenly, spectacularly, tragically?

Think of Jack's paramour, Marilyn. Try to envision her blonde hair transformed to gray, her body yielding to the effects of time. It does not compute. Same with Jack, the youthful king of Camelot. Can that be why fate sometimes takes the great ones in their prime, to spare them the indignity of decline? Or to spare the rest of us from seeing it? Dallas pondered the question as he stared at the photograph and grappled with Claire's question about the future: Who will still care when the bloom is off the rose?

Leafing through the book, two other photos stopped him, one he'd seen before but hadn't looked at in years. It was a grainy black-and-white shot taken from behind the president's limousine as it accelerated out of Dealey Plaza. In the background, a boy in a dark sweater could be seen on the grass clutching the ankle of a woman on her hands and knees. Both of them were facing the hill, away from the street, while next to them a young girl sat on the grass, eyes riveted to the president's car as it sped away. Dallas felt a chill as he struggled to imagine himself fitting into that sweater — into that adolescent body — yet still so firmly rooted in the mind's eye of the moment. It was incomprehensible to view oneself as a freeze-frame of history when time insists on dragging us relentlessly on. Strange to be depicted in black-and-white when the memory's vision is locked in vivid Technicolor.

The next page brought a greater shock. A photo taken during the assassination with the Grassy Knoll in the background revealed a shadowy figure standing behind the concrete wall next to the steps Dallas and Linda had dashed up when the blackbirds took off on July 4th. Assassination researchers refer to the figure as the Black Dog Man because the portion of his body that is visible creates the illusion of a dog sitting on the wall. The 1,000-watt jolt came from an extreme enlargement of the photo. Although the man's face is not discernible, there is an identifiable object on the wall next to him. Clearly, a Coke bottle. The caption said it was unknown what happened to the man and the bottle. Until now.

It's him! Just as he said. Devereaux is the Black Dog Man!

Dallas could still feel goosebumps on his arm when Body Odor plopped back into the aisle seat. Feeling another set of eyes on the book, he closed it slowly and stretched.

"I seen what you're looking at. I'm kind of a buff myself. Just visited the Sixth Floor Museum. Took the bus tour, the whole nine yards. Fascinating. Who d'ya think was behind it? To me, it had to be the Commies. That's why LBJ wanted it all covered up. He was afraid of setting off World War III."

The man reminded Dallas of Ned Beatty, the actor. He wore a dark blue business suit in dire need of pressing. Before Dallas could formulate an answer, Bad Breath chimed in from the window seat.

"If you ask me, all the conspiracy crap is a bunch of hooey. I've never seen a more clear-cut case, and the whole thing was wrapped up quicker than a Kojak rerun. I can't even believe anyone's still debating it?"

Dallas looked at this man for the first time and for an instant thought it was Jerry Van Dyke. The voice wasn't right but the resemblance was startling. He was into his second Scotch of the flight and itching for an argument.

"You mean you think Oswald was just some lone-nut assassin like the Warren Commission said?" Body Odor had twisted himself around in the seat so he could talk across Dallas.

"No damn doubt about it. He was a loser trying to justify his pathetic existence by taking out the most powerful man in the world. In 10 seconds, he goes from nobody to the history books."

"But they haven't been able to prove he was even in the window at the time. He was discovered downstairs drinking a soda about 30 seconds later. How did he get down there so fast? And if he was up there, he had to have been working for somebody, probably the Russians."

"You can believe whatever fairy tale you want, but there was plenty of evidence the guy was a crackpot. The Marines didn't want nothing to do with him. Neither did the Russians. That was his gun they found up there. He was seen carrying in a package it would have fit it. Thank God we never had to hear all the nonsense that would have been spouted by lawyers at the trial. I don't know why Ruby did it, but he did everyone a favor by turning out Oswald's lights. Boom, it was over. No muss, no fuss, no trial. Case closed. The Dallas police were smart. They let it happen. They probably set it up to happen."

Dallas felt like a ball boy at Wimbledon, center court, head on a swivel. He was sandwiched between the clone of Jerry Van Dyke debating the Kennedy assassination with Ned Beatty's body double. As they jabbered, he concentrated on making himself invisible, settling deeper into the seat. He slipped the headphones back on and pulled another tape out of his bag. ZZ Top. Perfect. Crank it up. Better than putting on dark sunglasses.

Even with eyes closed and guitars raging in his ears he was aware of the debate continuing for several minutes in an unintelligible rumble, much like the speech of an adult is depicted in a Peanuts cartoon. Then there was nothing but Billy Gibbons, Dusty Hill and Frank Beard filling his head with rockin' blues, for a mind-numbing half-hour taking him farther from worldly concerns than any jet plane could. Until in a lull between songs near the end of the tape another voice cut in on a separate frequency.

Dallas slipped off the headphones to hear the pilot's cheery announcement. "We're beginning our approach to the Miami area. Looks like we're going to have you on the ground a few minutes early."

Freed from the grip of the music, Dallas's thoughts were already chugging down U.S. 1 to Islamorada, where at the same moment another voice crackled over the P.A. system in the warehouse at Snapper Cove Boatworks.

#

"Captain Devereaux, please come to the front office. You have a package waiting."

Skeeter Devereaux was so worked up, so engrossed in his own tormented thoughts that the tinny blare of his name almost didn't register. Ever since the unsettling series of phone calls, he'd been pacing about the rear of the building like a bull with hives, cursing to himself and occasionally kicking at any object that happened to be in his path. The announcement jolted him back to the reason he had come to the yard today. The package had to be the part that would enable him to finish the rebuild on the sub's gearbox.

After what he'd heard on the phone, it didn't much matter if he fixed the damn thing or not. The more he thought about it, the more ticked off he became. Devereaux stood like a bandy-legged rooster, hands on hips, face red, a rusty-gray strand of hair flipped up like a plume. He was the meanest S.O.B. in the barnyard, and he wasn't about to take any crap from the quick brown fox or the lazy dog.

"Fucker thinks he's going to pull the rug out on me, I'll stomp mud holes in his back and walk them dry. The bastard's got no idea what we're on to here. He couldn't pour piss out of a boot if the directions were written on the heel."

When the phone rang, he stared at it for two rings before answering. The voice on the other end needed no introduction. Same one he'd been sparring with all day. The call lasted maybe 15 seconds. Devereaux said just two things: "Yeah" when he picked up the receiver and "Aw right" just before he clunked it back down. He strode off through the building with chin thrust forward and elbows pumping side to side, thinking, this will be for the best, set 'em straight face-to-face, get it over with, once and for all.

When he reached the front office, he paused to peer through the window. Sylvia Jernigan, the spitfire office assistant who kept this place from sinking into the mangroves by the sheer force of her personality, saw him and pointed toward a box on a counter near the door. Devereaux held up an index finger and shouted, "Be right back." Sylvia watched, puzzled, as he marched outside, got into his old red Ford pickup, backed up, stalled, restarted it, spun around and roared off, scattering stones. She went to the front window and looked out through the blinds as Devereaux made the right turn out of the yard and disappeared from view. She shrugged and hurried back to her desk to answer another call.

Although a portion of Snapper Cove Boatworks could be seen by traffic moving south on U.S. 1, the zigzag route that connects them is well secluded by a dense hammock of native Keys foliage. Devereaux pulled onto the narrow road that led to another smaller boatyard and a trailer park, then turned left onto Old Ironwood Road. He was rounding the bend that would bring him into sight of the main Keys highway when a dark-colored sedan pulled off the berm and headed toward him. Devereaux would have zoomed past without a thought until he realized the left-front fender of the other car was blocking his path. He hit the brakes and skidded, shouting, "Motherfucking tourists!"

The skid carried the pickup sideways across the gravelly shoulder and into the scrub brush next to the road, stopping just short of a limber caper tree. The tree was laden with pungent pods bearing the blood-red arils encasing ivory-white seeds that Mexicans equate with the teeth of decaying skulls and incorporate in their November "Festival of the Dead." Several pods swayed over the hood of the truck, but Devereaux didn't notice them. He was looking back through the rear window. He slammed the gear shift into reverse, spinning his wheels into the sandy soil until they bit and propelled the pickup back onto the roadway. He hit the brake again, ready to give the other driver an earful.

As the two vehicles came side-by-side facing in opposite directions, the tinted front window of the other car slid down to reveal a face Devereaux knew well but wasn't expecting, at least not then and there.

"What the fuck? What're you doing here? I thought we were. ... You damn near..."

The other driver grinned and said, "You thought, what? We were going to get together and talk? Frankly, I ain't got a damn thing left to talk to you about."

At that moment Devereaux noticed a second occupant in the car, crouched in the backseat. He saw the gun rise from behind the driver's seat, clenched in a double-handed grip, its cavernous bore staring him down like a cold, conscienceless eye. In the span of the second that he had to register a thought, Devereaux's eyes darted from the gun to the man behind it. There was an instant of recognition as the eyes of the two men locked, a momentary awareness of a circle being drawn through time and completed. Then blackness blotted out perception.

CHAPTER 43

You can rot in paradise. That takes time. The shock is in sudden, violent death. Then all pretense of paradise dissolves into a Chamber of Commerce nightmare. In a faux paradise as jaded as the Florida Keys, the murder of Capt. LaRue "Skeeter" Devereaux was primarily a jolt to the tourist industry. To others it was seen as a spicy tonic to the summer doldrums. While suntanned spin doctors in T-shirts representing resorts and restaurants were standing before television cameras assuring viewers that "This was just an isolated incident," patrons were bellying up to bars along both sides of U.S. 1 to speculate about who did it and why.

The consensus held that Devereaux was involved in something a lot more sinister than treasure hunting. Rumors spawned by cocktail hour chitchat quickly passed down the road as fact. The most popular theory was that Devereaux was using the mini-submarine to ferry cocaine and drug money to and from vessels offshore. Somebody remembered seeing him in the company of some Colombians. Or were they Cubans? And, hey, didn't he make a lot of trips to Miami or Hialeah or someplace?

One rumor turned out to be true. There was one witness, a woman on a bicycle on the way to her waitress job, who heard the shot and got a fleeting glimpse of the shooter's car, a black sedan. She thought it was a Mercedes. A navy blue Lexus was later found abandoned in Tavernier. It had been stolen in Fort Lauderdale and bore plates stolen in Miami. Police were dusting it for prints.

Nowhere among the speculation was much discernible sympathy for the victim.

Inhabitants of the Keys tend to be as wryly realistic as they are individualistic. When one chooses to reside defiantly on a narrow band of limestone smack in the middle of hurricane alley, death isn't that difficult to accept, provided it's someone else's. Add the Keys' fondness for its buccaneer past, both distant and recent, and the gangland-style slaying of a modern treasure hunter becomes another yarn for local legend that needs no embellishment.

By nightfall that Friday quite a few Islamorada drinking establishments were offering 2-for-1 "shooters." Creative bartenders whipped up variations of Deadman's Punch with grenadine or tomato juice as the distinguishing ingredient. One house band declared it Grateful Dead Night.

The hollowness of these tributes was due primarily to the identity of the deceased. Devereaux wasn't an esteemed dive boat or fishing captain or a popular bartender. He was an aloof character, not well known but merely known of through his efforts to salvage *Nuestra Senora de Carmelita*. That made him just another opportunistic outsider out for all he could grab of diminishing Keys resources.

The transient nature of the Keys was the other reason that Devereaux's spectacular demise was viewed more as a happening than a tragedy. A TV crew roaming for reaction at Holiday Isle Resort thrust its microphone toward a well-oiled mourner who captured prevailing sentiment in a slurred nutshell:

"I never heard of the poor bugger but, hey, any excuse for a party. So here's to the dead guy."

The one place that a sense of loss seemed to be genuine and heartfelt was the hole-in-the-wall dive where Devereaux was a fixture for the Saturday night crab races. It was the hangout where he was a familiar face, and on the night of his death described as a "good fella" in recognition of his habit of contributing any jackpot he won toward a round for the house. Thus, it was well received when the proprietor announced that henceforth the final crab race every week would be known officially as The Capt. Devereaux Memorial Stakes.

"He was just a crusty old coot doing his own thing. He wasn't no different than a lot of us," the bearded barkeep told another interviewer before throwing in a plug for his establishment.

That afternoon, Dallas had no inkling of the furor he was returning to as he exited the turnpike at Florida City and passed the first osprey nest high atop a telephone pole that signaled he was back in the Keys, where nature and man maintain a coexistence that is more quirky than cozy. He was thinking about the differences between the place he'd left that morning and where he was now, his former home and his for-the-moment home, and how neither really felt much like home to him at all.

Texas and the Florida Keys have little in common other than they are hot as Hades in the summer, but even in that they differ. Texas can be as dry as the throat of a bronco rider astride the nastiest bull. Florida in July is a slobbering bulldog's tongue on the back of your neck, and it just keeps coming at you, drooling, panting, showering droplets with the shake of its head that sting your eyes and tickle your cheeks. There is no respite, even in a cold shower, because there is no actual cold water. The water table is a sauna. So you settle for a lukewarm spritz and step out thinking you are refreshed, only to find that you can't towel off the moisture as fast as a fresh supply beads out of your pores.

Driving with the top down produced the same illusion. You don't realize you're sweating until the next stoplight or when traffic bogs down, which it did as Dallas approached Tavernier. A couple of police cars had dashed by, using the berm to avoid the snag of cars. Must be an accident, he figured. Typical Friday afternoon madness on U.S. 1. The two TV news remote trucks chugging south didn't set off any suspicions. His thoughts were channeled into getting off the road and into a pair of shorts, popping the lid on something cold and finding Claire as soon as possible.

He wondered about the reception he'd get from her and what he should say, and decided it was best to wait until he saw her face and just wing it. He wondered if he'd left any beer in the fridge or if he should stop. He was starting to wonder about the sirens.

Coming from the north, he reached his destination a couple of miles before the turnoff to Snapper Cove. So he was still thinking car wreck and someone else's problem when he pulled off and parked in his space under the shade tree that was the closest he had to a carport. The first shock came when he opened the door to his apartment and was knocked back a step by the locomotive breath of a room full of steam-pressed tropical air. Home, sweltering home. He cranked up the undersized window air-conditioning unit, which groaned in protest, and hit the replay button on the answering machine.

The second shock came with the first message he heard, Claire's voice hysterical, barely comprehensible. He could make out, "They shot him," and little else. Dallas's heart leaped into his throat, thinking something terrible happened to Lyle. He hit rewind and listened more closely, this time discerning the gist of it.

"It's terrible! ... They shot him! ... Somebody shot Skeeter outside Snapper Cove! ... Oh, God, Dallas, what's happening?"

The shower and the cold one would have to wait. Instead, it was back on the road where traffic was backed up despite the efforts of the police to keep it moving. They had the corner of Ironwood Road blocked off and Dallas had to continue on another quarter-mile before he could park by a restaurant and hike back. A crowd was milling about and the cops weren't letting anyone through, including an agitated trailer park resident complaining that her dinner was burning in the oven.

Identifying himself as a colleague of the victim wasn't Dallas's smartest move of the day. It earned him an uneasy interview with burly Detective Ken Carkner, who appeared as if he'd be delighted to arrest his own mother if it would enable him to close the case and get the hell out of the heat.

"So you're telling me you're unaware of any enemies the deceased may have had?" It was the third revision of essentially the same question.

"I'm aware that someone broke into his place a couple weeks ago. So, I guess he may have had a problem with somebody. I have no idea who it was or what it was about."

"And you say your relationship was strictly a working liaison?"

"We didn't hang out together, no. We may have had a bite to eat a couple of times, but I couldn't say I knew much about him other than to work with him out on the boat. Skeeter wasn't the sort of guy I'd pal around with. And he didn't talk much about himself."

Carkner was giving him the skeptical cop look, trying to read him. Dallas was conscious of not averting his eyes, not wanting to appear evasive. Actually, he knew quite a lot about Skeeter Devereaux, but he wasn't sure at that moment how to tie any of it to his murder.

"Skeeter?"

"That's his nickname — was."

"What about other acquaintances, anyone he may have had a beef with?"

Dallas thinking, cripes, do cops really talk like this? Must be because they watch TV cop shows, too. And why do they speak in terms of beef? At least relate it to a food with an edge. Something that could kill you, such as raw pork. Or what's that poisonous fish the Japanese eat, some kind of blowfish? That's it — *Anyone he may have had a blowfish with?*

"I know he had investors in the salvage operation. He never said anything about who they were. You have to understand, I haven't been part of his crew for long and it was just a part-time thing. I know he had to get a court order to keep the project going. He was fighting the government on that, but there may have been other people who wanted to stop him. I don't know, I'm kind of new around here."

Carkner did a once-over of Dallas's alibi, took his address and phone number and made a note of the number of the flight he said he took to Miami. The cop handed over his card with the usual instruction to call if anything helpful came to mind.

It was a relief when he was finally dismissed, though Dallas walked away feeling uneasy, his legs rubbery. A commotion on Ironwood Road caught his attention. Two patrol cars were approaching, leading the way for a police van that was removing the body. After they passed and turned north onto U.S. 1, Dallas noticed three figures walking along Ironwood, two uniformed officers flanking a woman. It took a minute before he realized the woman was Claire. She was wearing the tight aqua tanktop and white shorts, her typical attire for tending bar, which is what she was doing when word about Devereaux reached the Leaky Tiki. As she got closer, Dallas could see the expression of disorientation on her face. She looked utterly lost.

He waited until she parted from the cops, then called her name. She ran to embrace him, burying her face in his shoulder. Even under the circumstances, it felt good to hold her. He could feel the sobs shaking her body, so he held her tighter. It was the only thing that made sense at that moment.

On top of the disbelief that accompanies the death of anyone familiar was the shocking aspect of murder. It wasn't that Devereaux was a beloved figure in either of their lives, especially considering what Dallas now knew of his past. But in an odd way, he was sort of family.

"It was so cold. So crude. So … unbelievable."

"I know. I know."

It pained him to see the trauma on her face — eyes reddened and heavy, her skin creased by lines that usually were not visible. Those eyes were searching his face for answers he didn't have. All he could offer was solace.

"I keep thinking, what if Keith had been with him. Or you."

"Where is Keith?"

"Back there with more police.

"Come on, let's get out of here."

#

He drove them back to his place, where it at least felt safe. The air inside was still stale and lifeless, but the little air-conditioning unit grumbling and complaining in the window had succeeded in making it tolerable.

Neither of them intended for it to happen. It occurred as a natural reaction to pent-up emotions approaching the boil-over point. The door closed and he reached for her. Her eyes were brimming with need and her lips conveyed a sense of urgency that equaled his own. Somehow they ended up on the bed, though neither was conscious of who led the way or how their clothes were discarded. No words were spoken. This was solace with a solar intensity. The little air-conditioner was no match.

Afterward, both of them breathless and awash in sweat, the context of the moment dawned on Claire. She turned away and covered her eyes with a hand.

"My God, I can't believe we just did that. I mean, after what happened today."

"I know, I know. Don't feel bad. In times of stress and grief, people sometimes find refuge in sex. It's natural. It's an emotional safety valve. I remember, the day the space shuttle exploded, I had one of the, well, let's just say a pretty amazing experience with someone I'd only been friends with up to that time."

"Really, after the space shuttle? Didn't you feel guilty?"

She was propped up on an elbow, mouth open, staring in disbelief.

"Well, a little. Later, after I thought about it." Then, after a pause, "Naw, not really."

She started to laugh and rolled back into his arms. But after a moment the laughter reverted to sobbing. So he just held her like that, feeling the tension in her body, listening to the drone of the air-conditioner.

"I know he was no saint," Claire said after she cried herself out, "but nobody should end up like that. He probably didn't even mean to, but he meant a lot to me, helping me get back on my feet by giving me a chance and respecting me as part of the crew. I mean, it took a while. It enabled me to exert my independence and get my confidence back. Now, just like that he's gone. I can't believe it."

While she went to splash water on her face and phone Margie to check on Lyle, Dallas fetched the book he'd brought back from Dallas. When she returned, he showed her the page with the Black Dog Man.

"That's him."

She stared at the photos for a long time.

"How can you be sure?"

"If he was telling the truth about where he was, it's got to be him. It's just the way he described it. You can even see the Coke bottle."

"I keep looking for something familiar in the shoulders or the way he holds his head. It's really hard to tell. The pictures aren't that clear."

"It looks more like that character in *Mad* magazine," Dallas said. "Remember, "Spy vs. Spy?" It looks like the dark spy."

"Maybe Skeeter was a spy. Maybe that's what got him killed."

"It's always hard to know anything for sure about anybody. You look at him and you see a profane little man who never really made a mark. Even in the worst thing he probably ever did, that day in Dallas, he was invisible. Unknown. Forgettable. A chameleon."

"Don't you think it's like that with a lot of people, maybe most people. You think you have a reading on them, but deep inside there's something else, undiscovered. Maybe they don't even realize it's there."

"Yeah, look at you. Everyone thinks of you as Claire, the nice, friendly barmaid. Only I know how nasty you really are," he said, crinkling an eye at her.

"Hey, it isn't easy trying to be nice all the time. Sometimes you just want to off somebody. So you better watch out."

The remark caught him completely off-guard, and it tickled him. On this day, the surprise of laughter felt almost as good as the sex. It was one of the many things he loved about her, her ability to surprise. He had no doubt about her many hidden dimensions. He wondered how many he'd have the opportunity to discover.

"Everyone's on a treasure hunt of some sort," Dallas said. "Skeeter managed to turn his life into a hunt for real treasure. But I have a feeling that gold and galleons and green rock candy wasn't the essence of what he was really searching for."

"Whatever it was, he'll never find it now. Too bad. I can't help wondering how many people ever do."

Dallas didn't say so but he had a hunch about the object of Devereaux's unrequited quest: his soul.

"Did he ever say anything about the investors that were backing him? Did anyone like that ever come around?"

"I heard him on the phone with a lawyer a couple times. That was it. Skeeter was pretty secretive, as you know."

"It seems he had plenty of reasons to be."

"Keith might know more about it. He knew him better."

"That's what worries me, that Keith might know something that could make him a target, too."

That evening there was no shortage of experts on the subject, as the rest of the Middle Keys turned the treasure captain's murder into an excuse for a macabre sundown party. Dallas and Claire stayed away from all of it. They phoned out for pizza. They talked about traumatic details of past experiences that neither had shared before.

Dallas recounted the odd juxtaposition of recent unrelated deaths, which now ranged from the famous to the infamous. Later, they turned out the lights and lit a candle to the memory of Capt. LaRue "Skeeter" Devereaux. When they were talked out they made love again with the shadow of their joined bodies flickering on the bare wall next to the bed like a silent movie played on an antique film projector.

One thing they never got around to talking about was the question Claire posed on the phone a few nights before. What of the future? This night, they were living for the moment, in no hurry to face the dawn.

CHAPTER 44

In the morning, after he dropped Claire off at her place, Dallas headed for Snapper Cove. Driving slowly along Ironwood Road, the same sort of impulse that makes rubber-necking a national pastime compelled him to locate the spot of Devereaux's murder. He scanned the roadside until he saw the area where vegetation had been flattened by the previous day's activity, pulled over and shut off the engine.

In the distance a truck shifted gears clumsily on U.S. 1. Even that seemed far removed. At this spot the quiet was so profound it buzzed in his ears. Dallas tried to imagine the single, staccato crack of the gunshot. He had similar thoughts a few nights before in Dealey Plaza. It is what visitors do at historic battlefields such as Gettysburg, standing atop Little Round Top peeling away the overlays of time to visualize a battle raging on the hillside below.

Now Dallas was sitting in the car, top down, trying to comprehend that at this spot someone had died violently. Someone he knew. Only yesterday, and yet already history, an irrevocable moment. When had he last seen Devereaux alive? Had it really been — yes, the day of the confession. Linda's call had come that same night. Now Devereaux was gone and with him any more secrets he may have been harboring. Dallas hated to admit it, but he felt more of a loss about that than for the man.

Feeling creepy, he drove to the boat yard. Walking to Keith's boat, he paused by *Levante* and noted that it looked more rundown than he remembered it a couple of weeks before. Yes, you can rot quickly in paradise.

Keith was still asleep when Dallas knocked on the bulkhead of *Big Momma*. He emerged sleepy-eyed and scowling, but his face brightened when he saw Dallas.

"Happy homecoming, my man." He shook his head and held out a hand. Dallas took it, and Keith clenched Dallas's hand with both of his. They stood there like that for a moment, Keith shaking his head slightly, two friends sharing the burden of misery. "I tell you, ain't this some heavy shit?"

Keith made them each a tall Bloody Mary, extra stiff, and hacked a pineapple into thick wedges. They ate and drank without speaking for a while. Like at the murder scene, the silence in the cabin of *Big Momma* magnified the solemn mood. Usually the old ketch was filled with music. Dallas often suspected that was what really kept it afloat.

"Do you have any idea what it's about?"

Keith was staring past him, outside at the monotonous backdrop of mangroves, attempting to penetrate a dimension to which there was no admittance for the living.

"I knew something was up before that shit happened at his place. But you know Skeeter, you try to pry into his stuff and it just pisses him off. I try to make jokes, get his guard down, he just wave me away. With that man, if he don't want a door opened, you can't bust the lock off with dynamite."

"Do you know anything about the people backing him on the salvage, the investors he referred to sometimes?"

"I knew he had some pretty big muscle behind him. I never could figure it. I mean, here's this little man ain't got a penny to piss on and he comes up with that sub. Pretty sophisticated. Lot of people wondered about that. Even Mel Fisher never had anything like it. I say, 'Where the fuck you get that?' He say never mind about that, he's testing it for somebody. Like it's on loan and he's doing someone a favor."

"Probably a good thing if you don't know. Hopefully, whoever it is knows you don't know anything about it — whatever it is. Think you should maybe disappear for a while? I can't help wondering who else may be at risk. I worry about Claire. All of us."

Keith held his hands palms up. "I don't know what to think, man. He used to disappear sometimes for a day or two up to Miami or who knows where. As independent as that bugger was, he had bills to pay like everyone else, and maybe it wasn't in cash. Know what I mean? He used to talk about going back to Cuba, that he had people who would help him get there, when the time was right. And the whole time I think he knew his time was running out. Think that's why he was such a prick lot of the time."

Dallas made a snap decision and gave Keith an abbreviated version of the tale about Devereaux's past. Keith's expression went from incredulity to acceptance that there would be no reason for a friend to make up such a story.

"The fuck you get him to tell you all that? I knew about his wreck in Cuba and his lover, the widow who told him how to find it."

"The old lady was his lover?"

"Hell, yeah. She wasn't that old, just older. I always thought that was the real reason he wanted to go back there. That she was the real treasure he was after."

They looked at each other for a moment. Keith sucked Bloody Mary off the celery stalk in his glass, then held it in his teeth like a cigar. Without using a hand to steady it, he chewed the celery into his mouth, washed it down with a big gulp of the drink, swallowed deeply and said, "I repeat, how the *fuck* did you get him to tell you all that?"

Dallas shrugged. "If something's eating a person up inside, sooner or later they've got to spill it to somebody. Why do you think the Catholic Church still does so much business with confessions? Not exactly my calling, but I told him to say 20 Hail Mary's for good measure."

Dallas winked. Keith raised what was left of his Bloody Mary as a toast. "I'll grant you this much, you're a hell of a piece of work."

"I've been hearing that a lot lately — every time I talk religion."

#

On his way out, Dallas ducked into the boatyard office where Sylvia Jernigan was hanging up the phone. He noticed the sign on the wall behind her desk: "You say you need it NOW? Then go to Helen Hunt for it." Sylvia was crusty but competent. Dallas had found a way to soften the facade by leaving her jelly doughnuts on the mornings they worked the wreck.

This morning she appeared dazed. She jumped when the door opened, but her face brightened when she saw Dallas. She pointed to the package still on the counter that Devereaux never picked up and recounted his peculiar abrupt departure.

"Did he get a phone call just before then?"

"I don't know. That phone back on the bench where he works, that's a direct line. Those calls didn't have to come through the office." She thought a minute. "You know, I made a few trips out there yesterday and I did see him on the phone a couple times. But the only thing he said to me all day was when he left."

"What?"

"That he'd be right back."

"Did the police go back there at all? Do you know if they used the phone?"

"I don't know what they did. They looked around back there but didn't stay too long. Said they'd probably be back, but I haven't seen anyone yet today."

"Mind if I have a look before I go?"

"Be my guest. They didn't put crime scene tape to keep anyone out. Thank God it didn't happen in here. Thank God for that."

Devereaux's corner of Snapper Cove Boatworks looked like it always did: scattered machinery on the floor and workbench, a greasy rag here, a wrench there. The hatch to the sub was open. Dallas climbed up and peeked in. Clearly, Devereaux had been interrupted in the middle of some project. The panel to the power plant was off and there were parts and wires strewn about in the cockpit.

Backing out, Dallas noticed Devereaux's favorite hat on the deck of the sub, a black baseball cap with the Tabasco insignia above the bill — spicy Cajun through and through. Dallas took the cap with him and jumped to the floor.

He examined everything on the workbench but found nothing of interest. There was a pad of paper with some parts numbers written on it. Surely Columbo would have found a wealth of clues. Dallas just saw a bunch of junk, assorted tools and a grease-smeared phone. He was about to leave but found himself staring at the phone, a boxy brown standard-issue AT&T model. The ringer was set on high. Dark fingerprints marked all the buttons except the star and pound. In addition to all the numbered buttons, one in the far right row, second from the top, was particularly soiled. Dallas had to look closely to make out the partially obscured word there:

Redial.

Lifting the receiver to his ear, he pushed the button. The dial tone yielded to seven rapid beeps. Local call. He listened … one ring … two … three. On the upbeat of the fourth ring someone picked up and a voice said, "Yeah, what?"

Dallas waited, holding his breath.

"What is it? … Who the hell's there? … Aw, fuck."

Clunk.

Dallas slowly set the receiver in the cradle as the voice echoed in his head and he scoured his memory, desperately trying to recall. *Where have I heard that before?*

#

Several hours later it came to him, though not as a sudden lucid realization. It came unexpectedly, delivered by the ring of his own phone. He picked it up, expecting Claire or Keith or even Detective Carkner. Anything but the voice that had haunted him all day.

"Hello, Mr. Huston?"

"Ah. Yeah?"

The voice was deep and raspy. Southern something. Not Texas, more like Alabama.

"Is this Dallas Huston? The writer fella from the magazine?"

CHAPTER 45

The sign out front said, "Showgirls. Sophisticated adult entertainment." Good to see Edison Hawke III frequented only classy dives. The gorilla inside the door said, "We got a $5 cover. No touching the girls." Yes, very sophisticated.

Dallas went in and bumped into a gent with a catsup stain on his sport shirt — hopefully it was catsup. No sign of Hawke, so Dallas found a seat at the far end of the bar, opposite the main stage where a Caribbean queen with long legs and coconut-size breasts was wiggling her booty in front of a potential entrant in an Uncle Fester Lookalike Contest. Dallas ordered a Corona over the heavy-metal din of Hellfire and Damnation or some such head-banger atrocity.

"We've got Bud, Lite or Heineken, that's it," said the past-prime stripper turned barmaid.

At $4 for the Bud, he was glad he didn't go for the Heineken. Clearly, only the prices were sophisticated. At least it was cold and soothing to the throat, which felt like the sole of a loafer in the breathless atmosphere. As if it wasn't smoky enough, a fog machine on the stage was belching faux cumulonimbus that enveloped the dancer, creating an illusion of socked-in San Francisco Bay with an undulating Alcatraz.

As Dallas scanned the room uncomfortably, a brunette with pouty lips walked up and propped a foot on a rung of his stool, calling attention to her garter stuffed with grubby dollar bills.

"Would you like to show your appreciation for my dance?"

"Actually, I just got here. I didn't see it. Your dance, that is."

Her shoulders dropped in sync with her lips as she walked away without a word, but she perked up and repeated her routine at the next occupied stool.

Dallas felt like Admiral James Stockdale, the reluctant vice presidential candidate in the previous election, who expressed the bewilderment the rest of the country was feeling about his unlikely brush with prominence when he said, "Who am I? What am I doing here?"

Dallas's thoughts drifted to the two phone calls that led him to this unlikely rendezvous in a South Miami nudie bar with the strange man behind the mysterious *P-BJ-003*. Was it pure coincidence that Hawke phoned him a few hours after Dallas pushed the redial button on Devereaux's phone?

It seemed there was no way that call could have been traced to him. Or could Hawke have done a star-69 to find the source, then talked to Sylvia Jernigan about who may have been in the boatyard this morning?

And the most perplexing question: Why was Hawke's number the last one dialed by Skeeter Devereaux before he was murdered?

Why hadn't the police checked to see who Devereaux may have phoned before his death? Or had they, for whatever reason, placed that call to Hawke? Or had someone else done so after Devereaux's death?

Disoriented by the noise and commotion, Dallas squinted through the smoke as if stuck in an absurd dream. He *was* Admiral Stockdale. *What am I doing here?* Curiosity and the shock of realizing Hawke was the phantom voice on the phone at Snapper Cove must have cold-cocked his better judgment.

Since meeting Hawke at the Islamorada boat race, they had spoken once, when Dallas ambushed him at the Leaky Tiki on the way to take a leak. He'd handed him his *Florida Nautique* card and said, "Call when you're ready for me to do the big story on your flying boat." Dallas had spotted Hawke at the Key West race among Ramon Ortega's crowd but didn't catch his eye.

Now Hawke's words on the phone pin-balled through his mind.

"You said you wanted a story. I got one'll make your head spin, and could make you a heap of money in the process. Interested? Then take this down. ..."

Dallas was incredulous when he heard the name of the place Hawke referred to as a "gentleman's club."

"The what?"

"The Sweet Patootie. Hell of a place."

"You've got to be kidding. Why would you want to meet there?"

"Good place to talk. ... And maybe mix a little pleasure with business. Nothing wrong with that, eh buddy?"

Inexplicably, here he was, Admiral Stockdale on the campaign trail for the presidency of vice. He'd barreled through a gauntlet of caution signs. Hawke had said: "This is strictly confidential, understand, so don't bring no one with you, if ya want the story."

He'd tried to call Keith but couldn't reach him. Thought about calling Detective Carkner. Stared at his card for a minute before tucking it back in his wallet behind Kirby D'Arbonnell's. Probably should have told Claire where he was going but didn't want her to worry. Was thinking he'd find a phone and call her now, but how would he talk over the din in this place?

The song ended and the next one was worse, a rhythm-less rapper with a relentless mantra of, "Fuck, you, I won't do what you say. ... Fuck you, I won't do what you say ..." The dancer was now playing Dixie on Uncle Fester's bald pate with her fit-for-a-mannequin breasts. Dallas's eyes began to water. The apocalypse seemed very close at hand. He checked his watch: 11:15.

Dallas was thinking about bolting when in strode Edison Hawke III with the self-assurance of the Miami Hurricanes football coach emerging from the smoky tunnel during pregame introductions in the Orange Bowl. Stogie clenched in his teeth, Stetson tilting at every dancer he passed. He shook hands with a bouncer and paused to get a light from a cocktail waitress before plunking down on the barstool next to Dallas.

"Hiya, kid, you're in for a treat. This is what I call perfect timing. Five minutes till Tierra's final show of the night. Tierra Firma I call her; you'll see why. And, of course, the last show's always the best." Then to the waitress, "Sweetheart, fetch me a bourbon on the rocks. Lotsa rocks — got to keep the old radiator from overheating. It's gonna be gettin' hot and heavy in here. Whoo-ee."

Dallas glanced at the stage just in time to see the dancer take a header on a wet spot of the hardwood runway. The sight of a 6-foot naked black woman on 6-inch stiletto heels doing a pratfall leaves an impression. Dallas wished Keith were here to see it. Uncle Fester must have thought it was the finale of Queen o' Sherona's act because he began applauding wildly. The dancer picked herself up amid a stream of curses and began gesturing angrily toward the DJ in the glass booth next to the stage. A burly bouncer in an undersized tux hurried up with a towel and wiped the hardwood while the dancer pointed out the slick spots. She gathered her skimpy items of clothing and limped off the stage.

"Come on, guys, put your hands together for Jasmine," the DJ said over a tinny P.A., "and when she comes around for an up-close visit, don't be afraid to show your appreciation by stuffing her garter with something green bearing the face of a dead president. Now don't you envy those dead presidents?"

Dallas wondered if she'd show him her bruise.

"Come on, got to get a choice seat before they're all gone," Hawke said, leading the way to a small table with two chairs at the corner of the stage. Dallas followed reluctantly as the DJ began the introduction.

"And now, the moment you've been waiting for, we direct your attention to the main stage. The Erection Section is now closed. There will be no private dances during this show. You're going to want to pull up a chair, grab a handful of dollar bills and get ready to be entertained by our featured performer. You've seen her in

Penthouse. Now we are fortunate to have her here on our stage for your enjoyment. ..."

The crowd pressed closer stomping, whistling and hooting. Dallas felt hemmed in. It was like being in a forest full of horny parrots. Stragglers were still emerging from the backroom area, the so-called Erection Section, where nearly-nude women did lap dances for $10 a song.

"Look, Hawke, just tell me what you wanted to talk about."

"In due time, buddy. Now's the time for a little fun. Relax, it'll do you some good."

"... It is with great pleasure that I introduce our star attraction, the lovely Tierra!"

Jiggling out through a swirl of smoke illuminated by crisscrossing spotlights was a long-legged, teased blonde wearing a red thong, see-through robe and the obligatory spike heels. Yeah, she's been seen in more than a few penthouses. Dallas could see what Hawke meant by Tierra Firma, but the geographical allusion that seemed more apropos was Silicon Valley.

"Ain't she something," Hawke said, his eyes seemingly on a roller-coaster ride.

It wasn't really a question, but the crowd was offering enthusiastic affirmation with a crescendo of hoots and shrieks. Tierra's prepackaged smile didn't change as she wasted no time in shedding the robe and got right down to it with an assortment of contortions and bends. A strutting Latino with a cigarette in his teeth was the first to stuff a dollar in her garter. She left a quick kiss on his cheek and wiggled away down the runway, stopping in front of Dallas and Hawke's table, where she dropped down and began doing spread-eagle pushups.

As Dallas's eyes traveled up the gulf of thighs to that thin, taut red satin ribbon that was now the focus of every eye in the house, he was overcome by one thought: What a time to be a lip reader. He got as far as "once upon a time" before he felt a jab in the ribs from Hawke's elbow.

"Hypnotizing, ain't it?"

It wasn't Dallas's first time in a strip joint, though it was the first time he could recall being this sober in one. Hawke beamed and winked. "It gets better."

It got progressively more bizarre as Tierra, ahem, interacted with a suitcase full of props and topped it all off with a whipped cream surprise, which one lucky member of the audience, who looked like he hadn't tasted anything sweet in a while, got to sample. He returned to his seat looking like a mime with a sunburn.

It was entertaining. But Dallas kept hearing the echo of the original question: What am I doing here? He started to get up.

"I'm going to take a walk. I'll wait for you outside."

Hawke's hand clamped firmly on his arm.

"Hang on a minute. Can't walk out now. Wouldn't be polite. Besides, you'd miss the best part. Audience participation."

The DJ was explaining the concept of the finale of the act — "a little game we like to call Cooterball. Everybody dig out their dollar bills now and let them fly. You hit the cooter, you win a shooter."

Most members of the audience seemed well acquainted with the game. They were pressing closer to the stage and crumpling dollar bills into little balls. Tierra assumed the position on her back and pulled her G-string down just enough to form a — well, an inviting target.

"Now remember, to win, your shot has to stay on skin. If it ends up on the stage, you're out of luck."

Most of them did just that, but the sharpshooters weren't dissuaded. They continued to rain a fusillade of wadded bills on the dancer without a single protest from a dead president. Just when Dallas thought he'd seen practically everything, he learned there really is no limit to what someone will do for a buck, with the DJ's prodding.

"Come on, I *know* you all can do better than that."

The more bills flew, the more raucous the crowd became, oohing and ahhing with every hit and miss. The occasional success brought a rousing cheer. When two bills landed simultaneously and only one of them stayed on the target, a dispute ensued over who had fired the winning shot. The DJ, in an act aimed more at maintaining order than benevolence, awarded free shooters to both claimants.

Hawke contributed a couple attempts that went awry, then handed a bill to Dallas. "Here, big fella, let's see if you've got the winning touch."

Dallas stared at it for a moment, then thought, what the hell, George Washington could use a thrill. He balled up the bill and measured the shot the way a golfer does a chip onto a slick green, calculating the arc and adding reverse spin to make it grip and stick. For a moment, a hundred wild eyes followed the flight of Dallas's dollar as if it were a satellite of love with the power to deliver all of them to the doorstep of nirvana. The shot was on line, but when it descended it caught the elastic band of the red G-string, teetered there for a moment and fell back onto the floor.

Ohhhhhh!

"Close but no see-gar," the DJ said in a mocking tone. "Looks like we've got a lot of limp-wristed shooters in this crowd. Better luck next time, ladies!"

And that was it. Tierra began scooping one-dollar projectiles off the stage, and the crowd dispersed. Hawke grabbed his own drink and Dallas's beer and led the way to a table in the corner.

"Hoo, boy, tell me that wasn't more fun than a fart in a blizzard!"

Dallas retrieved his beer and took a swig. The old gun-slinger's instinct made him uncomfortable that he had the chair with his back to the door. He looked past Hawke and noticed a line forming for Polaroid snapshots with Tierra for $12 a pop.

"So what's the story? You going to tell me what's really behind the what-do-ya-call-it, your high-speed ocean skimmer?"

Hawke pulled his hat down a little tighter and leaned forward. His eyes narrowed and darted side to side, as if to ensure no one else was listening.

"That thing's just what it looks like, a revolutionary means of traveling fast across the water. There's a helluva lot of interest in that, and it's going to be a helluva enterprise. That's just one of the many irons I've got in the fire. If a man's going to make his mark in this world, he's got to diversify. That's a lesson for the new millennium, which is slipping up on us faster than moccasins on shit."

Dallas was studying Hawke's face, searching for clues. It was like trying to read a side of beef. Hawke paused, letting his chin drop to his chest so that all Dallas could see was the top of the Stetson. Dallas's throat was dry and his eyes burned in the smoky atmosphere. He took a big swig of beer as Hawke snapped his head up and fixed him with a conspiratorial look.

"Now I happen to know you are a man who can appreciate what I'm saying. One thing about me, I do my homework. I know you do more than write articles for that magazine, which are damn entertaining, by the way. I've read some of them. I have a hunch you have the right stuff for the sort of enterprise I have in mind."

Dallas folded his arms and leaned back in his seat, feeling uneasy. Hawke leaned closer.

"I know you have a bent for adventure and I suspect you have a hankering for a quick buck. But then, who among us don't. Am I right?" Hawke crossed his arms and leaned back in his chair, mimicking Dallas. He reached for his drink and took a long sip.

"What are you getting at and why would you be interested in doing business with me? We don't know each other."

"Look, I happen to know you've been salvaging sunken treasure with a certain LaRue Devereaux, who recently met with a tragic mishap and, unfortunately, won't be able to continue his work."

"The fuck do you know about that?"

"Just what I read in the papers and from talking to some buddies with the police. Frankly, I'm sickened by what happened. LaRue Devereaux was a good fella. He was an associate of mine for a long time."

"What do you mean by associate?"

"As you know, I'm a businessman. And a damn good one, if I may say so. I'm successful because I deal with a lot of different people who have a lot of different skills that I don't have. What I have is the ability to turn what they know into money. I help them make money, and that makes money for me. It's what you call a symbiotic relationship. That's what we're talking about here, understand?

"Now, your friend Mr. Devereaux, he was a treasure hunter. I was helping him pursue his dream."

"You were one of his investors?"

"Look, it costs a lot of money to do what he was doing. It's the same as trying to strike it big in Vegas. You can't hit the jackpot without a bankroll to play with. In the case of Mr. Devereaux, I was able to supply him with the equipment and cash flow he needed to operate. So you see, you've already been working for me, to answer one of your questions. Naturally, I was banking on a return on my investment. Mr. Devereaux's unfortunate death is a big loss to me. But that's all part of the risk you take in any enterprise. Look at horse racing. You can buy the fastest damn horse, and the son of a bitch can break a leg in the homestretch. Then what have you got? A pile of Alpo.

"Any idea who wanted him dead?"

Hawke shrugged. "Wish I did. Whoever it was took money out of my pocket. But what can you do?"

Dallas tried to look into the man's soul and saw no evidence of one. At that moment one of the dancers came by the table looking for a tip. Hawke slipped a ten spot into her garter and grabbed a handful of tanned hiney. She gave him a wet kiss on the cheek and moved on.

"Mmm, mmm, soft as a cloud but a helluva lot more to grab onto, don't ya know."

Dallas looked away and noticed that the line waiting for pictures with Tierra Firma hadn't diminished.

"So you want the rest of us to continue salvaging the wreck of the *Carmelita* so you can still get some return on your investment."

Hawke leaned forward again. "Hell no. What I got in mind in a hell of a lot bigger than that. More exciting, too."

"What are you talking about?"

Hawke's face was inches away from Dallas's. He said only one word before settling back in his seat with arms folded.

"Cuba."

As if that were a cue, he pulled two fresh cigars out of an inside pocket of his sport coat, handed one to Dallas and peeled the cellophane off the other. He lit his cigar and held the lighter out, but Dallas was still holding the wrapped stogie.

For a moment, Dallas thought Hawke was laughing, because his face appeared to be moving. He blinked and squinted, and realized Hawke was merely sitting back with a smug expression. His throat was so dry he couldn't swallow, and he felt an invisible hand gripping him at the shirt collar.

"The hell you talking about?"

"Your buddy, Devereaux. He found the mother lode down there, but Castro chased him out before he could tap into it. That's what he lived for, the chance to go back and get it. Funny how fate works sometimes. Now Fidel's strapped for cash, and he's receptive to the idea of salvaging some of the wrecks down there. There's a crapload of treasure sitting there like ripe fruit waiting to be picked. It could go a long way to solving his cash flow problem and make whoever brings it up for him very rich. I've got a group got its foot in the door, so to speak, and LaRue was going to lead the way to the promised land. Except now it looks like he's not going to be available."

Dallas could feel dizziness coming on. He closed his eyes to steady the room, not realizing until he opened them again that he had his chin on one hand supported by an elbow propped on the table and his other hand clenched on the edge of the table. The room had taken on the tilt of the *Titanic* in the death throes, and he was holding on tight to keep from sliding into the cold, cruel sea. He could see Hawke through the slits of his eyes and was having to concentrate intensely to keep him in focus.

"Why me?" His own voice seemed to come out of an echo chamber.

"Because you know how to run that little submarine LaRue's been using."

Dallas stared, trying to keep his thoughts clear. "The sub? You're going to ..."

"Hell, yes, that belongs to me."

Dallas lost his grip on the edge of the table and rocked sideways in his chair. It took all of his concentration to keep his eyelids from slamming shut. It was useless to try to keep up with the spinning room. He felt hands under his arms lifting. He was on his feet, legs moving but he had no control over them. Hawke's voice was close to his ear.

"Looks like you've had yourself too much to drink, boy. Better get you some fresh air before you pass right out on this ..."

Dallas tried to speak but the words wouldn't project. It seemed as if he were breathing into a balloon. The air he was inhaling seemed spent, void of oxygen. He felt himself being sucked through a tunnel, the skin on his face stretching as something propelled him through the vortex. There was a change in the light, and the din that gripped his head like a vise gave way to a soothing hollowness, leaving a single phrase ping-ponging in the echo chamber that remained of consciousness:

"Ya bet your sweet patootie ... Ya bet your sweet patootie."

CHAPTER 46

She was riding in the back of a vintage black convertible, seated on the rear deck like the grand marshal of a parade, white chiffon gown fluttering in the breeze. Streamers of multicolored paper rained from skyscrapers so tall the tops of the buildings on one side of the street seemed to meet those on the other, blotting out the sky. Yet the light was so bright Dallas could barely keep his eyes open. He kept straining for a better look at her while wincing at the pain searing his retinas.

He could see clearly enough to be sure, it was Mom. It was her in a younger incarnation, younger than he was now. He had to scan back to his earliest memories to recall her like that. Even then, it wasn't a perfect match. He couldn't remember her skin ever being this light, as white and smooth as alabaster. It was a stunning contrast to her jet-black hair flowing in the breeze. That's it, she was like a statue come to life, radiant and animated, basking in the adoration of the crowd that lined the streets. She kept blowing kisses and gesturing with a hand that held a silver cigarette holder half a foot long. Each time she waved, the cigarette emitted an arc of smoke that turned into a shower of Chicklets. People cheered and waved and scrambled for the candy.

Dallas was breathlessly trying to catch up, straining to hear what she was saying. Her lips were moving but the words were lost in the clamor of the crowd. He was chasing the limousine on a scooter, pumping madly with his left leg and gliding on the right. But every time he drew near, the wheels of the scooter would stick in the pink, bubble-gum-like droppings from the white stallions that strode in escort at each corner of the limo. He'd have to stop, jerk the scooter free and dash off in pursuit once again.

Finally, he pulled alongside between the car and the curb, passing the trailing horse on that side and pulling even with Mom. She was looking in his direction though not at him. Suddenly his attention was drawn to the four horsemen, who all turned in their saddles and pointed silver sabers at him. Dallas blinked in disbelief. Famine, Pestilence, Destruction and Death? Hardly. These weren't the Throwbacks of Notre Dame. There was Fred Gwynne on left point, his boots nearly dragging on the pavement as his stallion morphed into a sway-backed mare. That wasn't the only surprise. John Connally was riding the right point, his face contorted in familiar agony as he turned in the saddle to face Dallas. Bringing up the rear were Spanky McFarland and Curly Joe DeRita, each in a tuxedo at least two sizes too small. When Dallas looked at him, Curly Joe stuck out his tongue.

Dallas's head throbbed. He felt nausea returning. The scooter started to wobble, and he fought to steady it. The driver pivoted in his seat and waggled a finger at him. It was Drysdale, the old heartful Dodger himself.

"Your problem, kid, you were afraid to throw the high, hard one. Forget rock 'n' roll. Chin music! That's the magical beat. Ain't that right, Campy?"

Roy Campanella riding shotgun? The wide grin was unmistakable. Dallas knew he was losing it now. The front wheel of the scooter brushed the curb. Just before he went down, he glanced at Mom. She was looking at him now, saying something, like a mantra.

"You've got to marry the girl ... marry the girl ... marry the girl ..."

There was a loud sound, like a backfire. Then another. And another. Then they all disappeared.

#

Bang ... Thud ... Bang ... Thud ... Bang ... Thud ...

The noise had been maintaining a steady backbeat on a subconscious plane, an annoyance that can't quite be grasped. The voices, too, intruding, then fading like a distant radio station on a cross-country car trip. Even as the sands of consciousness built a foothill of awareness it was difficult to separate reality from dream. Or life from death. That thought was floating out there in the twisted circuitry of Dallas's mind, chilling yet elusive. Gradually an effort was emerging to relink body with soul, a sense that it still mattered. But there was nothing familiar in the orientation of time and space, no thread of normalcy to reach for. Just the persistent percussion: *Bang ... Thud ... Bang ... Thud ... Bang ... Thud...*

And the voices, returning again.

"Look, it's not ideal. I know that. We need someone who knows how to operate the sub. That's the bottom line."

"I don't like it at all. He could fuck everything up."

"It's not like he's got a choice. What's he going to do, swim home? It's cooperate or die. Besides, it's not like you haven't worked with an amateur before. I mean, what about that joker in the Texas thing."

There was a burst of throaty laughter that cut through the mental gloaming and elevated consciousness another notch.

"I prefer to work alone. I never even saw that son of a bitch. Never knew who the fuck he was."

"Oh, you should've got to know ol' Lee H. That boy was a piece of work. Some kind of major loony-tune festival going on in that attic. I'll tell you, was it ever fun to mess with that ol' boy's head. More fun than a riverboat full of whores on a sandbar."

Bang … Thud … Bang … Thud … Bang … Thud …

It took a moment to comprehend that his eyes were open, to reconnect sight with synapses, to perceive that through the darkness there was substance. A wall. A light fixture. A door? Focus was fuzzy, sound confusing. Then a jolt of recognition: The thud was his own shoe bumping against something solid. The bang was somewhere on the other side of a wall. Or?

Dallas bolted upright and smacked his forehead on a wooden beam. The impact crossed his eyes, but at the same time broke the spell. He lay back down, trying to reboot the mental processes. It wasn't a pleasant awakening. Gasping for breath in stale air that seemed low on oxygen. Impossible to swallow, throat like sandpaper. He felt as if he were inside a washing machine, sans suds. Was the room moving or was it all inside his head?

It was a compact room. He was on a tiny bed, with too little depth and breadth, his legs angled off the edge. No, a bunk. Dallas had spent enough time on the water to grasp, even in a disoriented state, that he was on a boat. No mistaking the sudden drop into a trough of a wave and lurch onto the next crest. He could feel the vibration of an engine through the thin mattress and hear the muffled rush of water against the hull.

He tried to roll off the bunk, to put feet on the floor, but inertia was in conflict. Using an elbow for leverage, he pushed off mightily. For an instant he was upright, albeit unsteadily, legs wobbly as if on stilts. Head felt as if clamped in a vise. Squinting through pain and darkness, searching for a handhold, all effort and concentration focused on reaching the doorknob. It was moving, dodging his grasp, taunting him. And then it faded to a vision that gave hope and haunted him at the same time — the vision of a face.

"Claire … Claire, help me."

The sound of his voice surprised him. It didn't sound like his voice, and he couldn't feel the vibration in his throat. It was as if the words were being spoken by someone else. He was trying to touch her face, but she remained just out of reach and showed no recognition."

"Claire, it's me. Please!"

She was farther away now, features less distinct as if enveloped by dense fog. He made one last futile attempt to reach her, and then he was falling, tumbling, down a hill or stairs or, hell, maybe off a cloud. Over and over, heels over head, spinning, sliding faster and faster. He was the Jamaican bobsled team out of control, careening hell bent on an upside-down descent to nowhere.

CHAPTER 47

When Keith got there, she was sitting on the step by the door into Dallas's part of the duplex, staring into the backyard. Staring at, what? Not much of a view — some trees and palmettos, a couple of mobile homes visible through the brush. The nearby ocean out of sight, this wasn't the most scenic spot along A1A. At the moment, Claire was staring at future uncertainty awash in a perplexing present.

"You OK?"

She looked up at him, and all he could see were question marks eclipsing those riveting green eyes.

"I should have known. I should have fucking known. Why didn't I see it coming? Why?"

"You sure?"

She jerked a thumb over her shoulder at the door that was open a crack and scooted aside to let him enter. It had never been a sweet home, but at the moment it was nobody's home. The basic furniture that came with the place, an eclectic collection of not-so-art deco, was still there. But all signs of human occupation were gone, except for the bed sheets, which were in a pile in the corner. Dresser drawers were open, and empty. Nothing left in the closet but a few hangers. Keith stuck his head into the bathroom. The medicine cabinet door was open and a green shower curtain hung bunched against the wall over the tub. The wastebasket was tipped over and a few tissues spilled on the floor. That was it. The only other signs of life were in microbe form.

More of the same in the kitchen, where several ants were picking over a smattering of crumbs on the counter. There were dishes and utensils in the cupboards but nothing edible. A detective could only deduce that the recent occupant had no plans of returning and may have left in a hurry.

Keith found a solitary can of root beer in the otherwise vacant refrigerator. He popped it open and downed half the contents in one swallow. The air-conditioner was off. It was hot and stuffy. His shirt was soaked through with sweat by the time he stepped back outside. Claire was standing under a large ficus tree. It broke Keith's heart when he looked into her eyes. The question marks had been replaced by tears. One flowed off her cheek and landed in the dust by her feet.

She looked up at him and repeated the question: "Why?"

"He say anything to the landlady or anybody?"

"The woman lives in the other part. She said the car was gone Saturday night. Nobody saw him go. Probably left in the dark. Didn't have all that much stuff here anyway. Door was open when I got here. Not even closed all the way. Ajar."

She was speaking in a monotone, thoughts spilling out. Just the bare facts. Too numb yet for emotions to kick in.

"Don't make no sense. No sense at all."

"I must have scared him. He bolted." She shrugged.

"Why would he just up and leave? Where's he got to go that's better than he's got here? The man's crazy about you. No doubt about it; it's as obvious as the man in the moon. I read people. I know these things. I know something ain't right about this. No sense. No sense at all."

"The man in the moon?"

"Yeah, you see him don't you?"

She smiled weakly. "I used to. Thought I did. You think you know someone. Guess you can't ever know them for sure. I should know that by now." She shrugged again. She wiped a tear from her cheek with the back of a hand. "You'd think he'd leave a note. At least have the decency to say, 'Sorry, I can't deal with this.' Maybe it'll come in the mail when he gets where he's going. Whatever."

Keith kicked a stone. It sent two garden lizards scurrying for cover. Claire didn't notice. Her mind felt thousands of miles removed from her body. Her heart felt the chill of the far side of the moon. The man wasn't home.

#

Which came first, his eyes opening or the click of the lock that preceded the opening of the door? Dallas's mind was still as mushy as the inside of a jelly coconut. When the thought process finally re-engaged, he was staring at the same face he remembered last seeing. Edison Hawke's Stetson bumped the top of the doorway. He ducked and quickly readjusted it.

"My, my, what a surprise, it is alive. The monster in the lab has opened its eyes."

Dallas pushed himself into a sitting position but words didn't come as easily. He had to swallow several times to cut through the desert in his throat.

"Where the fuck am I?"

"Questions, questions. When you sleep through whole days, one does have some catching up to do."

"Son of a ..."

When Dallas lurched off the bunk, his knees buckled. Hawke grabbed his arm and steadied him.

"Take it easy, for God's sake. This is no time to be sprinting out to get the newspaper. You're weak as hell. We need to get you something to eat and drink before you start doing calisthenics."

Dallas was too weak to protest. Another wave of nausea unleashed a fresh burst of sweat. He let Hawke lead him through a narrow passageway to a table in a cramped galley. The smell of food in a pot on the stove roused pangs of hunger to an acute level. As shaky as he was, he knew the only way to regain strength was to eat. He dug in to a steaming plate of biscuits and gravy Hawke served him.

"I'm a gourmet cook, you know, and this is an old southern favorite just like my grandmother used to fix on Sunday mornings. Made the biscuits from scratch this morning. They just sort of dissolve in your mouth."

Hawke grinned when Dallas emptied the plate and embraced a second helping. Fucker could cook. Dallas finished a bowl of grits even though they were a bit lumpy. The orange juice was cold and the coffee was hot. He had no complaints about the fare. Breakfast at Tiffany's couldn't have tasted better right then.

As hunger dissipated, Dallas became more aware of his surroundings. When he leaned across the table, he could see through a portion of a window in an adjoining cabin. The sunlight made him squint, but he could make out a shoreline some distance across a calm body of water. They apparently were at anchor now.

"Where are we and why have you taken me here?"

"Glad to see you enjoyed your breakfast. And, you're welcome. I was beginning to wonder when ..."

Dallas bolted past Hawke and out of the galley. The chamber with the window turned out to be the wheelhouse of the vessel. They were anchored in a bay about a quarter-mile from shore. Scanning the shoreline he saw a dock with a small powerboat moored but no other signs of civilization. Suddenly a strange realization swept through him. He knew this boat, though he had never seen it from this perspective.

"Is this the *Mary Lou II?*"

"Welcome aboard. Can finally say that, though you've already made yourself quite at home. Thought you were never going to wake up and join the party."

Hawke was standing behind Dallas, arms folded, watching him. Dallas spun to face him.

"You fuckin' kidnapped me. What the fuck did you give me to knock me out?"

"Kidnapped? Hold on a minute, boy, you're talking crazy now, throwing out all kinds of accusations and bad language. Nobody gave you anything you didn't ask for. After you accepted my offer to join our Cuban enterprise, we ordered a bottle of champagne and you proposed a toast. 'To new horizons and prosperity,' you said. I said, 'Here, here,' and you downed the whole glass like it was a drop of honey. But you were just getting warmed up. You wanted to drink shots then, and kept proposing one toast after another. Well, I did one or two, but there was no way I was going to keep up with you. And there was no stopping you, either. I've never seen anything like it. You practically drank yourself into a coma. But I figured, let him enjoy himself. The opportunity of a lifetime don't come along every day, and you obviously recognize one when you see one. I just never expected you to take so long to sleep it off. I was starting to get worried."

Dallas stared, dumbfounded. He had a slight headache and his leg muscles were the consistency of semi-soft caramel. His head was still fuzzy but strength was gradually returning.

"You're a lyin' sack of shit. I never agreed to anything."

Hawke blinked and took a step back in feign disbelief.

"I don't know what you're getting all riled up about. You drank like a fool, so we loaded you on the boat and set sail. We're on a tight time schedule here. Like I always say, time's money, so you got to go double-time to make twice as much. There's a heap of money to be made on this venture and you stand to rake in a good slice of it. Hell of a lot more worth your time than writing nonsense for that rag of a magazine. So I suggest you wise up and get with the program. If we get the OK, we shove off in the morning, and by tomorrow night you'll be in Havana smoking a Cohiba and stroking some Cuban chiquita."

Dallas looked around in exasperation but his feet remained rooted in confusion.

"Where the hell are we?"

"The Bahamas. Exuma chain. Just about friggin' paradise, if you could get room service. But that'll come. This is our jumping off point to the Promised Land. And just in case you were wondering, it's Monday afternoon."

"Monday?"

"That's right, Rip Van Winkle. Monday. You hopscotched right over Sunday. And speaking of Scotch, it is about time for Happy Hour, even on the Bahamian clock."

295

CHAPTER 48

Ramon Ortega liked to think he had a gift, and perhaps he was right. Something about his hands. It was as if they enabled him to see in another dimension when others were simply groping in the dark. Certainly there were women who would attest to his maestro's touch, and his record as a boat racer spoke of an ability to coax maximum performance from machinery.

It was a knack he carried throughout his life. Even at an early age when others in his family were stymied by a particularly challenging knot or tangle of string, Ramon was the one who would unravel it with confounding ease. When no one else could dislodge a stubborn lid from a jar, Ramon would remove it without apparent strain. His hands were ordinary in size but immense in intuitiveness.

His mother always said, her youngest son had blessed hands because they were kissed by an angel on the day he was born. She was certain he would become a fine artist or great surgeon. But while Ramon showed considerable talent when he chose to draw, he had neither the patience for art nor the inclination to embrace the discipline required to study medicine. He was a man intent on instant gratification. Whatever he got his hands on he could usually turn to his advantage.

Perhaps Ramon should have been a magician. He could have been a master. He loved to dazzle. And here, with as tough an audience as anyone ever perspired in front of, he had done it again, coolly and efficiently. *Voila!* He had made the old commando smile.

This dress rehearsal for the abduction of Fidel Castro hadn't gone smoothly at first. A balky latch on the hatch of the hidden compartment at the stern of the skimmer failed to release on cue. When Ortega and Miguel, playing the faux Fidel, succeeded in opening it from the outside, out flew an angry hornet's nest in khakis spitting nails. Ramon played the intimidation game as well as anyone, but even through the veil of Latin pride he recognized that his unlikely counterpart in this delicate undertaking wasn't one to engage in a war of wills.

He still couldn't bring himself to address the man as El Lagarto. In most dealings he chose to suppress the chill he felt anytime he stepped into the crosshairs of that steely stare. He kept communication as succinct as possible. On this matter Ortega chose the prudent course and moved well clear of the line of fire while underlings attended to the problem. From a safe distance he made a telling observation.

Even in a rage, Lagarto maintained focus and control. A dose of 3-in-1 oil eased the problem but didn't solve it. Lagarto quickly diagnosed a flaw in the way the latch was mounted. He ordered a slight adjustment to compensate for a curve in the hatch cover. When the alteration was complete, the hatch snapped open and the Jack in the Box of death popped out. This was not a young man. He was not lithely built. Yet he sprang with the stealth of a cobra.

From a discreet vantage point, Ortega took it all in. He noted the discomfort in the body language of Miguel and the man working on the latch. Their posture suggested fear that was understandable. At the same time, a wave of inner peace swept through Ortega. When he stepped aboard the skimmer again, it was with a renewed sense of self-assurance. The stakes of this venture, after all, were far greater than the prize purse for winning a powerboat race. One did not want to venture into a dangerous undertaking like this with Barney Fife for a sidekick. Ortega knew he had the genuine Terminator tucked away in that secret compartment, and the thought was oddly comforting. Yes, this was the right man for the job, quite possibly the only one who could pull it off. He would soon have the opportunity to demonstrate his merit as the other essential element of the equation.

The next few runs were successful, if not spectacular. The machinery worked. All the players hit their marks. Still, Lagarto was not satisfied.

"Again," he said.

So the ruse was enacted one more time. Miguel, phony beard in place, boarded the skimmer with a bodyguard named Carlos in tow. Ortega began the demonstration, running the skimmer alongside a Blue Thunder high-performance boat. When he goosed the throttle enough to romp away from the other vessel, Ortega turned to Miguel, *aka* the exulted leader, and said in Spanish, "Do you feel the power?"

Those words, picked up by a microphone and transmitted to Lagarto's headpiece, served as the call to action. The hatch snapped open and the dance began again, a deadly two-step that immobilized the victims with the quickness and ease of a handshake and a bow. Lagarto opened a second hatch to retrieve a rocket launcher and was eyeing the pursuit helicopter when nature threw a curve in the form of a sudden crosswind.

Maintaining stability is a challenge to everything that floats or flies, and the balance is doubly precarious for a craft having to contend simultaneously with the conflicting properties of air and water. For a moment, the Juergens Principle didn't compute. The *P-BJ-003* shuddered and shook. Lagarto grabbed a handhold and shot a concerned glance toward the cockpit, where Ortega stood at the controls, braced in the padded cradle of a racing bolster. Ortega didn't flinch. His left hand darted to a bank of levers as quick and purposeful as Sugar Ray Leonard throwing a jab in his prime. A touch of this one, a tweak of that one, and the skimmer not only leveled out but accelerated, as without hesitation Ortega ratcheted more power to the turbine.

Lagarto turned his attention back to the pursuit. The helicopter was falling behind. The threat passed. Getaway, assured, mission accomplished. Coup, coup, ca-choo.

Ortega brought the *P-BJ-003* back to the cove on the leeward side of the island that was being used as a staging area. As it settled onto the water, it skipped twice like a supercharged stone before slowing to idle speed. Approaching shore, he cut power and let momentum carry it the rest of the way to the beach. A small welcoming party greeted them with applause. Two men waded out to secure a line and pull the nose of the skimmer onto the sand.

Then came the shock of the day. Ortega removed his helmet and disengaged himself from the bolster. When he turned, he was face-to-face with Lagarto. For just a moment, the menacing countenance of the man succumbed to a smile. No words were spoken. None were necessary. It wasn't a smile of friendship. That brief gesture conveyed acceptance. Whether he was comfortable there or not, Ramon Ortega had entered an elite realm. There was no turning back now.

#

Jubilation of the moment was short-lived. Lagarto led the procession up a gravel path to the house atop a hill where a Bahamian lunch of fresh fish, conch salad, rice and beans was waiting. This was the house where Jorge Ortega had hidden and become bored with island living after his escape from the Dade-West Correctional Institution. The elder Ortega brother was waiting, just back from Venezuela, with a group of men that included Vittoria Figueroa, the venerable freedom fighter who would direct the exile force that was poised to step into the void once Fidel Castro was out of the way.

Edison Hawke, playing the role of mother hen, greeted the crew returning from the final trial run of what was being referred to as Operation Havana Ruse. His signature hat was off, revealing silvery hair strategically placed but inadequately covering a bald spot. He ran a hand through the thinning hair and shifted his weight uneasily as he prepared to deliver distressing news.

"Something's come up. Monkey wrench in the ointment," he began, face scrunched in a pained expression as he glanced warily at Lagarto, then at Ramon Ortega.

"A what?"

"A ... complication."

"What kind of fuckin' complication?"

"I'm afraid, one beyond anyone's control at the moment. It seems the tropical storm that was down below Puerto Rico just decided to turn into a hurricane, and it's aiming to put a boot up Cuba's ass. The Fidelistas are all in an uproar. Looks like we're going to be sitting here diddling our puds until that situation sorts itself out."

Lagarto was incredulous, his voice rising quickly to gale force. "Have we been watching this thing?"

"Senior Figueroa's people have had an eye on it. It was supposed to be turning out to sea like a lot of them do. But this one is as flighty as a flea on a faggot's dick. It's taken a different turn and is throwing us a curve like a hot poker up the caboose. The Cubans are running around like a bunch of Mexican jumping beans, and we're left to coagulate on a cold stove."

Hawke shrugged and grimaced again. Ramon, looking past Hawke toward his brother, said, "Where's this storm supposed to be heading now?"

"I dunno, we'll see." He shrugged. "We've got the Miami stations on the satellite. Should be another update any minute."

"Put it on Channel 4. See what Blanchard is saying."

The leaders of the latest in a long line of plots to dislodge Fidel Castro from power huddled around a television set watching the homespun weatherman who had been dubbed the Hero of Hurricane Andrew the year before. Morton Blanchard was credited with calmly talking South Florida through the killer storm that bowled over southern Dade County with winds exceeding 165 mph. Now, with another hurricane menacing the Caribbean, Blanchard was back on stage, a star grasping for an encore. He was in full-contact crisis mode, deploying the complete array of techno-wizardry — satellite photos, computer analysis, probability projections and surveillance planes. He had a graphic depicting the possible path of the storm with a blazing red arc that had everyone between Havana and Nassau scurrying to nail plywood over their windows and fill their bathtubs with water and bleach.

Senior Figueroa, standing closest to the television with arms folded, broke out in a surprisingly high-pitched cackle. "What the fuck's with this guy? Somebody poke him in the eye? He's blinking faster than the fuckin' wind."

"I think he's got stock in Home Depot. Probably gets a kickback from all the plywood they sell," said a wiry Cuban about the same age as Figueroa.

Jorge Ortega stared at the screen, brow furrowed. "I don't think they've got any clue where this thing's going. So he's trying to scare the bejesus out of everyone so nobody can say he didn't warn them. Question is, what do we do?"

"I think we stay here for now and see what's what," Ramon said. "Keeps going like it is now, it probably goes up into the Gulf."

"I think if this guy gets his way, it'll bounce around like a pinball and blow all of our asses to Kansas," Hawke said. "Then he can say he was the one who told us so."

CHAPTER 49

Morning came and the *Mary Lou II* remained at anchor. As Dallas regained his wits and strength, trepidation increased. He'd seen the activity across the bay the previous afternoon. Several powerboats coming and going, helicopters flitting about. And then, something streaking across the water. He recognized it immediately. Once you've seen the *P-BJ-003*, you couldn't mistake it for anything else.

This didn't look like the beginning of an ocean salvage operation. Something more sinister was afoot. Dallas guessed drug smuggling. What he couldn't figure was why they needed him? It was a question that led naturally, and ominously, to a bigger one: What happens when they no longer need him? He could almost feel the sticky, stifling strands of Edison Hawke's mysterious web tightening. He kept telling himself, don't panic. Problem was, the more he thought about it, the more helpless his predicament seemed.

Suddenly he felt the despair of every dramatization about hopeless captivity: *Papillion, Midnight Express, Gilligan's Island*. Well, maybe not Gilligan. But it did make him focus on the nearby island. He was beginning to think that was his best chance. Before the *Mary Lou II* left this bay, he had to find a way to get to that island. He could see foliage that would be useful for cover. It was less than a half-mile to shore, and the water was shallow. He had hoped nightfall would provide the chance to slip away. It didn't.

Hawke hadn't been aboard since their conversation the previous morning. His shadow since then was a burly, square-jawed fellow named Ellswick. He had the type of weathered, roughhewn looks that some women find irresistible combined with an elusive spirit that 10 women couldn't tame. He looked as if he could have been a stuntman or a linebacker. He said he'd been a powerboat racer and an ironworker, but now he was seeking greater return for his risk-taking. Dallas had met plenty of guys like Ellswick in bars and on boats. He was the sort you could enjoy trading tales with over a beer — and didn't trust for a minute.

"Let's be honest now," Dallas said late that first afternoon, as they watched the odd activity in the bay from the bow of the *Mary Lou II*, "We aren't really going to Cuba to salvage old shipwrecks. This isn't a treasure hunt, is it?"

Ellswick chuckled. He'd actually been working on some dive gear and attending to other tasks around the boat but never let Dallas out of his sight. "Hell yeah, it's a treasure hunt. That's exactly what it is." He chuckled again.

"Then why are we sitting out here while all of this, ah, preparation is going on? Why do I feel like a prisoner, or some kind of guinea pig?"

Ellswick laughed louder. "No one's a fucking prisoner. It's all a matter of teaming up and doing our individual parts. I'm going to be working with you in the sub, so they want us to get acquainted. And there are other details that need to be worked out that don't concern us. Understand, when you're dealing with Cuba, you're dealing with a sensitive situation."

The word sensitive sounded incongruous coming off the tongue of a lug like Ellswick. Alan Alda, he wasn't.

Ellswick wasn't a gourmet cook, either. He prepared grilled-cheese sandwiches and tomato-rice soup out of the can for dinner. Dallas didn't complain. He realized that if his plan to check out of the Hotel Hawke under the cover of darkness succeeded, it might be a while before he ate anything substantial again.

He and Ellswick were in the galley finishing their meal when noise from the stern of the *Mary Lou II* signaled the arrival of company. Ellswick hurried back to greet the visitors. When Dallas peeked around the corner a couple minutes later, he saw Ellswick and two other men hoisting the *P-BJ-003* out of the water. They lowered it carefully onto a cradle next to Devereaux's submarine.

Dallas figured the break of dawn would find this strange caravan bound for Havana, or wherever. It was his intention to part company well before then. As it turned out, neither happened. Soon after Dallas retired to his cabin and pretended to fall asleep, there was a firm click outside the door. Panic flared again. He tried the door. The handle turned but the door wouldn't budge. No prisoners, my ass.

Hours dragged. The walls closed in. Dallas struggled to keep his breathing under control. He was on the verge of hyperventilating. Felt like he was running a marathon but going nowhere. Then, inexplicably, he was asleep.

For how long, he had no idea. When his eyes opened, a strip of daylight showed along the bottom of the door. He turned the knob and it opened. Ellswick, seated in a swivel chair at the boat's helm with his feet on the console, looked up from a cup of coffee and grinned.

"About fucking time. Thought you were going to sleep the day away."

Dallas glared. He turned and saw the empty latch that had secured the door. The padlock had been hidden away.

"This is bullshit, you know. Whatever y'all are up to, I don't want any part of it. Just let me off here and the rest of you can build an underwater cocaine pipeline from Cuba to Key West, for all I care. Just keep me the fuck out of it."

Ellswick howled. "Take it easy, man. Don't sweat it, you won't regret it. This'll be worth your while." He laughed again. "Cocaine pipeline. Not a bad idea."

Dallas stormed out of the wheelhouse. The morning was hot and still, the cove as calm as a millpond, the sky cloudless. He headed toward the stern with Ellswick a couple of strides back.

"Hey, hold on."

The *Mary Lou II* had been thoroughly revamped since its days as a shrimp boat. Gone were the outriggers used to raise and lower the nets. A crane, similar but larger than the one on *Levante*, had been installed to launch and retrieve the *P-BJ-003* and the submarine, which rested side-by-side on the deck. Dallas had a brief thought that this would have been an improvement on Devereaux's tender. Yes, the *Mary Lou II* would have made a damn fine platform for a salvage operation. But what the hell?

Dallas had spent enough time with the submarine that the alteration caught his eye immediately. The robotic arms he had learned to manipulate like an extension of his own had been removed and replaced by an odd boxy framework attached to what appeared to be a swiveling apparatus. On either side of the framework were a pair of open-ended tubes, one atop the other. Dallas spun in his tracks and stopped face-to-face with Ellswick.

"What is that on the front of the sub? What the hell are you people planning to do in Cuba?"

Ellswick stood with arms folded, biceps bulging beneath his T-shirt, and a smug expression on his face.

"You'll have to direct those questions to Mr. Hawke. I'm just a hired hand. Same as you."

#

Hawke returned just before noon in a Cigarette boat along with three other men. Dallas watched from the bow as they pulled up amidships and tossed a line to Ellswick. Hawke was first to board. He spoke briefly with Ellswick, then hurried forward where Dallas was waiting.

"Getting a late start," Dallas said, grimly.

Hawke looked him in the eye. He wasn't in his usual gregarious mood.

"We've hit a bit of a snag. Should be temporary. There's a hurricane, looks like it's going to beat us to Havana. Hopefully won't be too bad. Might even veer off and miss them altogether. We've got to sit tight for a while and see what's what."

Dallas held his gaze.

"Look, it's about time you level with me. You drugged me, you kidnapped me, you've got me locked up out here in floating purgatory. What're you planning and what do you want with me? And don't give me this crap about salvaging treasure."

Hawke thought for a moment, then said, "Trust me, there'll be plenty of treasure for everybody who, ah, cooperates. But there's another mission we've got to take care of first. Your role is minor. You've just got to drive the sub, help us create a bit of a diversion. Just go where Ellswick tells you. He'll take care of the rest."

"What do you mean by diversion? Diversion for what? And, what is that apparatus on the front of the sub?"

Hawke's face twisted into a half-grin, his eyes narrowed. "Torpedo tubes."

Dallas felt a surge of invisible needles on the back of his scalp that can only spring from a bolt of sheer terror. His jaw actually dropped.

"You've got to be kidding. What is this, Bay of Pigs II?"

"You'll see. You'll have the best seat in the house, actually."

Dallas was incredulous. He felt the same dizzy, surreal sensation that overcame him in the strip bar, but this time it wasn't drug induced. It was sensory overload.

Torpedoes? They were asking — no, *ordering* — him to help invade Cuba. The swirl of mental images began clicking into realization like the spinning fruit icons on a slot machine. Bing! Bing! Bing! No jackpot, no payoff. But there they were, all in a row. Read 'em and weep.

Torpedoes. Boats exploding. Dallas could see the flash of the Coast Guard cutter erupting in flames and recall the concussion transmitted across the water. For the first time he saw his own inglorious arrival in South Florida in a different light: Was it a faulty gas stove, or …?

"This is crazy. You can't be serious. There's no way."

Hawke shrugged. "What we're planning, it's bold. Nothing crazy about it. And the reward will be tremendous for everyone who helps. Otherwise, well, that's not really an option."

The sound of the Cigarette's twin big-block engines revving caused both of them to turn. The mooring line was released, the speedboat started to pull away. There were two men in it. That meant someone else had come aboard the *Mary Lou II*.

That was confirmed a few minutes later when the newcomer came forward and entered the wheelhouse. An older man, about six feet tall, solid but with a burgeoning paunch. His salt-and-pepper hair was closely cropped. He was dressed for combat in camouflage pants and a dark green T-shirt. Sunglasses hung from a strap around his neck.

Just before he stepped inside the door, his eyes met and locked on Dallas's. The glare was like a blast of hot air when you open the door of a car that has been sitting for hours in a scorching hot parking lot. The impact of it felt like a punch in the gut.

It was more than a look of malice, it was intrusive. It wasn't that the man looks right through you, he looks inside of you, Dallas would reflect later. He recalled a relief pitcher he met in the minor leagues who boasted of doing the same thing to hitters. "I look right into their soul," he'd say. "I go into their head and find their weak spot, and they know it. That's when I've got them." That's what this guy does. He enters your mind and dissects you.

Dallas had paid his dues at a poker table or two and he was determined not to show his hand. With warning lights flashing and alarms squawking on the central nervous system control panel, he somehow mustered the verve to disconnect the circuits. As the master intimidator bore in, Dallas revealed the inside of a cloud. He stared back dispassionately until the other man turned and slipped inside the cabin.

When the door closed, Dallas felt his pulse throb in his temples. His own aplomb surprised himself. But as his mind regained its edge he realized, not only had he seen this man before, it was as if he'd expected to see him. This was the same man he'd observed aboard the *Mary Lou II* after his rescue from the sailboat explosion and again flipping the cigar off the balcony in Key West. It occurred to him that even on those occasions there was a familiarity that was disconcerting.

Dallas could feel eyes on him as he made small talk with Ellswick.

"So who's our new shipmate?"

Ellswick ducked his head. His shoulders sagged noticeably. He drew the back of his hand across his face, as if to wipe away sweat. In a muffled tone, he said, "What you're asking about could be your worst nightmare." He laughed nervously. "Once again, I'll defer to Mr. Hawke. If I were you, I'd call that one sir, or better yet, stay the fuck out of his way."

CHAPTER 50

As if on cue, Hawke emerged from the wheelhouse with the newcomer on his heels. The mystery man, whom Hawke addressed as Chief and other associates referred to as Lagarto, carried a small rectangular case. Dallas glanced at it surreptitiously, thinking it was too small for a briefcase. The two men walked to the rear deck and sat on a large storage trunk. Dallas moved into a position where he could observe them without being easily seen.

He watched as Lagarto set the case in the space between himself and Hawke and unzipped it. He extracted a slab, apparently wooden, and set in on the trunk. Dallas was flabbergasted. He recognized it immediately. As a boy he'd watched his grandfather and uncle hunkered over the same object for hours. Dallas stared in disbelief as Lagarto removed a deck of playing cards from the case, offered it to Hawke to cut, shuffled and dealt two hands of six cards. Each selected two cards and set them face-down next to Lagarto. Dallas stared agape.

With plans for an assault on the dictator of Cuba on hold because a hurricane was beating them to the punch, Hawke and Lagarto were passing time playing cribbage! A game invented by a poet, a sedentary gentleman's pastime, turned amusement for anarchists, for God's sake. Dallas stood transfixed, watching cards being played and the pegs used for scoring move around the board. At one point he saw Lagarto's back shake from a slight chuckle.

It was at about that moment that something came crashing into Dallas's consciousness with the impact a demolition ball. Something Devereaux had said; something about another game of cribbage on another boat during another Cuban crisis. Could it be? The wrecking ball swung again. Smashing. Crashing. Scattering shards of history in his brain, time unraveling in reverse. The Iron Curtain fell. *Challenger* exploded. Tanks rolled through Tiananmen Square. The last chopper fled Saigon. Bobby. Martin. Jack.

Dallas stood with his back pressed against the side of the former shrimp boat's superstructure, breathing heavily, sweating profusely. He couldn't run, couldn't hide. So he stood there as wave after wave of anxiety washed over him until he heard laughter, Hawke's familiar chortle. He was coming this way. Dallas stepped away from the bulkhead to the rail, pretending to be enjoying the view of the bay and shoreline.

"Gorgeous fucking day," Hawke said in passing. "Hard to believe there's a hurricane out there. They ain't kidding when they talk about the calm before the storm. Might as well work on your tan. Doesn't look like we're going anywhere for a while."

Dallas nodded. He was staring past Hawke at Lagarto, who was gathering up the cards, packing them away. Operating purely on instinct, not even thinking, he didn't hesitate. Panic vanished like a pickpocket in a train station. His stride was steady, purposeful. He barely felt the deck under his shoes as he closed the distance and stopped just short of the trunk and looked down at Lagarto, who was sliding the pegs into a tiny compartment in the side of the board.

"I wouldn't mind a game, if you still feel like playing — as long as we're killing time."

Lagarto looked up at him, incredulous. Dallas avoided eye contact, looking down at the board cradled in the man's beefy hands. It was a fine piece of craftsmanship, really. Obviously, custom work: dark wood, perhaps mahogany, brightly polished. The holes were perfectly aligned in twin columns of 30 on each side of the board. Horizontal lines scored in the wood separated each set of five holes, plus one more single row of game holes at the head of the board. On either side, alongside the holes, figures of lizards had been carved, long and lean, facing in opposite directions. The pegs, two for each player, looked as if they might be ivory. Definitely not plastic.

"Dallas Huston," he said, extending a hand.

Lagarto regarded the hand for a moment. Then without a word, he reached for the cards and began to shuffle. Dallas sat down. Lagarto started to deal.

"I learned the game a long time ago, from my grandfather. Must have been 30 years ago. In Texas."

Dallas picked up his cards, mind fumbling to dust off a vague recollection of the rules. He had played the quaint game occasionally with his Grandpa Earle but, shit, it was so long ago.

He sneaked a peak at Lagarto, who had already set down two cards for the crib. Damn, what was the object? Something about building face value of the cards to 30. No, 31. Good, it was coming back bit by bit. But what the hell was the strategy? He could sense Lagarto's impatience waiting for his discard. He had drawn a queen, eight, nine, three, five and an ace.

"Ace is low, counts one, right?"

"Always."

Dallas knew face cards were 10. He decided to keep the queen and ace. He remembered something about striving for runs. So he set down the three and five for the crib, and immediately regretted it. That's right, you get points for 15; the five may have come in handy.

Lagarto cut the rest of the deck and turned over the top card of the shorter stack for the starter. It was a jack.

"Two," he said, and moved one of his pegs ahead two holes.

It was a nuance Dallas would never have picked up on. His stomach knotted. What the hell was he doing letting on that he was an old hand at a game as complicated as cribbage? This wasn't "Go, Fish." And his opponent wasn't kind old Mister Greenjeans from the barnyard. This might very well be Devereaux's mystery man from the plumbing truck; quite possibly the shadowy figure behind the fence on the Grassy Knoll. The man who may have fired the shot that killed John F. Kennedy. Even as he pondered the incomprehensible, he knew it was true.

"Nice work on this board. Did you carve it?"

Lagarto, staring at his cards, grunted. More interesting was the carrying case, set nearby on the trunk. It was dark brown, obviously made from the rugged hide of some animal. "Is that leather?"

"Lizard."

He glanced at Lagarto and felt panic returning. This was crazy, mind-boggling. He'd seen this man for an instant in a moment of infamy, caught a reflection off his mirrored sunglasses. Had the assassin seen him looking back up the hill? Dallas always wondered what it would be like to encounter that man, if in fact he was still alive. And here they were, playing cribbage while waiting out a hurricane.

"What do you play, one time around the board?"

"Twice around, or it's not a goddamned game. Play to a hundred twenty-one."

Dallas realized it was up to him to begin play. He studied his hand for a moment, shrugged and laid the nine. Lagarto followed with a seven.

"Sixteen."

Hmmm, what now? Eenie, meenie …

He reached into his hand and set down the eight. "Ah, twenty-four."

Lagarto didn't move. Count of one, two, three. Dallas looked up and those eyes were on him again, bottomless, inscrutable. Suddenly, they narrowed and Dallas could almost feel the heat of their intensity.

"Muggins!"

Dallas stared back, uncomprehending. He looked down at the cards, then back at Lagarto.

"I said 'muggins.' You didn't score the run, so I take it." He pegged three.

"It doesn't have to be in sequence?"

"Hell, no. Do you know how to play this game or not?"

"I told you it's been a long time. I mean, who can remember the minute details from anything that happened 30 years ago?" Dallas looked directly at Lagarto for two, maybe three seconds, then back down at the board. He could feel the weight of those eyes still on him. "If you can bear with me and help me refresh my memory, it'll come back. I mean, as long as we're not going anywhere for a while."

Lagarto studied his cards, then played a five. "Twenty-nine."

"I can't go over 31, right?"

"If you can avoid it. If not, say Go."

Dallas played the ace. A diamond. "Thirty."

A malevolent grin flashed on Lagarto's face. He played another ace, a spade. "Thirty-one, and four." He reached for his peg. "Two for the pair. Two for thirty-one."

Dallas looked at the pegs. He felt like a jockey whose mount had refused to leave the starting gate. But the next hand was a different story. Dallas hit 15 on a pair, and the chase was on. He could feel the energy from across the board and sensed he was up against an opponent who relished matching wits.

It was Dallas's nature, as well. That was the one thing he had in common with this ruthless man. Whenever he settled into the nondescript flow of life, his senses dulled. It was in the face of a challenge, the stiffer the better, when he always felt most alive. His tendency was to glide through life until circumstances forced him to action. As a pitcher, he'd always made his best pitches in the most precarious situations. He could recall turning on the mound, seeing runners at every base and being overcome by a calming sensation. He'd turn back to face the batter feeling, incongruously, that he was actually dealing from an advantage.

Something similar was happening now. Panic subsided and his senses perked up to full alert. Competitive instinct took charge. He was in his element playing a game. Any game. Approaching the end of the first trip around the board, Lagarto still led, but Dallas was closing fast. After nailing a 31 on a run of three, he was tight on the tail of the lizard man.

"Story of my life. I'm a slow starter, but I catch on eventually."

"Don't expect any more favors. If you miss one, you miss it. Tough shit."

As if a shift in the wind, Lagarto surged further ahead with a strong hand. Challenge laid down, challenge accepted. Dallas was regaining a feel for the game but couldn't be sure if his instincts were always in tune with proper strategy. Cribbage is much more than the luck of the draw, it's knowing which cards to hold on to and when to play each to best advantage. Like so many things in life.

The two men were so intent on their objective, minds locked in mental combat, neither of them heard Hawke approach. Both looked up with surprise when he cleared his throat.

"Got some distressing news. Just been on the radio. Seems that hurricane made an unexpected turn. It's not aiming at Havana anymore."

"The hell you saying? Where is it now?"

Hawke shifted uneasily. "Well, I hate to have to tell you, but it's looking like it might be coming up this way. Pronto, I'm afraid."

"Might be? When did it make this turn? These assholes paying attention to this or what?"

Lagarto in a rage was a sight to behold, and to avoid, like a hurricane. His eyes bugged, his chest puffed. The hair on the back of his neck bristled.

"Look, I hear what you're saying, but it don't do no good getting riled. What we best do is go on in to shore and decide what we're going to do and get on with it."

Lagarto was already gathering up the cribbage board and slipping it into the case. As quickly as his temper flared he seemed to regain command of it. Dallas could see his mind turning over possible courses of action. As Lagarto and Hawke stomped off to the wheelhouse, Dallas called out, "Guess we'll just have to finish this thing later, then."

CHAPTER 51

Lt. Col. Eric Sanders glanced at his counterpart in the co-pilot's seat, Carl Wannemacher, and grinned.

"Pretty good bump there. Probably dropped us 150 feet."

The veteran Air Force meteorologist had flown more than a hundred missions into hurricanes. This was his first time up with Wannemacher, who seemed to know his stuff. But when you're running this tricky gauntlet you like to know the man in the next seat. He couldn't help missing former sidekick "Little Jack" Draper and his unique way of breaking the tension.

Last August, in the clutches of Hurricane Andrew, with hail obscuring all view and the wings rattling like a hummingbird on cocaine, ol' Drape turned to him, and in that high-pitched Arkansas twang, said, "Damn, that makes my butt crave a dip of snuff."

"Yeah, well, mine's chewing a hole through the seat about now," Sanders said, and they laughed. The thing about Draperisms, the imagery was always twisted, but somehow the meaning came through, as long as you didn't think about it too much.

"Still seeing some wrinkles in that eye wall, but I think it's a little better defined than before. Guess we'll have to wait and see the effect these upper-level currents are going to have," Wannemacher said, bringing Sanders back to the present.

"It ain't Andrew, but it's shaping up as a pretty decent Category 2. Enough to give them a pretty good knock down in Haiti about now."

"As if those poor bastards don't have enough trouble already. Probably feels more like Hades."

#

The wind was picking up and Dallas was thinking about his first brush with a hurricane. He'd spent a harrowing night on a 48-foot Hatteras in St. Thomas when Hugo bull-rushed the Virgin Islands en route to slamming North Carolina in 1989. With anchors dragging and one mooring line snapping, Dallas and two crewmates kept the engines running for 10 hours to maintain a foothold in the harbor. The hangover from the survival celebration lasted two days.

Despite the sweat soaking his shirt he shivered at the thought of this sunny Bahamian afternoon degenerating into that. He was standing outside the wheelhouse of the *Mary Lou II*, the salty sea mist a refreshing kiss on his face. As precarious as his situation appeared, it felt better to be on the move than anchored in that cove.

Hawke had been surprisingly candid when he and Lagarto returned from the powwow on shore, answering all of Dallas's questions as if he actually was accepted as a willing member of the crew. There'd been a flurry of activity from the anchorage: A helicopter left the island, a couple of go-fast boats zoomed out of the cove; several men in a small open-fisherman boarded a large yacht anchored a half-mile away. But when Ellswick weighed anchor, the *Mary Lou II* departed alone on what Dallas deemed to be a northwesterly heading, conveying an unlikely foursome along with Devereaux's mini-submarine and the strangest vessel in the Bahamas, the *P-BJ-003*, secured on deck.

"We're moving up a ways in the islands. The chief has a place that's as sturdy as a damned fortress. We'll tie everything down on the boat and ride it out there," Hawke said, his demeanor void of the usual bravado. "Won't take more than four or five hours. Should be there before dark, no problem. From what they're saying, the storm's still a good 12 hours away."

They were running the Old Mailboat Route, a well-traveled slot of protected water between the islands and the Great Bahama Bank stretching from George Town to Nassau. Dallas wasn't sure of their position, but he knew the general lay of the Exuma chain, angled northwest to southeast. He questioned why they weren't taking the less perilous deep-water route through Exuma Sound to the east of the islands.

"It'll be kicking up out there soon enough, and we'd lose time getting out there. This is quicker, a shortcut through the back alley," Hawke said. "Don't worry, the chief knows his way around these waters better'n a dog knows his own ass."

Conditions were still no more than vexing. A gust lifted Hawke's Stetson and sent it skittering across the deck. When he stooped to retrieve it, Dallas smiled at the sight of the perfectly rounded bald spot glistening with sweat like a polar icecap in meltdown. Hawke ducked back into the wheelhouse and stayed there. Dallas glanced through the window and saw him speaking animatedly to Lagarto, who stood impassive at the wheel.

Dallas eyed the endless procession of islands that appeared like spectators along a parade route. All of his experience had been in the northern Bahamas, but he'd heard more than a few island hoppers extol this 140-mile band of limestone steppingstones as the crown jewel of the archipelago. Still, the Exumas remain an enigma, a star-crossed paradise that trouble has a habit of finding. Situated a short punt away from Columbus' supposed first landfall at San Salvador, the chain has always been a sleepy outpost with more going on than meets the eye. It has been the haven of pirates, privateers and profiteers, as well as British Loyalists fleeing the American Revolution, Civil War blockade runners and modern-day bootleggers and drug smugglers.

As recently as the late 1970s, Norman's Cay in the Northern Exumas was the centerpiece of one of the most notorious marijuana and cocaine smuggling operations, headed by Carlos Lehder, whose connections purportedly included former Panamanian dictator Manuel Noriega, fugitive financier Robert Vesco and Fidel Casto himself. Lehder now was doing life plus 135 years in federal lockup, and only a wrecked cocaine transport plane in the shallows off Norman's Cay remains as a monument to another murky chapter in Exumas history.

Dallas was musing about a night in a bar in Freeport years ago with a group of sport fishermen, listening to a couple of shadowy characters relate the tale of a massive raid on Norman's Cay that left the DEA frustrated and fuming because someone in the Bahamian government apparently tipped off Lehder that it was coming. Dallas could still see the smirk on the face of the guy with long hair tied back in a ponytail saying, "Course, I'm getting this third or fourth hand, but from what I hear, when the Bahamian Defense Force went storming in there, Carlos's boys were playing volleyball, roasting a pig, having a big ol' party. One of the ones doing the cooking goes up to this DEA guy that came ashore and goes, 'Care for a conch fritter?' " He and his buddy laughed like hyenas and ordered another round for the fishermen, who guffawed along with them.

Who knew what other secrets lurked in these sleepy isles? Dallas glanced through the window of the wheelhouse at the man steering the *Mary Lou II* and thought about Devereaux's description of the similar character from the plumbing truck in Dallas and on the ship out of Cuba. It wasn't as much what Devereaux had said as it was an ominous feeling he conveyed, coupled with his subsequent murder, that completed the connection for Dallas. He kept watching Lagarto at the wheel, studying his posture, transferring it to events in his mind, trying to grasp the magnitude of having stumbled onto one of the great secrets of the century. There was plausibility in the man's age. And didn't it kind of figure? The Exumas sure beat the foothills of the Sierra Madras, as hideouts go.

Lost in thoughts that boggled the mind, it took several seconds for the sudden change to register. He saw Lagarto react with a flurry of herky-jerky movements at the same instant he realized the drone of the engines had stopped. They were still making headway on momentum, but the twin diesels were no longer propelling the heavy displacement hull through the water.

Ellswick materialized on the run and ducked into a hatch in the deck behind the main superstructure. A few seconds later, Lagarto appeared and followed him into the engine compartment. Dallas, standing next to the hatch with Hawke, scanned his memory of mechanical crises he'd encountered on boats. Breakdowns are as much a part of boating as sunburn. The marine environment puts an even more sobering twist on the familiar Murphy's Law: Anything that can go wrong, will, and at the worst possible time. Tough to imagine a more inopportune time than this.

Hawke, hovering over the open compartment, was getting antsy for a progress report.

"Some water down here but not too bad. I don't think that has anything to do with it," Ellswick said from below.

"Of all the goddamned things."

Dallas looked at Hawke and shrugged. Although he'd spent a lot of years around boats, he hated to admit his mechanical expertise could fit into the glove box of a Volkswagen. His experience was that no trouble with an engine ever carried a simple solution. The first thought was a fuel problem. But that wouldn't explain the loss of all power, or as Hawke put it, "full electrical crap-out."

Minutes passed. Curses erupted from the engine compartment. Hawke was down on his knees in classic ostrich position, head thrust into the hatch, backside creating an inviting target. Dallas saw the mental image of a field-goal kicker in slow motion: Two quick steps and the firm swing of a leg. It was tempting. One solid kick down the hatch, slam the cover down and he'd have the whole lot of them bottled up like hornets in a corked nest. But then what? Sit on this raft and wait for the hurricane? He glanced at the *P-BJ-003*. Didn't know the first thing about operating that. He knew the mini-sub, but it wasn't suitable for long-range transit, and without power he couldn't operate the hoist to launch it.

Suddenly, he had a sickening thought. Rushing to the side and peering into the water, his fears were confirmed. Even with the surface frothy with whitecaps, he could see the bottom through the gin-clear water. In the rush to pinpoint the engine failure, nobody had bothered to set the anchor, and they were drifting toward a sandy shoal. Not yet aground, but Dallas had been in deeper water in a bathtub.

He yelled to Hawke about their predicament and rushed to the bow. Hawke looked up from the hatch, his face flushed, dumbfounded. Dallas released the anchor line and immediately felt foolish. He heard the splash, but that was it; no line played out. Scanning the area off the port side, he could see water breaking over a sand bar not more than 100 yards away. Perhaps he had acted in time to at least keep them floating.

He secured the anchor line and went back for a progress report, there wasn't one. Racked with nervous energy, Hawke was becoming increasingly agitated, jitterbugging around the deck like the kid in the back row of the church choir who needs to take a leak and there's still a half-hour left in the service. His fractured melody would have made the congregation blush. With a "motherfucker" here and a "son-of-a-bitch" there, he was a troubled tenor yodeling into a deaf wind. His angst was understandable. Dallas felt it, too, in the knot growing in his stomach. Without electrical power, they were in a communications blackout with no way to check on the progress of the storm. It was like getting a postcard written in blood from Freddy Krueger: You know he's stalking you, you just don't know where he's coming from or when he'll get there.

The weather still gave little indication of the danger beyond the horizon. It was gusty but sunny as late afternoon pressed toward early evening. Daylight Saving Time held a couple hours of grace, if they could only get underway again.

"How much farther we have to go?" Dallas asked Hawke.

"Hour. Maybe a little more. Can't believe the rotten luck. Reminds me of the time I had this great run going at blackjack over on Paradise Island — $100 table, absolutely kicking ass. Just as I'm thinking I'm going to own the place, the damn lights go off in the casino. Took an hour to get 'em back, and after that I couldn't put two cards together to buy a fart in a tin can."

Dallas was trying to sort through Hawke-eyed logic to grasp how that related to this predicament in any way when word of the breakthrough came. Ellswick found the problem. Something about a balky relay switch. However, it took another 45 minutes to bypass it and get the power back. Dallas retreated to the bow to avoid Hawke's incessant pacing and chattering.

He sat on a nest of the coiled anchor line, his back against the wheelhouse bulkhead, listening to the wind. Even when he became aware of the next setback in this ill-fated voyage, he doubted the others had noticed: The *Mary Lou II* was no longer behaving like a boat. A quick peek over the side confirmed it. The tide was falling. They were firmly planted on a sandbar, listing slightly to starboard. No point mentioning it now. Dallas felt like the lonely unicorn without a ticket for Noah's *Ark*.

A flurry of hoo-haws from Hawke signaled success with the electrical problem. Dallas stayed where he was, waiting, mentally noting the time to recognition: 10, 15, 20 seconds ... 30. That was it, 30 seconds of jubilation before the shouting started. Dallas looked tentatively around the corner. Lagarto had Hawke backed against the gunwale, face in his face, spittle flying, railing at him. Hawke just stood there, taking it. It surprised Dallas that he felt vaguely sorry for him.

Perhaps Hawke was the catalyst of this mess. He certainly wasn't going to be browbeaten into a solution. This was beyond all of them. Nature had all the cards stacked so high it was suffocating. Ellswick, who'd emerged from the engine compartment moments before, filthy but triumphant, was staring over the side in disbelief. Lagarto calmed down but fixed Dallas with a wicked glare when he came forward.

There was a discussion of the options before them, brief consideration of using the P-BJ-003 to complete the journey. Ellswick shook his head.

"Forget it. That thing can handle some pretty rough stuff, but the way this wind is gusting now, it'll flip it over like a pancake and we can all kiss our asses goodbye."

The wind was showing its muscle now, whistling around the superstructure, rocking the old shrimp boat slightly, as if mocking their predicament. Just before dusk the sky took on an ominous amber hue. There was nothing to do but wait for high water and pray the brunt of the storm missed them.

When darkness set in, Dallas sought the only refuge available. He curled up on a bunk in fetal position and went to sleep.

CHAPTER 52

The woman in the white chiffon gown was coming directly toward him, skipping and laughing down the mountainside. A faceless mob of cartoon cutouts, scrambling to keep up with her, stretched to the peak and beyond, pouring over it like tumbleweeds. They were alternately oohing and ahhing, like the crowd at a fireworks display. Some carried long banners, others brandished signs at the end of long handles. Dallas got a look at one, which read: "Obladi, Oblada. Yeah, Yeah, Yeah!"

The sun was directly at her back, partially eclipsed by the material of the gown billowing around her. Squinting into the harsh light, Dallas couldn't see her face, but he knew it was Mom. He stepped aside, his heart beating faster as each stride brought her closer. Suddenly she was there, her face so young, so clear, looming larger than life like an extreme close-up on a movie screen. The image took Dallas's breath away. He was overcome by a wave of joy greater than he'd ever known. When she recognized him, her expression mirrored the sensation he was feeling.

"Where have you been, son? Why do you stand there, rooted like a tree?" She reached out and touched his cheek, her fingertips cool, invigorating. "Time to spread your wings and fly. You can do it. It's easy."

With that, she was off again. A hop, a skip and she was gliding, the material of the gown catching the wind and lifting her. She touched down, leaped and soared once more. Again and again she took flight down the mountainside as the crowd trailed along, oohing and ahhing.

Dallas glanced at his side and he had wings, too. Cardboard. But he didn't hesitate. He ran, leaped, and was airborne, rising above the crowd.

When he looked down, a row of gunners rose from the shrubbery. They were dressed as clowns wearing Richard Nixon masks. Their gun barrels gleamed in the sunlight, then fired as one. A sickening blast echoed across the mountain.

\#

Dallas was down, disoriented. His head throbbed. He blinked and was rocked again, his head smacking against something solid. Reality came rushing back. He was on the deck of the cabin, and the way it was rocking suggested they were no longer aground.

The deck dropped again. This time he braced himself and avoided another knock on the head. He scrambled to his feet, reaching for a handhold as the boat fell into another trough. He felt dizzy, nauseous, desperate for fresh air.

Finding the doorway, he lurched through it and collided with Edison Hawke, who at that moment was stumbling down the narrow passage toward the wheelhouse. Hawke's face was pale. He looked as sick as Dallas felt.

"We're off the bar?"

"Been off a couple hours. Something like that. Hard to know anything anymore. All hell's breaking loose. The chief's doing an amazing job pointing us in the right direction. Got our position on the satellite. We lose that, we're toast. If we can just hang in till daylight, he thinks we got a chance to make it."

Dallas tightened his grip on Hawke's forearm and stared into his eyes, dimly illuminated by light from the wheelhouse. They were red, droopy.

"Your friend. I was wondering, what's his name?"

Hawke's expression was full of disdain. "You dumb bastard. Right now, you just might want to call him 'Destiny.' "

Hawke pulled away. Dallas followed into the wheelhouse. Lagarto stood with a wide stance, both hands on the wheel, leaning into it. Ellswick was alternating between studying the navigational chart and the instruments, providing a steady flow of information and guidance.

"You're going to want to take it another 10 degrees to the right. Should be plenty of water over there, and a better angle on the waves. I think."

Hawke was right, it was difficult to be sure of anything. They were sailing through hell's back alley on a course for oblivion. There was a glow outside but no real visibility through the window, just torrents of rain pounding, pounding. Now and then, they'd plunge into a deep trough and be socked headlong by a solid wall of water that rattled the glass. It was like trying to fight Muhammad Ali and Joe Frazier at the same time: the persistent jab, jab, jab of the storm interspersed with the periodic rabbit punch from the sea.

"We should have life jackets on," Dallas said to Hawke. Dallas knew at any moment it could come, the jolt of something solid that would smash open the belly of the boat like a pinata and scatter them all as saltwater taffy. Hawke looked at him, expressionless. All they could do was try to hold on and hope to stay afloat.

Somehow they did — miraculously. Dallas had no idea how long he'd slept. It surprised him when the light outside the window brightened. It was dawn, though the sun was obscured. The storm had lost some intensity. Not as much rain at the moment, though the periodic wind gusts were still staggering. Dallas could see land through the gloom, a low-lying island off the starboard side.

The waves seemed to be converging from every direction at once with no defined pattern, the surface a quarry of potholes. The savagery of the sea was even more frightening now that it was visible. Now and then they'd fall off a wave so steep Dallas couldn't see the top of it, as if the sea was intent on swallowing the boat whole and dragging it to the bottom. Sometimes the concussion of the drop was so great he could feel the jolt from the keel transmitted along his own spine. How much of a beating could this old boat take? Each time they bottomed out, Dallas braced for the sound of the hull caving in. But each time they popped up again and readied for the next onslaught.

Hawke wedged into the space between Lagarto and Ellswick and peered through the window. "Any idea where the fuck we are?"

"Close," Lagarto said, his voice remarkably calm. "Close. If it don't get any worse..."

Before he could finish, there was another concern. Ellswick spotted it, a red light on the panel warning of overheating in the starboard engine. The tachometer indicated a drop in RPMs. Ellswick slipped on a yellow slicker and ducked out through the door. Just gaining access to the engine room with the deck awash and pitching would be horrendous. Dallas shuddered at the thought of having to descend into that dark hellhole.

The gauge showed more drop in power. Lagarto was cursing about the likely loss of the engine when Hawke began gesturing toward something he'd spotted through the window.

"That's it, isn't it. I recognize the son of a bitch. What a beautiful fucking sight."

Dallas could see it looming off the starboard bow, an elongated island that resembled a large lizard, the front half of its body raised. It faced southeast, head up, as if peering through the storm, awaiting their arrival. From the headland it sloped back to the northwest, tapering gradually to a tail that curled around to form a u-shaped harbor that was their objective.

The appearance of the island — or was it an apparition? — gave Dallas the creepiest feeling. He recalled Devereaux referring to the mysterious cribbage player on the freighter out of Havana as the Lizard Man. He had to consider the possibility that, in the midst of extraordinary circumstances, his mind was doing an Evel Knievel over the Snake River Canyon of conclusions. After all, what were the odds? And yet, with each glance at the face of the man at the wheel he felt more certain. The great irony, and it didn't escape him, was that at this moment his own hope of survival was in the hands of a man he firmly believed was responsible for perhaps the most notorious murder of the Twentieth Century.

Although they were almost even with the headland, the form of the island was becoming harder to discern. The storm was closing in again, more intense than before. An eerie growl rumbled through the wheelhouse. The walls seemed to flex inward. Dallas felt his ears pop, an indication that barometric pressure was dropping faster than a young lawyer's scruples. He remembered the same sensation just before the worst of it during Hugo, and the terror of that night came screaming back. The hurricane had them in a hammerlock now.

It seemed to be coming from every direction at once. A huge wall of water slammed the front of the wheelhouse. The door on the starboard side rattled, opened slightly, then banged shut. Dallas's first inclination was to throw his weight against it to keep it closed. He was headed that way when it swung inward and a figure appeared in the opening. He'd almost forgotten about Ellswick. His face was red, his hair soaked. There was a cut on his forehead, a stream of blood flowing down the temple past his right eye. His expression suggested a man who'd had a ringside seat at the devil's circus and the juggler dropped a flaming torch in his lap. He was shouting something, but it was difficult to make out through the din of the storm.

"Skimmer's loose back there. Strap broke!"

The message didn't immediately register with Dallas but it did with Hawke. Dallas had Ellswick by an arm, attempting to pull him into the cabin when he felt a push from behind. As the boat dipped suddenly toward that side, the three of them were catapulted out through the door. Dallas tried to scramble back, but something was pushing him in the other direction.

He turned his head and there was Hawke, face contorted, bellowing to be heard through the storm. "Gotta tie that fucker down. Can't lose it now."

Dallas was incredulous. They were on the brink of destruction and Hawke wouldn't let go of his selfish agenda, or Dallas's arm. He was the damn fool who runs back into a burning house to save his stamp collection, and he intended it to be a group outing.

Ducking low to use the gunwale as a windshield, they reached the rear deck where the *P-BJ-003* and Devereaux's sub were an odd couple in transit. The stern of the skimmer was off at a 45-degree angle from its mooring cradle. Ellswick had gotten a line on it, loosely fastened, but it was flopping around like a fish on a pier.

Strange how at such moments personal safety becomes a secondary concern. Engulfed in the madness of the storm, Dallas found himself responding to the crisis as if the skimmer were a child in peril. He could feel his legs buckling under the exertion of wrestling with an unruly obstacle on a deck bucking over the uneven waves, awash in frothy seawater. All that seemed to matter was helping two individuals who were, in fact, his captors, save a precious piece of machinery that had no value to his own hope for survival. In part, it was the chaos of the storm, screaming at him, overriding the ability to think logically. Dallas had a hold of the skimmer and the vague notion that the sooner they got it tied down the better his chances of getting back inside the cabin.

Ellswick had the rope rigged through a large pulley fastened to the deck and was using it for leverage to force the *P-BJ-003* back onto its cradle. Dallas and Hawke did their best to add impetus while fighting for footing. It was an unlikely crew on desperation detail. Somehow they were succeeding, bit by bit gaining purchase. Progress spurred greater effort. Another heave by Ellswick, another push coupled with a timely dip of the deck, and the skimmer slipped back into place.

Ellswick was tying it off. Hawke was pumping a fist in triumph, hoots of glee momentarily piercing the primal chorus of the wind. Dallas was crouched, shoulder tight against the side of the skimmer, attempting to regain his strength when nature's conspiracy yanked the rug out from under them.

The *Mary Lou II* broached so suddenly and violently that Dallas found himself staring directly into a hole in the sea so dark and malevolent it appeared as a wink from hell. Conflicting forces pulled at him with such veracity that for a moment he drifted free from gravity's chains. In that instant it felt as if he could float straight up and out of the storm. The sensation gave way to a tug so strong it seemed to touch the center of his soul. It was dragging him downward, claiming him, and he could see it happening as if he were watching someone else being sucked helplessly into the ocean's bottomless maw.

Just as terror was yielding to resignation, the jaws of the sea snapped shut and the boat reared back onto a level plane. The brief respite it provided was incongruous with the violence of the storm. It lifted Dallas onto his toes. He spun around in a perfect pirouette that was at once stunning and comical. He was on the verge of regaining balance when he was slammed from behind by a force that knocked the breath out of him. It wasn't Hawke or Ellswick — they were both in his field of view. This was inanimate, unyielding. It staggered him.

The boat yawed sharply again in the same direction as before. Dallas, gasping to recover his breath, felt a tremendous weight crashing down on him. As his knees buckled, he got a look at his tormentor. The mini-sub had broken free and was lurching about the deck like a drunken bull. One of the torpedo tubes swung and caught him below the left knee. Something had to give. It was his ankle. The snap of the bone sent a bolt of pain all the way to his hip, his cry of anguish lost in the cacophony of the elements that seemed to be focused on beating the old shrimp boat and its crew into submission.

The agony was indescribable, but the flip side was salvation. Dallas was momentarily pinned between the sub and the skimmer. The others weren't as fortunate. When the bottom dropped out, Ellswick lost his grip on the rope and staggered backward, arms windmilling. Dallas didn't see what happened to him, but he had a front-row seat for Hawke's grand exit.

It happened quickly yet seemed to take forever. As Hawke flailed about for something to grab on to, the stern of the skimmer caught him below the hip and bucked him into the air. He made a surprisingly graceful flip with a half twist. He remained suspended, inexplicably, on his back, feet up, as if lounging in an invisible hammock. With vision blurred by searing pain, Dallas watched in amazement as Hawke's jaw dropped and his eyes bugged. For an instant their eyes met and Dallas saw Hawke's expression change from surprise to disbelief just before the sea opened up again like the mouth of Jonah's whale and smacked its frothy lips around him.

Before Dallas could fully grasp what he'd witnessed, the sub seemed to come to life, sliding and dancing and finally plunging over the side at the same spot where Hawke had disappeared. As he began to slide, too, Dallas swung an arm and banged into something solid. It was the base of the cradle that held the skimmer. He just managed to wrap his arms around a steel rung. He closed his eyes and held on, fully expecting to join the exodus.

It didn't happen. He lay there with a bear hug around the rung, eyes clamped shut, the pain in his leg flogging him, each lurch of the deck another lash against frayed nerve endings. Waiting. Waiting, it seemed, for the end of time. For the end of his time, almost wishing for it. The storm seemed to be taunting him. The wail of the wind and agony of his broken ankle were overriding his will to hold on.

Gradually it dawned on him that something was different. When he finally opened his eyes and peaked around the bottom of the skimmer's roost, he was met by a stunning sight: trees and the slope of land. It was apparent that, for the second time on this ill-fated voyage, the *Mary Lou II* was aground.

That knowledge was a glass of cold water in the face of the survival instinct. The storm dropped its guard a couple of notches and Dallas dove through the opening. No time to think about it. If he had, he would have never released his grip on the skimmer's cradle. All concentration went into convincing his body it was still a functional entity. With his left leg screaming in protest, he felt like the Allied forces clawing for a foothold on Normandy Beach. Each inch of progress came with a price.

It didn't matter. Turning back was unthinkable. Every bit of focus was on getting back inside the cabin, even though there was no guarantee fate would be kinder there. It was simply a hope to cling to, a cause to strive for. He slithered and crawled, feeling like a sloth dragging a ball and chain down a road slathered in molasses.

At one point he was tossed violently against the outer wall of the wheelhouse. The audacity of the impact infuriated him, further setting his resolve. Sobbing and cursing, mouth and elbows bloody, he pressed on along the narrow passage on the starboard side until he glanced up and saw the edge of the wheelhouse door.

It took his remaining energy to summon the effort to tuck his left knee under him and push up with enough force to reach the door handle. His fingers hooked over it, then slid off. He teetered like an old tree with rotted roots no longer able to support its weight. Just as gravity was about to cash its chips, Dallas mustered one more lunge at the handle. He caught it. It gave way and the door swung inward. He tucked his head and tumbled into the cabin. The Russian judge hated the routine, deducted all the style points. Dallas was too exhausted to care. He managed to kick the door shut with his good leg and lay on his back feeling his heart pounding.

He arched his neck and looked quickly around the wheelhouse. Lagarto was not in sight. He wasn't Dallas's immediate concern, nor did he feel a significant sense of security about being back inside. The killer that worried him now was outside, pawing at the turf, waiting for the right moment to exploit its advantage. He could feel it building to a reckoning such as he had witnessed once before.

Suddenly he had a clear vision of John Kennedy in the calm before the fusillade, squinting and waving at the cheering crowd. He could imagine Mrs. Connally, the governor's wife, delivering the ironic line just before they rode into the teeth of hell's fire: "Mr. President, you can't say that Dallas doesn't love you." He wondered if Kennedy had any inkling what was coming.

This wasn't as subtle. The storm was closing in, rattling its saber, mustering for the decisive charge. Coming for him. Who else was left? Hawke and Ellswick, both gone. Mom and Devereaux, too. He thought of Claire and Keith, their faces indistinct in his mind. They couldn't help him now. There was only himself, and maybe Lagarto. But all he could see was fate's bony finger pointing — at him.

Dallas felt his ears pop again and he flashed back to the terror of Hugo, the deafening locomotive breath whistling through a hideous chasm. He could feel himself tumbling into a dream state where you are falling, and the sensation is so real your stomach drops and you actually feel yourself bounce on the bed. But there was no waking up from this to wash away the sweat of fright with a glass of water in the dark.

This was fright in full flight, like a chorus of all the ghosts of the spirit world sucking every bit of mortality out of the air and exhaling the resentment from the sum of every miserable life ever wasted. It manifested as an otherworldly wail that was not only chilling to the bone, it reached to the center of the soul and twisted, intent on wresting control. Dallas retreated toward the only haven of familiarity within reach.

He got as far as the threshold of the little cabin with the bunk. The door was wedged open and he tried to crawl through the opening. The boat was rocking violently like one of those mechanical bulls in the cowboy bars. To keep from being thrown, he wrapped himself around the edge of the doorway, his upper body inside the cabin, his legs in the hallway.

Revved to the red line and beyond, the storm made its run along Broadway with tires squealing. The deck rumbled, bulkheads flexed. Something had to give, and it was the main window of the wheelhouse, imploding and scattering shrouds of glass against the opposite side of the only interior wall shielding Dallas from the wind.

It might as well have been a cardboard rampart facing a torrent of flaming arrows. The beast was inside now, just around the corner. That added to the terror, the perception that it was alive. Dallas could feel the pulse of the hurricane. It wasn't a random burp of nature, it was death's henchman, shouting his name, stalking him. There was nowhere left to run. Dallas could feel the tendrils of the storm tighten. It had him now, and all he could do was jackknife himself tighter around the edge of the doorway and hold on like a human clamp.

What he couldn't counter was the relentless will of the wind, which was wearing him down from the inside out. He closed his eyes and uttered the plea of last resort, the mantra of lost causes.

"God, no. God, no. God, no. God, *no!!!*"

CHAPTER 53

The final defense of the doomed is to disconnect the mind. Time loses all depth and breadth as a dimension. The being floats, awaiting a new equilibrium. People who claim the near-death experience describe an unfathomable peacefulness they are reluctant to relinquish. Dallas wasn't sure how close he came to the great disappearing act or how long he'd hugged the bulkhead like the love of his life. The sudden calm that had replaced the torment was so unexpected and pleasant, it took a glimpse of the last face he wanted to see to realize he'd either gone directly to Hell or the storm had taken a pit stop.

Lagarto was standing over him.

"Where's Hawke?"

"He's, I don't know … gone. We almost capsized, and he just went over. Ellswick, too. I think."

Dallas tried to sit up and grimaced from a jolt of pain. He pulled up his pant leg to reveal an ankle swollen to grapefruit size. "I think I broke it."

He looked up almost expecting Lagarto to offer a hand. The other man stared back, expressionless. Without a word, he stepped over Dallas and exited through the door on the port side.

That wasn't so much a shock as it was a catalyst for sorting out certain realities. The process took several minutes as Dallas sat in the narrow hallway. He was in shock. Every part of him ached, though a merciful numbness was blotting out much of the pain in his ankle. He felt as if he'd been run over by an entire football team, including the water boys. But he was alive.

Despite the break in the storm, there was no guarantee he'd stay that way. He was injured and stranded with a man he had reason to believe was an inveterate killer. Where the hell was he, anyway, and how was he going to get away if he did survive? The weight of those questions was just beginning to settle when another memory from Hurricane Hugo caused him to exclaim aloud.

"It's the goddamned eye! Son of a bitch."

He practically leaped to his feet, bearing all the weight on his healthy right leg. Using a wooden slat from the bunk for support, he hopped and shuffled out the door. Pain be damned, he wasn't going to sit and wait for the counterpunch.

The *Mary Lou II* had wedged itself onto a u-shaped spit of land that projected from one end of an island to form a perfect harbor. The boat was situated broadside to the mouth of the cove. This was the low end of the island, which rose to a modest elevation at the other end, perhaps three-quarters of a mile away. Suddenly he remembered, that was the headland Hawke had pointed out. This was Lagarto's island.

Dallas couldn't see any buildings, but there was a dock across the cove. Obviously, that was Lagarto's objective. He had the *P-BJ-003* on the hoist and was lowering it over the side. The storm surge washing over this end of the island made it impossible to simply walk around. But if Lagarto could get to that dock before the backside of the storm slammed the window of opportunity shut, he was home free. He intended to use the skimmer as a dinghy to get there.

There was at least a small part of Dallas that believed — that *wanted* to believe — Lagarto intended to come back for him. It is a natural inclination to assume everyone possesses some measure of humanity. It is difficult to comprehend the mind of one who only values self-preservation. In his 40 years, Dallas couldn't recall ever knowingly interacting with such an individual. It became evident he was looking at one now, when Lagarto slipped over the rail and rode the skimmer down on the hoist without so much as a glance in his direction.

The realization was a shock, even though it would have been hard to imagine being holed up with this man, together against nature's wrath. It wouldn't have been surprising if Lagarto had shot him before he left the cabin. That would have seemed in character. But to just leave him, injured, as a sacrificial lamb for the wind and sea to fight over was unconscionable. It sickened him. It pissed him off.

Lagarto was struggling to get the skimmer launched and pointed in the right direction. The wind had taken a breather, but huge waves were plowing through the tiny harbor, breaking all around the *Mary Lou II*. Dallas worked his way along the rail toward the stern until he was just above Lagarto. He thought about switching off the motor that operated the hoist, but Lagarto was already releasing the harness.

Instead, he shouted, "Something to think about when you're sitting there safe, waiting for the storm to pass: I saw you."

Lagarto glanced at him quickly and continued to work on the skimmer, easing it into the water.

"I'm talking about 30 years ago. I might forget details about a card game but not about life. And death. I was there. I saw you. I've wondered about you for 30 years."

Now he had the attention of the man who fired the shot that killed JFK, felt the full impact of the eyes that looked through the sight at a spot on the president's head and willed the bullet into his brain. What surprised Dallas was how little fear he felt. Maybe it was shock from the broken ankle desensitizing his mind. Perhaps the hopelessness of the situation left him beyond caring. Now that he was locked on the eyes of the assassin, he didn't flinch. He was trying to look inside, to see if he could detect any semblance of a soul.

"You know what I'm talking about. My name is Dallas, same as the city. I was there. I even know how you made your getaway. Back of a plumbing truck, wasn't it?

Lagarto's eyes narrowed, jaw tensed. Dallas felt a flash of fear. His eyes scanned quickly for the lump of a holster. He didn't see one.

"Thing I want to know, were you just a hired gun? Or was there something more? Did you feel anything when you pulled the trigger or was it nothing more than scratching an itch?"

If there was any visible reaction, it passed like a blip on a radar screen. What was he expecting? Surprise? Some betrayal of guilt?

The expression of the killer remained unreadable. It was the same as Dallas had observed earlier when an outburst of anger dissolved to calm unflappability. He guessed this was a natural defense against any challenge, the way Lagarto responded to pressure. Dallas could imagine the steely eye peering through the telescopic sight, unblinking; the pulse slowing to an imperceptible pause just before the moment of decision when the finger clenched on the trigger. The thought brought a shiver, but his nerves were surprisingly placid.

"You CIA?"

The question was unexpected. "You think I'd be asking about this if I were?"

"You gonna write a book? Always room for one more. Think anyone would notice? Think anyone cares?"

"Fuck you."

It was the most banal of responses. Yet, the way it rolled off Dallas's tongue it bore the eloquence of Plato. It was spoken for the millions who still remember where they were when they heard the news that unleashed a nation's tears. It was spoken for the little boy who saluted like the bravest soldier the day they buried his father. It was spoken for everyone who still asks why? Yes, for those who do still care.

Lagarto laughed. He started to speak, but as he did a wave smacked the *P-BJ-003* and diverted his attention back to his mission. The wind was picking up again. Rain stung Dallas's eyes. He didn't blink. He kept staring at the man whose deed had haunted him for three decades and changed so much for so many.

Looking at him now, it seemed incomprehensible. The assassin was just a man, beholden to the same effects of gravity and time as the rest of us. From this vantage point, Dallas could see liver spots through thinning hair. Lagarto's posture suggested back problems. What set him apart was unparalleled cunning and a complete void of conscience.

Something else crept into Dallas's assessment as he watched Lagarto wrestle with the skimmer: Despite his capacity for intimidation, he was not infallible. Dallas watched him sweating, his breathing labored against the exertion of launching the skimmer. He saw an aging thug too vain to recognize his own decline.

With a determined leap, Lagarto boarded the skimmer and began using a long pole to shove it away from shore. Just before he hit the starter he turned back to face Dallas.

"Go ahead, motherfucker, tell the world. Better hurry. Make sure you put it in a bottle and seal it good. Hope someone finds it along with your corpse."

He signed off with another laugh that was eclipsed by the whine of the skimmer's turbine awakening. A shower of spray erupted from the stern as the strange craft surged into the harbor.

Dallas turned away angrily and began to retreat to the cabin. He had no plan for survival. The curtain was about to rise for Act II of the hurricane and he had the worst seat in the house, front row, center. The worst of Hugo had come on the backhand. Instinct said, seek shelter, any shelter. What other option was there?

He was moving along the rail, using it for support, skipping along on one good leg when the one he was dragging banged against something, igniting a fresh burst of pain. Crying aloud, he looked down in surprise as a small coconut rolled ahead on the deck. He hadn't noticed it before. It was insignificant to his predicament; food was not an immediate concern. Yet, an irresistible compulsion drew him to pick it up despite the difficulty in bending while maintaining balance on one leg.

It was puny for a coconut, about the size of a cantaloupe, weeks if not months away from maturing to bowling ball size when the wind had wrenched it off the tree and apparently flung it onto the *Mary Lou II*. Amazed at that coincidence, Dallas turned to scan the shore for the nearest coconut palms. When he did he was met with another surprise. The *P-BJ-003* was dead in the water, drifting back toward him while Lagarto attempted to restart the engine.

Dallas couldn't account for what happened next. Sometimes, at extraordinary moments, the subconscious becomes the locomotive of the will. Impulse asserts itself as a blustery Alexander Haig declaring on the day Ronald Reagan was shot, "I'm in charge here."

Dallas was holding the coconut. The hide was smooth and it felt good in his hands, a familiar sensation to cling to amid unsettling circumstances.

A voice echoed from a mothballed chamber of unessential memory. It wasn't Al Haig. It was his old baseball coach, Chuck Robison. Dallas could see him as clear as a Texas stampede, red-faced, cheek bulging from a wad of tobacco — Ol' Chewin' Chuck, they called him — stomping out to the mound to deliver the same message he brought every time Dallas got himself in a jam:

"Dadgummit, kid, pitching's simple if you've got the arm. See the target, follow through. Simple. Just throw the damned thing. Got it?"

Dallas simply responded the way he always had. He nodded, turned and hurled the coconut.

He almost didn't get to see the result. When his weight shifted forward on the follow through, his injured ankle collapsed and he crashed onto the portside gunwale. But he managed to keep his head up following the flight of the coconut.

At first it appeared it would sail high of the mark. It is difficult to judge the trajectory required to hit a target significantly lower than the point of release. However, if there was one thing that had always come easily to Dallas, it was throwing a sinker. Something about the way it rolled out of his hand, his crooked index finger imparting the distinctive spin he'd been known for. Dallas could always tell when he'd thrown a perfect strike the instant he released it.

His eyes were fixed on the green orb, almost mesmerized by the tightness of the rotation that bore it through the air. At the apex of its flight it hung for an excruciating moment like a harvest moon. Then, with the purpose and precision of a guided missile, it darted down and struck the lower right rear of Lagarto's skull.

It wasn't the fortuitousness of the throw that caused Dallas to gape in disbelief, it was the effect. Lagarto dropped like a rock. If the impact of the coconut wasn't sufficient to render him unconscious, the jolt from his jaw slamming into the skimmer's control panel as he went down ensured it.

Still lying with his chest across the gunwale, arms dangling over the side, Dallas expected his nemesis to pop up and come back to finish the job he'd entrusted to nature. Lagarto never moved.

When Dallas finally pushed himself up from the rail, he uttered the same phrase Lee Harvey Oswald shouted as he was being subdued in the Texas Theatre: "It's all over now."

#

If someone throws the pitch of a lifetime in the middle of a hurricane, does he hear applause? Does he take a bow? Doff his cap? Hell, it was dumb luck, he knew that: an imperfectly shaped sphere thrown from an unstable platform at a bobbing target through wind and rain. And nobody to witness it. He scarcely believed it himself. But, oh, what a feeling.

An imperfect pitcher named Don Larsen once pitched a perfect game for the Yankees in the World Series, etching a place in history with one superlative act. For every Don Larsen there are a million Dallas Hustons who paint their masterpiece in obscurity.

There was no time to savor the deed let alone analyze it. The hurricane was winding up again, ready to deliver more misery. Dallas barely made it back inside the wheelhouse before the wind, now coming from the opposite direction as before, rocked the *Mary Lou II* back on its keel and sent him sprawling.

Lying there, head fuzzy from the fall, a strange image came to him from the past, a wacky cartoonish decal that he had stuck to the mirror in his boyhood bedroom. It depicted a gangly character with a jowly face crouched inside a toilet bowl bearing an expression of resignation as his hand grasped the flush lever. The caption read, "Goodbye, cruel world." As the storm raged anew and the old shrimp boat floated free from its temporary sanctuary, he imagined the voice of Ricky Nelson in the wind singing goodbye to Mary Lou, and he saw a vision of the face of the pathetic figure in the toilet bowl pressed against the window grinning demonically. It stuck him how quick and easy it is to flush away a life, in the blink of an eye, the twitch of a finger.

Then it dawned on him why that decal had come to mind. He had spent hours staring at it that terrible afternoon after returning from Dealey Plaza following the assassination and an unsettling visit to the police station where Mom gave her statement. He'd locked his bedroom door and remained with his eyes fixed on the fool in the commode while the doomed day faded to night. It occurred to him that his thoughts had been the same then as they were now, about the swift finality of the royal flush. With one hand clutching the corner of a bulkhead, he held the other in front of his face and snapped his fingers. *Click, click.*

His thoughts drifted to another bleak moment, the night he was released by the Orioles. Despair found him in a bar in Baltimore. It happened to be Edgar Allan Poe night at the bar, and a man on the next stool, dressed as the poet, looked at Dallas and said, "Didn't I just see you on the news. Aren't you that pitcher the Orioles let go? Huston, right? Tough luck, pal. Ain't that the way it always goes, you only get a moment in the spotlight, then darkness descends forevermore." Dallas got up to retreat, head down, and walked into a man wearing a raven costume. The first man laughed and said, "Isn't that right, raven? Forevermore … Forevermore."

As Dallas hurried toward the door that night, he could hear the two of them croaking, "Forevermore … forevermore … forevermore …"

From where he was crouched in a corner of a tiny cabin, it sounded like the wind was taunting him with the same refrain. He closed his eyes but could still clearly see the head of that six-foot raven and hear the echoes of his cry:

Forevermore ... forevermore ... forevermore ...

CHAPTER 54

Keith watched her pull up in the dusty gray Toyota. Somehow it looked smaller than normal, and so did she tucked inside with the sum of her life. It contained all she had left that mattered, the boy in the passenger seat, and underscored how much was missing. The rest of it — their clothes, Lyle's toys, a few keepsakes — didn't even strain the capacity of the trunk and backseat. Claire had explained that to her friend Margie during the tearful goodbye that left her eyes red and necessitated a makeup repair.

"My whole marriage was about acquiring things. Seemed that was what we had in common. We accumulated things, we talked about accumulating things. We ended up with all this stuff that had no real meaning, and, it turned out, neither did the marriage. It made me want to get rid of all the stuff. Now the thing I treasure most is freedom."

Now even that seemed hollow, empty.

"Can't believe you're really leaving," Keith said, arms folded, watching her get out of the car. She pulled two bags of perishable food from the backseat and handed them to him. He stood cradling one bag in each arm. She squinted up at him and shrugged.

"It's time to go. It's been a great adventure. Helped me put some distance between myself and the past. Sometimes life flashes the lights and points the way to the door. You're a fool if you don't know when to leave. I'll go back to California. My family's there, what's left of it. Mom could use some help. My friend Mary Jo said I can work the front desk in her beauty salon until I land a regular job doing what I know."

Keith was studying her, thinking how fond he had become of her. Just then she looked like a wounded bird, and instinctively he wanted to protect her, throw her a lifeline, save the day. Even the emotional havoc showing on her face couldn't conceal that this was a fine-looking woman, on the backside of youth but in the full bloom of mature sensuality. She'd been derailed a few times but was no pushover. And as vulnerable as she might appear, he had no doubt she'd survive and thrive.

He was thinking about what he'd miss when she was gone. Claire had the ability to light up a moment and give everybody reason to smile. After all that had happened, a smile would be a luxury right now.

"Maybe you should stick around. We'll go out. I could kick myself for not making a play for you long ago. Only a damned fool would let a woman like you get away."

She forced a smile and pulled him down for a kiss on the cheek. "You're sweet. You will be missed. You won't be forgotten. A part of you stays right here."

She clutched both hands over her heart.

They stood there for a moment wrestling with king-size lumps in their throats. Keith started to say something, then looked away. "Make that a blind, damned fool."

She shuffled uncomfortably. "It's OK, really. Better to hurt a little than to feel nothing, numb. I've known that, and it means time wasted. Nothing's guaranteed forever. I mean, you start out as a clean page and everything you experience that means anything stays with you always. I came here, made some friends. Made a lot of memories. Got a tattoo. See."

She pulled aside the sleeveless tank top to reveal the little lizard on the back of her shoulder. Keith smiled, remembering the first time he'd seen it. The tattoo had been the conversation piece at the resort after Claire's impulsive weekend in Fort Lauderdale with Sami. She'd blushed so much from all the teasing and speculating about the events that accompanied it.

"That'll ensure you never forget about us, even when you're 70."

"Not sure that was my brightest moment," she said, peeking over her shoulder at the tattoo. "Funny, this guy's here for good. But when you catch one of these for real, usually you grab the tail and it comes off. The lizard's gone."

She looked up at Keith, and tears welled in her eyes again.

He said, "It's like that with a lot of things in life. They come and go. You get to hold on to them for a moment. You just don't know how long the moment's going to last. A song's like that. It's a moment, a good moment. You enjoy it while you have it. Really, life's just a moment, when you think about it."

"But a song, you can sing it again. With people, when they're gone, they're gone," she said. Her voice cracked and she paused to collect herself, and they both knew where her thoughts were. "You know, I can intellectualize it until the cows come home. That's what I learned to do to try to cope with a lot of things. I mean, this was a guy who has never settled down, doesn't have a real career or even a steady job. Not one with benefits, insurance, everything that goes with that. But you know, the heart doesn't want to hear any of it. The heart doesn't ask why it beats or for how long. It just goes on pumping. And feeling. And right now it feels like it's trying to pump a tennis ball through my arteries. Or maybe a grapefruit."

"I know what you mean. It's like when a snake eats a rabbit whole and you can see this big bulge in the middle of the snake," Keith said.

"I don't even know how he got in there. I don't know if he even meant to. But he's there, and right now it hurts."

That boulder of emotion won the battle for her throat and she had to turn away. Keith watched a couple of huge tears create a river of mascara as she struggled for composure.

"You know, it didn't matter that he was unsettled. Because so am I. I was married to an executive, and look what it got me. With Dallas, we were like a couple of stars adrift without a galaxy. Our paths crossed, and suddenly there was gravity. It didn't have to make sense, it just felt right. Now it looks like we were just star-crossed."

"Believe me, he felt it too. I know he did; I can read these things in people. I loved to tease him about it. He'd get that confused puppy face and I'd say, 'Damn, boy, you got it bad.' He was always talking about how you gave his life meaning and that you were the reason for sticking around. That's why it don't make no sense, why it feels like something had to have happened, like he's hiding somewhere from something."

"But he wasn't in that big a hurry. He packed up and left, without a word. He could call if it was something else."

Keith didn't have an answer other than to just hold her. She felt his arms around her, and sought momentary sanctuary in this bear of a man. She melted into him and just sobbed until her tears soaked through his T-shirt.

"Come on, Mom. Aren't we going?" Lyle gave the horn two quick beeps. She jumped and pulled back. Just before slipping into the driver's seat, Claire turned and said, "Everything that happened here will always stay a part of me, the good and the bad. I know that when I am very old I will look back and find myself transformed to a younger me. I'll think about all the trips to the wreck, about you, Skeeter, everybody — Dallas, of course. And I will know that I had something very special happen in my life."

Keith stood as still as a statue in the driveway of Snapper Cove Marina until her car was well out of sight.

#

It couldn't have been more than three hours later when the phone rang aboard *Big Momma*. Keith didn't hear it at first. He was in the galley cutting up veggies for chowder while several plump slabs of conch meat soaked in lime juice. Friends come and go but hunger lingers. And Marley, the songs never die. Claire was right about music, the real soul food. You've got music and a fragrant broth, the party will find itself.

Keith was feeling it already, the tropical "Auld Lang Syne," as he hummed along to Marley singing "Don't Worry About a Thing."

It took at least four rings before the sound that didn't fit slipped between riffs. Then there was the momentary disorientation of trying to locate the portable phone. So it was probably the sixth ring before he answered. Then he couldn't hear over Marley.

"Wait." He turned down the volume. "Hello."

There was a crackle of static, then a pause, and he thought it might be one of those automated solicitation calls cueing up the recorded spiel. Another burst of static followed by a voice barely audible breaking in and out like a war correspondent on a rooftop in Baghdad describing a flurry of smart bombs seeking an avenue up Saddam Hussein's ass.

"I say, yo, can't understand a damn thing. Terrible connection."

Keith shook the phone, for no logical reason, then listened again, squinting as if that would aid the reception. Surfing down the fragile ladder of electrons was a familiar intonation that couldn't have come as a greater surprise if it had been Ed McMahon telling him he'd just won $10 million.

"What?" His eyes widened, his jaw slacked in disbelief. He looked at the phone, then pressed it tighter against his ear. "Is it ... really you? ... Say what?"

....

"What the ... Where have you? ..."

....

"Where? What the hell ya doing in Nassau?"

....

"Some long damn story, I'm sure. We all thought. We didn't know what the hell to think. Oh, man!"

There was another pause on the other end of the line. It was Keith's turn to speak. To reply. He didn't know what to say, how to say it. Finally, he lowered his voice and spoke slowly.

"That phone's not out of order. It's disconnected. She's gone, man. She left. What do you expect? She thought. Well, you know."

....

"Today. You kind of just missed her."

....

"I don't know. She's on the road. Driving. Could be anywhere."

Keith pushed the stop button on Marley. It became painfully quiet, save for the squawk of a seagull outside and the voice in his ear. Even in a measured tone, his own voice sounded too loud.

"Look, man, I'm sorry. I really am. Don't know what to tell you."

....

"You hurting bad?"

....

"Look, I got an idea. Can you stick it out there for a few more days? With everything that's been happening I've been thinking of getting away myself. Could use a vacation. I'll come over, pick you up. We'll cruise the islands. Catch some fish, lobsters. Kick back, rehabilitate. You know what I mean? Re-ha-bil-i-tate. That's a good word. Get you well again, inside and out. Better medicine than you'll get in any hospital or just sitting around back here."

CHAPTER 55

Five days later Keith found Dallas perched on a low wall made of concrete and seashells outside the guesthouse where he'd been staying since his discharge from Nassau's Princess Margaret Hospital. A pair of crutches rested against a hibiscus bush loaded with lush red flowers. Keith glanced from the yellowish bruise on the side of Dallas's cheek to the cast encasing his lower left leg.

"You look like hell, man."

"Good to see you, too." Dallas grinned at his friend. "Whaddya expect, I've been to hell and back. It leaves an impression."

"You gonna make it?"

"Could've been worse. They were going to fly me back to Miami for surgery, but the break was pretty clean. There was a doctor over here from Jackson Memorial. He looked at the X-rays, thought it was best to get it set and stabilized. So here I am doing what you said: rehabilitating. The woman runs this place makes a mean Goombay Smash. Works wonders. Keeps everything numb. She's got a daughter with a sweet smile comes by and checks on me a lot. That helps, too."

Dallas said his good-byes, got a kiss on the cheek from the fresh-faced daughter with rich mocha skin. Waited while Keith flirted with her.

"She's only 17," Dallas said in the taxi.

"I'll be back next year."

They laughed, then rode in silence the rest of the way to the yacht harbor. Keith, sitting in the back, smiling, hummed softly. Same Marley tune, thinking, yeah, everything gonna work out fine. He waited until they were getting out of the cab.

"By the way, got a surprise for you."

Leaning on his crutches, Dallas peered down the slight incline toward the dock and spotted it right away. *Big Momma* stood out from the other boats like Roseanne at a meeting of Anorexics Anonymous.

"How did you get over here in that?"

"Been working on that engine for months. If I'm gonna leave home for an extended period, I'm gonna take home with me."

Dallas gingerly negotiated the asphalt down-slope to the marina, Keith walking close just in case. Setting his crutches carefully to ensure they didn't slip between the wooden slats of the dock, he felt like the Ancient Mariner bound for a farewell voyage to oblivion. Approaching the end of the pier, he paused to take in the squat splendor of *Big Momma*.

"So, that's the surprise?"

"Well, that's not all. See, I got a new hammock, just for you. You can kick back, put your leg up and soak up the rays. Rehabilitate in style."

Dallas studied the hammock swaying slightly between the masts and pondered the difficulty of getting in and out of it at sea with a leg in a cast. He looked quizzically at Keith, who had a bemused expression on his face. Something didn't fit, and it had to do with the giggle of a young voice that had an entirely different lilt than the two island boys who were struggling to land a jack from the adjacent pier. It didn't register, because he was pondering the step up from the dock to the deck of the boat when a shadow descended on him like a spell.

"Need a hand?"

She appeared as a vision from a ray of sunshine. He began to lose balance. She floated down as if out of a cloud and captured him in a hug that stole his breath. For an instant he thought he was still under the influence of Edison Hawke's mystery drug and would awaken to find himself still a prisoner in the tiny cabin. Or worse, in the throes of the storm.

"It really is you," she said.

The spell was broken. He glanced at her face and saw the smile and a tear. He kissed them both. He'd dreamed about the softness of her lips, the smoothness of her cheek, the sparkling emerald eyes. He noticed something else, a hibiscus tucked in her hair, same shade as the ones at the guesthouse. She plucked it out and held it for him to smell.

"It's you, too, my red flower lady. I didn't know if I'd see you again."

Her body trembled with a joy she couldn't and didn't want to contain. She kept alternately burying her face in his chest, then backing away to arm's length to stare at his face in disbelief. He was hopping on one leg as they spun around together in an impromptu lover's loop. So loopy, Keith could only shake his head and shrug at the boy who stood on the deck of the boat, rolling his eyes toward the sky with mock disgust.

Coming back to earth, Dallas cast a quizzical glance at Keith.

"You son of a bitch, you told me she left."

"She did. She called from Tampa. Thought she left something she needed. Turned out she was right. 'Scuse me, but does it say 'lost and found' on my business card? Or Keith's Broken Heart Repair Service?"

Dallas started to say something else, but a pair of persistent lips took the words out of his mouth. It would be a while before any more questions were asked.

#

If this were a movie, this is where they'd roll the credits and play the love song by someone like Sade or Bryan Adams as the happy couple sails off toward a tropical sunset. In reality, life is nothing like a movie. There is no such thing as a happy ending. Life is a journey, an odyssey. The best anyone can hope for is to avoid troubled waters as much as possible and enjoy pleasant side trips along the way.

The Great Rehabilitation Cruise of 1993 aboard the most unlikely love boat afloat in the Bahamas was one of those idyllic side trips for Dallas, Claire, her son Lyle and Capt. Keith Richards Salmon, who added "finder of lost loves" to his resume under musician, salvage expert, catering and snow removal. OK, the latter was a joke, but Keith was a man of many talents, several of which he demonstrated on the cruise. He taught Lyle to free-dive for spiny lobsters, the clawless relative of the Maine lobster, and how to fillet a fish leaving behind the bones. He gave Claire lessons in windsurfing and showed Dallas some basic reggae riffs on the guitar, which he practiced in the hammock while the others found relief from the afternoon heat in the gin-clear waters along the edge of the Great Bahama Bank.

They spent their days meandering amid the countless cays, coves and inlets, soaking up all the sun, salt air and scenery that go into the prescription for rehabbing fractured bones and tortured souls. They swam, fished, laughed, sang, danced and made up for lost time. They wore few clothes and showered in the rain. They ate fresh fish every day and sated their thirst with fruity boat drinks and clear-bottle Beck's. Keith kept a pot of his famous conch chowder simmering at all times, while Dallas assumed the duties of grill master.

At night Keith served his most important function, keeping Lyle occupied in the cabin with gin rummy and tall tales while Dallas and Claire retreated to a bed of boat cushions on the bow. There they made love under the stars until they were breathless, then slept so close it was as if one heart were beating for two.

One night while lying together wishing on stars, Claire granted one that Dallas had voiced months before. He finally got his song. She sang *a cappella*, a solitary voice emanating from the soul. Her eyes never left his as sweet strains of "Let Me Call You Sweetheart" took the loneliness out of the vast Bahamian night. At daybreak, the seagulls seemed to be carrying the refrain. Or was that Keith's whistle mocking the stars still in Dallas's eyes? He gave his friend an elbow to the ribs, just in case.

"Hey, man, I was impressed. She's good. We're going to have to get her singing with the band. But nothing quite so sappy."

Occasionally, they came ashore on uninhabited islands to wander the beach and explore. They had a memorable stopover at George Town, the unofficial capital of the Exumas, where they spent the night at the quaint Peace and Plenty Hotel, and took on provisions before turning back to the north.

The most notable stop came early in the trip on a small island unnamed on the navigational chart. Dallas had no trouble picking it out for the same reason that attracted a Bahamian fisherman the day after the recent hurricane that plowed through the Central Exumas. There at the tip of a strip of land that arced back from the northwest corner of the island to form a narrow harbor was the wreckage of a black boat. It rested on a rock formation at a 45-degree angle on the port side of its fractured hull with the bow pointing toward open water.

It wasn't until *Big Momma* was anchored and its crew came ashore in Keith's inflatable dinghy that the name of the wreck was visible on the upraised starboard bow: *Mary Lou II*. It was also then that Dallas and his companions gained a true appreciation for how close he had come to being swept to oblivion during the storm.

"It was grounded farther up in the harbor before the eye went through," he said. "Then when the wind went the other way, it floated off and I thought I was a goner."

Lyle had been studying the wreck and listening intently to Dallas's narration of the ordeal and the sequence of events leading to his rescue and transport to Nassau. Finally, the boy offered his assessment.

"This part of the island looks like the tail of Sami's lizard. Your boat got stuck on the tip of the tail. You're lucky a lizard has a long tail."

Keith noticed that Dallas kept glancing across the narrow harbor toward the remains of a dock torn asunder by the hurricane and scanning the shoreline.

"You're wondering about him, aren't you?"

He didn't have to answer. Dallas had told Claire and Keith separately about the demise of Hawke and Ellswick and the whole story of Lagarto. Now he felt a need for closure.

Dallas and Keith left Claire and Lyle aboard *Big Momma* and landed the dinghy next to the shattered dock. They stood there listening to the creak of broken timber before Keith removed the Browning .45 he had stuck in the back of his shorts, cocked it and started up a path leading toward the high ground at the opposite end of the island.

The path was a steady incline that quickly diverged from the shore and wound through the thickly wooded center of the island. It was slow going with Dallas on crutches, but more so because of debris strewn along the path. By all appearances, nobody had passed through there since the storm. At one point a rustling in the underbrush caused them both to duck and freeze until they realized it was a small animal scurrying out of harm's way.

The path led to a plateau at the south end of the island overlooking a picturesque vista of the ocean. The need for eyes to adjust from the shade of the woods to the bright backdrop momentarily obscured the fact that someone had already staked a claim to the view. There, among a shroud of tall pines was a dome-shaped dwelling painted dark green to blend in with the surroundings.

Seeing it sent a chill through Dallas, and he motioned Keith back to cover behind trees at the terminus of the path. It took several minutes to muster the nerve to approach. Trepidation churned in his stomach, but each step brought him closer to the conclusion he'd sought. It wasn't merely that the building was sealed like a vault with steel shutters covering every opening. The telling sign was the uprooted Australian pine that blocked the primary entrance.

"Looks like nobody's home," Keith said. "Think we should leave a note?"

Both resisted the temptation of a smile, but each felt the same release of tension. It didn't take long to determine there was little chance of gaining entry without a blow torch or dynamite. And who knew what surprises might await an intruder. So after a quick circuit of the building, they were about to make a grateful departure when Keith grabbed Dallas by the arm.

"Check it out. Looks like I was wrong about nobody home."

Dallas hadn't noticed and would have overlooked the silent sentinel. There on the trunk of the fallen tree on Lagarto's threshold was an iguana doing its best imitation of a bump on a log. The lizard looked different than others he'd seen in the Bahamas. It was green, sleeker, most likely from somewhere else. Most striking was the stubby tail, in the process of regenerating from some sort of trauma.

Without so much as a twitch, the animal answered another question that had plagued Dallas for months.

"Rambo!"

"What?"

"Remember, I told you about the one I lost off the sailboat. Lagarto was there when I was rescued. I thought he picked up remains. Guess my friend was more resilient than he was."

Dallas noticed that the tree had fallen across one side of a wire-mesh cage. The whole puzzle was clear now. The smile finally broke through on his face. He reached out and rubbed the back of the lizard's neck, then ran his fingers along either side of the comb extending the length of its back. The iguana lifted its head, opened its eyes and flexed the fan-shaped dewlap beneath its chin.

Dallas continued to bond with the strange animal while Keith watched in silent amazement until, finally, he moved away and said, "Sweet dreams, old friend."

EPILOGUE

August is a turbulent time in the Caribbean and adjacent waters, a time when tropical storms often stack up like commuter flights waiting for clearance at LaGuardia. Not the best time for island hopping. So, after 2½ weeks the enchanted cruise of *Big Momma* ended when another hurricane menacing the region hastened retreat to the Florida Keys.

It would be easy to report that Dallas and Claire lived happily ever after. Life is not so simply summarized. With the caution of dipping a toe into water of indeterminate temperature, Dallas and Claire decided to give cohabitation a chance on a trial basis. As Dallas confided to Keith, "Until fun do us part." They sublet the canal-side stilt house vacated by Sami the waitress/massage therapist, who moved back to San Francisco. As part of the deal they inherited Mandrake the iguana, who soon became a fixture on Lyle's shoulder.

There was a notable event that occurred early in the Cross Your Fingers and Toes Living Together Experiment that followed the Great Rehabilitation Cruise of 1993. One morning in September, Dallas, Claire, Lyle and Keith embarked from Snapper Cove Marina aboard *Levante* and steered a familiar heading to a spot where the continental shelf begins its descent toward the deep canyons of the Atlantic Ocean. The Loran-C told them precisely where to set the anchor, in a spot they had visited many times in previous months.

Because he still had a walking cast on his left ankle, Dallas remained on the boat with Lyle while Claire and Keith donned scuba gear and headed for the wreck of *Nuestra Senora de Carmelita* with an urn bearing the ashes of Capt. LaRue "Skeeter" Devereaux.

They didn't immediately recognize the site and had to backtrack until they found the rock formation where the friendly Warsaw grouper Lech Walesa resided to ensure they were in the right spot. Finally they located a portion of grid work that marked an excavation site. Already the ocean, perhaps aided by the surge of currents from the recent hurricane, had obscured much of their progress in unearthing the centuries old Spanish booty. It was a moot issue now, with Devereaux gone and new federal regulations putting a hammerlock on treasure hunting in the Keys.

Keith dug a hole for the new captain's quarters and set the urn inside along with a laminated photograph of Devereaux. Facing one another, Keith and Claire locked hands for a minute of silent prayer. Then together they pushed sand into the hole. With nitrogen-laced melancholy, the two divers closed the book on a 300-year-old saga.

If fate hadn't intervened, Claire would have missed the denouement. She and Keith were making their final exit from the wreck site when her hand bumped something protruding from the sand. She felt it give and realized it wasn't a rock. Her first thought was it might be the end of a tool they may have left behind on another dive. She nearly swallowed her regulator when she saw what she'd found.

Back aboard Levante, the scene was reminiscent of the day they discovered the trove of emeralds. But this was a far more remarkable find, an ornate gold cross, five inches long, bulging with emeralds. They stared in disbelief and exulted until reality seemed to hit them all at once. Claire was the first to speak.

"What are we going to do?"

"Guess we're going to have to tell someone. Probably Culpepper would be the best one to call," Dallas said.

"Bullshit!"

Dallas and Claire looked at Keith in surprise. Lyle giggled.

Keith stood before them barechested, water dripping from his dreadlocks, looking like a funky player from Neptune's undersea ensemble.

"We ain't even supposed to be out here digging stuff up. I don't need the hassle. Neither do the rest of you. So I'll tell you what you're going to do: Nothing. Nothing! Sometimes the sea taketh, sometimes it giveth. You're going to do what you should do when you receive a special gift — say thanks and be grateful."

With that, he put the cross in Claire's hands and closed her fingers around it.

It was on the way back to Islamorada that Lyle tugged on his mother's arm and spoke close to her ear so only she could hear above the engine noise. Claire waited until they were back at Snapper Cove before informing Dallas that Lyle had something to tell him.

Fidgeting under the weight of three sets of eyes, the boy looked up and said, "Captain Skeeter, he gave me something to hide for him. Said if anything happened to him, I should show it to you. I just remembered."

"Where is it?"

"I buried it next to Lucky O'Brien's tree."

Lyle made them agree to wait in a nearby parking lot while he slipped into the yard behind Dallas's former duplex apartment and retrieve his buried treasure. It was contained in a small metal box such as is commonly used to store petty cash. Keith used a hammer and chisel to bust the lock.

Inside was an object wrapped in a faded red handkerchief and a note. With quivering hands, Dallas removed the cloth to reveal the second shock of the day, a jeweled lizard made of gold with a row of oval-shaped emeralds along its back.

The note read: "Sometimes the treasure you seek is closer than you think. Skeeter."

"Look," said Lyle, "The tail curls around like that island where your boat got stuck."

#

The summer of high water gave way to an autumn of raging wildfires that consumed 1,000 homes in Southern California, including 300 in ritzy Malibu. That led to several frantic phone calls for Claire until she determined that family and friends back home were safe. Otherwise, concerns of the outside world roused little fervor in Islamorada, where greater interest centered on the current state of fishing and continuing controversy over the new federal restrictions in the Keys Marine Sanctuary. TV news was regarded primarily for entertainment value, fodder for barstool philosophers in the many watering holes along U.S. 1. There was plenty to talk about.

In the fall of 1993, troops loyal to Russian President Boris Yeltsin quelled a rebellion by storming their own Parliament building in the bloodiest confrontation in Moscow since the Bolshevik Revolution. Former Panamanian dictator Manuel Noriega, already serving 40 years in Miami for drug trafficking, was convicted in his own country for ordering the murder of a political opponent years before. On the domestic front, President Clinton's proposal to guarantee affordable healthcare to all citizens was being met with skepticism and political opposition.

Meanwhile, 90 miles from Key West, Fidel Castro continued to perpetrate his illusion of revolution in Cuba, oblivious to the latest plot to send him to the great despot depot in the sky. While Fidel fiddled with ideology his comrades staggered under the burden of deepening economic hardship compounded by severe weather that devastated the sugar harvest and other cash crops.

Dallas and Claire had their own financial worries as they settled in to make a life together. One source of income dried up when Kirby D'Arbonnell deep-sixed *Florida Nautique* and took a job as editor of a publication put out by Peepers Restaurants, which featured waitresses in black Speedo bike shorts and bright yellow tank tops. The magazine was called *Peepers' Eye-Poppers.*

"Surprised it's not *Peep Show*, if you've got anything to do with it," Dallas said.

D'Arbonnell said the career move made sense. "A lot more people are into eating and ogling than fishing."

Dallas did receive inspiration from his former editor, who encouraged him to write about his recent adventures. D'Arbonnell had some experience as a literary agent and promised to "take your book to the top of the best-seller list." With recovery from the broken ankle hampering his employment prospects and Claire working full time at the Leaky Tiki, he set to work pounding the keys of the old Smith-Corona, the one item overlooked by Edison Hawke's lackeys when they moved him out of his duplex apartment.

As the words began to flow in a torrent, he was reminded of what he'd read about how Jack Kerouac composed "On the Road" in a month of marathon writing while his wife supported them with a waitress job. The story goes that Kerouac, subsisting on coffee and pea soup and working around the clock, typed on tracing paper taped together to form 12-foot-long sheets that he fed through his typewriter in a continuous roll.

Claire gave Dallas one of those you've-got-to-be-nuts looks when she saw him taping paper end-to-end, but otherwise supported the project, frequently bringing home pots of Keith's conch chowder to fortify his creativity. Dallas didn't have Kerouac's single-minded focus. He was easily sidetracked by the impulse to cast his spinning rod into the canal. But, with the beat bard's photograph propped up opposite the Smith-Corona for inspiration and jazz tapes to stir the soul, a compulsion became an obsession.

By early November, Dallas sent D'Arbonnell a rough draft of a manuscript titled "Tail of the Lizard." He mailed it the same day that Ramon Ortega won the Offshore World Championship in Key West and was arrested during the victory celebration by federal agents on charges of conspiring to sell a large cache of automatic weapons to a Cuban exile group. The arrest was big news in South Florida and prompted a rehash of the dramatic escape of Ramon's brother Jorge, who remained at large despite more than 100 reported sightings. Ramon was held under extreme security in the same facility that his brother broke out of. Strands of wire had since been strung in a crisscrossed pattern above the exercise area to thwart anyone with similar ambitions.

However, once again an Ortega slipped through the hands of the government. A week after his arrest, Ramon was suddenly released and a terse statement issued about insufficient evidence. Rumors circulated that the real reason was that Ramon was brokering the weapons on behalf of the CIA, but not a word about that was ever reported in the media.

A few days later, Dallas received a call from D'Arbonnell, who already had a friend at a publishing house interested in the manuscript.

"It's going to need a lot of work, though."

"What do you mean?"

"For starters, it's going to have to be published as a work of fiction."

"But it's all true. Everything I wrote about happened."

"If you say so, sport. I'm just telling you what's going to sell. They want to get rid of the Kennedy stuff — that's ancient history — and play up the sunken treasure angle. They want to see a lot more treasure and how it corrupts the characters. That's what leads to Devereaux's murder."

"But ..."

"And, of course you're going to need a lot more sex. You've got to get the Asian waitress involved more and set up a love triangle with her and the brunette."

Dallas was still coping with disillusionment about his introduction to the publishing business when he and Claire flew to Texas. He needed to help Linda close the sale on Mom's house and wanted Claire to see his boyhood home. With Lyle staying at Margie's, it was their first trip alone together.

The closing on the house was Friday afternoon. That night they partied with Linda in the Deep Ellum entertainment district. On Saturday, they attended a barbecue hosted by Chuck Robison, Dallas's old baseball coach. On Sunday, they had brunch at Dick's Last Resort and took a drive to South Fork Ranch, home of J.R. Ewing's fictional TV clan. As the weekend progressed, Claire was aware of one point of interest she hadn't seen. She didn't mention it.

Monday morning, Dallas drove them into the city and parked the rental car near West End Market. Without a word, he took her hand and led the way along Houston Street, across railroad tracks to an intersection next to a squat red brick building. There they bore off on Elm, which curved to the right down a gentle slope toward a highway underpass. Claire recognized the scene immediately and felt a chill on the back of her neck.

She turned and looked questioningly into Dallas's eyes.

"Are you sure?"

"It's November 22nd. It was 30 years ago today."

A large crowd was milling about on a grassy area next to the street. They had come for the dedication of a bronze plaque designating the site as a national historic landmark. Nellie Connally, wife of the former Texas governor who also was wounded that day, spoke to the crowd about not looking back with grief but forward with hope.

When the ceremony ended, Dallas turned to Claire and smiled. Choked up by the emotion of the moment, she was surprised to see a mischievous gleam in his eyes.

As the crowd began to thin, he gave her his guided tour of the infamous mountain of a molehill that millions refer to as the Grassy Knoll. He showed her the concrete pedestal where Abraham Zapruder recorded his famous home movie and led her up the steps to the area behind a rickety stockade fence where many witnesses, including police, rushed after the shots were fired at John F. Kennedy's motorcade.

That drab, wooden fence atop the Grassy Knoll is littered with graffiti, most of it relating to the event that occurred there on November 22, 1963. While Claire was occupied reading the observations of plebeian poets, Dallas pulled out a black felt-tip marker and added a message of his own. It read:

"Dallas & Claire

Let's make it forevermore"

When she looked up, he was standing there grinning again.

"What? *What?*"

"I just thought you should know, there is something on this fence for your eyes only. You have to find it."

With that he retreated down the steps. He stood next to the wall where Devereaux drank his Coke and stared back at one face on the other side of the picket fence. It was almost exactly where he once spied the face of death and heartbreak. Same place, different world.

Now, looking through the same eyes at the same spot, he saw the face of hope and everything worth living for. On the 30th anniversary of the murder of a president, they were two faces in a large crowd paying homage to a national tragedy. But in his mind, his world, he was looking at the only one that mattered. He watched and waited, overcome by a sense of peace that was so foreign he didn't yet fully comprehend it.

There was no doubt when Claire discovered her destiny on the Grassy Knoll. It was the moment her face turned very red.

Thank you for reading

I hope you enjoyed reading "Tail of the Lizard." I'd be honored if you'd consider posting a review of the book on Amazon. My hope is you found my first novel entertaining, but I would like your feedback either way.

Craig Davis

About the author

Craig Davis has been a sports journalist in South Florida for more than four decades, covering all of the major team sports as well as niche sports including fishing and boating. It was during a 10-year run as an outdoors writer that ideas for characters, setting and events of "Tail of the Lizard" took root. He lives near Fort Lauderdale, Florida, with his wife, Fran.